The Adoption

ANNE BERRY

EBURY
PRESS

13 5 7 9 10 8 6 4 2

Published in the UK in 2012 by Ebury Press, an imprint of Ebury Publishing
A Random House Group Company
This edition published in the UK in 2013 by Ebury Press, an imprint of
Ebury Publishing
A Random House Group Company

The Random House Group Limited Reg. No. 954009

Addresses for companies within the Random House Group can be found at:
www.randomhouse.co.uk

A CIP catalogue record for this book is available from the British Library

The Random House Group Limited supports The Forest Stewardship
Council® (FSC®), the leading international forest-certification organisation.
Our books carrying the FSC label are printed on FSC®-certified paper.
FSC is the only forest-certification scheme supported by the leading
environmental organisations, including Greenpeace. Our
paper procurement policy can be found at
www.randomhouse.co.uk/environment

Printed and bound in Great Britain by Clays Ltd, St Ives plc

ISBN 9780091947057

To buy books by your favourite authors and register for offers visit
www.randomhouse.co.uk

Anne Berry was born in London in 1956, then spent much of her infancy in Aden, before moving to Hong Kong at the age of six, where she was educated. She worked for a short period as a journalist for the *South China Morning Post*, before returning to Britain. After completing a three-year acting course, she embarked on a career in theatre, playing everything from pantomime to Shakespeare. She now lives in Surrey with her husband and four children. She is the author of the critically acclaimed, award-winning novels *The Hungry Ghosts* and *The Water Children*.

Praise for Anne Berry:

'Anne Berry is a wonderful writer with a poetic imagination and use of language; startling metaphors and images flow effortlessly from one to line and, from page one, the plotting is heart-in-the-mouth stuff. What more could you ask?' *Daily Mail*

'A highly acclaimed debut novel from Anne Berry, *The Hungry Ghosts*, which is about a young girl living in Hong Kong who is haunted by a spirit. You will simply love this story of a broken family and its many hidden secrets' *Sunday Express*

'A most extraordinary debut novel since *The Lovely Bones*. Astonishing!' *The Lady Magazine*

'Epic in scope and voice so skilfully crafted, and the writing so elegant, it's hard to believe it is a first novel' *Psychologies*

'A stunning debut' *Woman and Home*

Also by Anne Berry:

The Hungry Ghosts
The Water Children

My sincere thanks to my inspirational publisher and editor, Gillian Green, and to my lovely publicist, Hannah Robinson, and to all the production team at Ebury Books.

My especial thanks also to my wonderful agent Judith Murdoch.

Chapter 1

Bethan, 1948

My hands are shaking uncontrollably, so that it takes a full minute to open the flimsy letter. Silly that I am so afraid when I know the likely contents. I allow my eyes to linger a moment on their motto, before I devour the rest whole. I taste not a word but knock it back like medicine. Cold. It is cold, so cold that I can see the steamy vapour of my breaths. I feel like . . . like . . . the air is being beaten out of me. And the thought makes me picture my mam beating the fireside rug outdoors in spring, little explosions of pearly dust. Barefoot, I pick my way across the rough floorboards to where a drawer lined with a quilt serves as a crib. Close by, the chest minus its middle gapes contemptuously at me. Will it poke its tongue out? I peer into its splintered gullet desolately and placate it with this thought. Soon now, very soon, your drawer will be returned – empty. Kneeling as if at chapel, I gaze down at my babe in her makeshift manger. Oh what a dark star led me here?

I must not touch her. When I look I must not touch. When I touch I must not look. In this way Mam says no bond will form. There is a milk blister on her upper lip, brushstrokes of rose pink on her cheeks and a curl of golden hair fine as gossamer on the crown of her head. Her eyes are tight shut, a gentle blush of mauve on their lids. But let me tell you what you're missing. They are turquoise, pale turquoise exactly like mine, the colour of dreams. In my dressing gown pocket

1

is a compact. I lift it out, open it up, hold the mirror in front of her nose, her tiny mouth. A fine veil mists the silver surface. My baby is as alive as I am. I read her a story, whisper the tale into her perfect ear no bigger than a half-crown coin.

'The Homeless Child for the Childless Home'
The Church Adoption Society
(Founded in 1913 in Cambridge by Rev. W. F. Buttle, M.A.)

Telegrams
4A BLOOMSBURY SQUARE,
BABICHANGE, LONDON
LONDON, W.C. 1
Telephone HOLBORN 3310

23rd April, 1948

Miss Haverd,
42 Rochester Row,
Westminster

Dear Miss Haverd,
    We have a very nice couple who are interested in Lucilla and would like to see her. All being well they will take her straight home with them. Could you arrange to be at this office at 2.45 pm on Tuesday next, the 27th of April?
    Yours sincerely,
    Valeria Mulholland
    Secretary

When my story is finished I do not say, 'And they all lived happily ever after.' But the ending I offer in its place is a fair exchange.

'"The Homeless Child for the Childless Home". Surely?'

Chapter 2

Lucilla, 1995

The muscles of my cheeks hurt tensed for so long in such a stupid, simpering smile. I wonder how dancers accomplish it, their faces portraits of bliss while their toes cramp mercilessly. I was woken at dawn by squabbling magpies, flapping and hopping about in the dove-grey light. Such a to-do! Spring has taken us unawares. The sun is at the window making the inside seem tired and dowdy, and the outside bright as fresh paint. The pear blossom is out. The bluebells are slowly unfurling their shy heads. And here am I confined indoors, having to listen to Cousin Frank prattle on endlessly about his daft wife and his obnoxious sons.

'Oh, they're smashing lads. A credit to us both. No surprise that they've done really well for themselves. Like father like son, eh? A quantity surveyor and a banker. You can't say better than that, can you, Lucilla?' Certain that I can, wisely I hold my peace. There comes a pause, a lengthy pause into which Merlin, my golden King Charles spaniel, gives an enormous gummy yawn. Glancing down, I see him slumped at my feet. He's partially blind, poor old gentleman. His right pupil and retina are a swirl of milky white, giving a piratical slant to his adorable pugnacious face. Now he rolls his liquid eyes up at me, his expression skew-whiff. In them, I see he has surpassed my state of boredom and is inching his canine way into a coma. The urge to

3

replace my look of feigned interest with one of genuine fond amusement, is almost irresistible. Across the way from me I see Henry, my
husband, lever himself out of his chair. At the welcome sight of him
my heart gives its familiar tug, as if an invisible cord fastens us together.

'Anyone for . . . for more coffee?' he offers hesitantly, smoothing
his greying handsome cinnamon-brown beard and moustache. There
is something of the chivalrous musketeer about my Henry. He should
have a cap adorned with swirling feathers to sweep off, now and then,
from his bowing head. Whereas Frank is more the scurvy rascal, bent
on rape and pillage rather than acts of selfless gallantry. I mark the
disparaging twitch of his pompous mouth, the subtle quarter rotation
of his wrist where his imitation Rolex is strapped.

'*Tempus fugit*, Henry. *Tempus fugit.*' Another glance at his fake
watch. 'Time waits for no man.'

'*Sic transit gloria mundi*,' returns Henry in his element, elbows
propped on the arms of his chair, hands clasped, fingers linked, face
expectant. He opens out his hands inviting Frank to translate. Frank
frowns, annoyed and at a loss. And I reflect that there are many
industrial diamonds that are worthless in value and only one Star of
Africa, which is priceless. 'Thus passes the glory of the world,' Henry
supplies with a magnanimous smile.

'Quite so. Quite so,' mumbles Frank, recovering himself with a
show of latent comprehension. He stretches out his stick-insect limbs
and pedals his right foot, as if revving the engine of a car. 'Alas, I must
wend.' Henry, reading my rapturous reception at this long-overdue
cherub-of-departure, silences me with a look of whiskery Victorian
censure. My pretentious cousin is on his feet now. He wears of all
ridiculous get-ups on this lovely day, a day that demands a frivolous
butterfly palette, a workaday suit, a dung-brown tie and black lace-ups
buffed to the shine of a policeman's boots. Tall, imposing, with his
irritating sermonising way of speaking, he appears more like a funeral

director than a man at his leisure on a fine Saturday. 'The lunch was awfully nice. Home cooking. Can't beat it,' Franks oozes.

'Shop bought,' I mutter rebelliously. A white lie but then I suddenly wish it had been, that I had expended no culinary effort at all on our lunch.

'Marks and Spencer, I bet. You can always tell.' The snobbery of my cousin is legendary.

'Tesco – economy brand,' I retort without missing a beat, embellishing my white lie with wicked delight. Disappointingly he bypasses this. I stay seated for a few moments more listening to birdsong, and enjoying the feeling that this is my space, my chair, my domain. It is the home I share with my man, my Henry, worth a thousand Franks even on a bad day. We are downstairs in the long room in the cottage, the one that does for a lounge and dining area, both. Frank is fussing with his papers, spread out on the oak dining table, pedantically putting them into his briefcase. He licks his finger as he flicks through them, something I have always held to be a disgusting and unhygienic habit. His black hair, salted generously with dandruff, looks as if it has been varnished onto his skull.

'So, Lucilla, how's your job going in that dinky little tea shop?'

I wince at the sound of the name. To me it sounds like a scream, which is ironic really because it often was – screamed at me, I mean. I do not believe anyone loathes their name as much as I do. The lucky ones store up early memories of their names spoken with wondrous love, mine is of the three syllables being picked at like leftovers on a plate. Was Lucilla worth saving for tomorrow when, with imagination, she might be transformed into something more palatable, or should they just scrape me into a bin and wait for the dustmen to take me away? Sensing my preoccupation, Frank leers at me, his proximity together with his halitosis eliciting the unspoken observation that a visit to the dentist is long overdue, my cousin.

'Getting on all right are we?' he asks patronisingly.

We are definitely not getting on all right. 'It's bloody hard work,' I choke out.

His face spasms momentarily in shock. He reviles women using foul language. I am tempted to give vent to a diatribe of the filthiest, most offensive swear words I know. Henry's hands are thrust deep into his jeans pockets, a bad sign, and I see them wriggle now in agitation. I catch his eye and the gentle reproach I see there brings swift repentance. With a soft sigh, I harness my wayward tongue and remind myself that, God willing, for miracles do occasionally happen, he will soon be gone.

Our cosy abode is one of several small cottages leased out to employees on the Brightmore Estate. The main house, Brightmore Hall, is a grand imposing structure built in the Regency style. The tall maize-gold walls are softened with mauve wisteria in spring. During winter, the dark-green topiaries, sculpted into chess pieces, the kings and queens, the bishops, the castles and the knights, lined up on opposing sides of the front lawn, seem to spring out at you from their jonquil background. The property situated on the North Downs is set in over six hundred acres of rolling fields and woodlands, while hugging the fairy-tale building, with its central tower, are walled rose, lavender and dahlia gardens, cottage borders that fringe the pleasant walkways, a rockery, a herb garden, a vegetable garden, and the stables, now used to other purposes, surrounding a cobbled courtyard. Henry, with his patient green hands, is head gardener here, conjuring magical beanstalks to sprout tall and majestic from a pinch of dull brown seeds. I am a general dogsbody, sometimes serving in the café, sometimes in the gift shop and sometimes in the offices. And occasionally I am seconded to the main house to show visiting parties around. Here I confess to spicing up Brightmore family scandals with more poetic licence than fact, until gratifyingly eyes pop, mouths gape and maiden aunts mutter disapprovingly. Very occasionally I find myself scurrying between all four to keep the great house running smoothly.

'Of course my wife doesn't work. Never has. Lady of luxury. Life of ease,' Frank boasts with quite revolting prehistoric manly pride. Me, hunter-gatherer, you, stay-at-home-twiddle-your-fingers wife. 'She likes to sew. To stitch me up, eh, Henry?' Frank hee-haws with disproportionate hilarity at his own humourless joke. The padded shoulders of his suit jacket lift with laughter in a fair imitation of Edward Heath, spittle flies and eyes vanish in porcine creases.

I grimace. I do not like to sew. In verity I hold that needlecraft is a vile occupation, one that should be bracketed alongside consorting with the devil. It should have perished with pitiable, oppressed, medieval damsels. Poor dears, sitting uncomfortably on clunky chastity belts stitching away at interminable tapestries, while their husbands went galloping around lopping off infidels' heads on jolly capers and crusades. Confidentially, I despise sewing nearly as much as I do my name. And, after all, the afternoon is wearing on. It is ticking by without me and Merlin bounding through it, watching the land waking up, feeling the earth soften under foot and paw, and the shoots thrust up through it. Frank counts his papers, then repeats the exercise pedantically.

'Keep the hands busy and the mind pure. That's what your dear mother used to say,' he reminds me, smothering his nostrils with a damp hanky to suppress a sneeze. The whites of his eyes are tinged with pink. He's a wee bit allergic to pet fur. Must be finding this a trial. What a shame. Actually, I don't care a hoot what my dead mother might say. If the devil wants my hands he can have them and welcome. I'd prefer to give them to him than waste my time going blind trying to thread eensy-weensy needles. But my smile remains fixed in place as if nailed there. 'I don't know how you cope with working, even if it is part-time, Lucilla. I know your children are both

. . . out and . . . and about. Such a colourful pair. Gina a married woman – and a park ranger. A park ranger! I expect that means doing all sorts of jolly things with squirrels and trees and acorns. Such fun.' He frowns, trying to imagine it, but it proves beyond his scope. 'Can Tim actually scrape a living making musical instruments? I can't imagine how he goes about that. Still, I'm sure they bring all their hiccups home to Mum.'

As he talks, his shallow grey eyes take in a corner cobweb, Henry's crumpled shirt, the layer of homely dust on the wooden mantelpiece, finally coming to rest on the cork-tiled floor, worn to a dullness by the many scrabbling muddy paws it has been trampled under.

'I manage,' I say shortly, not the least abashed by my lovely lived-in home. I fondle Merlin's head, sculpt the comforting dome of his faithful skull under the silky fur cap. Etiquette demands that a hostess see her guest to the door. My enthusiasm for this last duty is betrayed when I shoot up, as if bitten on my derrière by a starving mouse. And at last Frank's briefcase snaps closed. I still have the cheque in my hand. Twelve thousand pounds. It isn't a great deal really. Not by today's standards. What can you get for twelve thousand pounds? A decent car, a new kitchen at a stretch, a few designer frocks, a round-the-world sea voyage. Probably wouldn't get you all the way round either. More likely only to the Indian Ocean to maroon you on some godforsaken island in the middle of nowhere. Is the legacy sufficient to purchase a baby? To buy off a child. To bribe a teenager. To gag a woman. I think not. We migrate into the kitchen where unconventionally the main entrance to our cottage is located.

Helpfully, I open the door. But it is Henry who exits it with a kindly wink, preparing to conduct Frank to the estate's communal car park. Unfortunately, Frank's broad shoulders lodge inside the door frame, making me want to uncork him and send him popping into the wild blue yonder.

'Well, Lucilla?' he says, bowing ingratiatingly, fingering a brown envelope tucked under one arm and swinging his briefcase.

'Well, Frank?' I return. I inhale the scent of coffee grounds and burned toast and warm dog, trying to rid myself of the taint of stale cigarettes that clings to the fabric of his drab suit.

'Are you pleased?' he inquires, his tone that of a generous benefactor.

'That my mum's dead?' I rejoin angelically.

To my satisfaction I see that he loses a bit of his composure then, working his block jaw in irritation. 'No, of course not. About the money, I mean.' His stained teeth are crooked, leaning drunkenly against one another in his wide mouth. They appear an encumbrance to his speech, rather than tools for sharpening up his diction. Merlin waddles in from the lounge-diner, positioning himself between us, staring up from face to face, possibly waiting to see who will land the first punch.

'If you really want to know, I don't think it is very fair.' I fold my arms in place of slapping a gauntlet across his smarmy face. He looks slightly taken aback – a statue wobbling on its plinth.

'I assure you that I have performed my duties as executor and trustee of her will scrupulously,' he blusters.

'Oh, I don't doubt it.' I shrink back from the door reclaiming my snug in the bosom of Brightmore, and lean on the kitchen work surface. My gaze idles over the dishes piled in the sink as I say, 'Do you really think you deserve a share of her money though?'

'A third. Your cousin Rachel and I got a third each,' he interjects, gobbling like a turkey. He sounds defensive, even annoyed. Perhaps he expected to get more, to bank the lot. Then, under his breath, 'There would have been a small fortune, if it wasn't for that interfering damn busybody Whatmore. He was a fraudster taking advantage of Aunt Harriet like that. It was despicable.'

Like attracts like, I muse dryly. But I let pass this reference to my mother's ill-advised decision to sell her pretty house, to purchase an ugly bungalow on the Pembroke Dock road. 'Wasn't she *my* mother?' I query delicately. My inflexion implies sincere confusion, as if I really am undecided. After all, biologically there was no bridge adjoining us. I was not blood of her blood, flesh of her flesh – thank God! I spare a charitable thought for my poor cousin Rachel whose silver spoon was filled with the gall of fertility problems. Ultimately, however materially well off she became, motherhood was denied her.

I worshipped Rachel when I was little. She was kind to me, and pretty, and there were notable occasions when she broke from the herd to gallop to my aid. But then a day came when the ease with which I produced offspring fostered a resentment in her that soured our relationship. Rachel, like my adoptive mother, had problems down below, problems talked of in hushed whispers. She was unable to carry to term, having a succession of miscarriages. The longest she went was her first pregnancy, nearly six months. The tiny alien scrap, a boy, skin raw as a skinned rabbit's and wizened as an old man, dwindled through three days before expiring. I visited Rachel in hospital. Eerily, she didn't weep. There were no marks of her vacuous fathomless sorrow. Though what I did fasten on was a disturbing opacity in the irises of her chalk-green eyes, as if overnight they had changed colour. I would eventually come to recognise this as the lustreless matted shade of madness. After that, as the years went by, we drifted apart: cards at Christmas, birthdays, the occasional stilted phone call.

Incredibly, Cousin Frank is still whistling through his bad teeth, justifying his slice of inheritance. It was no surprise to me, this three-way split. My mother told me of the division in advance. But once in a vanilla spring sun it rankled with me, so I cut in icily. 'I was the adopted daughter.' He doesn't answer that, but I note how his eyelids fall and his disparaging gaze travels at the mention of adoption. I go on, undeterred. 'When *your* mother, Aunty Enid, died, I don't recall her leaving me a penny.' I can feel the heat coming to my cheeks, my militant feet tapping in a war dance. 'You and Rachel own your homes. I don't.' Again he is sullenly tight-lipped. 'This cottage comes with Henry's job. When he retires, we will effectively be homeless. We will have to buy somewhere with our modest savings.'

His small, slug-grey eyes crinkle at the corners and he shrugs. 'You have to respect the wishes of the dead,' he says, gorging himself on humble pie. Then, as if suddenly remembering something, 'Oh, I've brought along a few documents you should have.' He takes the envelope from under his arm and holds it out to me. He blots out the light, his shadow lying like a corpse on the kitchen floor. The features of his face blur, so that I can only detect the buff glow of his leaning-tombstone teeth.

'I suppose I must be satisfied with that then.' I reach for the envelope. Merlin backs a pace and growls. He has gained weight in his declining years. But, bless him, there is a wolf in that roly-poly pudding yet. I can hear distant steps on the cobbles and the murmur of the lawn mowers far off. I conjure the scent of freshly cut grass, inhale it deep down, let it purge me of my past.

'The photographs you asked for, they're in here. Including the one you mentioned. I tracked it down.' Frank waits as if for a round of applause, and I recall our telephone conversation of a month or so ago. He asked me if there were any of my mother's possessions I had my eye on. I was about to say, no, that there was nothing, no keepsakes I coveted, when I remembered the photograph. It is hard to explain what it means to me, so I shall merely say that I had a yearning for it.

'There's a photograph taken in August 1950. I was two and half. I'm on a donkey at the seaside. Not a real one, a stuffed donkey. Life size,' I reported. He gave a bemused grunt.

I'm alone in the picture. My adoptive parents aren't there. Perhaps they're supervising me. I don't know. But I'm not posing, not smiling at anyone, not trying to be anything other than what I am. A tiny girl in a white dress, sitting proudly astride a donkey on a seaside promenade. I suddenly felt hot tears coming, and sensations crowding in on me. Rows of deckchairs and the backs of people's hatted heads, the flat of a calm sea, the slap of sunlight, the salty dead smell, the cries of gulls. And me sitting alone on a furry donkey, in command, gripping the reins. The sea breeze was blowing back my hair. I leaned forwards and stroked the big floppy ears. They were like soft toys nestling in my small hands. The donkey had a funny face. The forelock of its fluffy black mane fringed bulging eyes, cartoon eyes, white with big inky pupils. Its mouth was open in a broad toothy grin. I imagined it whinnying. 'Giddy up, giddy up,' I chivvied it on, kicking its flanks and jiggling my bottom on the leather saddle. I was absurdly, momentously happy. The emotion was so foreign that I wouldn't have been able to name it, although I have no trouble identifying it today. Now I can say, ah yes, that was happiness, and this . . . well, this is sadness. And this? This is sorrow. And this is regret. And this is despair.

'Yes, I'd like that photograph if you can find it,' I said.

'Oh. Well, I'm sure I'll be able to dig it out. Anything else?'

'No, no, thank you.'

'There's a ring you know, an engagement ring. Your mother's engagement ring. A diamond set in gold, no less.'

'Is there?'

'You must have seen it a million times.'

'I don't recall.'

'I've had it valued. It's worth two thousand pounds. Shall I send it to you?'

'If you like.'

If Frank was expecting me to grovel he was sorely disappointed. He kept his word though and posted it to me. Actually it was rather grubby and scratched. I hocked it round the local jewellers, but no one would give me two thousand pounds for it, or even one thousand. In the end, grudgingly, one chap gave me three hundred and fifty. I bought a colour television. Henry was thrilled. Now we can watch wildlife programmes together.

But the donkey photograph was priceless to me. And today I will have it in my possession. Frank continues, still seemingly reluctant to hand over my legacy. 'There are some other things, documents I thought you might want to have. Probably sensible not to open it until I've gone.' Is that the Cheshire cat or my cousin, face divided with a hideous grin? I step forwards and my hand closes on the envelope. I hear it crackle temptingly. But he still refuses to relinquish it, so that we have an extraordinary tug of war on my doorstep.

'Lucilla, what's in here . . . well, you may find it difficult to accept. Try to remember it was complicated for them too.'

I want to say, oh just give it to me and bugger off. But I wait, suddenly feeling a frisson of fear. You see, I grew up in a conspiracy of silence. He takes a breath, as if he wants to say something more. Then, clearing his throat, he seems to change his mind, at last letting go. He makes a move to peck me on the cheek. I lean backwards and Merlin bares his teeth. 'I'll be in touch,' is all he says, ducking through the doorway and skulking out into the sunlight.

I take the envelope upstairs to my bedroom and sit on the end of our bed. I turn it slowly around and around in my hands, staring into my dressing-table mirror. In it a middle-aged woman, Lucilla Ryan, slim, with fine strawberry-blonde hair, an oval face, pale skin, delicate features, and guarded watery turquoise eyes, gazes back at me. She wears a pastel-blue cotton sweater. And there is a silk scarf patterned with tropical parrots tied at her throat. The loose knot is pinned with a brooch fashioned from a peacock feather, silver-framed under glass. This woman is suddenly a stranger. I don't recognise her at all. I don't know how long I sit here. I've fallen into one of those odd pockets where the treadmill of time seems to grind to a standstill.

'Well, Cousin Frank has gone,' Henry says. I look round and there he is, a reassuring comforting presence, as he has been throughout my bleakest days.

'Did I behave?' My tone is querulous. But my apprehension is reserved entirely for my husband and his pacifistic nature.

'Well, you passed,' he grants generously, coming to sit beside me on our bedside, the envelope sandwiched between us.

'A merit?' I push, biting my lip and leaning away from him, the better to assess his verdict.

He pauses and gives his shaggy-haired head a little shake. 'Barely scraped through,' comes his judgement. Another pause, then with his trademark frankness he adds, 'You owe it to creative marking if I'm perfectly truthful.'

'Oh!' I sigh and then we both giggle. Merlin joins us, panting from the exertion of the stairs, and collapses at our feet, nosing our shoes experimentally. It seems Henry's have the finest bouquet, and he rests his head on the worn leather of his loafers with a wine connoisseur's appreciative wheeze. We both stare down at the envelope. Only Henry can absorb the emotions that are storming through me. He scrunches his lips together. The oddest expression but well known to me, as if his mouth, trimmed with beard and moustache, is frowning deeply, cognitively.

'It isn't sealed,' he observes at last.

'Mmm . . . so I see.'

'Are you going to . . .' His gruff voice breaks and he gulps a breath, then speaks again with more control. '*Fortes fortuna adiuvat*,' Henry pronounces levelly. My husband is a gardener of philosophy, as opposed to a doctor. Learning the Latin names for plants was the branch that led to the trunk of Latin proverbs. And his ability to memorise them, reams of them, and supply them when symptoms of life require such sagacity is legendary.

'Translation?' I ask with trepidation.

'Fortune favours the brave,' my husband intones sonorously. Then he spoils it and grins.

Now I am smiling in spite of myself. Merlin shifts his head to Henry's other foot. Through the window, out of the corner of my eye, I see the sun-kissed leaves all atremble. Spurred on by the ancient wisdom of Greece and Rome, I draw a breath and fish inside the envelope. I take out the photographs first, shuffle them through my hands. There aren't very many of them, not when you consider that this is a lifetime's worth. And, weirdly, none after I am about four and a half. As if, like Peter Pan, I didn't grow up. They are all black and white. One. Aerial shot. I am lying in a pram with cuddly toy. The toy is an animal of indeterminate breed, the possible progeny of a lamb and a bear. The label says three months. 'It's an odd-looking beast.' I glance quickly up at Henry but he is sober-faced, agreeing. 'I mean the toy . . . not the baby. Not me,' I say.

'Oh no, not you. You're beautiful,' he whispers. I give him the snapshot and move on.

In the second I am a baby in my mother's arms. I look solid, round-faced and plump-cheeked. I am certainly not being deprived of food. What of her?

'She looks old, far too old to be the mother of that baby,' I mumble. Henry nods. And that's another curious detail. 'Do you see the way she's holding me?' She is tipping me forwards, and craning her neck as if to examine me. She appears to be screwing up her eyes behind her glasses and squinting at me. Her expression is . . . doubtful. 'What do you think is going through her mind?' I ask and answer myself before Henry can, my voice tiny. 'Is this really it? A baby? Nothing more to it?' She was always a big woman, not fat but almost masculine in her build, domineering in her stance. In the photograph, she wears a patterned dress and a wool coat that has fallen open. We do not interlock. We might be images in separate photographs. 'It says four months,' I say, handing it to Henry.

In the third photograph, labelled five months, I am recumbent on a rug spread over grass. 'My eyes are half open. As though . . . as though I'm dazed,' I reflect. Henry looks perturbed and takes the photo from me before I drop it. In the next, six months, Mother is sitting on a bench, an arm strapping me in position on her lap. She wears a dark dress with a light collar. There is a little girl in a fussy smock, face shaded by the brim of a white bonnet beside us. 'That's my cousin Rachel,' I identify, tapping the figure with a forefinger.

'I guessed as much,' says Henry, taking a closer look as I give it to him.

'One year.' I am peeping out from under a sun hat, holding a beach ball and staring in wonder at it. 'It's as if I'm carrying the world in my arms.' I stand legs apart on a pebble beach. I keep hold of this one as I sift through the remainder. 'Two years old.'

'A nautical pose! You don't look very happy,' Henry remarks in perturbation, as though he would like to extract me from the photograph.

'No! Mother and I in a boat.' Instantly a wave of nausea grips me. 'I'm not a good sailor even now.'

'I know you're not.' Henry rubs my shoulder. He is such a kind man. There is a shortage of kindness in life, a dearth of it. But somehow Henry got the lion's portion, which is liberally distributed throughout his character.

'I look very distressed, don't I?' Henry nods. No argument from him. He knows my expressions. 'My mother has on her long-suffering face.' I sigh in remembrance.

I sift through the rest more quickly. Mother, looking less of a mother and more of a grandmother, bending down to drag me through shallow water. The sea? A lake? Me, sitting at the edge of a sandpit surveying a sandcastle I have built. Then an image of me by myself, and one of me with my mother in a park, both dated 1950 on the back. 'I think these two must have been taken together. Look.' Henry obliges, our shoulders nudging each other. 'I'm wearing the same dress in each.' I have a side parting in my shoulder-length hair. 'It must be summer because all the trees are in full leaf.'

'August I'd guess,' Henry contributes with confidence, on safe ground with his expertise in all things that sprout from the earth. 'Mmm . . . yes, early August. I'd put money on it.'

Mother wears a short-sleeved dress, belted at the waist. Her face is a long and angular, presided over by a large nose. Lines may be detected on her brow, despite the distance between us and the photographer. What strikes me about this mini album is that I am not saying 'cheese'. 'My lips look as if they've been sewn together,' I remark recalling the frustration of stopped-up feelings. My eyes are haunted.

On to the next. I flip it over and read the date. 'Easter 1952. I would have been four.' I am in a dark coat and dark beret, clutching a doll. And I do mean clutching, with those same pensive eyes, anxious what-happens-next eyes. 'And here's one of me with my father.' A business suit, hair clipped close, large glasses with chunky frames. He is swinging me between his legs. 'I'm giggling.' My note is one of wonder. 'Proof that I could do it, that I could giggle if I had reason to.' Finally, the last photograph. 'Oh, Henry, it's the picture I wanted. Me and the donkey. The donkey and me. I was in bliss on that donkey. I can remember those ears, those flippy-floppy ears. How soft they were.'

Henry clears his throat importantly. 'If I might make an observation.' Our eyes lock for a moment as I attempt to gauge what he is going to say. 'You have a jolly good seat on a horse.' We share a smile. Then I rummage once more in the envelope, lift out a letter and start to digest its significance. Seconds later and I am sobbing, Henry gathering me into his arms, Merlin displaced, up and whining fretfully.

Chapter 3

Bethan, 1943

If I'm honest when the war came it was sort of a relief. I was eleven years old. And really what I do remember most was a kind of charge of concentrated energy. It was as though electricity was running through my veins and not blood. It meant change, see, something different. There was lots of talk before it happened, know-it-alls saying this and that. Grave faces, raised voices. I can remember Dad losing his temper and thumping his fist down on more than one occasion. Didn't really understand why at the time, but I do now. I was too young to take it all in, see.

Brice was in a flurry, too. You could see it in his eyes. They sparkled like the starry heavens on a clear night. He had gorgeous eyes my big brother, the fern green of the Preseli Mountains. And he was always so patient. Bethan, *cariad*, he would say, stop running about like a rat on a mound of grain. Round and round you go making yourself dizzy, getting nowhere fast. Sometimes he used to catch me up in his arms. And that was so nice. Though I was getting too big for those swinging hugs by the time he left. All that quiet, that inner calm drained out of him when the buzz of war began. He was seventeen at the time. The thought of leaving off books to help on the farm, well, it felt like freedom to me. Just the way joining up felt to him, I s'ppose. To hear him chatter you'd have thought he was going to win single-handed, shoot the German army dead all by himself, that it would be over in a month or so. Like I said, neither of us really knew what lay ahead.

Our dad frowned even more than usual. He said the country needed our farm to feed it, more now than ever before. I thought he was crazy when he spoke like that. Our little farm feeding all of Wales? It made me smile, and brought to mind of the story of Jesus feeding a few loaves and fishes to all those hundreds who'd come to listen to him preach. He managed it with a miracle. I realised soon enough that we'd need a miracle, as well, if we weren't to expire with exhaustion. Our mam realised what it meant though, what was happening to us. She cried most every day.

'Mam, why are you so sad?' I asked her. 'Everyone's saying we'll win and teach those beastly Germans a lesson.' I won't forget what she replied.

'I expect we will, Bethan, *bach*. Eventually.' And she wiped her wet eyes with the corner of her apron. She didn't cry, though, when Brice came home in his smart uniform. I gasped he looked so handsome. But all the blood left her face and she had to be helped to a chair. She made a noise then that was a moan and a sigh all mixed up. She gripped his arms and looked into his shiny, shiny eyes. I don't know what she saw there but it wasn't good. She didn't say anything but I heard her all the same. *Don't go*, she begged with her eyes. *Don't go, my Brice, my darling boy, my darling, darling boy.* And he grinned and bragged he'd be back on leave before she knew it, with lots of gory stories to make us girls scream. He was my roundabout, spinning me until I didn't know up from down. Then he complained that I was getting too fat. I scowled at that. No girl wants to be told she's filling out like a squashy cushion. He winked at my screwed-up face. He said that soldiers got extra rations of chocolate, and if I was good he'd bring back a whole trunk for me.

My mam, Seren Haverd, is as small as my dad's tall. Her figure used to be rounded, what you'd call cuddly. And the lines on her face came from having a laugh. Her eyes are green like my brother's . . . were, but richer, steadier, you know. She had a mischievous streak that in a blink could turn a sulk into a giggle. Before Brice left she had thick brown hair. Although she tidied it into a bun, it spent the days escaping, tumbling about her face like a waterfall. She threatened to chop it all off she said it was such nuisance. Then Brice joined up and that glorious mane seemed to go grey overnight, the lustre quite gone out of it, so that it lay limp and lifeless wherever she put it. The weight fell off her as well. Now when she enfolds you in her arms she's all brittle bone. You feel you have to be careful because she may break.

The day Brice went to war he shook Dad's hand and said he was sorry he wouldn't be here to help on Bedwyr. Our farm, Bedwyr Farm, is named for Sir Bedivere. He was a knight of the Round Table, the fellow who returned the sword Excalibur to the Lady of the Lake. It's in Newport, South Wales. Our farmhouse is over a hundred years old, Dad says. That's why it's all higgledy-piggledy, with bits fallen down and bits stuck on. It's white with a slate roof. There's a small barn, a milking shed, a stable, a sty and a few old outbuildings that Dad is always promising to do up for lodgers. I'm afraid the way things are going it'll be full of evacuees, not rent-paying lodgers. We keep sheep, a small herd of dairy cows, a few pigs, chickens and a couple of bad-tempered geese that I'd far prefer to see on a plate. We have forty acres laid to corn, wheat, barley, oats and turnips. And then there's Mam's vegetable garden, the mainstay of our meals.

When my brother surveyed the land he looked so worried that I flexed my arm and told him not to fret, as I'd be doing all the chores from here on. We all laughed at that. But I tell you, I wouldn't have found it half so funny if I'd known how true it was going to be. He said goodbye to Mam upstairs in her bedroom, so I'll never know what sentiments were exchanged. She didn't come outside but I saw her curtain twitch. Instead of him arriving home on leave though we got a telegram. Mam read it out, and her face, which was all kind and gentle, set hard as a rock. That was the day she stopped smiling. It won't ever leave me. It was 22 February 1941. I was suffering with one of those earaches I'm prone to. Mam's troubled with them as well. A family weakness she says. There were reports on the radio that Swansea had been blitzed by German bombers, that the town was all but gone. They say you don't value a thing until it's taken away. So that was when I learned my mam's smile was more precious than gold.

The bits and bobs I think I'll remember about the war are nonsense really. Not what you'd think a girl would store up in her head, while all around her is death and grief, droning planes and marching men. No church bells, see. I warned you. Daft, isn't it? I think church can be really boring, but I miss those bells. Hearing them on a winter's morning chiming out in the frosty air, and in the summer ding-danging over fields of poppies. I s'ppose I should be grateful that the bell ringers are idle, because we all know they'd only peal if the Germans were invading, come to take away our beloved Cymru.

And the dark, that's another thing. Oh I imagine you think you know what dark is. It's when the sun goes down and you switch on the lights, get a fire going in the grate, and if you're in town watch as the street lamps are switched on like blazing sunflowers. But there are no street lamps in war. And if the lights are on in the houses you don't know, not with the blackout curtains we all have. The night is so dark you think you've vanished. You don't know where you begin or end. Once or twice I've pinched myself to make sure I'm real. It's all so ditchwater dull, too. No colour, see. And how I long for colour, for marshmallow pinks, and minty greens, and marigold oranges and yellows.

I almost didn't mention the shops being empty. I miss the shops. I used to like browsing the shop windows in Newport thinking what I'd buy one day. On the bus heading home, I'd recall my favourites, what had tickled my particular fancy. And as I closed my eyes, pulled the eiderdown over my head and felt with my toes for the hot water bottle, I'd flick through my wished-for purchases. A satin dress, a glittery piece of jewellery, a box of chocolates with a big velvet bow on top. But when there isn't anything in the windows and half the places are boarded up, or have queues outside them a mile long, you have to employ your imagination. I stock up in my head. On the dreariest of days, I look forward to it so much, unpacking my bags and boxes before I drop off to sleep. I'm very well dressed in my dreams you know.

And I have so many books up here in my imagination, my head might as well be a library. I can't believe that I was so eager to slam them shut. Who needs books, I used to grumble. Well, I've my answer now – I do! I picture my school, too. I want so badly to go back there, chewing a pencil and puzzling out sums. Though I haven't got a head for numbers and facts. They seem to trickle in and trickle out again, as if there's a plughole but no plug in my skull. I had such fun playing skipping games in the playground with my friend Aeron Powell, the vet's daughter, and sharing our lunch pieces. Aeron sat next to me in class and she helped me out with maths when the teacher wasn't looking. She was clever at maths, Aeron was. She had long red hair that mostly she wore in braids, and she was shorter than me so that I felt protective over her, especially when the boys got stupid and tried to bully her. Oh, what I'd give to be back there, starting again, but without the war.

After Brice died I became a daughter and a son all in one. I think Dad has forgotten I'm a girl inside these dungarees. Or p'rhaps I should say a woman. Because you see, I developed in the blackness, like a mole in a hole. My body changed while I was digging potatoes. My breasts swelled while I was driving the tractor. My periods started one morning when I was milking. I felt sort of warm and wet down there, like I'd had an accident in my knickers. It wasn't a shock. I live on a farm for goodness' sake. Nature's everywhere.

'Dad?' I said. 'Dad, I've got go inside for a moment.'

'What you talking about, Bethan Modron? We aren't nearly done here.' My dad only uses my middle name when he's getting impatient with me. Modron is the Celtic goddess of motherhood – a bit grand for me. When I hear it, I know his temper's stirring and I best be careful. He's a large man, my dad, Ifan Haverd, very stern. He's got wild grey hair the colour of Welsh slate, a square face with a big bumpy nose in the middle of it and startling turquoise eyes, deep set, that look out of place, as if they've been stolen. Mam says I've got my father's eyes. They're exact same shade, though I think they suit me with my pale skin and my strawberry-blonde hair. Unlike him, I look like the rightful owner.

Dad's skin is wind-burned and craggy. He wears his farm clothes as if they are an army uniform and he's a Welsh Fusilier moving on the enemy in Belgium. I love him, I do. But I'm a bit scared of him, too. I know how tired he gets, how he's up nights fretting about yields, and lambing, and ringworm and vegetable blight. I wish I could control the weather for him, make the rain stop and start with a snap of my fingers, make the sun beat down before the harvest. I wish I could stop the seagulls and crows gobbling up the seed, and prevent the pests from burrowing into the vegetables. But no one can stop nature, that's plain to see.

Also, I do try to make up for Brice being gone. We were never told the details of his death but I think about him sometimes at night. He pops up among the satin dresses and the chocolates decorated with candied violets, and in the pages of the books. I think about the Germans blowing him up with a grenade, or shooting him through his lovely heart, or stabbing him dead. I don't want to but I can't tie down my thoughts. I try to see the Jerries' ugly faces, but that's hopeless as well. As I bring them closer and peer under their helmets, all I discover is other young men like my brother, men whose eyes are shiny, too, but with terror now.

I did my damnedest to ignore my period when it began, but like the weather it wasn't going away. So I left off milking and risked Dad's wrath. 'I've really got to go, Dad. I won't be long.' He sighed angrily and squeezed his mouth with a hand, as if that was the only way he could delay giving me a telling-off. I got up then and walked a bit awkwardly to the door of the milking shed. But if I was anxious about him seeing a stain, I shouldn't have been. It's gloomy in there. It's always gloomy, steamy with the breath of the cows and the cold. And besides, he wasn't even looking at me. I didn't tell Mam either. What would have been the purpose? She was as busy in the house as Dad was outside it. I coped perfectly well. A bit of a wash down, rags and clean trousers. Soon sorted.

Dad didn't even notice I'd changed my clothes. No one guessed what was going on, which seemed unbelievable when I was so acutely aware of it. Some days I could feel my chest swelling and tingling like twin buds opening. Underneath these clothes, I'm a woman, though no one has made the observation. But if you think I'm miffed, that I go about mooning at my face in the bathroom mirror, pouting like a movie star and wiggling my hips, if you think I ferret in the linen cupboard and drape the old curtains around me like a bride, or that I mix coal dust with water and try painting my face, you'd be wrong. Why not? No harm in it, I know. Well, it's because I'm just too knackered. I get up at six and keep on the go till nine, fall into bed and start the whole rigmarole again. You have a try and see if you have the strength to play at being a fine lady.

At supper Dad often says furious things about the Germans, about what he'd like to do them, how he wants to make them pay for Brice. He says that Hitler is the devil come to earth to make his hell. He says the SS are his henchmen. He says our brave boys are infiltrating Germany this very second, that a day's coming soon when one of them will blow Hitler to smithereens. He says he despises the filthy Hun. The way his voice grinds out of him is horrible. It's like his hands are gripped about the neck of some young German boy, strangling the life out of his thrashing body. But I'll tell you what bothers me most of all: that boy, he'd have a mam at home as well. And a dad. And maybe even a sister like me. And if you stabbed him he'd bleed the same as Brice. Before the war I used say that I hated things most days, getting up for school, lava bread, going to chapel, the earaches I get. But I don't think I meant it, really. When Dad's eyes seem to disappear into his head, and his face pulls all one way so that I don't recognise him, that's hate, that's killing hatred festering inside him looking for an outlet.

So it's an especial surprise when one evening sitting about the fire he says he can't cope no more. He says that he needs as many arms as an octopus. He says that two German prisoners of war are going to be working on the Bedwyr Farm, starting next week.

Chapter 4

Harriet, 1947

The world wars have robbed me of both my parents. I was born in 1912, a toddler when the First World War broke out, six years old and motherless by the time it ended. Of course, I recollect nothing whatsoever about it. At the outset of the Second World War, I was twenty-seven, living in Finsbury Park, had been married three years to Merfyn Pritchard, was childless by circumstance not design, and had been employed as a dressmaker and in a munitions factory. And when it was over, I remembered everything about it, though I would have preferred to forget.

My mother died in a Zeppelin bombing raid on London in September 1915. It raised the house we were living in at the time to the ground. God knows how, but providentially for me I was pulled from the rubble alive. My father took sole responsibility for my upbringing then, with the able assistance of our housekeeper. Papa was a strict parent, a tower of a man, austere in disposition. His features carved into a pale mottled complexion, he reminded me of a Roman bust – but without a scalp of coiled hair. His own, though swept back from his high pleated brow, fell in loose squirrel-grey waves to his starched collar. He lived by the highest moral standards himself and he expected no less of his only daughter. So I've got him to thank for my acute sense of right and wrong, of good and evil, of sin and virtue. Sadly, he was also taken from me during the Second World War in a car accident in the blackout. So you could say that Germany orphaned me.

Among his rules was one of total abstinence from alcohol. If this was an irrelevance to a girl accustomed to mugs of milk and water, it came as I grew up to have a significance I could not have foretold. 'Drinking liquor is a degrading vice, Harriet. It eats into the soul of man like a cancer. It robs him of his self-respect. It teaches him to squander his wages. It leads to domestic violence and crime. It destroys the family. Never doubt that ever since man has trodden the grape and partaken of its fermented poison, chaos has resulted,' he lectured, as if from the pulpit, shaking a finger in my face. Every night and every morning, he came to my room and we prayed together for temperance, for restraint in all appetites of the flesh, for moderation, for self-control.

'The body is a vessel of debauchery, Harriet. It is a carnal cesspit of greed and lust and bestial depraved urges. It must be cleansed with fervent prayer and constant communion with God. In his infinite mercy may he grant you purity in mind and body and soul. For you can ask no greater gift.'

We knelt down at the foot of my bed when we petitioned our maker. We said the Lord's Prayer in unison, his thunderous delivery drowning out my child's treble. He schooled me that this invocation should be my sunrise and my sunset. 'Lead us not into temptation,' he shouted, lifting my sagging arms up to heaven. 'The devil with his prodigious cunning will place forbidden fruit in your path, Harriet. Most assuredly he will. As a soldier of the Lord you must fast. Put on your suit of holy armour. Leave no chink in it for Satan, that slippery viper, to worm through. Remember evil is crafty and baffling. You must be vigilant, child.' He laid his hand like a clod of earth on my head and buried me under it, so that my neck ached and my knees wobbled. 'Do you feel it, Harriet? Do you feel the devil driving into you?'

I opened my eyes and tears trickled from them. 'Yes, yes, I do, Papa. Help me,' I pleaded earnestly. And he called upon the Holy Spirit to wash away any thought of sin. 'Lord God give us the strength to fend off mortal desires. "Wine is a mocker, strong drink is raging: and whoever is deceived thereby is not wise." Proverbs 20, verse 1.' Though, of course, I was far too young to understand that drink corrodes the mental faculties.

Sometimes prayer alone could absolve me. Sometimes he needed to beat the badness out of me. 'I do this to demonstrate God's love,' my father would say hoarsely, crouching down before me, his grey eyes meeting mine, his warm stale breath on my face. Seeing his eyes well up along with mine I was moved, so sorrowful was my papa that he must castigate me.

Unsurprisingly, Papa was not an advocate of the suffragette movement. He held that equality between the sexes, like the unicorn, owed more to myth than reality. 'Only trouble will come of women having the vote,' he prophesied. It was his opinion that the fairer sex should be adorned like birds of paradise in pretty dresses and gathered skirts, hemmed to reveal no more than your ankles, in high-necked blouses with modest sleeves that hid both elbows and wrists. He was very disappointed to see the war eroding this edict, and more and more females swaggering about in men's attire. By the way, I abide by his code. And this not simply out of respect to a principled man, but because I have come to share his dictum: 'Let men be men and women be women.' You only have to look at Romans 1, verse 26 and 27: 'For their women exchanged the natural function for that which is unnatural, and in the same way also the men abandoned the natural function of the women and burned in their desire towards one another.' I think that clarifies the Almighty's position on cross-dressing rather succinctly, don't you?

Papa did not hold with face painting either. I am not my father's clone, and yet I have come to share his views. Women seem to have gone mad since the war ended, smearing their faces with anything they can get their hands on. 'What are they trying to hide, Harriet, with their cow eyes and their mouths all red and greasy?' Papa used to say with a sneer. 'Trollops, every one. Soap, water and truth is all you should require. What need of the tricks of Jezebel here?'

Papa did not encourage friendships with other girls. And socialising with boys was an unbreakable taboo. I was twenty-three before he permitted me to interact with men. I met Merfyn at a church social. I had come, by then, to reconcile myself to the fact that marriage might not be God's will for me. It certainly did not seem to be my father's. Perhaps it was my lot to care for him, I reasoned, and not for a husband. But no sooner had I resigned myself to spinsterhood than Merfyn Pritchard, a member of our Baptist church's congregation, asked my father for permission to court me. The resemblance between them was uncanny. My suitor was scholarly, sober and dependable. An exponent of the Bible, he held it was the only book that repaid regular revision, that publishers of the modern prurient novel were in league with Satan.

Besides these attributes, he possessed a trump card, his rigorous adherence to punctuality. Papa venerated punctuality in others. Living his creed, he referred constantly to the silver pocket watch tucked into his waistcoat. 'If you say you will arrive at seven o'clock in the evening, then it behoves you to do precisely that. Indeed should you be either premature or tardy, you are less of a man in my opinion, for you have given your bond and failed in the expectation of it.' Merfyn did not have a pocket watch, he had a wristwatch. Nevertheless he consulted it quite as much as my father did, if not more. They were also of one mind regarding the importance of temperance. 'To imbibe,' Merfyn told my papa before taking me to a tea dance, 'is to descend the stairway to damnation.'

The Adoption

I am no wavering daisy, more of the hollyhock in build and stature. I have my father's firm chin, his pointed nose. And if I am the hollyhock, then Merfyn is the sturdy oak. With rumours of war flying about, I needed a crutch to prop me up. It may not sound romantic to you but then I am a realist. Regarding me through his horn-rimmed spectacles, Merfyn also appeared content. He saw a tall woman, a woman who did not baulk at physical toil, a woman with an honest open face, brown eyes and curly ebony hair, a woman who valued modesty over vanity in dress. The curls are my one indulgence – curling irons. Through my own round lenses, I perceived a man an inch or so shorter than myself, a man who, in suit and tie, his frizzed hair oiled down, did not offend the eye. He'll do, I thought. And no doubt he thought, she'll do, and the match was made.

Merfyn is originally from Wales, Pembrokeshire, a Buster Keaton lookalike, though somewhat heavier set. If he had an accent once all but the barest trace of it is gone. He's prudent with money. So between him and Papa, our wedding was an exercise in economy. I made the dress, arranged the flowers in margarine tubs, and the tea, sausage rolls and fruitcake were provided by my mother-in-law. Afterwards, we moved into our small house in Stroud Green. In truth, it felt rather like going home when we returned there after the ceremony. At night, I continue to fall to my knees, but now Merfyn heads up the prayers for temperance, sobriety and abstinence. He does not beat me. But once a week on Saturday nights, with the lights off and the curtains pulled tight, we have sexual intercourse.

Apparently my mother was a gifted seamstress. My father encouraged me to work at my needlecraft, to emanate her skill. He said I had inherited her aptitude for it, even went so far as to praise my efforts. Merfyn is also proud of me, and I like to think pleased with the way I manage our home. In wartime he remarked that I was wonderfully inventive, unpicking worn jumpers and making them anew, fashioning dresses from curtains, faded tablecloths and the like. And, as for my cooking, he told me that he didn't know how I put dinner on the table with the paucity of our weekly ration.

'You do not slack, Harriet. You are a plough horse. I admire that,' he said.

Merfyn has angina. So instead of fighting overseas he did his bit at home, working as an air-raid warden. When he went out at night, I worried that he might be buried under a mountain of bricks the way my mother was, the way I was. But, like a homing pigeon, he always returned. Then we would sit sharing a pot of tea companionably, undeniably weak and stewed from recycled leaves, but a comfort all the same. He would complain about the people he had rousted on his rounds, windows bare, lights on. 'Can't afford the curtains, a woman cheeked me tonight. Then turn the light off, I hollered back. Will they ever learn? Do they want to give Jerry an illuminated map showing the blighters where to drop their blessed bombs?' The general malaise regarding the gas-mask drill was another of his niggles. 'Hardly anyone has the vision to carry their masks with them. I've told them that it's essential, even demonstrated how to put it on in seconds. But I wear glasses, they moan. And here, what about my hat? So I quote verbatim from the radio broadcasts: "If you are wearing spectacles take them off first. If you are wearing a hat, take it off calmly but quickly. Always hold your breath so that you don't take gas into your lungs." They look at me as if I'm touched. Still, I've done my job. If Hitler gases the lot of them it won't be my fault.'

By then we had already signed the pledge of lifelong abstinence from drink, and I am proud to say are venerable members of the increasingly popular Sons of Temperance. The organisation was founded in the nineteenth century to battle an epidemic of drunkenness, and to offer an alternative to the dissolute lifestyles rife in Britain. The Band of Hope that started up in Leeds in the 1840s was all part of it. Our members live entirely without intoxicating substances, vowing for evermore to refresh minds and bodies in the way God intended, with health-giving recreation, fresh air and non-alcoholic cordials and beverages. And I am happy to say that Brothers and Sisters join us and take up the good cause every day.

'With the war on and the stuff being so difficult to get hold of it's not so bad. But you mark my words, Harriet, once it's all over the rot will speedily set back in,' Merfyn predicted, his face clouded with pessimism. And he was correct. We are kept busy spreading the word, converting the fallen. People are so easily led astray. Though I have to confess that Merfyn and myself do have a mutual weakness of the flesh, one neither of us feels able to deny. I blush when I reflect on the condemnation Papa would most certainly have rained down on us for this shared defect. I confess it. We both have a sweet tooth. There is nothing more soothing I find than sharing a quarter-pound of barley sugars of an evening, or crunching on a bit of slab toffee. It was one of the few treats we permitted ourselves before the war. And we all need something sweet to take the bitter edge off these bleak days now it's finished.

I had seen quite enough of death when the Second World War was finally over. So had we all. These days everyone you meet has lost a relative, a son, a brother, a husband. Here countless homes have been destroyed, and hundreds of thousands are dead, Papa among them. I don't like to contemplate how many of our brave boys are buried under foreign soil. The Germans have much to atone for. Hitler is gone. They say he took the coward's route committing suicide at the last. The Nazis are obliterated. But it will take decades for the wounds to heal. I suppose I should count myself lucky. I am one of the few who still has her husband by her side. But I do not have a baby in my arms.

We have been trying for some years now, letting nothing disrupt our routine. During the war, Merfyn became so keen on having a baby, on becoming a father, that I gave my consent. He duly abandoned the use of prophylactics. However I have not conceived. Unlike many women, I do not have the excuse that my husband has been away either. Merfyn thought that frequency, or rather the lack of it, might be the culprit. So we followed a twice-weekly schedule for in excess of six months – but to no avail. My menses come like clockwork.

I dislike being thwarted. Besides, it is vinegar to me to see my sister-in-law, Enid, with her two children, Frank and Rachel, my nephew and niece. She doesn't seem to appreciate how fortunate she is. And Rachel is such a darling. True, it must have been tough for her with Gethin invalided at Dunkirk. Gethin was Merfyn's younger brother. He hobbled home more a burden than a boon and, despite Enid's constant nursing, eventually caught influenza and died. Widowhood, and with so few men returned home no hope of a second husband . . . awful! Still, I'm sure her children are a comfort to her.

I want a child, a daughter. I have been mulling it over. A son would be too messy. Muddy boots and cricket bats. Dirty kit. Meccano all over the floor, tripping me up. Matchbox toys and rowdy cowboy and Indian games? What a headache! But a daughter? A pretty girl who I can dress up in the clothes I make, dress up like a dear little doll, me teaching her sewing, knitting, crochet, cooking, housework. I have had myself checked out. It seemed common sense. As far as the doctors can tell there is nothing amiss, which leads me to conclude that the fault lies with Merfyn. But how to tackle the subject?

An evening while Britain is busy throwing off the millstone of war, and a Labour government is getting into its stride, I approach Merfyn. 'Are you planning to go to the doctor,' I enquire delicately. 'To see if . . . if any problems you might be unaware of are holding us back from having a . . . a family?' My cheeks flame and quiver with shame. Head down, I peer through my glasses at an intricate bit of pearl stitching around the snowy toe of a hopeful baby's bootie. We are listening to

Gracie Fields singing 'Now is the Hour' on the radio.

'No, I don't think I am, Harriet,' Merfyn, rejoins, rolling the pipe clenched between his teeth to allow his words through passage. Like me his head is bowed as if he is intent on his paper.

I unwind a bit of two-ply, and moisten my lips with the tip of my tongue. Haven't I undergone an examination, embarrassing and intrusive as it was? From beyond the grave my papa's chill grey eyes bore into me. Outside our front door they are constructing a new city from London's rubble, and I want our daughter to be a part of it. My knitting needles click in irritation. 'So that's that,' I mutter.

A pause that I take for my answer abruptly and unexpectedly ends. 'Not altogether,' Merfyn says. He has resumed his previous job working as a stock manager for the Ever Ready Company. He remains, I observe, in his work suit trousers, though not his jacket. In place of it, he is wearing a pullover I knitted for him. It is a Fair Isle design in cobalt blue and cream and seal grey. It looks rather fetching, though I say so myself. It was a devil to get hold of the wool though. He turns the page meditatively. It has been a bitterly cold winter. When the heavy snows started to melt it led to widespread flooding. They have cut down radio broadcasts, and suspended television altogether to conserve energy supplies. And morale, as we struggle through to the spring, is desperately low. I am beginning to feel as if rationing will persist to eternity. I miss my slab toffee as an injured soldier might miss a limb. An exaggeration? Not really. These years are proving a trial to us all.

When the war was won everyone was jubilant. Street parties, bonfires, and so forth. Spontaneous celebrations erupting like miniature volcanoes. The mood was ebullient. And then? Well, you logically assumed things would quickly get back to normal, to how they were prior to the years of hellish nights pierced with air-raid sirens, and dawns of discovered mayhem. But they didn't. The shops still look empty. Rationing drags on. And day-to-day life, particularly with these arctic conditions, this interminable winter, seems worse than ever. It is the rolls of fabric I pine for most, after the toffee that is. Georgette, organdie, voile, tulle, bombazine, crepe, taffeta, chambray, lawn, seersucker or even just plain cotton. Just plain cotton will do. It will do very well. The day I choose a new pattern, buy yards of fabric, and get my treadle machine going, then and only then will I believe the war is truly over and done with.

Merfyn interrupts my reverie. 'Have you thought about us adopting, Harriet?'

I admit I haven't. The idea has not occurred to me before. In a way, I ruminate, as the mantelpiece clock strikes eight, it is not utterly repellent. No discomfort for me, no morning sickness, no pounds to gain. I own that there is something vaguely distasteful about the notion of something growing inside you. And I am, with my fondness for sugar, prone to putting on weight. I progress my thoughts. No labour, no painful childbirth. No risk of congenital abnormalities. We will know that the baby is perfect in advance. After all, it will have been previously checked over, literally top to bottom. Besides, being that much older, thirty-five to be accurate, I have to accept there is a chance of me having one of those . . . those mongol children, or a kiddy who is retarded, or disabled. And that would be horrible. When you consider it, there are no guarantees after such an ordeal that you will produce a normal baby. And it is worth remembering that you can't send it back. You'll be lumbered with it for year after year until you are old, and perhaps even beyond to the very limits of decrepitude. Oh! I acknowledge that most get away with it and are perfectly content with the result. But . . . well, you'd be foolish not to open your eyes wide to the possibilities.

The Cossor radio Papa bought me as a wedding gift bursts into song with a Judy Garland number, making us both start. 'Somewhere Over the Rainbow'. There is static. The rainbow must indeed be far off. I lay my knitting aside and get up to twiddle the knob and adjust it. Once I am satisfied with Judy's dulcet notes, I stand and stare at it for a bit, daring it to misbehave. A ready-made baby, I muse, tapping an index finger over my mouth. A memory surfaces, a rare fossil of Papa escorting me around a toy shop in the build-up to Christmas. He instructed me to point at the doll I wanted. There were so many, all of them dressed in beautiful outfits complete with accessories, all of them competing for my attention. Lacy parasols, brocade purses, leather handbags, bouquets of silk flowers, buckets and spades, satin scarves, velvet bonnets, straw hats, tooled belts, tiaras and jewels. Painted and glass eyes followed me from under fringed lashes. I counted tiny shoes with silver and brass buckles, and boots with laces fine as embroidery thread.

I directed Papa's gaze behind the counter, flapping my hand excitedly in the direction of a doll propped at a far end of a low shelf. I must have her. She had skin of light peach porcelain, crimped hair of the finest gold and a pair of glass eyes, sky blue and iridescent. And I could glimpse pearl-white teeth, minute as rice grains between parted smiling sugar-pink lips. The shopkeeper lifted her down for me to touch her silky dress. He said her name was Francesca. But when I unwrapped my present on Christmas morning after church, it was not Francesca I discovered but an inferior cloth doll with a printed face and straggly wool hair. Her dress had not even been properly hemmed.

Now Merfyn is offering me an opportunity to pick again. Surely this time with Papa at rest no one can prevent me from having my Francesca. But still a doubt nags. What about the things you can't see, the things the doctors can't detect, the qualities that are inbred, the character traits that might emerge gradually? What if the birth parents are simpletons? Or immoral? The unwise union of a thief and a murderer say? What if the infant is the fruit of an alcoholic father?

Imagine this! Now here really is a dilemma. Some of the brethren in our temperance group believe that alcoholism, a proclivity for drink, can be inherited, passed on from a mother or a father to their child. Or am I being paranoid? It is training that counts. Any taint of evil can soon be eradicated. It is a bit like buying a length of fabric. It doesn't matter what the design is, because you can make it up into any style you like.

I conjecture that there must be lots of wartime babies needing homes, an entire catalogue of them. Some, very probably, have been fathered by American soldiers. I grimace envisioning them armed with silk stockings, cigarettes, chocolates and their bold brash Yankee charm. Many gullible young women will have had their heads turned by easy promises and rare luxuries. Few possess my moral backbone. Ambrose's Big Band is kicking off with 'Memphis Blues' as I return to my seat. Merfyn's eagle eyes spy me interestedly through his large lenses. A measure of Yankee blood? After all, didn't we sail over there on the *Mayflower*? Weren't they English through and through when they set out?

'I suppose we could give it a try,' I agree slowly, taking up my knitting again. 'Or at least make some preliminary inquiries without committing ourselves.' Merfyn leans across to me and pats my leg approvingly through the wool of my skirt. 'I'd have to see the baby first, of course, decide if I like the look of it.'

'That goes without saying,' Merfyn concurs. I hear the enamel of my husband's teeth scrape on the stem of his pipe and he puffs contentedly for a few seconds. Then, 'We'd do it all properly,' he adds. 'Officially.' Hmm . . . *officially* – I like that. It has the ring of a money-back guarantee. My husband's attention vacillates and he returns to his paper, flapping the pages with a rustle.

'I think I'd like a girl,' I say after a gap. I might try to get hold of some pink wool next.

Chapter 5

Bethan, 1947

The night before the Germans came I had a scary dream about them. I saw them far off at the other end of a newly ploughed field running towards me. They were both carrying guns and shouting. I wanted to escape so badly, but my feet were planted in the ground, really planted, as if there were roots coming out of my boots going deep down into the soil. It was a glorious day. Spring and the great greenness coming up. Birdsong, the distant treetops visible over swell of the ground, like sphagnum moss. I kept pulling and pulling, but I was stuck fast, and they were getting closer now. I crouched down and started frantically to undo my laces. And glancing up, I saw they had stopped as well, about twenty feet from me, that they had both raised their rifles and were taking aim. 'Bethan,' one of them called out in a German accent sighting me, 'keep still. How can we kill you if you keep wriggling?' Their voices were regimental barks, their hands were all covered in blood and their faces were scarred terrible. I woke with a fright when their guns went off. Listening to the hammering of my heart, I realised to my astonishment that I was still alive.

My heart was still hammering when they arrived for real, striding down the lane towards us. And my throat was so parched that I couldn't swallow or speak or anything. I think Dad hadn't slept very well either. The whites of his eyes were all bloodshot, and under them were purple pouches. He pulled his hat down and his expression soured. He told me I was to work on the vegetable patch and see to the pigs today, that I was to tell him immediately if I spotted them up to anything. He said that I was to be his spy. He had his hunting gun with him. And as they got closer, he hissed that he would shoot them both dead if they put a foot out of line. They wore dark clothes, jackets, caps, navy, brown, khaki. Blended in with the surroundings. They stopped about two yards away, took the caps off and spoke. I thought it'd be nonsense, the words all German and bitten up. But it was English I heard. A bit stilted, but English all the same. And their voices were soft as a breath of wind tickling the leaves in a tree. Very polite, apologetic almost.

'Good morning. My name is Jonas Faust, and this is Thorston Engel.' I'd dropped my gaze, both shy and scared. But I forced myself to look back up, to grit my teeth and face the enemy. Stunned, I saw the taller of the two reach inside his jacket. I was sure that he was going to pull a revolver out, but it was papers he held towards my dad. 'We are from the POW camp at Llanmartin.' He hesitated and cleared his throat. 'I think you have been expecting us. Is it Mr Haverd?'

My dad grunted sullenly, snatched the papers and studied them for several minutes. I took the opportunity to hastily appraise the monsters who had come to labour on Bedwyr Farm, the monsters who might have thrown the grenade, pulled the trigger, or plunged the knife that ended our Brice's life. The spokesman, Jonas, I estimated to be in his early thirties, broad across the chest but with a slim waist, his hair shaved close to his skull and fair. His eyes were greyish green but he kept them lowered, not once meeting mine. His friend was even leaner, and younger, his features gentler, kinder, his hair white blond with a touch of red in it. And his eyes . . . his eyes were blue, the blue of morning glory, and they *did* meet mine and held them for a long moment. Then Dad was shouting orders and the Germans were following him.

For the first few months, Dad didn't like me ever to be alone with Faust and Engel. He refused to call them by their first names. And when I asked him how I should address them, he said that I shouldn't as I'd have no cause to talk with them. His suspicious eyes tracked their every move, waiting for them to flatten us with the tractor, or jump us from behind and string us up with rope from the barn rafters, or smash our brains out with a shovel. He mumbled we should keep alert in case they tried to rob us, as if we had anything worth stealing. It was as though they were invisible to Mam though. She didn't use any name for them, first or second. She sent me out with a bit of bread and cheese or bacon rinds for them at lunch, and a mug of tea. But that was it. When she gave me the food she just jerked her chin in the direction of the fields. If it was raining they ate in the shelter of the barn. I knew she couldn't bring herself to wash up their plates or their mugs, so I did it. They left them at the back door and I rinsed them, dried them and put them away.

And nothing did happen. They didn't try to murder us. They arrived on time every day, kept their heads down, spoke only to each other in German in subdued voices, or in English to answer a question, or query a direction. They were always well mannered and deferential, worked very hard and never complained. They didn't make any attempt to break down the wall between us. It was there and that was it. But we all felt the benefits of them coming. They undertook the heaviest tasks automatically, digging, lifting, loading and unloading. Three times Jonas mended the tractor when it broke down. He said he knew about engines and if Sir, that was what they called Dad, would permit him to, he thought he could fix it. At first Dad was scathing. But when the only alternative was putting Jessy our horse to the plough, he relented and let him have a go. When he did it and the engine began to purr and chug again, I think secretly Dad was impressed, though he didn't say so, or thank Jonas either.

We'd taken in an evacuee in the autumn of 1944, Tilley Draper, from Bethnal Green in London. She was twelve years old, with a fluffy head of peanut-gold hair, slightly cross-eyed, her irises a vivid green. And she had a snub nose and the cheeriest smile I think I'd ever seen, apart from Mam's – and I didn't see that any more. She slept in Brice's room, and helped in the kitchen mostly and around the house. She proved a tonic for Mam, and company for me, a little sister, kind of. During the days she couldn't be serious for more than five minutes, which was terrific. She worried about her mam in London, and her dad who was a sailor in the navy. Sometimes she woke in the nights and came to me, and we had a bit of a cry together. But in the morning it was as if it hadn't been. She dried her tears, put on her valiant smile and came to breakfast humming, an example to us all.

It was the day one of the cows got stuck in the mud that something altered. We'd had a dreadful spate of wet weather. Torrential rain for weeks. I made a joke at breakfast about us having to build an ark. But only Tilley laughed. One of our fields slopes down very steeply in the corner furthest from the farm. And there's a bit of a ditch and beyond that a stream. Well, it gets awful muddy there, like sinking sand Dad says. He fences it off when cattle are grazing that land. Only this March day one of the cows had broken through and got stuck in the boggy ground. We tried everything to get her out, but she just kept on sinking further down. The rain was sheeting horizontal and the poor beast was lowing and lowing, neck all stretched and roped with straining muscles, her eyes wild and rolling with panic. Piteous it was.

By noon, Dad declared there was nothing for it but to shoot the creature and butcher her where she lay. He was setting off to fetch his gun when Thorston said he had an idea, and would Dad let him have a last go before he shot her. Dad shrugged as if he didn't care one way or another. Thorston and Jonas put their heads together, and the next thing they'd brought the tractor over and ropes from the barn. Thorston stripped off his jacket and his shirt, then jumped down into the mud with the struggling cow. It was dangerous because one of her back legs was still free and kicking about, and it was fearful slippery. Jonas threw two lengths of rope down to him. Dad stood looking on, frowning, shaking his head and driving back the other cows who'd come to investigate what was going on. Curious creatures cows are. We were all drenched and trembling with the cold. But even with the noise of the rain, which mercifully was easing off now, I could hear Thorston talking to the heifer in German, gentling her and stroking her back. Somehow he managed to get the ropes under her, to either side of her belly. Then he tossed the ends up to Jonas, who tied them to the tractor's towing hook. Our eyes met just before he clambered up the bank. He was as brown as a Negro, head to foot plastered in mud, and those melting blue eyes peered up at me. I wanted to laugh. But not a mocking laugh, look you, just because it was funny. Though I wanted to cry a bit too. I was so frightened he'd fail, and that Dad would fetch his gun and the cow would be dead.

Thorston didn't ride on the tractor with Jonas. He was too filthy. Jonas put it into gear and started to drive away very slowly. The rope whipped taut and mud splattered on my cheeks. You could see the wheels grinding in the sodden earth, and smell the burning petrol. The cow started up her lowing again, louder now, more panicky, and then all of a sudden more and more of her appeared. The tractor moved, slow and steady, and the cow was pulled from the mud like a stopper from a bottle. As soon as the animal could, she got a foothold and began scrambling up the bank. She was filthy too, though the rain was already washing them both off. Thorston undid the ropes. She heaved herself up the last few steps, then ambled off to join the herd none the worse for her encounter. All my dad did was nod curtly at Thorston, and tell him to go and clean up.

That night I lay in bed thinking about it, about the way he had talked to the panicking beast, his determination to save her, the sound of his voice like balm on a sting. Afterwards, I began taking notice of the way he looked up at the sky as if it was speaking to him, the way the wind flattened his hair, the way on the hottest day when we were wracking hay he stripped to the waist and the sunbeams slid over his torso. And I felt his blue eyes on me, fastening on me, looking at me in the way he did the shifting skies. I imagined touching his skin, tasting him, what his lips would feel like pushing against mine, what it would be to have him pull me out of the numbing, back-breaking quagmire of this war. I imagined him jostling my five slumbering senses, making them stand to attention tingling with life, making my blood burn.

I waited for Brice's ghost to come wailing at me through the nights, telling me what a wicked sister I was, how I was betraying him with my lustful longings. But he didn't. He was dead, see. I'd thought I was dead, too. But I wasn't. I was alive, starved for the sensual, beset with cravings I didn't know I had. I very nearly told Tilley one night when she came to me, but then I changed my mind. I s'ppose I knew deep down what a taboo it was to hunger after a German, a soldier who'd probably killed one or more of our boys.

When the war was over and Tilley went home, I missed her dreadful. I really did. I thought we'd revert back to how it was, that the shops would fill up, that rationing would cease, that I might even get to go back to school, pick up where I left off. But things seemed just as hard, only there wasn't Tilley's giggling to make it bearable. By then we'd got so accustomed to having Jonas and Thorston about the farm that Dad had stopped watching them so much. You could say he'd got so as he trusted them. He still didn't call them by their first names though.

Jonas went back to Germany, back to his family. But Thorston stayed on. He said he didn't have anyone waiting for him, that he was an only child and that his mother had died when he was twelve years old. His father was also dead; gassed in the First World War his health had never recovered. Thorston had no memory of him. He had been a baby when a respiratory infection had claimed his father's life. His mother had remarried but he did not have a good relationship with his stepfather. He also told me that he came from East Germany, from Saxony, an area now under Soviet control, and that he was not sure what the future held for him there. He volunteered all this information piecemeal and without elaboration. He said he was content working the land, and that this was reason enough for him to want to stay, that he was even considering trying to immigrate, to make Wales his permanent home. I did wonder though if there was something more, something he was holding back, something which might explain his reluctance to leave Bedwyr Farm. He didn't have to report to the camp any more though. The prisoner-of-war camps were gradually closing down, the functions of the buildings being reinvented. He was effectively a free man and, while he made his contribution to British agriculture, providing unpaid labour, his presence was tolerated by my dad. We cleaned up one of the outbuildings and he moved in there for a bit. It was much more convenient really, him being on the spot, for all of us. No travelling, see. And he was able to put in longer hours, which with Jonas gone was a bit of a blessing.

We are having the bitterest of winters. Tonight I can't settle for fretting about Thorston, all alone in that tumbledown outbuilding with the icy gales whistling in through the cracks in the windows. He stuffs them full of old newspaper but it still seems to slice in. I slip out after supper, leave Mam dozing by the fireside. Dad has braved the conditions to visit a neighbouring farm, the Mortimers. Their son, back from the Far East, has been taken bad with some mystery fever. I trudge through the snow to bring Thorston a flask of hot tea and a couple of extra blankets. I knock on the door and when he opens it the wind fair blows me in. He battles to close it behind me, quite a feat, and stands staring at me, sort of bemused, like he's just woken up.

'Bethan? Is everything all right?'

'Oh yes. I brought you a couple of blankets and a flask of tea,' I say, breathless with cold. I stamp the snow off my boots, offering him the small comforts.

He is wearing his spectacles, wire-rimmed, and he looks so bookish and lonely. 'That is most kind of you,' he says, taking them from me. He sets the blankets down on the wooden bed he made for himself, and puts the flask on the small table in the centre of the room. I found him a spare mattress, and a box to keep his few things in, a couple of chairs and the table. There is an oil lamp placed there, casting eerie shapes on the wall. Outside the wind is having a fit of the heebie-jeebies, screeching and yowling. Heebie-jeebies! That's an expression I learned from an American soldier when I was shopping in town. It means an extremity of nervous agitation coming over you. He told me so with a twinkle in his eye. We are walled in with heavy snow, mislaid in the amnesia of the whiteout.

I wring my hands to try to get the circulation going again. 'It's so . . . ssso . . . cold,' I stutter. Thorston takes them in his and rubs his own heat back into them. And the friction of his skin on mine, the pressure of his fingers is like the electric shock I got trying to lever a plug out of its socket once. And then he stops, but carries on holding them. He looks like a golden boy, his thick jumper, the lumpy knit of it, his skin, his hair. I can smell the cigarettes he smokes, and wool, and the male scent of him. Even his blue eyes seem gold. Our breaths mist the air, and they mingle and gleam, a spin of golden motes.

'Would you like to stay and share the tea?' he asks politely.

'I'd better get back,' I say but do not move. I slip my hands from his. My eyes stray to the table. On it lies an open notebook, a pencil, a penknife, some wood shavings and a small carved wooden horse, the hind legs unfinished. 'Can I have a look?'

He nods, hastily clearing a few folded clothes from off the two chairs. I sit down, my fingers exploring the smooth wood.

'It's not very good. My knife is blunt and I have not any talent,' he excuses his craft, his tone self-depreciatory.

'No, it's so . . . so fine,' I sigh, all the stiffness of my mind gone with the slide of the polished oak.

'You judge this to be accept?'

'*Accept*. Oh yes it is accept,' I echo his faulty English as if it is the highest praise. His face lights up at the unlooked-for compliment. 'It looks real, alive, just like Jessy.'

'I enjoy to make things, to . . . to draw.' He fiddles with an arm of his spectacles, adjusts it around his ear. 'Mmm . . . if . . . if it had been different, I should like to have been an artist.' He comes to stand beside me. I pick up the notebook. 'I do not think those are accept. Not worth your attention.'

I catch my breath as I turn the gilded pages and see picture after picture of Bedwyr Farm, the animals, the sheep, the pigs, the chickens, the cows and Jessy the horse, from every angle. I study the trees and fields I know like my own body, the valley, the sky turning the land on its head, the changing seasons, and me . . . me . . . drawings of me. I pick up the book and inspect it more closely. Me at all my tasks observed in intricate detail. It is over three-quarters full. The last sketch is a portrait of my face, my strawberry-blonde hair loose for once and not bound up in a scarf. My eyes look wistful, distant, focused on something only I can see.

'You are very gifted, Thorston. You have captured such a likeness.' And the utterance is low with admiration and respect.

'And you,' he responds, his voice the rustle of corn cobs tousled by a breeze on a summer's day, 'you . . . you are most beautiful, Bethan.'

He takes the book from me, closes it and places it back on the table. He pulls me to my feet, undoes the buttons of my coat and slides his hands inside it until his arms encircle me. My heart is jumping and every inch of me seems grated raw. I lean into him, my body craving his, wrapping him round here . . . and here . . . and here too. And then I know what it is to have our lips come together, to feel his energy sprint like a hare beyond the plodding tortoise of me, to have it tunnel into my belly, then lower . . . and lower. He undresses me under the coat. Then he lifts me, still folded in it onto the bed, and covers me with the blankets while he sheds his own clothes. He is molten gold, the lamplight ladling gold over the hollows and ridges and plains and arches of him.

When he climbs in beside me, I try to remember who I am. You are Bethan Modron Haverd. You are the only surviving child of Seren and Ifan Haverd. Your country has been at war with Germany for almost six years. German soldiers killed your brother, Brice. You are lying naked in bed with a German soldier who might have shot your brother, who would certainly have murdered him if he'd had a chance.

'I am Bethan Modron Haverd,' I mutter. 'I am Bethan Modron Haverd.' But my identity lies under an avalanche, and the snow press beyond our little shack rubs out my name.

'*Schatz. Ich liebe dich*, Bethan.' His words scald my ear and make my reason deaf. Thorston kisses a fugue, light as clouds, into every cell of my body. I am floating into him. He is breathing into me. Who am I? I am snowmelt. I am the coming of spring. I am the conception of life. In some distant part of my senses this registers, as, with a momentary tear of pain, his seed sinks into the virgin earth of me.

The times we lie together in the coming months may be counted on my fingers. I know a dreadful reckoning is coming. I sense the chemistry of me changing. I stare at the shivering pools of amber light flickering on the walls, and I follow our shadows making love. I know this is my entire harvest of happiness, these hours, these minutes, these seconds, spent here with him. There is the rough of the blankets, abrasive on my bare skin, and me soaking up the scent of him like blotting paper, making him mine, and the song of the keening wind whistling away all caution. Soon I will have gambled all of myself, and the remainder of my days will be taken up with repaying the debt.

Chapter 6

Lucilla, 1995

'The Homeless Child for the Childless Home'
The Church Adoption Society
(Founded in 1913 in Cambridge by Rev. W. F. Buttle, M.A.)

Telegrams
4A BLOOMSBURY SQUARE,
BABICHANGE, LONDON
LONDON, W.C. 1
Telephone HOLBORN 3310

21st April, 1948

Dear Mr and Mrs Pritchard,

    We have heard of a little girl, although we do not have her full documents in our possession, and we are wondering if you would feel interested in her. If so, we could arrange for you to see her in the very near future and take her home if she appeals to you.

    The baby is Lucilla Haverd, born on 14th January, 1948. She weighed 7lbs 6oz at her birth and is now about 9lbs 7oz. Her medical report is satisfactory and Wassermann blood tests are negative.

The Adoption

The baby's mother is 20 years old, unmarried and lives at home helping on her father's farm in Wales. The baby's father is 26 years old and has been working on the farm for the last few years. He was a German prisoner of war. Both parents are said to be in good health. The baby has fair hair and blue eyes.

We look forward to hearing from you as soon as possible, letting us know whether you are interested or not. We have to find Lucilla a home in the very near future, and it would be a great help to us if you could telephone your decision.

Yours sincerely,

Valeria Mulholland

Secretary

I have read the letter in so many frames of mind, analysing every word, every comma, every full stop. What made me sob when I first saw it was not learning that my father was a German prisoner of war, a POW, but that they had concealed this from me all these years.

Henry was a tonic, telling me that deep down he had sensed a tantalising foreign allure in me that he found altogether irresistible. As if in testimony, he made love to me so tenderly and attentively that I began to wonder if he was telling the truth, that my interesting ancestry gave me added sex appeal. The fact of it, far from distressing me, made me timidly curious. Already my mind was preoccupied with this new German father; blond, blue-eyed, I hazarded. And I pictured him in a dark grey trench coat, leaning over the deck rail of a ship (I'm not sure why), his cap at a rakish angle, smiling out at the wide, wide ocean and the broad, broad sky. The problem was not with me. I rather liked the thought of distant relatives across the seas. It was the family, my family. They had known, my adopted parents, my grandparents, my aunt Enid and very probably my cousins too. If as children Frank and Rachel were kept in ignorance of this sooty sheep in their midst with her part

Teutonic ancestry, they had certainly been informed later on. The war is all history to me, if not ancient then out of my realm. It was over by the time I arrived. I harbour no hatred, no prejudice. I have no one to grieve. But my mother's parents were both killed in the great wars, and my aunt Enid's husband grew ill and died as a result of battle fatigue and a weakened constitution. Even my grandmother had harboured hatred, a dark residue left over from the First World War.

'So much of it makes sense to me now,' I tell Henry, as we sit together at the dining table that overlooks the small garden, enjoying our coffees after a sandwich lunch. That's one of the nice things about working and living on the estate. Henry comes home for lunch and we pool our morning's events, his of the vagaries of gardening, mine of customers and tourists. 'She often relayed to me in gory detail the fate of her own parents.' Henry has heard this before, but repeating it now with my newly acquired knowledge gives it fresh meaning. 'A mother who had died in a Zeppelin bombing raid in the First World War, and a father who had perished in a car accident during the blackout in the Second World War.' I shake my head ruefully.

Henry blows on his coffee then sets down his cup. 'Mmm . . . your mother, with her dislike and mistrust of anything foreign. Now it all falls into place.'

'My mother who blamed the wars for depriving her of her parents,' I contribute.

'Your mother who believed the Nazis were in league with Lucifer,' Henry continues my train of thought, the two of us only just starting to grasp the far-reaching effects of my paternal origin. 'She lived through the Second World War, slept in air-raid shelters, listened to the British propaganda, probably sang the anti-German songs. There must have been more than a few people she was acquainted with who had lost their loved ones.'

I felt suddenly uncomfortable with my mother's deep-seated

prejudice. All around us were the colours of hope, the harlequin green of virgin grass pricking the wakening ground, a tub of pansies, their heads wavering in a tumult of lavender blues, thistle and plum purples, and creamy yellows. The sky was a jubilant shout of blue that made you want to kick off your shoes, throw yourself down on the earth, lock your hands behind your head and let the aerial show hypnotise you. But there was an adjustment to be made in my perception that currently handicapped me, preventing such freedom of expression. Another ghost from the past, my father, had arrived to perplex me. 'She would have monitored me closely for any indication that the blackness was in me, my German blood. In her twisted way, she would have seen it as inherited evil.'

Henry drinks his coffee and we both contemplate the letter in my lap. 'It's the casual, offhand style of writing that bothers me,' he says when he has finished. 'It's as if you were a commodity, a model baby to be viewed and judged as either appealing enough to take home, or a disappointment to window-shopping prospective parents. Actually we wanted one who was a bit more . . . a bit less . . . she isn't really what we . . . we'd prefer it if she wasn't so . . . you can't help but notice . . .' He sighs and strokes his beard sagely.

'But I was a baby, a living breathing human being. Not a puppy who might have desirable traits bred into me, and who could be bludgeoned into obedience.' I offer Henry another cup of coffee and he declines.

'I must get back.' His tone is apologetic, as if he would like stay the afternoon and tend to me and not his plants. He stoops to kiss my cheek, his whiskers tickling me. 'You're not to brood,' he commands, remembering that I have the afternoon off. 'Go and work on your painting.'

I nod and rise as if I mean to act on his advice. But as soon as he is gone I sink back down into my rattan sun chair. Some of the weave is unravelling on the arm, and I pick at a strip until it is also at a loose end. I paint. I am an amateur artist. I should like to have been professional, but like so many other things it wasn't to be. But today had I the skill of Michelangelo all I could manage would be a coat of emulsion on the ceiling of the Sistine Chapel. I ignore Henry's appeal and give myself up to a storm of memories.

I was fourteen when I found out that *Mum* was not my mother, that *Dad* was not my father, that the genetic imprint in me came from neither of them. I returned home from school one day, and Mother said that she needed to speak to me.

Sit down, Lucilla. I have something to say, she announced. And I did. I sat down at the dining table. She stood opposite me and I stared up at her. I breathed in a rotten sulphurous smell. She had burned the eggs again. She frequently dished up peeled hard-boiled eggs with salad for tea, the whites discoloured to a disconcerting pebble grey or even a witchy green, or burned sausages, which were marginally tastier. Burned sausages with burned chips: a makeshift supper. Or burned toast that was like eating charcoal dust. She was more pyromaniac than cook. And then she told me – just like that, and I forgot about the stink-bomb smell.

'I'm afraid . . . I'm afraid that you're not our little girl. The truth is that you are adopted.'

And what I felt was not shock or grief, but the most enormous sense of relief. This woman was not my mother. At a subconscious level I had always known it. I suppose that was the start of it, the quest for my real mother. All my adoptive mother told me that day was that she was Welsh and very young, that she'd lived on a Welsh farm. Nothing about my father. Well, now I know.

I project my imagination back to those post-war years. A dull room with walls the colour of sand, full of uncomfortable office furniture. Me bundled up in my biological mother's arms. My adoptive parents sitting side by side on two upright wooden chairs. And someone from the Church Adoption Society, perhaps the secretary, Valeria Mulholland, supervising the prospective parents' introduction to Lucilla Haverd. There she is, adjusting the baby shawl to show her daughter off to best advantage. I see my adoptive mother scrutinising me critically, my adoptive father nodding ruminatively. But my birth mother's face is a blank as she wordlessly hands me over. If I did not fit before I was told the truth, afterwards I became the aeroplane missing that vital piece, the steel bird grounded in the hangar for the foreseeable future.

I last left my past in 1984. That was when the endless wondering progressed to an appointment with a social worker in Dorking. My adoptive father had died that year. I didn't go to his funeral. Mum asked me if I'd like to attend but I said no. I am not a hypocrite. They had moved back to Wales after Dad retired, to Pembrokeshire, something he had always wanted to do. He was full of national pride for his corner of the British Isles. I expect he was overjoyed when the Adoption Society found a baby girl with a Welsh birth mother. I expect all he focused on was the Welsh blood, the Welsh ancestry in the infant. I expect it neutralised the German blight in the otherwise ideal child. Anyway he died in the land he loved. After Dad had gone, Mum said she was downsizing, moving to the Pembroke Dock Road, that she didn't have room for Father's piano in this new, much smaller bungalow she was buying, and would I like it. We spoke on the phone.

At the mention of the piano, my stomach clenched and bile rose at the back of my throat making me gag. I willed that gloomy instrument to the bottom of the ocean, where only ugly mutant fish could fan their fins over its ivory keys. 'It is very kind of you to think of me, Mum,' but I'm afraid I don't have any room either. You know how tiny our cottage is. And then there's the transport, the expense. Why don't you donate it to a youth group?' I suggested. 'They might really appreciate the generous gesture.' I didn't want it. There were gremlins lurking under its lid, gremlins ready to reach up and seize my hands, to scratch my palms until they burned as if steeped in acid, to wrench my fingers so that the knuckles cracked painfully.

'It's a shame, Lucilla. But you've made up your mind.'

'Yes I have, Mum.'

'Lucilla?' Whenever she spoke my name it sounded accusatory, more accost than address, a punch to the abdomen.

'Yes?'

'There's something else. It's about the will. I thought you ought to know that your father wanted it split three ways.'

'Three ways?' I rifled my brain for the sisters or brothers I had neglected to notice as I was clawing my way up.

'Frank and Rachel.'

'Oh yes, Frank and Rachel. Of course,' I sang back with a twang of cynicism.

'Frank's the executor and trustee of my will. I hope you understand. Ought to be a man left in charge.'

So there it was. I was not blood, not their blood anyway. I was not kith and kin in the true meaning of the words. And they were. Even though Aunt Enid, their mother, hadn't left me a penny, this was fair – justice packaged and branded specifically for an artificial daughter, the stand-in, the understudy. A few months after that call, the haunting refrain started up again. I'd heard it all my life drifting on the air, background noise. *Who are you?* it said. *I'm Lucilla,* I replied. *No, who are you really? Who am I really?* I was listening to it when I sat down to write the letter to the social worker in the council offices in Dorking. Henry encouraged me. He said it was time for some answers. The jumping-off platform we settled on was my birth certificate, my full birth certificate. 'If this fish can be landed,' Henry said, 'surely one day you might harpoon the whale of your true identity.' The imagery was original coming from my borrower of Latin wisdom, and I told him so, if not a tad brutal. I was not sure I found the prospect of harpooning my identity attractive. Looking back, perhaps Henry had intuited that it was going to be a bloody business. But I was in the grip of a compulsion that I could no more have shrugged off than my own skin. I reported what scraps I had gleaned so far.

> *I would greatly appreciate it if you could assist me in attaining my full birth certificate. I enclose a photocopy of the only one that I have in my possession, passed on to me by my adoptive mother, Harriet Pritchard. As you will see, printed in red, it is not much bigger than a theatre ticket. It gives only the scantest of information, my name, my sex, my date of birth.*

With an alcoholic's morning tremble, I'd put a stamp on the envelope. I could have delivered it personally, but it felt as if the wretched thing might explode any second fracturing me further. When the letter came allocating me an appointment with a social worker, Clarice Goss, the alcoholic jitters spread from head to toe. I had some insane notion that my mother, my real mother, my Welsh mother, would suddenly appear, bouncing out of a cupboard in Welsh national costume, black and white checked woollen skirt, crisp white apron, shawl, lace cap and tall black chimney hat. And while I was sipping tea with the social worker, she would keep the pair of us entertained with a reel, or a melancholy Welsh ballad. I had no concept of what kind of a trek I was embarking on, of how treacherous a path the abandoned babes in the wood stumbled along. Gina was seventeen then and studying for her A levels. Like her father she supported me in my voyage to establish where I began. But unlike Henry, I believe she wanted this as much for herself as she did for me. A romantic teenager, she had been intrigued by the idea of more relations – potentially exotic creatures.

'I have a grandparents somewhere, and perhaps aunts and uncles. Cousins!' she exclaimed excitedly, springing up and abandoning the piles of books spread over the dining table for the purposes of revision. My Gina, though she tried, had an allergy to sedentary study. She might endure it for short periods, but then she would hare outside slamming the door so hard that Pear Tree Cottage was left behind quaking at her abrupt departure. Like me it was the countryside she adored, and forestry that claimed her restless nature. 'I expect finding your father will be too difficult if he's not named anywhere, but your real mother . . . I'm sure that's possible.' She prowled the small room as if pacing out her thought process. 'I would love to meet her, your mother, my real grandmother. Oh gosh, think of that. I wonder what she looks like. If we stood in a line, us three, my real grandmother, then you, then me, would the resemblance be obvious, the family characteristics stamped on our features? Oh, Mum, you must do it. You must find her.' Her powder-blue eyes were glowing with a fierce intensity, and the features of her pretty heart-shaped face were arranged in such a positive expression that it suddenly seemed incredibly easy.

Tim was less enthusiastic. Fifteen and in his first GCSE year, it was fast becoming clear that he had a real gift for carpentry. When storms tumbled the trees on the estate and some of the older ones came down, he was there like shot wood combing for branches or segments of the trunks to transform into carvings. 'We're all right as we are,' he said when I told him I was going to write to the social worker. 'If you start delving you might chance on something . . . well, not so great. Something that upsets you.' He was in the kitchen rummaging for food. Are teenage boys ever full up? In my experience thin though Tim is, you could shovel food into his mouth all day and half the night, a bit like coal into the voracious flaming mouth of steam engine, and he would still be the first down for breakfast.

'Or I might discover something wonderful, that there was a famous person in our family, a musician, or an actor or maybe a scientist?'

He shook his head and gave me hug. 'Or a serial killer,' he mumbled lugubriously.

I laughed. 'This is real life, Tim, my life, not a thriller,' I said breezily.

'*Our* lives actually,' Tim retorted, speaking with a custard cream crammed in his mouth, and helping himself to another two biscuits. Then, resignedly, still chomping, he added, 'Well, if you must.'

'I must,' I retorted, putting the lid back firmly on the biscuit tin.

Henry was keen to come with me, but it somehow felt right to go alone, and besides it would have meant him taking a day off work. Miss Goss was young and forthright, someone who you knew would scoff at superstition, who would go out of her way to stroll nonchalantly under precarious ladders. She wore a tight black skirt, a cream blouse and a fitted olive-green jacket. Her hair, a rather fetching hazelnut brown, had been drawn back into a French plait. She did not sugar her tea. I took three lumps, which plopped messily into my cup.

'Well, Mrs Ryan, you will be happy to know I have tracked down your original birth certificate.' She pushed a brown envelope towards me. The flap wasn't stuck down. I pulled out the sheet of paper and devoured the information greedily, eyes flicking to right and left. It was registered in Hampstead. It told me in part what I already knew; in part what I did not. I was born to Bethan Modron Haverd, a Welsh farm girl, on 14 January 1948 in New End Hospital, Hampstead. At the time apparently she was residing in a flat with her mother, Seren Haverd, the address Rochester Row, Westminster. Presumably my grandmother, Seren Haverd, and my mother stayed here until I was handed over to the Pritchards. I saw that the birth was registered on the 16 January, two days later. The name of my father was left blank.

It was June and sunlight poured through the open window, the drone of traffic reaching us like drowsy bees. The air smelled vaguely of mothballs, as if something or someone was being lifted out of the cedar chest they had been preserved in. 'A lot to think about, I imagine,' Miss Goss interrupted my reverie. 'You know you really ought to do a bit of research at Highgate, nose about in the archives. That's where your mother would have gone to court for the adoption.' Her bangles, gilt and enamel in a range of contrasting bright shades, chinked as she stroked her graceful neck.

I thanked her and took my leave. I had my full birth certificate, my real birth certificate. But the delight at this achievement was short-lived when, browsing through the papers a short while later, I read a report that there had been a fire at Highgate Archives. It appeared many records had been lost, mine among them. And so I was thrown off the scent, resigning myself to being not quite anyone again for the time being. Another eleven years drifted by before my past confronted me again in the shape of Cousin Frank, reluctantly handing over a second brown envelope. So now I have a father too, a German who had been a soldier, and who lived on my mother's farm for a few years after the war, which was intriguing in itself.

The air in Pear Tree Cottage throngs with phantom relatives. My Welsh birth mother, my German father, my grandmother, all are becoming steadily more substantial, colliding as they glide about, beckoning me to join them in yesterday's waltz. I think Henry is attuned to the psychic atmosphere as well. He smokes his pipe in the evenings, and eyes the wreaths of blue-grey smoke warily, as if expecting them to coalesce into identifiable spectres. It's as though I am in a huge rambling house, running from room to room. As I fling the doors wide, divergent scenes play out before my eyes, different characters, different plots with subtle variations to dramatic swings from the tragic to the comic. But there are constants, and among them is a kind of Romeo and Juliet effect. You see my natural parents are forever young in my mind's eye. Behind a door in the attic of this gothic house, I spy on them lovemaking. They are in a hayloft, lying on a bed illuminated by rose-tinted light, straw prickling under their bare bottoms. A mouse looks on, upright, frozen, its beaded jet eyes mesmerised by the commotion, its inquisitive whiskers twitching.

There is, however, a version of events that no matter how many times I explore my house of speculation is entirely absent. It's the one in which a young Welsh farm girl is brutally raped by a German POW, where her screams are smothered by a rough hand clamped over her bleeding mouth. I can't say why but I am absolutely sure that I was conceived in an act of supreme love. My natural parents fell in love while bombs bloomed in the night sky, and planes buzzed overhead on raids, and women wept abjectly for their wasted men. He stayed in Wales after the war because of her. I'm sure of it. Will Henry call me romantic if I tell him? But then he's romantic himself. No, it was not violent, not furtive, but unstoppable. While the world was bent on self-destruction, my mother and my father were intoxicated with the champagne of creation.

Chapter 7

Bethan, 1947

She has an energetic wriggle in the middle of the night, when I can't sleep, perhaps when neither of us can sleep. As if she's restless, in a hurry to get out, to peek at what's on offer. If she had any idea she'd stay put for sure. She? Goodness knows why, but I feel certain it's a girl, that the baby growing inside me is a girl, my daughter.

Damn! Oh damn, damn, damn! Why can't I stop this wheel of thought? I want to. I really want to. She isn't real, I say severely to myself. She's not there, filling me up, pushing the boundaries every day, testing the limits. She's as insubstantial as feathers stuffing a pillow. Tear it open and she'll float off in cahoots with the wind. I'll have her, you see, and they'll take her, someone will take her, someone else will be her mam. She'll be abducted. And I'll be empty, empty inside. The pillow will sag. My shape will come back. We'll return to the farm and everything will be the way it was, the routine unchanged. All the same, all familiar. She gives me a kick as if she's tuned in, as if she's listening to my internal broadcast, a bulletin of her future, of what's to come. Seems to me she's not very glad about it. Oh, *cariad*, I'm not either. But I can't do anything to prevent what's coming. Funny when you dwell on it, birth is as inevitable as death.

I'm lying on my side. I'm far too big now to rest on my tummy, and I get indigestion when I roll onto my back. I have to pee all the time as well, get up in the middle of the night. There's only one toilet in the flat and it's next to Mrs Heppell's bedroom. I get terrible worried that the noise of the flush will wake her. I try to hang on until the last moment, but I can't help myself and I don't want to go wetting the bed. Her flat's in London, Rochester Row, not far from Westminster Cathedral, from the River Thames, from St James's Park. But oh dear, so many miles from Wales, from Bedwyr Farm. That's where I go most days, to the park. I wander around and feed the ducks. I sit on benches and watch the birds all fluffed up with the cold, or pecking in the grass. I can't bear it really, having nothing to occupy me. Mam says knit, do a bit of crochet, embroider a cushion cover. She should know better. I despise sewing. Always have. All dainty and still. I like to be out and about, to fill my lungs with fresh air, to work with the animals, to pitch in.

The smutty oxygen here half chokes you to death, full of exhaust fumes and dust it is. At home I'd near as be off to sleep the second my head hit the pillow I was so tired. On the go, always on the go, muscles like frayed ropes, dreaming of my bed. Now I'm an insomniac. Only I don't count sheep because that only makes me want to cry. I'm idle, a big lumpy thing, heaving myself about, with no company but my own rambling thoughts. And they do buzz on, my thoughts. They stick to me like a maddened swarm.

I've got a roomy coat, navy blue, serviceable wool. A bit threadbare at the elbows, but who's looking? It's baggy and that's the important thing. It pretty much hides the bump. Otherwise I don't think Mam and Mrs Heppell would like me going out. They're mortified by the sight of me, the condition I'm in. Mam's eyes are so cynical when they meet mine, though they seldom do these days. I know she can't help it, that along with Dad she thinks I've betrayed Brice, that I've done an unforgivable thing to my dead brother. He came to me in a vision the other night, like the angel Gabriel appearing to Mary – only the tidings he brought weren't such a shock. I opened my eyes and he was sitting on the windowsill smoking a cigarette, the outline of him all silvery and shimmering.

'Hello, Bethan,' he said in a low rumble. 'I've been waiting for you to wake up. I hope you don't mind me making an observation but you've got dreadful fat. And I don't suppose it's the chocolate that's done it either.'

I shuffled up the bed and manoeuvred myself into a sitting position. There weren't any bushes in the bedroom so I didn't waste time beating about imaginary ones. 'I'm pregnant, Brice,' I announced baldly.

'Well, what do you know. My little sister, a mam.' Then, 'I didn't think you were married.'

'I'm not,' I confessed.

'Oh dear, whatever do Mam and Dad feel about this?'

I bit my lip and heaved a hefty breath. Not as easy as you might suppose, with no room in there for my lungs to expand. I decided to divulge the lot. Besides, being as he was sort of intangible he could be a mind-reader. 'Brice, I'm ever so sorry but the father, he's a German, a POW who came to work on the farm.' No reaction so I raced on. 'But he's not what you think. He's kind and gentle. I love him, Brice. I really do.'

He levitated to his feet and in a wink was at my bedside. He tipped my face up to his and his hands were chiselled ice. He didn't say a word, only shook his head all mournful like and vanished. I haven't seen him since. I wish he'd come back because I need to explain how it was, how it is. So with maudlin fancies like this in my head, you'll see why I can't cope with sitting around in the flat all day. I'll go bonkers. And it's worse when Mrs Heppell is around. She makes me feel uneasy, her eyes drilling into me and her mouth all prim and rosebud tight, saying nothing. She's an odd one, Mrs Heppell. Eira. She told me to call her by her first name, but she said it in the tone you use when you mean the opposite.

She works at Barkers department store, South Kensington, she says. She's employed by a ticket agency, selling tickets for all performances at London theatres. They have a booth there. In the war though it closed down, and she moved temporarily to the rationing office they set up on the premises. She was employed as a supervisor, in charge of staff she's fond of saying.

'I had countless responsibilities and I shouldered the lot. I could be relied on. So many can't,' she said, her eyes sliding like soap over my bump. Probably why she has such a posh voice. Mam says it's a telephone manner. You cultivate it so that when people ring in, they're so impressed they buy lots of tickets. But I don't know, it would just put me off and make me want to slam the phone down, I think.

'You needn't call me Mrs Heppell. After all, we're near enough in age. You can call me Eira, if you like.'

That's what she said. But she paused before the 'if you like' bit, tagged it on in a way that meant 'don't you dare'. Well daring had nothing to with it. I didn't *like*. Snooty cow hates me. Or p'raps I should say the snooty cow hates me as well. She's the daughter of one of Mam's old school friends who married an Englishman. Went to live in London, she did. Consequently, Mrs Heppell's a city lady, fashionable, high heels that I don't know how she walks in, tube skirts that make her bum look huge, and not a hint of a Welsh accent. When I speak she won't meet my eyes. Condescension, that's what it is, that and loathing and disgust. Well, I s'ppose I shouldn't blame her. Her husband was one of the parachute troopers. First jump. Sicily. Killed by a sniper shot. And here am I invading her flat, a miniature half-German growing in my belly.

She's tall and scrawny, though she does have an arse the width of Poppit Sands. And she's all blocked up, if you know what I mean. She's a head of hair the colour of weak tea. Not to my taste. If you're going to have a brew it should be a shade of dark honey so you can really taste the cuppa, or why bother. That's what I say anyway. What's more, it's all frazzled she uses those curling irons on it so much. She's got a pointy chin, a thin squiggle of a mouth, down turned, sour, and a large nose with a bump in the middle of it. Her eyes are pale, a shade of hazel, with a look in them as hard as gravel. I sound as if I'm being bitchy. It's not that she's ugly. If she smiled she might look tolerable, attractive even. Only I haven't seen her smile or heard her laugh. Mam and her are a right old pair, gloomy as crypts.

Mam's been back and forth a bit. She says Dad needs her on the farm. Of course he does. I mustn't be so selfish. He must be struggling with all of us gone, me and Mam and . . . and Thorston. He has a couple of young lads helping him out, come over from Ashton's Farm. So he's getting by. That makes me feel less guilty. If you must know, I had a weak moment a night or two ago. It all got too much. I felt so homesick, so out of place. We were listening to the radio, Henry Hall and his orchestra, hunched up by the fire, though God knows why. Mrs Heppell won't burn more than four pieces of coal a night. And there's no hot water either, so you have to boil a kettle if you want a wash down. She doesn't like you doing that, frets about the gas. I grab my chance when she's at work. I'm not going to pong, and besides a wash makes me feel better somehow.

So you can picture it, just the two of us, chairs pulled up close to a dying fire, and me fair shivering, teeth chattering with the cold. Oh! It was freezing. Rain spitting against the windowpanes, and that bloody bulldog of hers wheezing and farting. It's so fat that dog. Hardly ever gets out of its basket. Well, before I knew where I was, I had started to weep. I didn't make a row, not much really. I was so embarrassed, but they kept coming, hot tears running down my cold cheeks.

'I'd stop that right away if I was you,' she says, her mouth all knotted. 'Your tears are wasted on me. Save them for someone more gullible.'

'I'm sorry,' I sobbed back, making an effort to pull myself together. But it was no good.

She stood up then and looked down at me for ages. Then after a bit she folded her arms and said, 'Let's get one thing clear if you're going to be staying here. I'm not your friend. I'm tolerating you for one reason and one reason only.' She was using her telephone voice, and that made what she was saying even more nasty. 'My mother asked me to put you up as a favour to your mam. Now I care about my mother. And so because this means a lot to her, it being that she was so close to your mam back in the day, I agreed. I'll sit at the table and have my tea with you. And I'll sit like this of an evening and try not to mind too much if you're here. But that's it.' And then her eyes narrowed and her tone became thistledown soft, so that I had to strain to hear it. 'In my opinion you're a whore, opening your legs to some German lout, some soldier who more than likely wasted the blood of our fine British men without a second thought. When that brat of yours arrives you keep it away from me, understand. Or I just might strangle it where it lies and throw the fiend out with the rubbish.'

I blinked away my tears then and started protesting. 'Please, let me explain how it –'

'Oh no you don't,' she hissed, butting in and taking a step back. 'You can't fool me you little slut. I know what you did and so does God.' Her cheeks were a constellation of red stars and even her neck had flushed crimson, and her nostrils were flaring.

'Look, I'm sorry for your loss, for what happened to your Douglas.'

She dashed forwards at that and raised her hand to me. The dog snarled and I thought that she was going to slap my face. But she didn't, just kept her hand in the air as if she was swearing an oath in court. 'Don't you even mention his name. You're not worthy to speak it.'

'I lost my brother as well. Brice. I know how you feel but the war's –'

'No you don't,' she axed in, 'because if you did, if you had felt a fraction of the grief I've had to bear, you wouldn't have let that German violate you. You'd have preferred to die than have a murdering Nazi have sex with you.'

We neither of us said any more. After a minute, I staggered up and went to bed. We haven't spoken since. Well, what more can you say after that. And maybe she's right. Maybe I don't understand and I haven't felt her misery. Maybe she's only voicing what Mam thinks but won't say, what Dad thinks, what everyone would think if they knew. So I'd best dry my tears, best get used to enduring things, the awfulness of being separated from the man I love, the only man I will ever love, carrying his child in the certain knowledge that I have to give her up, to hand her over to strangers, going home and spending the rest of my life trying to do penance for the heinous sin I've committed.

During the days the baby's so motionless that sometimes I forget I'm pregnant. It's as though she knows she shouldn't be coming, that she wasn't invited, that she's about as welcome as heavy rainfall the night before the harvest begins.. It's New Year's Day, month nine now. She could arrive any hour. Mam's staying permanently and I'm grateful for that. She talks to Mrs Heppell, mostly about her mam, what they did when they were girls at school, how naughty they were. And I go for my walks and remember. It's a guilty pleasure.

I despise this city with its hullabaloo and its grime and its rush, rush, rush. You get trampled down here. Buildings everywhere, some all bombed and scarred. Hardly any grass or flowers. And no animals to mention. Oh how I miss the animals, the sheepdogs, Fflur and Gwil. Fflur's black with a white patch over one eye, and Gwil's light brown and cream and likes to have his tummy rubbed. When you do, his eyes glaze over as if he's in paradise. And I miss the cows, the sheep, the chickens and the horse. I even miss the pigs. And I don't know what to do with myself. My earache has been bad again. It's the cold I expect. I've become a dreadful fidget. I walk to the river, beside the river, and up and down the street, as if I'm ploughing a field. I tread in puddles the way I did when I was a girl. Sometimes I ride on the buses. I don't go anywhere in particular, just ride for a while on the top deck, then get off, cross the road and ride another bus back again. As I said, I go to the park. But the only place that seems to calm me is the cathedral. When you sit in there it's like being inside a great bell.

It's very grey is London, and it rains like the sky is a dishcloth being wrung out. But that's not a novel experience to me. We have more than our fair share of rain in Wales, and it's the farm's blood. Nothing grows without water. But when it's not too grey in the city, when the sky breaks open like an egg, I amuse myself stepping into the shafts of light that slash through the windows of the great cathedral. I know it's a stupid whim, one child might have, but I've taken to fantasising that I'm sucked up into a beam of light, as if God's sucking me up through a straw. And he deposits me far, far away, in a peaceful land where there hasn't been a war, a land where the graveyards aren't full up with dead men, and where women aren't stooped with anguish, where they cluck like crotchety hens as their sons grow up strong and healthy and their husbands grow old and grumpy.

And Thorston's there, in that land, waiting for me, open-armed. '*Ich liebe dich*, Bethan,' I love you, he says, as he pulls me close. And we have the prettiest little house, painted white, with blue window boxes full of gay flowers. And there's a rectangle of brilliant green lawn, with a path winding through it and a picket fence running round it. Positioned like a mouth in the front door is a letterbox, polished brass lips and flapping tongue. Through it the postman feeds our letters, lovely letters and greeting cards with not a bill among them. I pick them up and read who they're addressed to. 'Mr and Mrs Engel,' they say. And while I open them, I gaze out over the back garden where there's a pram standing in the cool shade of an oak tree. And I can just glimpse our baby's chubby hands reaching up to catch at the green leaves fluttering in the breeze.

Then a soggy grey cloud bowls up and the limbs of light wither, and it feels dreadfully sombre and chilly in the cathedral, like a dungeon must feel I expect. I try to hold on to the days of snow in that most cruel of winters last year. The whole of Wales seemed to be sealed in ice, held in suspense, one great glacier. There was no heat to be had anywhere save in his bed, his rickety bed on the tick mattress, with the wind serenading our lovemaking. I close my eyes and I am back there, with his mouth moving against my ears, the nectar of his wondrous words dripping into me, the only witness in that opaque bone-white desert where silence breeds silence. I open up like a rose, a single winter rose blossoming for him. His hair has grown longer, and a darker blond without the sun. He is so tender, so giving, so patient that my want becomes a frenzy.

I gloat over my tiny hoard of memories. I only wish they could have multiplied. But we had to be careful, make certain we gave no cause for suspicion, that our nocturnal couplings remained secret. I recall the coming of that spring, the onset of a thaw like no other. I recall us sitting in the corner of a field far from prying eyes, eating buns and jam, our sticky fingers linked in the tangled grass. Bringing the sheep down from the high pastures and stealing a kiss behind a tree. His lips tasted like spring water, cool and pure, leaving the honey of his sweetness on my tongue. Bending over him as he drew, the pencil seeming to guide his hand, not the other way round. And that intense look on his face coupled with humility, as if he recognised his skill was a gift, really a gift, something that God had given to him. And his round spectacles shining like gold coins in the candlelight.

'I love you,' he said. He pushed the hair behind my ears. I could see the mist of our breaths rising in the frosted air. We rubbed noses. Eskimos do that, don't they? And he climbed to his feet and unbuttoned my shirt, then laid his head against my breast. 'I can hear your heart, Bethan. I can hear it talking to me,' he said. And later, in bed, I rested my head on his chest and watched daffodils of light bobbing their heads on the whitewashed walls.

'And I can hear your heart, Thorston, hear it replying,' I said.

After the summer came and went, I said it again, feeling the ridges of his ribs against my cheek, letting my thoughts keep pace with its beat. But what I did not add is that sometimes when we lay like this I imagined I heard another heart, a minute heart flickering like the batting of a dragonfly's wing deep inside me. My bump was starting to show. The sun was hot and Dad wanted to know why I kept my jacket on, buttoned up over my dungarees, sweat dewing my brow.

'Get some air to your arms, Bethan,' he grumbled. 'What's up with you? Are you sickening for something?' And he took his hat off and scratched his scalp. I'd felt the babe quickening for some while by then. Such a weird sensation. Like a petal brushing inside you, and you having no control over it. With the arrival of autumn, I knew time was running out for me. It was like being propelled forwards and not being able to apply the brakes. And I wasn't just moving forward, I was accelerating. I felt Mam's eyes on me at the close of the day, at breakfast when I couldn't stomach anything, at supper when I was so starving I was truly ready to eat our horse. She didn't look at my thickening waist but at my face, as if she detected something in it that had not been there before.

Some may find this hard to credit but I didn't make an announcement to Thorston. It was as though it was happening to the three of us. He put his hand on the tiny dome of my bump one day, and when she moved wonder wiped his face. He told me that we would marry, very soon, that we could live in Germany or in Wales, either, that I could choose. And I smiled and said that I didn't mind Alaska, not so long as we were together. He said we should start to make plans. And I begged him, not yet, not quite yet. I asked him to kiss me again, over and over again, because I knew I would have to commit to memory that sensation, to record it in its most minute detail. The weightlessness that came first. And the light, bright and radiant, a comb of fire making me crackle down to my toes. And then the pressure that was not like pressure, not like persuasion, but fusion. And, after that, the flowering of me, so that I became exquisite. I think if there is a heaven that is how it feels being there, as if from moment to moment you are flowering, always coming to glory, untarnished, immortal, perfection.

We went together to tell my parents. I don't know if Thorston really believed in his fables, if he thought my dad would frown for a moment, then take him into the front room to question him as to his intentions. I don't know if he thought Mam and I would walk the kitchen floor, to and fro, to and fro. I don't know if he thought they would re-emerge after an hour, Dad with a huge smile on his face and him looking sheepish. Then my mam would rummage in the dresser and bring out the dusty old bottle of sherry she keeps there, and we would all share a glass, musty and syrupy. And there would be lots of back slapping and chortling. Was this the happy ending he idealistically envisaged?

'Mam,' I said. And she spun round as if she was expecting this, spun round, interrupting her washing up at the sink, suds on her hands, studying the pair of us. We weren't touching, only standing together shoulder to shoulder. I didn't have to say no more. She gave a barely perceptible nod, and there was such a forlorn darkening of her eyes, such a withdrawal from me. My dad came in then, through the kitchen door. He'd taken his boots off in the porch. I remember spotting a hole in his knitted sock that one of his big toes was peeping through. He was frowning, but it was a black frown, a malignant frown, a dangerous frown. He didn't like Thorston coming into the house even after all these years. He was bare-headed, his grey hair standing up. Then he drew his hands over the stubble on his chin, over his whole face, both hands as if he was scrubbing it clean.

'What's all this then?' he said quietly. We'd swivelled round to face him. Slowly, I rolled up my baggy sweater and showed him my bump, my bump pushing against the print of my dress. First his face drained of colour, and after it went a ghastly yellowish grey. His eyes flashed, and the turquoise of his irises was the hue of dreams no more. They had transformed into the impenetrable hardness of nightmares. They looked, bulging as they did, as if they might fly from their sockets. He's a stocky man and his muscles seemed to bunch up, making him even more solid, like stones under his skin. The dogs had come in with him and were lying by the range warming themselves. Now they seemed to sense the disturbance in their master's mood, to smell his rage. They lifted their heads in quick succession and snarled, teeth bared.

'Mr Haverd, please do not be angry. I love your daughter and I want to marry her. I shall –' But Thorston didn't get any further. My dad made a fist and slammed it into his face. I heard a crack, a terrible noise. Thorston's spectacles fell to the floor, broken. His nose was like pulp, all bleeding and mashed up. He cannot see very well without his spectacles, and he dropped to his knees and began scrabbling on the floor trying to find them. Blood was dripping from his face. I stepped between him and my dad. I can't recall what I said. Speech gushed out, pleas, pleas against all the injustices of this world that ever were. Mam was gasping and crying, arms bound around herself as if to ensure she remain upright, that she did not crumple. The dogs came growling and snapping at Thorston's heels. My dad's hand sang through the air and he landed me such a slap against my cheek that I nearly over-balanced. He hadn't struck me before. He is a stern man, and he can speak to you in a tone that makes you shrivel with fear, but before this he had not once raised his hand to me. Thorston scrambled to his feet, the broken glasses hanging off one ear now, looking askew, almost comical.

'There is no need for this. I beg you, Mr Haverd.' And he began to comfort me. He tried to draw me into his arms, but my dad gave him an almighty shove and he fell down again. This time the lenses popped out of his spectacles. He made no attempt to retrieve them. The dogs were slathering and clacking their teeth. I pushed them back and told them to shut up. Dad stood there, legs astride, his barrel chest heaving. Thorston clambered shakily to his feet, stepping on the lenses as he did so, splintering them. He hauled up his head bravely, blinking like some nocturnal creature that has just crawled out from the safe shadows of its burrow into a blaze of boiling light. The dogs crept forwards and began to lick up the spatters of blood. He looked so vulnerable, a small slight boy. And then tears came to his eyes and began spilling down his cheeks. And the tears mixed with his blood so that they were red, streaking his pale face with red lines. And it was the most awful thing I had ever seen, each tear tugging on the sinews of my heart. I thought that it was going to stop, that my heart, the heart whose drumming had soothed him, would give up with a final squeeze.

'Get out!' my dad rasped. 'Get out of my house, you Nazi scum!' His voice was a millstone grinding the air. Thorston turned his tear-stained face to my mother in appeal but she repelled him, casting her eyes down at the floor. Then my dad issued his ultimatum: 'I will give you fifteen minutes. If you are not off my property by then I will fetch my gun. I will load it. I will hunt you down with my dogs. And when I find you I will put a bullet in your head.'

It was very quiet then. Even the dogs slunk off, tails between their legs. I felt as if I wasn't quite there, as if I was invisible. Thorston and I exchanged a look. Not a long look, a second, perhaps two or three. I could smell his blood, and some stew bubbling on the stove, and the tarry scent of the soapy washing-up water. And I wanted to be sick.

My dad stood back from the door, snorting in and out his breaths. And then the man I loved seemed to melt into the basalt black essence of the night.

My dad's eyes took me in, head to toe and back again, as if he did not recognise me, as if he was filled with revulsion at what he saw before him. 'May God forgive you, Bethan, for what you have done because I never shall!' he said.

Without responding I went upstairs to my room. I did not switch on the light. I used the tip of a finger to draw a circle on the condensation that clung to the windowpane. I spied Thorston through its lens, a bent figure, crushed then swallowed by the night. And it came to me then, with our baby banging on the door of me, that I would not love again. I would go through the motions of my life, and uncomplainingly I would do what was asked of me. I would submit. From this moment to the moment of my death I would make no fuss, cause no further disruption. I would make reparation. I sold my soul that day, not to the devil but to my father. Although there was nothing to choose between them.

Over the next week my parents treated me as if I was a curse, as if being in the same room as me they risked eternal damnation. They looked away or dropped their gazes when I walked by. We ate our meals without a word. It was as if someone had died. I recalled when we heard that Brice was dead, and it was the same, like every day was a funeral, only this wasn't grief it was blind hatred and bigotry and dogmatism. The hell of it was that I didn't have death in my belly but life, a life made from love. I ached for my love, I ached all over the way I did when I had the mumps as a child. Dad didn't want me working on the farm now that they knew about the baby, as if I was an abomination, an incarnation of evil, of original sin. He made me stay in the house all day. It felt like I was suffocating for want of fresh air and the feel of the wind buffeting my cheeks. Lying on my bed through those long hours, staring up the ceiling, I began to have wild thoughts of running away, of finding my love, of us escaping together. Only they wouldn't let me out, not even for a walk. That was when the idea of writing to him came to me, writing a letter. He had been a prisoner of war staying in the camp in Llanmartin and I thought, well . . . I hoped, prayed actually, that he'd gone back there, and not left for Germany already. Of course it was no longer a POW camp but if he hadn't returned there he might have left a forwarding address. Someone might recognise the name. They might remember him. They might know where to send it.

I firmed up my plan in middle of the night. I would write, explain that I had made a dreadful mistake, that I should have left with him, that we were destined to spend our lives together, to marry and bring up our child. I realised as I lay there feeling our baby flutter inside me and imagining the little arms and legs paddling in the warm safe pool beneath my linked fingers that I was being irrational. Even if I wrote him a letter, how would I get it to him when I might as well be in prison? And if I did find a way of posting it, honestly what were the odds that he had gone back to Llanmartin, or that they had a record of his address? The war was over, and most probably he'd journeyed to his homeland by now, Germany. If not there, then I could take a pin, shut my eyes and stick it in a map of Europe. It was an unwinnable lottery. And if I was lucky and he was still in Britain he might be anywhere – Ireland, or Scotland or England. Only a miracle would put me where I belonged, with the man I love so much, so very much, that it hurts, physically hurts. But you know, my love was a fever, it was a fire raging through my body and I couldn't be logical, practical. So I got up and wrote my letter by candlelight. I decided that if I switched on the light my mam and dad might be disturbed and come to investigate. I keep a candle by my bed to pray by at night. So I s'ppose it was apt because this would be a prayer, a prayer from the heart. The proper writing paper was downstairs and I didn't dare fetch it. I made do with scribbling my letter to Thorston in a notebook I keep in the drawer by my bed.

Dear Thorston,

I miss you. I miss the feel of your body holding mine. I miss your kisses. I miss you inside me, part of me. I miss your eyes, so kind and loving behind the lenses of your spectacles. Only you don't have spectacles now. They're broken. But the day after you left I crept to the bins when Mam was busy, and I found some of pieces of glass, still with your blood on them, and the tiny wire frame all screwed up, and I kept them in my pocket. I have them hidden under my mattress now in a small box. Thorston, I believe I shall die if I can't see you again. You're the father of my baby. We are meant to be together. I am sending this to the camp at Llanmartin. I don't know how yet but I'll find a way. I must find a way. If you're not there perhaps they know where you are, where you've gone to, perhaps they'll forward it on. If this reaches you, get word to me, tell me where to go and when, and I promise I'll be there. I don't care about the rest, so long as when I wake up in the morning it's your head on the pillow next to mine.

I love you – always and forever.

Bethan x.

Next day I stole an envelope, from the drawer in Dad's desk, and addressed it to Mr Thorston Engel, POW Camp Llanmartin, Newport, Wales. I'd nowhere else to turn and it was worth a try. I didn't have a stamp either and that's where I thought I was going to flounder, that the letter would stay tucked under a scrap of carpet in my bedroom. And then the most wonderful thing happened, and it *was* a miracle, a real miracle. Mr Powell the vet came to look at one of the cows that was in calf and very sickly. And I was peeping out of the window at his car when I saw his daughter Aeron climbing out from the back seat. Aeron – Aeron my friend! We used to sit together at the same desk in school. It was before the war and it felt like another lifetime, but if I remembered her then there was a good chance that she would remember me. When her father was on his rounds and called in, she'd never been with him before. Don't you see? It was a sign. The miracle I needed. And then I heard her ask my dad where I was, if she could see me. Oh Lord, I held my breath until I was so light-headed I almost fainted. And I clutched my hands together and my eyes bored straight through the ceiling and the roof of the house and up into the sky where God sits. When my dad said yes, and nodded in the direction of the house, I fell to my knees. God be praised, I thought. God and all your angels be praised. I dashed to the carpet, lifted up a corner, grabbed the letter and stuffed it in my pocket. Then I smoothed out the wrinkles in the pile hurriedly so nobody would suspect.

Next moment and Mam knocked on my door. She checked what I was wearing, a baggy jumper and trousers. You couldn't see my bump. I didn't show under all the folds of a green, orange and beige hand knit that she made for Brice. She didn't meet my eye, just looked at the floor, at the scrap of carpet that only minutes ago was shielding my letter – ironic that.

'You have a visitor,' she said stiffly.

'Oh! And who might that be, Mam?' I acted all surprised as if I couldn't imagine who had come calling.

'Aeron. Aeron Powell, the vet's girl. You can see her for five minutes in the front room.' I jumped up but Mam immediately barred the doorway, arms flung wide like a prison guard. 'You're not to tell her about . . . about . . .' She broke off and nipped in a breath as if to fortify her. 'About that,' she whispered, indicating my belly with a nod.

'No Mam, of course not,' I retorted as if I was shocked that she should ever suggest such a thing. 'It's secret. I understand.'

'Fine,' she returned all clipped, her mouth paying the word out like a miser, a lifetime's ration of disillusionment framing it with her bitter expression. 'Five minutes mind, no more.'

'I'll watch the clock Mam. I promise,' I vowed solemnly. I considered saying cross my heart and hope to die but thought better of it. If there was a hope that I would see my Thorston again then I didn't want to die. I wanted to live.

'I'll come and fetch you,' Mam called after me as I clattered downstairs, as if she couldn't so much as trust me to tell the time.

Aeron was standing by window and she swivelled as I came in. Her long red hair was plaited in one thick plait down her back, and she was wearing a plain Hunter green dress and a grey cardigan. She had grown a lot taller so that she had caught up with me. She used to be much shorter. She smiled shyly.

'Hello, Bethan. I've been wondering how you were. So when Dad said he was coming over I asked if I could come along for the ride.' She had grown up a lot, so that she seemed more of a woman than a girl, as I expected I did. And yet she had retained an external layer of finicky neatness, which served as an efficient deterrent to untidy emotional advances. 'Your mam says you're not well so I can only say hello. She says she's frightened I could catch something.' She scratched her shoulder with a delicate finger and took a precautionary step backwards. I glanced at the clock face, and saw that a whole minute had gone. I had to speed up, but I didn't want her to sense that I was panicking either.

'Hello, Aeron, how nice to see you,' I greeted her, crossing to where she stood. She inspected me and the expression on her face was one of disparagement. 'It's a bit of a cold, that's all.'

She looked down her nose at me. I recognised I must look scruffy, my hair loose and tangled, my clothes more suited to a man. But anyone kept indoors for five days, pale, pregnant, sick with love and desperate, would have trouble putting on a happy face. Another swift glimpse at the clock. Oh why was the minute hand moving so fast? I lowered my voice. The door was open, but I could hear Mam banging the broom about in the kitchen so I felt safe. 'Aeron, perhaps could you do me a small favour. We were such great friends at school and I know I can trust you,' I started, my tone friendly, appealing to our childhood bond. I could feel the envelope in my pocket and I drew it out, trying as hard as I could to maintain a casual air, as if I was going to ask her to perform the most ordinary errand in Wales. 'I have a letter.'

'So I see,' observed Aeron, a touch of asperity in her tone. I presented the back of the envelope to her, preventing her from reading the address.

I had to dive in or I would be too late. My miracle would fade and be trampled into the dust. My letter would be good for nothing but the fire. 'I want you to post this for me. It's terribly important.' Her green eyes lit with interest. She was intrigued, if not the ideal reaction then a close second. 'But you have to swear that you won't tell your parents, that you'll keep this between us, for the sake of our friendship, for the sake of all the hours we shared, in the classroom and in the playground.' A pause while I racked my brain for something that would tip the balance. 'The skipping games. The daisy chains. The friendship bracelets we plaited from grass.'

She nodded, her round face sliced into a quick smile of passing fondness. And I wanted to sing the 'Hallelujah Chorus' and hug her. But that would have been unwise in my condition and, I was certain, would cause her to recoil and change her mind. She took the letter from me more curious than hesitant. 'Who's it going to?' she wanted to know, flipping it over and then giving a little gasp.

We were into the last minute, and really it might as well have been an hourglass, the trickling sands my lifeblood draining from me. 'It's for a friend. Just a friend. Nothing more than that. We want to be pen pals.' I fidgeted in my jumper and the baby gave a kick, as if my lie about its father had angered the tiny being.

'German?' Aeron came back at me in an unflinching slow reptilian blink.

I fingered my neck nervously, and gave a pronounced nod. Then, moistening my lips, I added this targeted reinforcement, 'He's a friend. A friend like you and I were.' I blushed. I could feel the burn on my cheeks and Aeron made a mental note of it as if she were ticking off something in her head.

'Your parents don't know.' She stated this as fact, and not a question.

Again I nodded. 'But it means nothing. We simply want to write to each other when he gets back to Germany.' I could hear my mother's approaching footsteps. 'Will you do it?'

'Yes,' agreed Aeron and I wanted to kiss her.

'You have to hide the letter.' I glanced at the door expecting to see my mam coming through it. 'Quickly,' I urged.

And Aeron concealed my letter to Thorston, my love letter, in her pocket a second before my mother entered the room.

Chapter 8

Lucilla, 1995

Prompted by my adoptive mother's death, the letter and a sense of the ephemeral that medieval paintings of skulls are apt to evoke, I turn to the Church Adoption Society, the organisation who arranged my adoption. But my attempts to contact them at the address I have are thwarted. They are no longer in residence at Bloomsbury Square. They may have disbanded, or changed their name and their location, or they may have merged with another organisation. Disappointed but not dismayed, (after so many years I expected complications) I pursue another lead – the Salvation Army.

'A library assistant mentioned that they have a family tracing service,' I report to Henry. We are strolling through the walled rose gardens in the regal golden excesses of an early November afternoon. The estate is closed to the public for the day and this is when I dearly love to roam the grounds, when they are deserted and peaceful, the house and gardens putting on a private show just for us.

'Fate,' Henry deduces simply. 'Clear as a signpost I'd say.' The roses are over, of course, and the beds mulched with well-rotted horse manure and all tucked up for their nourishing winter slumber. A warm earthy fragrance is detectable, faint in the chill but undeniably wholesome. We both breathe deep, and Merlin, trotting in front of us, pauses to nose the rich brown fleece appreciatively.

That same evening together we write the letter to the Salvation Army, Henry interjecting if he thinks I've missed some vital clue. I explain that I was not handed over to the Pritchards until April 1948, the formal adoption taking place later that year. I suggest that it is entirely possible that Bethan, my birth mother, kept me from my birth until then. I tell them that I am eager to get in touch with her, for her to learn that I now have a family of my own.

I have been very lucky. I am happily married to a good man, Henry. We have two children, Gina and Tim – well, they are adults now. We have lived on the Brightmore Hall Estate outside Dorking, where Henry has been head gardener, for over 20 years.

'They won't be interested in that bit about me,' Henry insists, leaning over my shoulder. 'A mention of the children perhaps, but not me.' I adore the waft of pipe tobacco that lingers about him, a world apart from the sharp acrid smell of cigarettes.

'Oh yes they will. After all you're my real mother's son-in-law. Have you thought of that?' I counter. The twinkle mirrored in my husband's eyes, tells me that secretly he's gratified to have confirmation he is a member of the cast in my unfolding drama. I end on a polite respectful note, whilst at the same stroke trying to stress how much this means to me.

I understand the work pressures that a large organisation such as yours, the Salvation Army, must be under, especially at this festive time of year. But if there is any chance at all of you being able to assist me I would be so grateful.

The following day, brimming with hope, I mail my letter to: The Salvation Army, Family Tracing Service,105–109 Judd Street, King's

Cross, London WC1H 9TS. On 16 November, I have my reply, as devastating as Dorothy's was from the Great Oz.

> *Thank you for your recent enquiry, in which you ask about the possibility of tracing your birth mother. It is noted that you were placed for adoption as a baby. We fully comprehend your motives in pursuing this. Unfortunately we have to advise you that our programme does not include tracking down birth parents in circumstances such as you have outlined. We are therefore sorry to disappoint you. There are few, if any, responsible agencies in the United Kingdom that carry out investigations of this kind, although there are a small number of private agents who may do so. Their fees, of course, can be quite high, depending on the amount of research that is entailed.*
>
> *You might also consider the possibility of getting in touch with the Adoption Contact Register. They will explain what facilities are available for adopted people. The address is: Office of Population Censuses and Surveys, The General Register Office, Adoptions Section, Smedly Hydro, Trafalgar Road, Birkdale, Southport PR8 2HH.*
>
> *We regret being unable to assist you with your request, and enclose an information sheet explaining some of the difficulties that might be involved in your undertaking.*
>
> *Yours sincerely,*
> *Cedric Lamb*
> *Lieutenant-Colonel*
> *Director – Family Tracing Service*

A Christian church and a registered charity – with heart to God and hand to man

The Adoption

It is the afternoon, a Thursday, and a good couple of hours before Henry is due home. Wishing he were with me, bolstering me up, I sink into an armchair utterly deflated. I have a sharp pang under my ribs and am visited by a sudden desire to hug our children close to me, to hold on to them, letting them define me in the tight circle of their small possessive arms. I recall the weight of their heads propped so trustingly against me, and their piping voices clamouring in my ears, chorusing for me to fill myself up with the needs of my precious tinies. That's what we called them when they were little. The tinies. Our tinies. Mummy, mummy, mummy. But Gina and Tim are no longer tiny. Gina is twenty-eight and Tim is twenty-six and they have long since moved out. And with the loss of their constant demands the malaise of anonymity has returned to torment me.

Now I notice, stapled to the missive and delivering a secondary blow, that there is a standard page of advice to all those foolish enough to embark on a journey to find their origins, to all those determined to prise apart the oyster shell in which their natural parents are cloistered. It is as though I am a child again being scolded for wanting something more, something that is mine and mine alone, some seductive identity that beckons from beyond the claustrophobic confines of the oppressive Finchley house. As if their inability to assist me is not decimating enough, they are trying to put me off the scent, to stop me in my tracks, to derail me. A sudden flare of anger, and I snatch a breath and purse my lips in resolution. I am flesh of *their* flesh and blood of *their* blood. There is no gainsaying this. And yet the conundrum I face is that despite this visceral connection they gave me away. I have to presume that they have lived perfectly contented lives minus their child, without speculating about me the way I speculate about them – every day. Every single day, I ponder where they are, what they are doing, if they have families. I want their hearts to have been pierced by the images of me, moving down the catwalk of my life at various ages, modelling a wardrobe of outfits. Their five-year-old daughter on her first day at school, of her at ten having a piano lesson, a young woman of seventeen wearing a dress she hated to a temperance dance, at twenty-two pushing her babies in a pram, at thirty-two having a fireworks party in the garden, at forty-seven finding out that her father had been a German POW.

The overriding tone of the advice sheet is critical. It reminds me that prior to 1976 a mother who placed her baby for adoption would be promised an absolutely confidential service, that her desire to remain anonymous would be honoured by the Salvation Army at all costs. It continues to explain the embarrassment and distress the adopted person may bring to their natural parents' current families, the disruption they may cause to their lives. What about my distress? I ruminate bitterly. What about my desires? What about my rights? Basically it aims to put me off, to discourage me. It reads more like a warning not to advance another step, not to trespass where I am prohibited, or more than likely the four horsemen of the apocalypse might come clip-clopping by.

Distracted, I am behind with preparations for supper. Scrambled eggs may have to suffice. I get up and make myself a consoling cup of coffee, fresh coffee, a dash of cream, double cream, and a spoonful, heaped, of rich golden honey – pure indulgence! And I give Merlin a biscuit dipped in gravy, which he sets about with the relish of a puppy, gazing up at me adoringly, his single good eye asquint. Perhaps I will live and die in ignorance, and perhaps, as the saying goes, ignorance is bliss. But for me it feels more akin to hell. Better to know and drop down into the bubbling cauldron, than live with question marks.

I put myself in my real mother's position. As the dusk creeps up to the windows, I put on a CD, a favourite piece of baroque, Scarlatti. I curl up in the armchair and recall the births of both my children in turn. Gina, a slow painful labour, an episiotomy, a forceps delivery, and then my daughter's cry, watery, as if she had swum up from the depths of the sea. A wave of love that was tidal in its proportions sweeping over me. Tim was a monstrous nine and a half pounds. The placenta had to be manually removed, making me feel remarkably like a cow being delivered by a hardy vet.

'You really cannot go on having babies of this size,' the registrar had remonstrated with me in irritation, his green skullcap dotted with sweat – as if I had deliberately conspired to have an enormous baby.

Could I have given either of them up? Could I have handed them over with a few useful tips? She likes to be well swaddled. It makes her feel secure. He's fond of having his lower back rubbed. It sends him directly to sleep. Try to slow down her feed or she'll be up for hours with wind. He adores his dummy. Never leave home without it. Could I have disengaged them from my arms and walked away, then picked up the threads of my life and started spinning, as carefree as if they had never been? The truth fell with a resounding clang into my conscious- ness. For me it would simply have been an impossibility. To cleave us apart would have meant the suspension of my life. No matter where I went or what I did, I would have carried the moment of our parting with me always, ironically like a birthmark. Why did you do it, Bethan? Was there really no other option? Did you want keep me? Or were you raring to be rid of me? And my father, my German father, who was imprisoned in a foreign land, and while death was everywhere set about making a new life with the enemy, what of him?

The rolling wheel of the seasons duly delivers a snip of frost and blue- black afternoons, a stark Christmas fanfare that results in the usual frenetic activity. We dress up in Victorian costume, and serve mince pies with cream or brandy butter and mulled wine in the restaurant. Very popular with the customers. We light candles and sing carols and have a collection for the nearby Wildlife Shelter. On 23 December, as per tradition, Henry dresses up as Santa Claus. We have a lucky dip. Token prizes that each year I'm afraid the children will scoff at. But so far I've seen nothing but delight illuminating their small faces. Admittedly only the *tinies* toddle forwards. Though I have seen older brothers and sisters looking on with something resembling envy clouding their carefully arranged sophisticated countenance.

We sit, Henry in his crimson suit trimmed with fake fur, me, in a red and green elf costume, in a grotto adjacent to the plant stands. We have decorated it with yards of cotton wool and tinsel. You'd be surprised how popular our Santa is. Some of the children want to know why his moustache and beard are an unconventional cinnamon brown. The explanation he volunteers is that he dyed them because he was getting sick of all that white.

'Where I live in the North Pole there's snow everywhere, and you can get bored of it, you know,' he elaborates with a ho-ho. Boredom is something they can all relate to, and they nod in understanding. Sometimes he lets them tug on his beard to prove that it's real. He's been a wonderful father to our two children, and he'll be a wonderful grandfather in time. Would the German have been a marvellous father to me if he'd had the opportunity? The children descend for lunch on Christmas Day. Gina, who did a BA at Huddersfield University in Human Ecology, is employed by Kirklees County Council. She lives in Meltham in West Yorkshire, with her husband, Nathan. She has recently been promoted to Senior Ranger Officer, supervising nature trails on the Pennine Way. And Tim, who attended Merton College for three years on a course making and repairing musical instruments, now one of a small team in a specialist workshop in Haslemere, is considering retraining as a psychiatric nurse. Music and psychiatry – I have not yet discovered their common ground, and Tim has yet to enlighten me.

Gina and our son-in-law Nathan are staying over. After the ritually ridiculously huge lunch, rosy-cheeked with sherry, my daughter and I opt for a walk and a blow in the reviving wintry air. Merlin, whose flesh is weak these days, but whose nose is as sharp as a starling's beak, hobbles along in our wake. It is one of those winter days that cannot be bettered. We have had light snowfall, and a wintery sun, a ghostly opal suspended low in the sky, kisses a sparkle into the Christmas card scene. The air is bracing, sobering my tipsy-turvy spirit. I feel the dead weight of overindulgence evanesce as my digestion squares up to its onerous task. We are strolling past the open-air theatre, a raised plateau backed by a thatch of fir trees, when Gina returns to a theme I thought she had all but forgotten.

'Did anything come of the Salvation Army?' she asks, her tone deceptively offhand. I have told her of recent developments. That I know now that my father was a German prisoner of war who stayed behind on the farm he worked on. It has reawakened Gina's romantic streak.

'No. They don't trace missing family members.' We both halt and wait for Merlin to catch up. He is panting from his lopsided exertions, his shallow powder-puff breaths melting away as they are forcefully expelled. 'Well, not in my circumstances anyway.'

'What's that supposed to mean?' erupts my tempestuous daughter, quick to champion my cause.

'Oh, I'm not sure really,' I admit lamely. I hunker down to pat Merlin's head and whisper some encouragement for him to keep going. 'Possibly it's the slightly scandalous association they're referring to. I don't know.'

'What rot!' Gina declares forthrightly. 'So your mother was unmarried – big deal! It's an everyday occurrence. And your father was German. The war was over . . .'

'Just barely,' I reply, 'And back then a child out of wedlock, let alone a child fathered by the enemy . . .' I remind her gently. 'Let's just say it wasn't considered quite the thing. The letter they sent came with a caution about proceeding.' I give a dry mirthless laugh. 'Like a contraindication on a medicine bottle.'

'Hypocrites,' Gina mutters under her breath. I stand rubbing my arms. On the move, the cold is refreshing, bracing, but we have been stationary for some minutes. Our extremities are gradually freezing. Neither of us is wearing gloves or a hat, and only Gina has her neck wreathed in a cheerful red and pink wool scarf. My daughter sets a remedial brisk pace, and Merlin and I bring up the rear. The sun is slipping away and with it the festive cheer. 'Well, damn it, I want to know who my grandparents are!' Gina's brow furrows into creases not yet set in lines. 'There may be important genetic history Tim and I should know about. A blueprint for some mysterious ailment? Huntington's or Crohn's disease? We could be carriers, and just not be aware of it. Have you considered that? Does our grandmother have glaucoma, or is there a tendency to conceive twins in the family?'

'Oh, darling, I'm sure there's nothing,' I reassure, catching up and patting her on the shoulder. But my daughter shrugs me off, her corn-gold hair loose and flying about her reddened cheeks. I suddenly realise that she is really upset, that this loss of identity that strikes me down as unexpectedly as an epileptic fit is not solely my selfish preserve. I am not the only relative who wants answers. 'Gina, what is it?' I call as she strides ahead. 'Gina!' To begin with she feigns deafness, then she whirls around and almost running rushes back to me. Merlin has quite given up and has collapsed on the path, legs splayed inelegantly. I fear I shall have to carry him home.

'It's just that . . . just that it's as though I've come into a story in the middle, and I may never know how it started, how I started.' She is very nearly in tears, her shoulders quaking with her dry sobs.

'Oh, darling . . . darling, I didn't understand that it mattered so much to you,' I confess, guilty that I have hoarded my misery and perhaps wallowed in it, believing I alone have suffered, I alone have been cheated of a past. I pull her into my arms, and though she puts up superficial resistance, she soon relents.

'It is far more horrible for you. I know,' she mumbles into my shoulder. 'And I didn't think I was very bothered, not deep down. 'But now Nathan and I are thinking . . . well, we are thinking of starting a family.'

'But Gina that's wonderful,' I say into her tangle of hair that smells sweetly of rosemary shampoo.

'You see that's when it hit me. The need, like hunger, to give a family to your child, a wide all-encompassing family that will give him or her a real sense of belonging. I don't want my baby born into a sealed capsule. We're part of a continuum. Am I making sense? I reckoned . . . oh I'm being ridiculous.' Her arms belting my waist lock for a moment, then speedily she detaches herself and regains her composure. Merlin reacts decisively, heaving himself up and rotating through one hundred and eighty degrees, poised for the route home. 'Granny Pritchard was always such a beast. I know we hardly ever saw her, but she wasn't cosy the way grannies should be. And Grandpa Pritchard seemed rather strange as well. Gramps and Nanny Ryan were lovely, but because they both died when we were so young we barely got to know them. When you told me you were adopted and that you hadn't met your real mum, that you didn't know where she was, I used to dream her up last thing at night. Do you remember when I did that history project on the war back in school?' I nodded. Now I wanted to cry too. 'Well, everybody was talking about their grandparents and what they got up to in the war. But I didn't feel able to ask Granny and Grandpa Pritchard to tell me their experiences. Even on the phone it felt awkward. So I had nothing to contribute, nothing to give. And here it seems like we had this . . . amazing story in our past – a German soldier and a Welsh girl fell in love, in spite of everything.' Brightmore

Hall hoves into view, the lights on the upper floors, where the family lives, shining out into encroaching dark like golden ingots. I sigh at the enormity of the chasm at my back, at my daughter's back. 'Please don't be put off so easily,' she implores with a sideways look that is my undoing. And as we trudge on I feel utterly torn, divided by love and the lack of it.

Tim is philosophic about the inadequacies of the Salvation Army. He discusses the situation in desultory fashion, in between serenading us with a ballad on a really quite splendid home-made guitar. Before he leaves, he expresses yet again his tenet that many adopted children regret tracing their birth parents. 'Think on, Ma,' he advises, giving me a peck on cheek at our cottage door. 'I know you're a dog person but look what curiosity did to cats.' He does up his duffel coat and grins. 'Dinner was excellent as per usual, Mother dear. Up to your usual standard, though the pudding could have done with more brandy. But now I'm nit-picking. Tea was good too. Your Christmas cake will keep me going for a good couple of hours.'

'You are incorrigible,' I say with affection, as he marches off guitar slung over one shoulder, a hand lifted in a backwards wave. Privately, I muse that fear of the unknown was a problem for Tim even as a toddler!

On 1 January, I walk up to Ranmore Church, with Henry at my side. Merlin refused to be lured from his cushion at the fireside. We listen to the bells ringing in the New Year. The chimes are so clear and optimistic, reverberating through the crisp air. I notice that the snowdrops are showing too, thrusting their deceptively delicate heads through the compacted ground. I shall paint them one day, make a watercolour of their pale feistiness. My easel is set up permanently in one of the bedrooms vacated when the children left home. We joke that it is my studio. I have a painting on the go all the time, all seasons. I like to work in differing light. It inspires me as though it is a living entity, an artist's model available continuously if you make allowances for her moods.

I am in the middle of a landscape of the bluebell woods when I make up my mind. Henry pops his head round the door, sucking contemplatively on the stem of his pipe. With the spicy fragrance of his tobacco, a certain calm descends upon me.

My husband takes the pipe from his mouth, cupping the bowl in one hand and holding it aloft. 'May one be allowed a preview of the great artist's latest masterpiece,' he ventures tentatively.

'Henry, oh Henry! You do talk nonsense,' I say, glancing back at him, amused.

'Ah now,' he continues as if I have flattered him, 'your perception is accurate to an astonishing degree. I am in point of fact fluent in the complex language of nonsense. It is no small boast either. I will have you know I have been taken as a native of nonsense, the listener completely convinced that it is my natural tongue.'

Now I laugh accepting when I am beaten. Henry takes a step forwards and shoots me a questioning look. When I nod in acquiescence, he levelly studies my painting.

'I'm giving up.' I throw away my resolve in a contradictory tone heavy with defeat. I pause and grief wells in my chest, making breathing a chore that requires concentration. Then sketching an 'S' mid-air, I add quietly, 'The Salvation Army have been successful in dissuading me.' I force a closing chord into my voice. 'My New Year's resolution is to curtail my search, to abandon my past, and to get on with my life.' I dab at my canvas, deliberately blurring the stinging blue of the inclined graceful flower heads, creating a delicate spectral film. When the haze ghosts the acid green of the pencil leaf clusters, the finest web of spun bluebells, I exhale a breath, content. 'Well?' I demand, counting the beats to his appraisal, both of my brushstrokes and of my determination to sound the retreat.

'Ah!' exclaims Henry. '*Per aspera ad astra!*' A few more puffs on his pipe. The dulcet notes of Judy Garland emanating from the radio in the lounge sail upstairs. 'Get Happy', not a favourite of mine, especially this year.

'And what pray is the meaning of that?' I probe hesitantly.

'A translation for my wife,' Henry announces portentously. He gives a theatrical pause then inhales a breath like a seasoned Shakespearian actor prior to a mouthful of linguistically challenging Bard. 'Through difficulties to the stars, my dear,' he declaims extravagantly. 'Through difficulties to the stars!'

Chapter 9

Harriet, 1948

We've had a communication from the Church Adoption Society. They have an available baby, a girl, which I concede is a plus. Apparently, she needs adopting as a matter of some urgency. The less said about that the better. So far the business has been more protracted than I anticipated. I was under the misapprehension that it would take a matter of weeks. It has however been closer to a year. Admittedly there were a couple of boys, but by then I had set my sights on a girl. Even hearing that they have the correct sex in stock does not overly thrill me. I hoped we would be offered more variety, that Merfyn and I might wander a row of cribs all occupied with potential candidates, that we would select the ideal baby for our daughter from the assorted homeless. I express something of my dissatisfaction with the process to my husband, and he reassures me that if this baby isn't to our liking we can hang on for another one. He does not seem to grasp that the delay of itself will be disadvantageous to us. I am thirty-six and Merfyn is forty-one. We are neither of us in our prime, and really it would be advisable not to waste another day.

About the baby (lately everything seems to concern the baby), it appears that they haven't collated all her documentation yet. But apparently this technicality is not an insurmountable obstacle to us taking her home then and there – if we find her engaging of course.

Merfyn called the secretary last week, Valeria Mulholland. It was she who signed the letter. He has already fixed up a meeting. It is tomorrow, Tuesday, 27 April, scheduled for 2.45 pm, at their offices in Bloomsbury Square. It's been rather a rush really. The mother, I'm reliably informed, is Welsh, a *Miss* Haverd. Envisage Merfyn's delight when we discovered this. She lives on her father's farm in Wales, helps out by all accounts. The identity of the father fills me with dread though. I was unprepared for the news. I had to sit down to absorb it. He is a German, was a prisoner of war, and has been working on the farm for a few years – though I imagine he's been sent packing now. I can't pretend that I'm not full of consternation. German! A Nazi, though Merfyn says they aren't all Nazis, so we can't be sure of this. It's not as easy to stomach as he assumes.

'They killed my mother,' I remind Merfyn, needled at how dismissive he is being. 'A Zeppelin raid in 1915 that blew our house to smithereens.'

'That was the First World War,' Merfyn placates, unwrapping a toffee. We've had our tea and are tuning in for *Dick Barton – Special Agent*, on the radio.

'They nearly killed *me*,' I add, blowing my nose and ramming my handkerchief into my skirt pocket. I am sewing buttons on a well-worn coat, brass buttons, and turning the collar. Giving it a new lease of life. Can't afford to be wasteful these days.

'She's a baby. Half-Welsh. An innocent,' he cajoles, popping the toffee in his mouth and concentrating on his paper again. 'They'll be running the Olympic games on a shoestring,' he mutters, his brow crinkling. 'Seems an odd time for us to host them, with no money to spare. Surely we should be using every penny to get back on our feet after the war.'

I set aside my sewing to scrutinise the letter yet again. 'It says here that the mother's given the baby a name: Lucilla.'

The Adoption

'You don't like it?' Merfyn asks, glancing over his paper at me. 'The Devil's Galop' starts up, Dick Barton's signature melody.

'Actually I like it very much. It's . . . feminine sounding. A fitting name for a girl. Born on the fourteenth of January, so she's over three months old already. You don't think she will have become attached to her birth mother by now?'

'Goodness no!' exclaims Merfyn. 'Babies don't have that kind of awareness until much later on. I have an idea that they start recognising people, places and things around the twelve-month mark. Another cup of tea in the pot?' His head rises over the parapet of the newspaper then lowers again.

I lean forwards as Dick Barton tells a police inspector that he wants more than a humdrum existence, that he's not afraid of hard graft. The brown teapot is set on the table in front of us. I lift the lid and peer inside it. 'I don't think so. I'll make another pot.'

'That'd be most welcome.' He turns the page fussily, shaking out the creases.

'She weighed seven pounds six ounces at her birth and she's nine pounds seven ounces now,' I report, without getting up.

'Oh, a good weight then,' he remarks absently.

'According to this overall she's in decent condition,' I continue. Then with less confidence, 'Her Wassermann test is negative.' I pause awaiting enlightenment. But as none is forthcoming I wade in, breath bated, 'What's that? The Wassermann test?'

'A test for syphilis,' Merfyn mumbles apologetically.

'Oh!' I gulp down my distaste and my mind strays inevitably to the father, the German soldier, and what escapades he might have got up to on his travels. 'That seems rather . . . rather unpleasant,' I cannot prevent myself from saying.

'It was negative, dear,' asserts Merfyn unruffled.

I give an explosive sigh. Unfortunately, at present, I am incapable of erasing the crude image that assails me. On the farm. Not being properly chaperoned. No one about to keep an eye on their licentious behaviour. A sordid roll in God knows what filth. A young naive girl letting the moment run away with her. A girl who, blatantly, is dismally lacking in moral fibre. 'So the mother is twenty and the father is twenty-six. Both healthy, or so they say. But then they would, wouldn't they? They're not going to tell you they've got some fungus running amuck in their family tree, spreading from branch to branch. Or a lunacy that resurfaces every few decades. If they did, no one would take their unwanted baby.'

'I think you're worrying unnecessarily. Have a toffee?' Merfyn offers.

'Not just now.' I drum my fingers lightly on the letter. 'Mmm . . . the baby has blonde hair and blue eyes.' I pick up the teapot and rise to my feet. 'I'd have preferred a brunette with brown eyes. Like my own.' I adjust my glasses and wrinkle my nose. I smell mildew. I'll have to give this sitting room a spring clean. 'Blue eyes and blonde hair. A frivolous combination I've always evinced.'

'Exceptionally pretty is my verdict,' Merfyn chuckles, a sparkle in his eyes.

'I fail to find this humorous,' I rejoin. 'Adoption is not a laughing matter.'

'Absolutely not,' concurs Merfyn, sobering in a second. Then he spoils it by digging about infuriatingly in the toffee tin.

'You shouldn't have too many of those, Merfyn. There's still rationing, you know.' He ignores me and helps himself. 'If we take her back with us tomorrow, how can we be sure she'll be fine? In the long term I mean.'

'There are no cast-iron guarantees with anything in life. You should know that,' Merfyn points out equably, sucking and chewing alternately. 'But we've done our research. And we're going to provide her with a stable, secure home. She's sure to flourish. It will be splendid.' He folds his paper and lays it on the table, his manner suddenly conciliatory. 'Look, the room's all ready. The cot's made up. You've knitted her an entire wardrobe. If she's what we're looking for then tomorrow we'll buy formula, feed and nappies. It's going to be tremendous. In under twenty-four hours we may be picking up our brand-new daughter. Aren't you tickled pink? I am.'

I take a deep breath and contemplate the German and the farm girl rutting like beasts. Why pretend it was otherwise? Might as well accept the fact now. The baby's natural father is a member of Hitler's tyrannical brigade. There's no evading this. I reflect, only fleetingly mind, on my deceased parents. How would they have viewed a half-German grandchild? 'Yes, yes, I am pleased. You know I am. I only want to make sure we've covered everything. Once we've adopted her, there will be no turning back, no returns, no refunds for faulty goods.'

'What a thing to say, dear. If I thought you meant it, I'd be shocked. It's the same when you have your own child,' Merfyn says still on an even keel. 'No different.'

He doesn't seem to have a handle on the risks that may be involved. 'You could be right. But it's a colossal decision.' I speak up more emphatically. 'We'd do well to remember this.'

'It is. And we have made it,' he retorts in a tone bordering on glib, considering the irrevocable circumstances that lie ahead. He stands up and pats my shoulder. 'I'm going to be a father and you're going to be a mother. Lucilla Pritchard. Has a ring to it, don't you think?'

I smile, regardless. It really is a lovely name. Only time will tell if she does it justice though. Later, in bed, I am wakeful. Merfyn is a good sleeper. It takes quite a rumpus to arouse him, especially when he's just dozed off. I close my eyes and have a go at visualising our baby. One of the things about this that's bothering me is the dearth of selection. We shall have no yardstick to measure her by. How are we to rate her?

How can you gauge quality if you have nothing to compare her with? I am vexed. If we were acquiring a puppy the science would be more exact.

I haven't had much experience with babies, well, any really. So how can I rely on my own discernment? Merfyn seems convinced that babies do little more than eat and sleep in the early days. I hope she won't be restless, up nights and so forth. I shouldn't think this chit of a girl has got Lucilla into any kind of routine at all. The vital thing is to establish a pattern immediately, set perimeters. I've got the house to run, the temperance meetings to attend. I don't want anything to upset our equilibrium. She's going to have to learn to fit in. Simple as that. If we have a few rebellious days, a squall of crying and kicking, well then, we shall have to block our ears and muddle through. I'm not dashing about at the beck and call of a spoiled baby. I'm far too busy.

The day we become a family dawns optimistically bright and crisp. Merfyn has taken a holiday from work. We're both edgy in the morning. He makes a show of sitting at his desk, getting on with some paperwork for the Sons of Temperance. I tackle some overdue housework, make inroads into my regime for annual cleaning, take down the net curtains, scrub the skirting boards, give the light bulbs a dust. Industrious action – the only antidote for anxiety. We have an early lunch, cods' roes on toast and very moreish too, then set off. We've both dressed smartly for the occasion. Merfyn wears a suit, a waistcoat and his temperance tie. I wear my navy crepe dress with the plaid design and scarf collar, purchased from Debenham & Freebody in Wigmore Street. We don't want them thinking we're not respectable. We take the bus and then the tube to Holborn. We don't run a car. Far too expensive, and really more of a handicap than an asset in London. It's quite a posh area when we come to it, Bloomsbury Square, so it's just as well we spruced ourselves up.

The Adoption

We're greeted at the front door by the Church Adoption Society's secretary. She's a tall woman, her short, straight, silver hair drawn back off her face in quite a severe manner. She has a dark streak in it that I'm not sure I like, and a beauty spot by her mouth. Adorning her neck are some rather lovely beads that trail very nearly to her waist. Her dress looks like silk, a William Morris print in peacock blues and greens and yellows. Goodness knows where she bought it. I haven't seen anything so lavish since well before the war.

'Mr Pritchard, Mrs Pritchard, welcome. I am Miss Mulholland, the society's secretary.' She shakes both our hands. She sounds as if she has spent a lifetime having elocution lessons her diction is so perfect.

In replying, I wish that I had, and attempt to mimic her faultless articulation. 'Oh yes, it's a pleasure to make your acquaintance, Miss Mulholland.'

'I expect you're both feeling quite nervous?' I nod and Merfyn waggles an index finger in his ear, something he does when he's feeling self-conscious. It is a foible of his that reminds me of riddling a poker in a dying fire, and one that I have advised him may not create a favourable impression. However, if Miss Mulholland is dismayed by its vulgarity, she disguises it seamlessly. 'Well, you really don't need to be. Won't you come this way?' She leads us to a room that resembles the waiting room on a train platform. It is in almost every respect nondescript: beige walls, a lead-grey cord carpet and utilitarian furniture. There are chairs and a low table. The seat covers are bottle-green plastic, their arms little more than wooden struts, so it all feels very formal.

'Do sit down,' she invites and we both oblige. Tall windows front on to the street, light flooding through them making me feel exposed somehow. I glance about expectantly. She rightly interprets my inspection and smiles sympathetically. 'I can tell you're eager to see the baby,' she says on an upwards inflexion. 'Well, Miss Haverd is here with her own mother, and Lucilla naturally. We want to make sure that the handover is as relaxed as possible. I'm sure you will realise that the potential for the birth mother to become anxious is ever present. The calmer the atmosphere, I believe, the more beneficial for both parties. Above all we want to make this pleasant.'

We nod. Merfyn mumbles something about how perceptive Miss Mulholland is, that we will trust entirely to her experience in matters such as ours. She offers tea, and although neither of us really feels like it we accept. A tray is brought, the beverage is sipped, biscuits are nibbled. I determine not to let my impatience show. Miss Mulholland keeps disappearing. She gives no explanation of these frequent absences, only reiterating that she will be back in a moment. But I have the distinct feeling that she is a go-between, scurrying down the corridor to another room where Miss Haverd, her mother and our soon-to-be daughter, Lucilla, are huddled. They are also probably drinking tea they don't want and eating biscuits they have no appetite for. An hour limps by. We are entertained with tapping feet approaching and departing outside the closed door of the room we are in, distant phones ringing, typewriter keys rat-tatting, when Miss Mulholland reappears wearing a positive smile.

'They are saying their final goodbyes now. It's preferable that they do this by themselves, don't you think?' She clasps and unclasps her hands in a gesture resembling a slow-motion clap, as if applauding the stage we have finally reached.

'Oh yes, no doubt about it,' agrees Merfyn, fearing an outpouring of embarrassing womanish sentiment, I hazard inwardly.

I suppress a sigh and incline my head. There follows a briefing as if we are about to go over the trenches. 'What's going to happen is this. Miss Haverd will bring Baby in. Somewhat unusual but she has insisted. She will put Baby –' She breaks off in a self-deprecatory titter.

'She will put *Lucilla* in your arms, Mrs Pritchard, and then without dawdling she will go. I have taken the liberty of applying a condition to this personal delivery. I have told her that there is to be no conversation. That's safest, I think. We don't want this to be a drawn-out process, do we?'

I resist the temptation of commenting that it has already been more drawn out than Neville Chamberlain's unsuccessful peace negotiations with the tyrant Hitler, and can we please get it over with. 'Like pulling off a plaster. So much less painful if you're quick,' approves Merfyn with unwarranted joviality.

'So, Mrs Pritchard, if you're ready?' Miss Mulholland checks, pencilled eyebrows rising quizzically.

I am not terribly sure what the apposite response to this should be, so I improvise. 'Oh yes, quite ready,' I respond putting down my teacup and making a cradle of my arms in preparation.

Merfyn looks as if he has suddenly been seized with a fit of stage fright and, hands on knees, rumples up the fabric of his trousers. But oddly I am not averse to the idea of seeing *her*, the birth mother, giving her a surreptitious appraisal. Who knows what clues she may hold as to the kind of butterfly that will in due course hatch from the pupa we are collecting. In fact, in that instant I am more curious about her than I am about the baby. 'Well then, if we are all content I will go and fetch Miss Haverd, and . . . and Lucilla.'

We nod yet again. It is another ten minutes before the door opens hesitantly and in *she* comes, gripping on to a woolly bundle like a lifesaver it seems. She is shepherded by Miss Mulholland. It goes without a hitch. No civilities are exchanged, for we are all struck dumb. The girl, she appears no more than that, eyes modestly downcast, approaches me. I give her an encouraging smile, but I'm not sure if she sees it. Her focus is riveted on the baby swathed in knitted blankets – garter stitch. And I trace the woolly worms of two runs. I take stock furtively. We will not meet again, and I decide that I want to take a mental photograph of her . . . for . . . for posterity?

She looks absurdly young, making me feel somewhat staid, like a maiden aunt. I have to grant though that she is tolerably pretty, with the most unusual turquoise eyes. Her hair is a light shade, I think they call it strawberry-blonde. She has on, of all get-ups, trousers cut in some coarse cloth – as if her farm is only five minutes from us and she has just left off minding her sheep. And really they look most unattractive on her slender frame. Her blouse is buttoned to the neck, and over it she wears a scruffy beige cardigan, stockinette stitch. There are two holes in the elbows. She is transparently ill equipped to raise a child. Why she is no more than a child herself. I restrain a sneer. In advance of today I am gratified to see that I summed her up correctly. She is a simple, ill-educated creature in whom the baser appetites of woman hold sway.

As she is putting Lucilla into my arms our eyes do meet and lock for several seconds. I know what you are, is the thought at the forefront of my mind. What does she think, if the chit is capable of cognitive reasoning? I honestly couldn't say. If she has any common sense she should be feeling thankful that Merfyn and I have come to her rescue. After all, we have been willing to put aside the less than savoury aspects of her unmarried liaison, to shoulder the responsibility of its inevitable outcome. We are giving her back her life and taking the by-blow of her sin off her hands. She very nearly runs from the room. Miss Mulholland hastens after her. Merfyn stands and, hands quivering, bends from the waist and brushes a crooked finger over Lucilla's round cheek. The baby blinks up at us with her birth mother's unsettling turquoise eyes, and gives an involuntary start.

'Hello, Lucilla,' says Merfyn in a funny voice I have not heard before, twee as Annette Mills joshing with Muffin the Mule. 'We're your new mother and father.'

Later, riding home on the bus with the baby on my lap, Merfyn tucks an arm about my waist. 'Oh, Mother,' he says beaming down at Lucilla, 'isn't she grand?' Like a schooner in the doldrums my sails sag. I realise suddenly that he is addressing me.

Chapter 10

Bethan, 1948

6th August, 1948

Dear Miss Haverd,

We are enclosing herewith the 'Consent to Adoption' form for you to complete and return to us, if possible, by Wednesday, 11th August, so that the case may be heard in the next session of court. It will be necessary for your signature to be witnessed by a Justice of the Peace, and you should complete the Declaration at the foot of the page in his presence.

We are happy to say that Lucilla is progressing very well indeed, and thriving with her adoptive parents who are devoted to her.

With best wishes.

Yours sincerely,

Valeria Mulholland

Secretary

10th Aug, 1948

Dear Madam,

I am very pleased to hear that Lucilla is getting on well, and that her parents dote on her. I only wish that I could have kept her. But I am happy to know that she is definitely in a very good home. I am afraid it is not possible for me to attend court in London for the adoption. But I have signed the form and enclosed it.

Thanking you for your great kindness,

Yours sincerely,

Bethan Modron Haverd.

18th August, 1948

Dear Miss Haverd,

I am afraid the form you sent will not do. It is necessary for you to attend the court hearing personally for the Adoption of your baby. Will you let me know by return if there are any days on which you could not be present? We will give you good notice of the date settled on.

If you have nowhere to stay in London overnight, I will try to make arrangements for accommodation for you. Are you in a position to pay your own expenses?

Yours sincerely,

Valeria Mulholland

Secretary

20th Aug, 1948

Dear Madam,

Received your letter this morning. I was surprised in reading it. It is impossible for me to journey to London as I am a land worker on the farm. I could not have leave for an hour because the corn harvest has just commenced. I am at my work from 6 am in the morning till nine o'clock in the evening. Every person here's the same and each one at different jobs.

So I hope you will quite understand my position.

Yours truly,

B. M. Haverd

2nd September, 1948

Dear Miss Haverd,

Thank you for your letter. I am very sorry to inform you that the adoption cannot proceed unless you attend the court in person. The Justices are adamant in this regard, and they will not make any exceptions. The court is being held on 14th September, 10 am at Highgate. You will be kept there no longer than 12 noon. It would be possible for you to catch the night train from Newport and return the day of the hearing. Mr Johnston, who is acting for the Justices, is writing to you to explain these conditions. The Justices will not dispense with your attendance.

We shall be only too pleased to meet you and accompany you to the court, as well as booking your accommodation should that be necessary.

Please write by return,

Yours sincerely,

Valeria Mulholland

Secretary

6th Sept, 1948

Dear Madam,

Thank you for yours of the 2nd Sept with instructions. I trust that my daughter will be able to carry them out. She understands punctuality is of the utmost importance. Once again I would be grateful if you could see that her expenses are covered, as we are not in a position to pay for her.

Faithfully yours,

Ifan Havard

Thorston didn't answer my letter, so there wasn't a miracle after all. I have to believe that he didn't receive it, that it's at the bottom of a sack in the sorting office with all the other undelivered letters. I can't live with the possibility that he did get it. But by then, what with the scene and my father punching him, and the dogs, he may have made the decision that I wasn't worth it, worth the suffering our relationship would inevitably entail. No, I won't have that. My letter has gone astray, the way we did, diverting from paths that our heritage had laid down for us. So please have some compassion for me, some forgiveness. The doors were slammed behind me, and not merely slammed but locked and bolted. I had no other option. God of mercy I had no other option.

I set off on a train rattling through the night, the beginning of what seems an unending journey. Stiff as a rake I am, in my seat in the carriage. My spine feels as if I couldn't bend it if I wanted to. I am by the window but there is no advantage to it. The lights reflect on the glass making it extremely difficult to see anything at all. Exhaustion overwhelms me, bodily exhaustion. But I can't sleep. It's a weird sensation, my head spinning with tiredness, and me riding in a pod rocketing through space. Outside is nothing. Inside is nothing too, so they match. There is a man, a middle-aged man I'd guess, with a briefcase, sitting by the compartment door. He has a drooping moustache and I think it must be tickling his nose because he keeps wiggling it, then blowing it noisily into a big white hanky.

Opposite me is an elderly woman with a worn face. Her hair is thin and grey, and tidied into a bun that looks like a hedgehog there are so many hairpins sticking out of it. Her skin looks grey too, like elastic with the twang gone out of it. Her eyes are dull as juniper berries, and the whites don't look white at all but tinted blue. She has whiskers like a man's growing from her chin and her nose. She's wearing a tweed skirt and jacket. And there's a silver brooch of a sailing boat pinned at her neck. Both her and the man start their journey reading, him, papers from his briefcase, her, a journal. Then after an hour or so the lady nods off, her mouth dropping open so that I can see the few yellow teeth she has left. Minutes pass and the man falls asleep as well. But he's very tidy about it, crossing his arms over his briefcase, and pushing the hat he is wearing down over his eyes. It's weird but when I stare at the lady it's like looking at myself. I'm being dotty, I know. I'm young and she's old. All the same, it's my reflection.

I am altered. I can't really say how because I'm no longer sure of the way I was before. The girl who went to London and stayed in a flat in Rochester Row, growing fat as a beer barrel day by day until she burst open, well . . . she's someone else. And this is healthy really, this division. No, it is. So don't feel pity for me. I have no feelings any more. Honestly, if you took a hatpin and pushed it into me, my leg, my arm . . . I don't believe I would feel a thing. I am anaesthetised. As for my heart, I am as certain as I can be that it stopped beating months ago.

That other Bethan – you might like to know that she gave birth in New End Hospital, Hampstead, in January of this year, the 14th. She was very frightened. The pains began on one of her walks. They weren't bad at the outset, something like chronic period pains, and she was so relieved. If it continued at this level she thought that she would breeze through it. She would be like the sheep that dropped their lambs in the field and then went on grazing. But it didn't stay like this. Rapidly it doubled, then trebled, then quadrupled, until it was as though the agony was a masochist within her. And it had its own rhythm as it bit into her. Then, when she was on the brink of fainting, when she wanted to die it was so excruciating, it paused in a kind of menacing manner. And even those pauses were horrid because she knew they would end soon, and that those teeth would again become fangs locked on her innards. They weren't very charitable to her at the hospital. They knew that the baby she was giving birth to was not like the others, that it was illegitimate. Her mam was kind to her when it came to it. She stayed with her all through that endless hard labour, held her hand, spoke about how she was as a little girl, skipping around outdoors all weathers, a wild child.

What she did not expect, what she had not figured into this equation, was how the birth would turn her anguish into exultation. It was magic. If the love she felt for Thorston had been forbidden, then she knew the savage immediate love that possessed her for his baby, for their daughter, was outlawed. Over the next three months she starred in the theatre of the absurd. The baby must be fed, but not breastfed. Her mam was adamant about this. The infant would be given the bottle, formula milk. The less contact Bethan had with the baby the safer for all of them. So her breasts were swollen and sore. When she heard the baby whimper, they leaked milk. Weeks it took for the supply to finally dry up. Her mam dictated that she would be the baby's carer, changing and feeding her, getting up to her in the night, rocking and cuddling her. They should take every precaution to prevent a maternal bond developing, she told her. So Bethan left her mam with the baby and ambled the streets alone, out nearly all day sometimes.

But when the baby became sick, very sick with gastro-enteritis, they were both frantic. They forgot about who should have a bond and who should not. She was treated in the hospital. Bethan was petrified that she might die. The thought of living in a world robbed of her baby made her lose her balance and fall to the floor. As her mam helped her up, a look passed between them. In that instant their limitless love was seen for what it was, an indelible brand on both their lives. Her mam owned her treachery and prayed that Brice would forgive her. Bethan owned the betrayal of her baby, and prayed that one day she would have absolution for the premeditated act she was going to commit. They did not share with each other their deep-rooted suspicions that Eira Heppell had in some devilish way doctored the baby's feed, that she had tried to poison it. From then on the baby was never left unattended.

During the pregnancy they had both avoided giving the baby a name. They knew the power a name would bestow, the undeniable sorcery of it. A name would transform their fairy child, their changeling into a human girl knitted not of angel dust, but flesh and blood, skin and bone, with a tiny pumping heart in the jewel box of her chest. In the event a café supplied it. It served fruit buns, teacakes and jam tarts, tea and coffee, and it was called Lucilla's. They all frequented it, all three of them.

'If it's a girl shall we call her Lucilla then?' Bethan suggested as they paid their bill one afternoon, only days before her confinement.

Her mam nodded. 'Mmm . . . why not?' she said. 'Lucilla will do.' They both felt indifferent to the name. They did not consider what to call the baby if it was a boy.

'It's quite pretty really,' they muttered in overlapping voices and the deal was done. Bethan had a moment of weakness in the Registry Office in Hampstead. Asked to provide the baby's name, she threw her head back and gazed at the ceiling. She didn't actually like it. It was too elaborate, too complicated. Saying it made her feel all breathless, as if she was suffocating. But like everything else it seemed a bit too late by then. So on 16 January her daughter's name was registered as Lucilla Haverd.

Her mam rang the Church Adoption Society and spoke to their contact, a Miss Mulholland, Valeria Mulholland. She said that the baby had been born, that it was a healthy girl, that they had called her Lucilla. Miss Mulholland gave effusive assurances that they were on the lookout for the ideal home for Lucilla. They realised how pressing the situation was, that it was a race to remedy their plight and locate a secure home with excellent adoptive parents.

They asked Bethan to fill out a form, to sign a certificate. She had stared at it for nearly a quarter of an hour. Phrases had leaped out at her and tolled in her head like the church bells had done at funerals:

'Adoption of Children (Regulation) Act (1939). To be furnished by a registered Adoption Society to every parent or guardian who proposes to place a child at the disposition of the Society. If an adoption order is made in respect of your child, all your rights and duties with regard to the child will be transferred permanently to the adopter.' She had been sitting in the Church Adoption Society's office, the office where the secretary, Miss Mulholland, typed letters to suicidal young women. It was the office where she answered the telephone and arranged for the babies to be collected, like undelivered parcels that were returned to the post office.

Her mam had been with her. She had also studied it, puzzling over the unfamiliar vocabulary. Since arriving in London, having the baby, tending to her, actively avoiding physical contact, as if Lucilla had leprosy and was not the most beautiful thing in all creation, Bethan had struggled to think coherently. She sometimes entertained the delusion that she had been in a car crash and was now brain-damaged. Her thoughts lacked logical progression, the snowballing ideas fragmenting or dropping into nothingness long before she could extract any sense from them. Her head wasn't wired. She had blown a fuse, more like a dozen. It was a bother and a blessing besides, because nothing concluded. She couldn't stay aboard trains of thought, ride them like bucking broncos till she broke them in. They threw her off in seconds. Oh the train went hurtling on, disappearing in the distance. But where it was going who knew? She was left in the fog, in the humane fog.

She pounded her brow hoping to hone her concentration. She might be back at school, chomping on a pencil end, hunched over an exercise book working out her sums. And they had been so baffling, she remembered, all those numbers to add, divide, multiply, subtract. She was subtracting that moment. Last year, she'd been adding, adding Thorston into her life, adding the heat of his body to hers. And then she'd been multiplying. Isn't that what the Bible said, go forth and multiply. Well, she had multiplied. She'd become two, Bethan and a baby. And then she'd been divided from her baby when Lucilla was born. She'd wanted to keep her inside for eternity. But that was obviously idiotic. And now, last sum of all, but inversely the most difficult one, torturous she might say, she was subtracting, subtracting the baby from her.

'It should all work out, dear,' she recalled her teacher telling her, her distant eyes zipping over the disastrous workings Bethan had scrawled on the page. 'Have another go and you'll see, it will all work out.' But it hadn't and it wasn't. The answer was wrong, and no matter how many times she did the complicated sum, she got the same result.

'If you have taken out an insurance policy against funeral expenses for your child, the insurers will be able to advise you whether the policy can be transferred to the adopters.' That's what it had said on the form, really! She'd only recently given birth and now they were talking about her baby dying. It had to be a joke, and like all jokes there was a grain of truth embedded in it. Because this birth felt like death. It did. She didn't care if it was a morbid thing to dwell on. And now they had presented her with their form, as if creepily they were telepathic, asking her to anticipate the costs of her baby's funeral. But it didn't feel as if Lucilla was in mortal danger, in spite of being so sick with the gastric upset. Gazing into her turquoise eyes, so like her own, like her grandfather's honestly, Lucilla exuded life force. It was Bethan who had received a fatal wound, Bethan who was fading with every passing hour. 'I hereby certify that I received from you a memorandum headed "Adoption of Children (Regulation) Act, 1939", and that I have read the memorandum and understand it.' And the dead person she had mutated into, the spectre, took up the pen and signed.

She had more in common with her brother, Brice, now that she was nearer death. They were both as good as ghosts, shadows of their former selves. Afterwards, after giving her baby away, she wished she hadn't insisted on seeing them, on physically putting her daughter into that woman's arms. She could have made them perfect if she hadn't done that, perfect parents for her perfect baby, and not been witness to their flawed selves. They were old. They appeared more like grandparents than parents. And the woman was sort of stolid and lifeless, like a felled tree. Not fat exactly but broad and wooden as a heavy door. Her hair, shoulder length, was a frizzy lifeless cap. It was no shade at all really, not brown nor grey, but an indiscriminate mix of the two. Most disturbing were her eyes. They *were* brown, brown as coffee grits, passionless, eyes that the soul, if she had one, did not reach. Both she and her husband wore glasses, the lenses thick as paperbacks, making them seem still more detached and aloof. The man was wearing a suit like her father's Sunday best, the one he saved for church. And he had his finger stuck in his ear, wiggling, as if he was giving his brains a stir.

More depressing, there was something used about them, weary, a stifling properness that made her want to fight for air. It would smother her daughter. They would systematically douse the light in those stunning turquoise eyes. She may not, by deliberate design, have known the intimacy of her baby suckling from her breasts. She may have shunned holding her. She may have held her breath when Lucilla came too close, in case she inhaled that unique, intrinsic, indefinable scent that was her daughter's, but she had locked eyes with her. And in that clasp a whole discourse of love had been spoken, a lifetime of it. She could no more quash her love, no more sever her emotional tie, than she could take a knife and hack off her own legs.

In her baby's eyes chapters of faraway tropical oceans were inscribed. And there was a gossamer dreaminess, a whimsical insight that would resist any kind of alphabetical order. She had a fey quality that meant, like her own mother, like herself, Lucilla would forever be spellbound. She would marvel at the way a field of ripe wheat could ripple like an amber sea, would marvel at the way the sky was the changing tide of your emotions. She didn't have to glimpse a crystal ball to know what was going to happen. Her daughter would not be allowed to run barefoot in the grass, to scramble up trees and swing in their upper branches, to ride horses bareback, feeling their warm flanks heaving against the grip of her thighs. These were the kinds of parents who made rules, who demanded obedience, who made you conform, who forced you into a mould. They would wait for years if that's what it took, for you to set. They would clock-watch. They would extol absolutism. They would be the dictators. They would yoke Lucilla's spirit. Her daughter would strive to battle her own nature. In vain she would try to resist gazing up at the unique character of each day, try to withstand the temptation of stringing the stars into necklaces and bracelets, try to still her imagination from pencilling a smile on the mottled silver moon.

But with full knowledge of all the tomorrows lining up like dominoes, Bethan did it. She let her go. She gave her baby into another's arms. And then she turned and walked from the room. She did it the way the condemned climb the steps to a gallows, the way they accept the eternal darkness of the hood, the way they raise their head to the collar of the noose. When they got back to Bedwyr Farm it had been rebuilt, her family substituted for another. Her mam no longer chatted comfortably with her. She treated her in the guarded way you might a dog that has bitten you, handling her carefully.

Her dad would not meet her eye, and in the unconscious curl of his lip was repugnance. He drove her relentlessly, from the second she was shaken from her sleep while it was still pitch black outside, to the second she fell, faint with weariness, back into her bed. He made her work on the land harder than she had ever done before. She did the job of a man twice her age and twice her size. He spied on her every waking minute. By taciturn agreement, she kept mute. It was something like solitary confinement, she thought. And she was never, never ever permitted to be alone with the farm labourers her dad had taken on in their absence: thickset Barris who spat into the mud when she was near, and lanky Jestin who sneered behind her back.

Towards her dad for his brutal treatment of her she felt nothing but gratitude. He was meting out the punishment she deserved. She bore it with the joy of a martyr. The more he pushed her, the less able she was to unpack the burden of her guilt, the less able to review the prospect of her life sentence. When the summons came for her to go to London in September to witness the adoption, she was overcome with disbelief. It was a second thrust of the knife in a fresh wound. Her dad was adamant that she could not be spared, not even for one day. But the the Church Adoption Society was equally adamant that she must obey, that the adoption would not go ahead without her, that the Justices would not be thwarted. And so he finally consented to the trip, but only if she left on the night train to Paddington on 13 September, returning to Newport by the midday train the following day.

The station is deserted when she arrives in the early hours of the morning. She hasn't slept. She hasn't eaten or drunk. She feels lightheaded, dehydrated, giddy as a revolving door. She sits in the waiting room and memorises its drabness. Saucepan-grey walls, varnished wooden benches, a concrete floor. She listens to the echoing announcements. Her stomach rumbles and she is taken by a wave of nausea so powerful that she retches, though all she can bring up is a mouthful of bile, brownish yellow and bitter. Her limbs are starch stiff and her bottom is numb from sitting too long. She has a crick in her neck and she can smell her own sweat. But it is not clean and honest, the way it smells at the end of a day on the farm. The stink is offensive to her, like the rank smell of an infection. In the toilet she undoes her blouse and tries to wash under her arms with a damp paper towel. But it falls apart, and when she finishes the stink is still with her.

Afterwards, she finds her way to the tube and travels underground with the rush hour. It's insanity. All the people are racing to their places of work and she races as well, carried along with the flow of them, rushing to her exam, the subtraction of her baby. She has the sudden impulse to interrupt a couple of women who are nattering about their children. She wants to tell them that her daughter has the most extraordinary turquoise eyes you have ever seen. She doesn't of course, but she dearly wants to.

Holborn and she stands by the red post box outside the premises of the Church Adoption Society. I hate this city, she thinks. I don't want to come back. I don't want to hear its name uttered in my presence ever again. It is September and the leaves are turning red and yellow and orange. Strands of silky white cloud are stretched across the loom of a duck-egg blue sky. Car horns blare and a welter of people jostle and chatter, purpose in their steps. A lady, Mrs Parish, salt-and-pepper hair piled high, comes and claims her. She asks her if she's had a comfortable trip, and if she has eaten breakfast. Bethan nods to both enquiries. Mrs Parish steers her to the juvenile court, Petty Sessional Division of Highgate, sitting at Avenue House in Finchley.

And she is here. Her baby Lucilla is here, and so are the adoptive parents, the parents who look like grandparents. She did not expect to see her, her beautiful daughter now eight months old. They are sitting to the rear of the courtroom, the woman clutching her baby. All she dares is a quick glance in their direction while she is being led to her seat. But the image that burns her retina will remain for a lifetime. Lucilla is restless, grizzling, squirming in her arms. And the woman is jigging her up and down, up and down. She doesn't like it. Her daughter doesn't like it. Why doesn't someone tell her to stop it? Why don't the Justices order her to desist? The impulse to turn and walk slowly towards them, to take her baby back, to hug her close and run from this frightful place is overwhelming. But the formal setting, the intimidating suited men, the Justices staring down at her with their long sober faces, the booming chesty voices speaking legal jargon she does not begin to understand, all these inhibit her. She keeps her eyes down, her body rigid, the scream in her throat gagged. Too fast. It is happening too fast. They race through the proceedings. And then she is summoned to sign her name on a document. And it is done. They hurry her out, leaving her baby, her daughter, her precious child behind her for the second, the final time.

'Well, that wasn't too bad, was it?' says Mrs Parish glancing at her gold wristwatch, and then frowning at a snag in her stockings. She has a pug dog's nose, Bethan observes. 'Will you be all right finding your way back to Paddington? Only I've an appointment.' Her thin mouth stretches like a rubber band and snaps back. 'I'm sure the society will keep in touch. Anyway it's been very nice meeting you . . . Miss Haverd.' She shakes hand but only with her fingers, as if she is concerned that she may sully herself. And then abruptly she ditches her outside the court.

For a minute Bethan just loiters at a loss, as though she has been jilted. She knows she has a train to catch, and that she should get a move on or she will miss it. But she doesn't care. She isn't bothered. She may stay here and lie in wait for them, for her baby, and follow them home. She may kidnap her own daughter. Or she may wander the streets like a bag lady. She may beg for a copper or two to buy a cup of tea. She may sleep on the clipped grass in St James's Park and dream of the green valleys of home. But even as she toys with this inviting inactivity, her feet begin to tramp towards the underground station. On the ride home, she sheds her skin. The woman who loved a German soldier and lay with him, the woman who conceived his baby and carried it to term, the woman who gave birth in New End Hospital in Hampstead, the woman who nursed her baby through gastro-enteritis as if both their lives depended on her daughter's recovery, that woman has gone as surely as if spades of earth are being thrown on her coffin lid.

Before she chugs into Newport she comes to herself. I am like the cloth doll that has been mauled by a rabid dog. I have holes and through my holes all the stuffing of me has come out. It would be a wasted effort to try to stitch me up. I am undone. I must make do. No one will notice I'm not really here. And she is right, they don't.

15th September
Dear Miss Haverd,

I do hope you managed to find your way to Paddington, and that you had a leisurely journey home. We were so glad to find such a nice couple to adopt Lucilla. I am sending you some snapshots of the baby. These were, of course, taken earlier in the year but I expect you will be interested to see them.

With very best wishes.

Yours sincerely,

Valeria Mulholland

Secretary

Chapter 11

Harriet, 1950

She has been such a good baby up until recently. Merfyn is garrulous in his praise for *our golden girl*. And let there be no mistake, so was I to start with. I have encountered some minor irritants, but none that compete with the magnitude of her Germanic ancestry. For example, it is a pity that her hair is so straight. My preferment would have been for curls, natural curls. Still this is not without remedy. When she is older I will simply have to perm it, to make it curl. As for her features, she is developing into a plainer child than I had hoped for. But she eats well, and sleeps well. And life, I am pleased to say, more or less is continuing on its accustomed round. What more can we ask for? Yet as things go on, I cannot rid myself of a heightened uneasiness in respect of our adopted daughter.

'I don't know what you were making such a fuss about, Mother,' says Merfyn one night as we sit by the fire. 'She is ideal.'

I nod and crease my lips in a thin smile. I dislike him calling me *Mother*. I am not his mother. And in reality I am not Lucilla's mother either, not genetically anyway. Therefore it seems nonsensical to let this new maternal role define me altogether. But if I argue the point he may take offence. He can be sentimental about such things, so I let it be.

Merfyn's job for the Ever Ready Company means that he is

employed for lengthy hours, alternate Saturdays included. I'm not saying his adulation is misplaced, but he misses the minutiae of Lucilla's emerging personality – like hangnails these traits are not necessarily a cause for rejoicing. I pride myself on keeping a sense of proportion. And granted they are only tiny indiscretions. But then if Adam and Eve had been more vigilant we might have avoided original sin. I don't wish to state the obvious but Merfyn is a man. So he is hardly best qualified to judge the progress Lucilla is making. I, solely, am alone with her all day. I am the one who has to spend tedious mornings and afternoons correcting her misdemeanours.

I am not dim-witted. I fully comprehend that infants do not arrive house-trained as it were. But the incontrovertible fact is that we have a problem. Frankly, I would talk it over with Merfyn, but it is rather delicate. At twenty months exactly, I started potty training our daughter. One month passed and Lucilla was doing magnificently. Two, then three, and really I was feeling quite smug. She appeared to be clean and dry, except at nights and that was understandable for the present. Please excuse the crudity of what I am imparting, but in the lieu of a mother you have to deal with these distasteful bodily functions.

However, as she approached her second birthday I am sorry to say I detected a deviation. Generally, she has a bowel movement after tea, and is accustomed to sitting on the potty while I run her bath or turn back her cot. Then one night she refused to stay seated, hopping up after only a few seconds. I peered inside the bowl. Empty. Meanwhile she was gambolling off down the corridor like a spring lamb.

'Lucilla!' I called. 'Lucilla, come here!' My tone was perhaps more peremptory than I intended, but then it was a situation that warranted it. This kind of thing must not under any circumstances be allowed to escalate. I heard a clatter of footsteps, and she peeped around the bathroom door. She was naked, dragging her toy bear behind her.

'Lucilla, sit back down right now.' She stood for a moment, head falling to one side, those odd turquoise eyes of hers unreadable. 'Lucilla, do you hear me?' I said imperiously. 'None of this silliness, miss.' I pointed at her and directed her to the potty. It is white plastic, and was sitting like a giant eggcup on the linoleum of the bathroom floor. She crossed to it and gingerly lowered her bottom down on the seat. 'You will sit there, miss, until you perform,' I said, wagging a finger warningly at her.

She screwed up her eyes and hung her head as if she was trying to do a complicated sum. We waited and waited and waited, me tapping a foot by now. I glanced at my watch. It was 6 pm. We had a temperance do on that night and I needed to get ready. 'Push,' I ordered taking a threatening step towards her. 'Go on, push! Take a big breath and push.' She took a breath obligingly, and puffed out her cheeks until they looked rouged. 'Hurry up, Lucilla.' My patience was being stretched to its limits. 'Lucilla!' I shrilled.

She closed one eye and looked up at me with the other. 'Can't,' she whimpered.

'You can,' I insisted. I knew what this was – a war of wills. And I would be the victor. If there was any dragon slaying to be done, mine would be the killing stroke. 'Do it or you'll have a smacked bottom.' Another five minutes crawled past, then ten. 'Lucilla!' I rasped, my voice now hoarse with anger.

Her little mouth set firm. 'Can't,' she said again.

I flew at her, lifting her by one arm off her potty with such force that her feet left the ground for a moment. Once more I scrutinised the interior of the bowl. It was clean as a freshly scrubbed basin. I glowered at her and undiminished she stared back. Was that defiance in those lucid turquoise eyes? And then suddenly I had it. I sent her to her bedroom in disgrace. Grasping the towel rail for support, the unwelcome realisation trumpeted in my head. It was deliberate. The child was resisting me on purpose, in order that she might spite me.

This obstinacy, and please don't assume I am overreacting, this obstinacy was a source of pleasure for her. She liked to see how it irked me. She liked the power it gave her. Well, we'd soon counteract that. Cod liver oil and syrup of figs – that would do the trick. And if they gave her tummy ache so much the better. Fair punishment for her naughtiness. There is a stubborn streak in that child. She will have to be cured of it. She is half German after all. It is vital that this carry-on is sorted out without delay. If I give way on this, if I let her believe she has the upper hand, where will it end? I have come to the conclusion that the remedy is more prayer. Each night I prescribe that our daughter confess her sins. 'Kneel down, Lucilla, and ask God to forgive you,' I say. We go through her day together and I make a list of her transgressions.

'Knees hurty,' is her usual whine. But not until she has repeated the catechism of her wrongdoings, not until I'm sure she is truly repentant, do we say our amen.

'Vanity of vanities, saith the Preacher, vanity of vanities; all is vanity', Ecclesiastes 1:2. A new biblical quote each week. So much more beneficial than bedtime stories, don't you think? We commit it to memory before selecting another. Yet my anxieties are not wholly allayed. Call me a pessimist but I think this is a forerunner of the future, of insurrections to be visited upon us in days to come.

'She's a pearl and she's all ours,' Merfyn says, as he sits after supper doing the crossword. 'We're so fortunate, Mother. "The Homeless Child for the Childless Home". The Church Adoption Society's slogan. It's very catchy, isn't it?' The question is rhetorical and Merfyn does not pause for a reply. 'We're proof that it really does work,' he adds, setting his paper aside and reaching for a malted milk biscuit. I let this pass without comment.

Chapter 12

Lucilla, 1998

The close of August and already the year is turning. The air has a lemon juice tartness to it. The flowers are looking papery and flyblown, like tipsy ladies on the town after midnight. Soon the trees will be weeping copious tears of butter yellow, of moth brown, of blood red, tears that drip-flutter-drop into the crumbling dusky-skinned earth. I want to capture the fire of it in oils, something of its richness, its decadence. Watercolours simply won't do. Too insipid. They lack that gamey high pigment, the rich meat of the oily shades. The magpie nursery rhyme pops into my head.

> *One for sorrow, two for joy;*
> *Three for a girl, four for a boy;*
> *Five for silver, six for gold;*
> *Seven for a secret, never to be told;*
> *Eight for a wish, nine for a kiss;*
> *Ten for a bird that's best to miss.*

I'm fond of it. I knew it by heart as a child, sang it out in skipping games. 'Three for a girl.' It's special for me. 'Three for a girl.' You see, three is my lucky number. I like the lopsidedness of it, the fact that it undoes that most hare-brained of human aspirations – the attainment of perfection. No such thing. It is the errors, the accidents, the mistakes that should be celebrated.

Brightmore Hall has a stately sweeping drive lined with green beech trees, seventeen to each side. You feel like a great lady even if you're only cycling up it on a battered pushbike. But you know what I love the most about the vista. All those years ago when the saplings were planted the gardeners bungled up. They must have been inattentive, had a lapse in concentration while they cocked an ear to a thrush in full song, or closed their eyes the better to bask in the mellow sunshine. Because one of those trees isn't green at all. It is a full-bodied wine red. A copper beech has snuck in to stand tall and proud among the frippery of green. I recollect how comfortable I felt when I first set eyes upon that tree, how I was instantly at ease with the asymmetrical avenue. As I say three is an eccentric number, the *numero tre* that upsets the symmetry, that tips the scale, that sinks the ark, and has Noah ripping his hair out by its roots. It is the arrival of three that makes an unpredictable crowd of two.

I am strolling in the grounds with Merlin, all he can manage these days with his endearingly drunken gait. We are soaking up the autumnal splendour, when I see a wisp of a girl playing at hopscotch on the path ahead. She wears jeans and a pink sweatshirt. She must be about seven, I estimate. One of the braids that her long brown hair has been plaited into is unravelling. Her cheeks look carnation pink and there is the tail of a yellow ribbon dangling from her fisted hand. When she spots us approaching, her eyes brighten, dancing with interest. She skips up to Merlin.

'Oh he's lovely. May I pat him?' she asks, crouching down, her voice high and energetic as her young self. Merlin deigns to halt, and waits with an air of nobility for his female admirer to pay him abeyance.

'Of course,' I say. 'He's awfully friendly.'

She strokes his head gently. 'What's his name?'

'Merlin.'

'Like the magician, King Arthur's magician.'

'That's right.'

'I've read stories about him at school. It suits him. His fur feels like my hair when it's loose.' I smile. 'Why is he panting?'

'Oh, he's quite an old gentleman now,' I inform her.

'So was Merlin. But he's still very handsome,' she says and my patrician Merlin licks her in appreciation of the munificent compliment. 'Is it rude to ask why that eye is a bit cloudy?'

'No, not rude at all. I'm afraid he is going blind. It's sad, but he doesn't seem to mind. He copes with the other good eye. He likes licking the cream that's left around the neck of the empty milk bottles. He's very adept at it. You'd find it funny to watch.'

She laughs. 'I wish I had a dog,' she says, feelingly.

'Well, you must ask –'

But here I am interrupted. A woman comes running from the direction of the house. She is screaming like a banshee. 'Lucy! Lucy! Get over here! Where have you been, you naughty girl?'

The child springs up, all traces of her previous enjoyment expunged in an instant. Her eyes are wide and alarmed. She bites her lower lip, bites and bites at it, and suddenly I notice how inflamed and sore it is. 'I'd better go,' she says. And she pivots and sprints up to the harridan. A minute or so later and the woman is still shrieking at her, pulling her by the arm towards the house. And in a trick of time I am that child again, alert, on guard, a constant swilling in my tummy, never knowing when to duck.

'Explain yourself,' demands my mother. And that is what I do, back-to-front words scatter falteringly from my trembling lips. The onslaught continues unabated. I have misbehaved. I have shown her up. 'Wicked child,' she hisses. 'Wicked, wicked child!' Then her close-up voice comes from all corners. 'You are a little liar.'

The back-to-front words go heels over head out of my mouth. 'I didn't. I never. I wasn't. I haven't. I can't.' But even when they form an orderly queue it is futile.

Over the last months, I have stopped using the name Lucilla in an experiment of sorts. I won't call it *my* name because it isn't. It is not my size, like shoes that are too small. It pinches my toes and stunts my growth. I am calling myself Laura now, Laura Ryan. Denying Lucilla is causing a disproportionate amount of confusion. Henry's adapted without much kerfuffle. Well aware of how much I loathe Lucilla, he has always abbreviated my name to Lucy. But like a severe allergy, exposure even to a syllable has begun to rankle. At work in the estate's gift shop and in the café, they are discomfited by this new pseudonym.

'It's not the name on your payslip,' the manager told me huffily the other day when I asked her outright not to call me Lucilla.

'I realise this. But I want to be known by the name of Laura now,' I petitioned with a winsome smile. And it took pluck because she's a battleaxe, her blade blunted with felling a forest of staff.

Her mouth narrowed to a plughole of disapproval. 'It doesn't seem proper messing about with your God-given name,' she continued disregarding me. And, oh, I did not have to simply bite my tongue here, but eat it up, every last taste bud of it. Because God didn't give me that frilly, fussy, lisping name, a name that spoken in anger is a scream, a snake's hiss of a name. If God had known, if he was a decent sort of bloke, he would have hurled a javelin of forked lightning, and intervened, shaking the columns of his heaven. He'd have taken it away, not given it to me. He'd have boomed, I created her and anyone can see she's not a Lucilla. Now the manager, still in full throat, is called Constance. And it's obvious that God didn't just give her that name, he chucked it at her. 'And besides', she went on, 'it's muddling when I'm dealing with the council or the tax man.'

I inhaled as if it was the last cigarette before giving up the habit evermore. My heart was slamming in my throat, or so it seemed. All I was requesting was that she called me Laura. 'It may seem a trifle out of the ordinary but that's what I want.' She worked her mouth, and the shoulder pads of her jacket shifted as if readying themselves to make a break for freedom. So far she's avoided calling me anything at all, but I'll fence to the end of this duel. Win or die, that's my motto.

Maybe it is the magpie rhyme, it being three years since I got in touch with the Salvation Army, or maybe it is hearing a little girl whose name is Lucy being harshly berated for petting a dog, or possibly it is a combination of both that are the triggers. Paradoxically, I am mired in the present, unable to proceed unless I reverse. Gina is now thirty-one. I can scarcely credit it, and mother to our beautiful granddaughter, Lisa. And Tim is in and out of relationships with the ease of someone switching seats on a bus. Our children are moving on, establishing their own families, planting their own gardens. And as the demands of being their mother lessen, as their needs are met elsewhere, the void expands. I feel like an empty gourd.

For archaeologists excavating the past is irresistible. So it is for me. I kid myself that after the dig is complete, after I have finished examining the detritus of days gone by, I shall be free to decamp and vault back into the here and now. All I want . . . all I want is to tailor my own shadow. Is that so much to ask? And when I have, Lucilla won't possess the tiniest particle of me. And so I get in touch with Norcap, the adoption support agency. It is the new cook in the café who refers to it quite by chance, relaying how helpful they were to an adopted friend of hers. Research on the internet soon leads me to the door of this organisation. I speak to a lovely lady on the phone, Patricia. She asks me to write in sum-marising my situation, and enclosing the now ubiquitous photocopies of all documentation that I currently possess.

I close by telling her how desperate I am to locate my real mother, and how welcome any assistance they provide will be. I also include my joining fee of thirty-five pounds. A week later and an information pack thuds on our mat. Now that I am a paid-up member of Norcap, membership number 34806, it feels as if my investigation has been legitimised. My contact leader is Hermione. Norcap advises me that adoption is frequently romanticised in fiction, in plays and in the media. They stress that the reality of tracing my birth mother may be the antithesis to any fantasy I am feeding. They underscore the value of keeping emotions reined in. They emphasise how crucial it is for the initial contact to be made by an experienced intermediary. If I do track down my mother, they urge me to come back to them and let their experts handle that fragile thread of communication on my behalf, lest, God forbid, it breaks. Shuffling through the pack again a tiny slip of paper flutters from its pages.

> *CHILDLINK – 12 Lion Yard, Tremadoc Road, London, SW4 7NQ.*
> *CHILDLINK holds the records of the following society:-*
> *The Church Adoption Society of Bloomsbury Square and Vauxhall*
> *Bridge Road.*

A sudden pressure on my chest as if some demon has selected that moment to stamp on my heart. Childlink may have my records, my full adoption records. I may unearth more from them than I have so far from my uncommunicative adoptive parents, my conceited cousin Frank, Dorking Social Services, and the Salvation Army, from Norcap itself in fact. How many pieces of my puzzle they may supply is dizzying after so many decades. I should be euphoric. But I feel as if, out without a brolly, I have been drenched in a deluge. There is only one thing more dire than not knowing – knowing! I will write to Childlink. I will open the box and let the evils of the world fly out, all in the name of hope. But not this afternoon. Just for today let Lucilla and her history slumber on.

Chapter 13

Bethan, 1950

It is Sunday. We go to church. We go every Sunday. I used to get bored, but now I don't mind so much. Oh I don't pray. I can't pray. But I do listen. I've noticed that the minister preaches a tremendous lot about hell, that he gets a bit carried away describing it. His face goes red as ripe tomatoes, and his hair becomes untidy he throws his head around so much, like he's imitating a musical conductor. He's ever so clever with his adjectives, because I can really visualise it when I close my eyes. All fiery pits and pitchforks and people screaming in agony. Not so different from working down the mines really, I reflect wryly. Aeron gave my letter to Thorston to her dad that same day, and he gave it to my dad the next time they met. After the court, when the adoption was legal and there was no going back, he confronted me in the lounge, the letter open and in his hand. He didn't shout. It was more vile than that. He smiled. He was smiling when he told me he'd had it all this time, since a few days after I entrusted it to Aeron, that he'd read the filth of it so often he could recite it in his sleep. He tore it up in front of me and threw it in the fire.

'I saw two letters, Dad!' I cried. 'One hidden behind my letter.'

'No, you didn't.' My dad denied it, riddling the fire so that the scraps of paper went up in a whoosh.'

'Yes, I did. I did! I saw another letter in your hand. Who wrote that letter? Was it for me? Did he send it to me?' I was shouting as I witnessed the flames burning brighter, gobbling up my last shred of hope. 'Please tell me if it was him, if it was from Thorston? I have to know!' I made a dash for the fire, but my father blocked me. I was beating my fists against his chest, and I do believe if he had stepped aside I would have thrown myself on the pyre. He shoved me backwards and I fell to floor.

'You're a slut,' he said, with a smile so broad it almost fell off his face. 'A whore. You confess your sins every day to God. You hear me, Bethan, every day you pray for forgiveness. You shan't go to heaven, daughter. But maybe God will spare you hell and send you to purgatory, eh?'

I just nodded meekly and stared at the black ashes. There were no tears left, see. I was dry as baked stone. I couldn't shed one, not a single one. My letters were burned up, mine to him and his to me. My dad would prefer to die than tell me where he was, where we might be reunited.

'I shall, Dad. I shall fall on my knees and pray for forgiveness every day. I'm not good enough for heaven. I know that, Dad,' I confessed, my head drooping. Ah, it was so heavy, my head, and I was so tired having to hold it up, so shattered with the effort.

The minister doesn't concern himself much with heaven though, so it's not so easy to envisage that. But I do have a go sometimes. I sketch green fields in my head, dot them with flowers, all colours, very pretty, you know. And the air is perfumed with the fragrance of dry hay on a warm evening. There are babbling silver streams, and a haze of lavender mountains, and a sky that's like a wash of buttermilk. I stroll along barefoot. There are no stones and the grass is cool and spongy like a cushion under the soles of my feet. What strikes me about my feelings as I wander through heaven is that there aren't any. No hunger, no thirst, no tiredness . . . no anguish, and no guilt. No guilt!

The thousands of nails of guilt that have been embedded so deep into my flesh that I don't think they'll ever come out, aren't there. I'm smooth as a peach.

Anyway I don't want to go to heaven. I've made up my mind. It'll only be full of Brice, and Mam and Dad, and the adoptive parents, and my baby. I'm going to roast in hell. It's where I belong. By the way, I can't spot God in the heaven I've constructed. I've had a good hunt but he's nowhere to be seen. I'm not dreadfully sure what he looks like. But I am certain that I'll recognise him if he appears. My knees throb after the service and that's a good sign of repentance, don't you agree? Despite not being able to pray, I do believe God might take that into account. Sore knees. When we get back to the farm, it's my habit to head upstairs to change into my dungarees and start work. Then a Sunday morning arrives when Dad waylays me.

'Not today, Bethan. I want you to stay dressed up,' he says terrible serious.

I pause and swivel on the stairs, bewildered by his request. 'But, Dad, there's so much to do,' I protest. I can smell dinner cooking. We're having roast pork, and the delicious aroma is making my mouth water.

'Never mind that,' my dad tells me. 'We've company coming for lunch. I want you to look presentable.'

'Oh,' I say, none the wiser. He's wearing his suit. Normally, he'd first in line to take it off, hang it up and slip into his comfortable clothes. But now he hovers in front of the hall mirror, whips out a comb from his top pocket and pulls it through the tangle of his grey hair. 'Who's coming then, Dad?' I ask. We don't often have guests for a meal. And I can't help feeling on account of how jumpy my dad is, that it must be someone really important.

'Mr Sterry,' he says, eyes shuttered so I can't see the expression in them.

'Oh,' I repeat, mystified. Of course I know Mr Sterry. He lives at Carwyn Farm over Hebron way. He's a contractor, an agricultural contractor. Sounds impressive, doesn't it? But it only means that he organises the hire of farming equipment, extra labourers, that kind of thing. He's been over here several times in the last months. Not that I've spoken to him, you understand. Besides they've been fleeting visits, business trips. He's not family, not a friend.

'Mr Sterry? Are you thrashing out a deal with him, Dad?' I feel timid but I want a reply, an answer to dispel my unease.

'Mmm . . . one or two things to discuss,' my dad replies, vaguely shuffling his feet. He's in a peculiar frame of mind. Sort of awkward, nervy. Not his commanding self at all. 'I want you to let down your hair,' he adds. 'It looks well like that.'

It as though an organist has slammed his arms down on the keys and the chords are blaring out altogether. Since London, I've been invisible to my dad, invisible to myself as well actually. He makes me feel as if I'm no more substantial than a puff of smoke. My hair and the style it's in is of no interest to him whatsoever. I've pinned it up today. I've ceased fussing with it. When I'm working, I knot it in a headscarf. Otherwise, I tie it back or plait it. 'All . . . all right,' I stammer. 'If that's what you want, Dad.'

'I do,' he maintains stoutly, sliding the comb back in his pocket. 'When you're ready come down and help your mam.'

I nod. Minutes later, as I stand before the bathroom mirror pulling out hairpins, I catch sight of myself. My hands are all aquiver. It's like the moment a deer freezes, the moment it scents the air sniffing change, the hunter, death. When I join Mam and start peeling carrots, my appetite, so acute earlier that I could taste the sweet tender pork on my tongue, has disappeared. I know a mouthful of bread would choke me if I tried to swallow it now. After an hour, Mr Sterry arrives in his green pickup. Mam goes to greet him and leaves me supervising the dinner.

When she gets back, my dad calls me into the front room. I go as if my feet are clad in iron boots. I shake hands with Mr Sterry, and he says that I must call him Leslie. I nod, but I can't. He's one of my dad's colleagues and I don't use their first names. It seems a liberty. For a few minutes, he and my dad talk business, milk yields, hoof rot and the weather. But his eyes keep drifting over to me, eyes the colour of our oak dresser. I hear pots and pans clang in the kitchen and get up.

'P'rhaps I'd better go and give Mam a hand,' I excuse myself.

'She can spare you for a while,' my dad rejoins curtly. 'Sit back down, Bethan, will you.'

And so I lower myself back into my seat. I grasp the arms tightly, like I'm in a rowing boat being tossed about in a storm. I'd say Mr Sterry is about thirty, taller than average, with sloping shoulders. He has a wide face and small sticking-out ears. He's missing one of his front teeth, and his tongue constantly probes the gap. He has a large nose, with a smattering of blackheads on its blunt tip. And he has dark sticking-up hair, cut short and parted at the side. His hairline is receding. But it's not that apparent because he has a sort of fringe that hangs down. His eyebrows are dark and bushy, and his brown eyes are small and deep set. They are not unkind but they are straightforward. He is, I think, peeking at him jawing with my dad, a man's man, a man who sees the world as an ordered place.

I eat next to nothing at dinner. When I get up and reach for their plates, scraped clean with chunks of bread, my dad stops me. 'I'll clear, Dad. Mam and I will wash up together.'

My dad shakes his head. 'No, not this afternoon. I want you to join us, Leslie and myself. We're going to take a tour of the farm.' I know the farm the way I know my own face. Why on earth does Dad want me to trail about after them? But I can see that there's no gain to be had in refusing, that I'll only enrage him if I argue it. And so I go, meek as if I am a cow and have a halter round my neck.

Mr Sterry – can't get used to calling him Leslie – Mr Sterry, he visits twice more before my dad tells me what's to be done. On the third occasion after he goes, my dad calls me into the front room. Mam comes too. We all sit on the high-back chairs facing one another. It feels very formal.

'I have some splendid news for you, Bethan,' my dad announces, rubbing his large hands together as if he's cold. My eyes veer between my mam and my dad, while under my skin it's like a landslide, like nowhere's safe, like I can't anchor myself to the spot. I go to wet my lips but there is no spit in my mouth. 'Leslie has asked me for your hand in marriage,' Dad continues, nodding. I take a breath to speak, but he growls at me to hold my peace. 'I know, I know what you're going to say.'

Mam smiles weakly. I stare at Brice's portrait photograph on the mantelpiece. He's in his uniform. The fabric was like thick cardboard and scratchy, I remember. He hardly got to wear it in at all. My dad clears his throat and then scrubs at his face with his hands – like he did the night he came into the kitchen and saw me and Thorston, side by side, and the round belly on me. I wonder at him knowing what I am going to say before I do. I haven't a clue what sentences my lips might form.

'I *know* what you're going to say,' Dad reiterates. I want to utter, you do, in an amazed tone. But I let him give me the script. 'You don't want to deceive him into thinking you are virginal,' he astonishes me by saying. And suddenly I do know what I was going to say, the words are stacking up there on the tip of my tongue. I was going to say, only my hand? He only wants my hand in marriage? I can keep the rest? Oh well, that's not too bad then is it? 'Bethan? Bethan?'

I am staring down at my hands in my lap. I am considering which one I should give him, which one I can manage without. You probably reason that this is hardly a complex dilemma. If you are right-handed give him the left one. If you are left-handed give him the right one. The problem is that I am ambidextrous. I can use either of them equally well. My teacher didn't really like that in school. She made me copy my letters down and do my sums with my right hand. But nevertheless my left hand served just as well. 'Bethan? Bethan, are you listening to me?'

I lift my head and meet my dad's eyes. I'd forgotten how similar to mine they are, similar to his granddaughter's. 'Yes, yes I am, Dad. I'm sorry. I . . . I'm taking it all in.'

'Well now,' says my dad appeased, pushing himself forwards on his seat, 'that's understandable. You've had a surprise. But look you, Bethan, he knows about . . . about your degradation. He knows about the . . . the baby. He knows you've been spoiled.' Sounds like he's swapped roles with Mam, because she talks about dishes spoiling, food going off, curdling and souring and rotting and so forth. Am I decaying inwardly? It's a spooky notion. He rubs the wooden arms of his chair, as if he's a shoeshine boy giving a pair of boots a polish. I look to my mam and she confirms what Dad's said with a bob of her head. Her fingernails peck at the fabric of her skirt. She has lost more pounds and so have I. They'll be nothing of the pair of us if we go on like this. The wind will blow us away with the chaff.

'Does he? Does he now? He knows about my . . . my degradation,' I parrot.

My dad springs up and struts proudly before the grate, where a fire has died down to its embers. It'll soon be out if it's not raked. I think of my letters, our words of love come to ashes. 'Yes, yes, he does. He, Leslie, expressed an interest in you. And after mulling things over for a stretch, I came to the conclusion that if he was in earnest, we had to be truthful with him. To tell him everything. The whole shameful secret. So I did. It was a gamble. But your dad's an astute judge of character. And I'm pleased to say that I had the measure of him aright.

He was staggered when he heard, but after a few days he adjusted to it. "She's young. She made a mistake. I expect this German forced himself on her," he said generously. "She's paid her dues. I believe I can forgive her and we can start over fresh."' My dad smacks the mantelpiece with the flat of his hand, making me flinch, and nearly knocking over Brice's photograph.

My mam leans across to me and squeezes my hand. The corners of her eyes crinkle encouragingly. 'It's going to be OK, you'll see,' she says.

It is late afternoon on a changeable spring day. There's been rain but it let up about an hour ago. Bales of cloud tumble away then and it's like the sun's been peeled. Segments of citrus light rock into the room, as if these tidings are cause for gaiety.

'"I believe I can forgive her and we can start over fresh,"' my dad says again in wonderment, but more to himself than to my mam or me. 'It's God's grace. God is merciful.' Forgetting he is still in his suit, he feels for braces that aren't there. 'He's a fine man. A few years older than you, but that's no bad thing. Mature, reliable, a stable influence. Thirty-three, still young by my reckoning. Owns his own farm. Has his own business. He'll provide a fitting home for you. I've met his father, Dafydd Sterry, and he's given his consent. But before I did, I chatted it over with Leslie, and we decided no one else should know about . . . about what occurred.' His drops his braying to hushed tones. 'Only your husband. That's proper, fitting. It'll be your secret, yours and ours. Not everyone will have Leslie's charity.' He stares at me, expectancy lighting his eyes, as if readying himself for my rapturous reaction, a show of teary gratitude. 'Well?' he nudges, the brusqueness stealing back into his speech. 'Well, Bethan Modrun? Isn't this an excellent turn of events?'

My ears are popping. The room is closing in, the walls sliding towards each other. 'It's . . . it's tip-top, Dad. I'm . . . I'm . . .' I run out of fuel and slump in my chair.

'You're overwhelmed. Happiness has that effect sometimes,' my dad observes blindly.

I lever myself up as if in a trance. 'Shall I change my clothes, get on with my chores.'

'Oh, I think we can let you have one afternoon off,' my dad decrees magnanimously. 'We've set a date for the wedding, by the way. Soon as the banns have been read. The thirteenth of May. Nevern Parish Church. You and mam will have lots to plan, so I'll leave you to get on with it.' He presents his cheek and I kiss it dutifully. The stubble is rough on my lips. He has the air of a man who has set down his load.

When we are alone, Mam and me, she gets up and takes my hands in hers. 'They're so cold,' she says, trying to glove my frigid fingers with hers. 'Now you can do it all decently, be respectable. I'm going to go and fetch my notebook. We can draw up a list of things to do before the special day comes. You'd like that, wouldn't you?' I try to nod but I can't. She hesitates at the door. Lowering her voice to a frail whisper she tweezers out her words. 'Next time . . . next time you have a . . . a baby, you won't have to . . . to give it away, *cariad*. Think . . . think on that.'

It isn't so abominable really. The marriage went ahead. The wedding night was tolerable. He was considerate, in no rush. Though actually I wanted him to get it over with. It didn't hurt anyhow. Well, I wasn't a virgin, was I? What happened between me and Thorston was another act altogether though. It was . . . paradise, a piece of paradise on earth. I don't compare the invasion of Leslie to that. Carwyn Farm is OK, not dissimilar from Bedwyr Farm. In fact, some days I have to remind myself I've moved, become Mrs Sterry. And it's not as if Leslie ever brings it up, my other life, my sordid past. He genuinely doesn't seem troubled by it.

On our wedding night, I began confiding in him. Couldn't help myself. But he waved it away. 'It's gone, Bethan. You're my wife now and all of that is behind you. We need to focus on our future, look ahead at what's coming up.'

Six weeks later, my head down the toilet, I can tell you what's coming up – my breakfast! 'I'm going to have a baby,' I croak into the toilet bowl. 'Another baby. And it'll be like Mam said, I won't have to give it up this time. I can keep it.' I wait for the rush of elation to come. But it doesn't. I contemplate this baby and then my gift baby. My gift baby populates my head, an image for every day I've missed. She's two and half now, my gift baby. Tottering about all over the place she'll be, and running her adoptive mam ragged, I've no doubt. The truth has a nasty habit of ambushing you. A few months later and 'Boo!' there it is. 'I'd swap this baby in the blink of an eye to have my gift baby back,' I admit to myself as I watch my husband striding out to the yard. In my belly the second baby, the echo baby, chooses that moment to make its presence felt, quickening within me.

Chapter 14

Lucilla, 1953

Dawn silvers strands of the little girl's hair, a fan against the pillow. A single tress, like a flower, is pressed into the book of her damp cheek. She is flushed with the opiate of slumber, in the throes of a dreamscape that is as native to her as it is alien. She is perched on the cliff's edge. All there is looms above her in the infinite carousel of blue. Clouds scud. The sun smoulders. And although they are extinguished in the fierce daylight, there is the certainty of treasure, the stars, the moon, an expanding universe buried in the China-blue sands. She totters on the brink of the steep chalky precipice, skyscraper high. The frill of broken waves, the gold bar of the beach, the dark uncut diamonds of rock, all hurtle up at her from the giddying depths below. Gusts of salty wind pummel at her, make her cheeks tingle and her eyes water. They sing their secret in her small ears.

'You can fly. You can fly. You can fly,' they keen.

She wills herself to lift off from the top rung of her chalk ladder, to let the strength of the wind overcome her, let it kidnap her. They are at her back, the mother and the father. They loom over her and the lighthouse looms over them. She leans out and feels aerial muscles flex, braced to take her sparrow's weight. Further and further out into the kick of the current. Further and further . . . But her wings have been clipped so that she cannot soar. Her faith is moth-eaten. She does not believe. She has doubts. She will fall. A shaving of a second – all that is left to her before the rocks racket up her tiny body. Suddenly the hand, the giant's hand, hooks her and reels her in. She jerks involuntarily. Her eyelids flicker open.

Now, as with most mornings, she lies gazing up out of the skylight above her bed. Rachel, her cousin, comes into her head, her last visit with her. She had to be quieter than in church, not make a peep. If Rachel heard her, the game of hide-and-seek would be over. She was having such fun that she wanted it to go on all afternoon. She had been very clever picking her hiding place. No one would ever find her there, unless she gave herself away with a tinkle of laughter. And so even though it almost hurt, she trapped the giggle in her chest.

'Lucilla? Lucilla? I know you're in here somewhere.' Rachel's inflexion sang up and down musically as she pulled open the wardrobe doors. The hinges creaked, then the hangers skidded on the pole while she searched among Aunt Enid's dresses for her cousin. But Lucilla was not just under the bed. If she had been, then when Rachel had bent down and lifted a corner of the bedspread, she would have spotted her. No, Lucilla was hanging like a spider from the bedsprings. She had dead men's fingers, and her spine ached from holding herself at such a difficult angle on the rock face of iron coils. But it was worth it because her cousin couldn't find her.

'Don't think I've given up. I've got a trick to play on you. Back in a moment,' Rachel trilled. Lucilla's heart was pounding so loudly she thought that it might betray her hidey-hole. After a minute, her cousin was back and a glug-glug, slopping, farting chorus reached Lucilla's ears. It seemed to be coming from everywhere. She tried to keep a cushion pressed down on her giggles, but they started to hiccup out of her. And a second later Rachel was on her knees, and then crawling under the bed. 'There! Got you, you mischievous monkey,' she cried jubilantly, as Lucilla dropped down onto the floor. There was more farting and glugging and slip-slopping, from the hot water bottle Rachel was holding and shaking by the neck. She slapped it on the floor and tickled Lucilla with her free hand. In the gloom under the bed, the pair were seized by a fit of hysteria, flopping about like landed fish.

Now Rachel disappears and, as she does so, Lucilla yawns and smiles all in one. These are lovely minutes spent bumbling from flower to flower, overloaded with the nectar of her imagination. Let us suppose . . . oh, let us suppose that the sky is a pale-blue sheet of paper. Let us suppose she can draw clouds on it with a cream crayon big as a lamppost. Drawing is magic. She is a witch, with witch's hands, and a pencil for a wand. The pictures she creates, although they aren't of her, somehow contain more of *her* than anything else in her life. She often feels as if the rest has been borrowed, the home, the bedroom, the toys, the clothes, and even . . . yes, even the mother and the father. Though she doesn't talk about this. She keeps it to herself, keeps it hush-hush. But the 'not belonging' is with her constantly. The clattering and knocking jars on her ears. It is her mother on the stairs slamming about with a dustpan and brush. Thump, bang, crash, wallop, and then her door flies open.

'Lucilla! Lucilla, didn't you hear me calling you? Why aren't you up yet?' And Lucilla leaps up from her bed guiltily, her momentary reprieve over. As the hands revolve on the face of the mantelpiece clock, as it upbraids her with its ticking, chiming soliloquy, she is reminded that there are chores to be done. Every minute is bagged. 'You mustn't sit idle, Lucilla,' her mother berates her. 'You don't know when the devil is lurking, on the lookout for a suitable apprentice, ready to purloin you for his evil deeds.' She doesn't know what *purloin* means but it has a nasty slimy ring to it. '"By slothfulness the building decayeth; and through idleness of the hands the house droppeth through. Ecclesiastes 10:18." If the devil espies a lazy girl he will roost on her soul, and work her hands as though she is his creature. Do you want to be the devil's creature, Lucilla?' That's what her mother says. Lucilla shakes her head. But her enchanted hands are already possessed by pencil, crayon, paint and paper.

Her mother has given her a description of the devil. It is so detailed that she knows she can capture his likeness from memory. He has bull's horns and a crocodile's tail, and his skin is all red and covered in pus-filled boils. He *can* fly. He doesn't have any doubts. He skulks in the corners of her ceiling like an inkblot. When the light is switched off, he swoops, a great bat diving so close that his leathery wings flap against her head. She wants to be good so much. She wants to please her mother, to make her say kind things. But every day she sins and lets her down. She will have to try harder or the devil bat will get her.

They have moved to East Finchley. Mostly there is only her and Mother in their new home. Father is out at work counting batteries, and generally he doesn't return till nightfall. Oh! There is the lodger, Mrs Fortinbrass. She is grey-haired and teeny-weeny, as though she has shrunk in the wash. And she moves in a flurry like the busy wren Lucilla watches in the garden. She came with the house. Not the wren. She's free to make her nest anywhere – but Mrs Fortinbrass. She lives upstairs with Lucilla. They both have their own bedrooms, but the lodger has a sitting room and a cupboard kitchen. When her parents go to the temperance meetings, which is often, Mrs Fortinbrass cares for her. She gives her hot Ribena and Rich Tea biscuits spread with butter and sprinkled with crunchy sugar – delicious.

Downstairs is another bedroom where her mother and father sleep, and a living room with a piano in it and a desk. The desk is where her father does his paperwork for the Sons of Temperance. There is also a dining room, a kitchen and a lean-to greenhouse and a garden shed. They have their very own train, which huffs steamily by on tracks running along a high bank at the rear of the garden. If it slows down, if a day comes when it screeches to a halt, Lucilla thinks that she will buy a ticket and clamber aboard.

A morning dawns when her mother takes her firmly by the hand and leads her to the mouth of a maze. She drags her into it and deserts her. Lucilla is surrounded by dozens of corridors and rooms the size of church halls. There are so many children all crowding her in. She is unsure if she will manage to escape. She squints into a kaleidoscope of changing faces. A farmyard cacophony makes her ears tingle. Will her mother ever collect her? She feels like next door's canary locked in its cage. She doesn't like birds in cages, hopping aimlessly from perch to perch. Birds should be in trees or whizzing through the air. She is having another of her earaches. She gets them regularly, these attacks. Her mother says that it is a weakness of hers, an inherited *infirmity*. When they are severe it is like having an insect burrowing in her head, eating through her brain. At home she rests her head on the settee arm, and prays that the stabbing sensation will go away. She visits the doctor. He puts a pipette in her ears and he squeezes medicine into them. She shivers as the freezing drops trickle in. Afterwards, they itch and it is as though she is underwater. Voices quiver.

The teacher has been telling them things all day. She is called Mrs Dean. There is so much to remember besides this. Which desk is hers. Where her peg is. The correct way to line up. Not to run in the corridors. How to find the room they have lunch in. When you are forbidden to talk. The names of all the grown-ups and the children. The place to change for games. The corner where you go to read. The corner where you are sent if you misbehave. She studies this corner for several minutes – because she is frequently bad. The whereabouts of the toilets. Lucilla needs the toilet now; she needs it very urgently. But she is too scared to ask, to raise her arm and ask if she can have permission to leave the class. Her mother says that she was such a perfect baby, but that she has developed into a wicked, wayward girl.

She hits her often, and calls her a liar. It make her ears buzz when her mother slaps her head. Suddenly the teacher picks up a bell on her desk and swings it enthusiastically. The clanging startles Lucilla and inside her something loosens. She feels the mess slip out of her into her pants, while the din of the bell makes her ears ring.

'Children, it is the end of school now. Go and fetch your coats and satchels from their pegs, put them on and line up outside the classroom. And no pushing.' Lucilla steals unheeded through the turmoil. Mrs Dean guides them out into the playground where their mothers are waiting to pick them up. Lucilla moves in slow motion. Luckily no one seems to bother with her. They are all too excited at seeing their own mothers and hurrying home. She is the only child dreading the reunion.

Her mother stands apart from the others. The large furry turban on her head makes her look even taller. From a distance it could be a dozing cat. There is a gaudy brooch pinned to it that flashes in the sunshine like a third eye, winking purple and green. With tortoise steps, Lucilla approaches her. Frustration brimming over at her daughter's dawdling, her mother strides forwards, stoops and presses her powdery cheek to Lucilla's. 'Hello, Lucilla. Did you have a nice time at school?' she demands briskly. 'And were you a good girl?'

Lucilla is still deciding on her reply when her mother grasps her hand in exasperation. With her in tow, she marches towards the bus stop. 'We're going to have tea with Granny in Archway,' she announces as they board a bus. Usually Lucilla enjoys riding on buses, spotting all the buildings and people going by. The game that is the greatest fun is counting the dogs and pretending that they are hers, her very own to stroke and cuddle. But today she would prefer to drive straight home, then she could run upstairs and closet her shame in the toilet.

'Miss Mousey, Miss Mousey. You haven't told me anything about school yet, Miss Mousey? What's the matter Miss Mousey?' her mother goads. 'Cat got your tongue?'

'No. Nothing happened,' Lucilla rejoins softly, her head tipping forwards.

'Oh, you are a peculiar child. Don't you want to tell me what it was like?' she badgers, dissatisfied.

'No,' says Lucilla in a vanishing voice.

At this her mother gives a pained sigh. 'Did you make any new friends?' She raises her eyebrows in an exaggerated way.

'No,' repeats Lucilla.

'Shan't tell, won't tell, Miss Mousey, eh? Very well. You keep your mouth zipped, Miss Mousey. Not a squeak.'

As they walk up the front path of the Archway house, Granny's cheerful face peeps out veiled in net curtains like an ancient bride. She ducks out of sight. Before they reach the doorstep the front door swings open. Despite her predicament, Lucilla's heart lifts at the sight of the rounded back, the wooden stick, the crimped salt-white hair. Her grandmother looks as if she has been wrapped in an omelette in her yellow dress. Normally, Lucilla yearns for her all-enveloping hugs. But today she quickly wriggles free. In the front room, Granny has set the tea table with a starched snowy cloth and the best bone china. This tea set only comes out of the cupboard to mark special events.

It is quite a spread, so that Lucilla regrets her lack of appetite. Miserably she ogles the plates of meat paste sandwiches, the lemon curd tarts, her especial favourites, and the macaroons with glacé cherries glistening like navels in the centre of their sugared tummies. A Victoria sponge on a lacy doily has place of honour. The golden-brown top is sprinkled with a mouth-watering dusting of icing sugar. Her Aunt Enid and her cousins, Frank and Rachel, who all live with Granny, materialise.

Frank is eight and Rachel is seven. Frank is bossy and boorish, but she is very fond of Rachel. They have all put on their best clothes, which makes it more frightful. Aunt Enid wears a silvery-green dress with a pleated skirt, an appliqué lace flower to the side of her square collar. Rachel has put on her navy and white sailor dress, and her hazelnut-brown hair is tied in a ponytail with a spotted ribbon. Frank has charcoal shorts on and a white shirt, and his nearly grown-up tie with the elastic neckband.

Lucilla scurries under the table with Rachel, their usual refuge when the adults are conversing. Terrified that she will be detected, she begs God to make the evidence of her accident vanish. But even as her desperation surfaces, Rachel wrinkles her pert nose. She flashes her little cousin a questioning look in the gloom under the tablecloth. The china chinks overhead. And Frank can be heard making zooming noises for his toy aeroplane, which he says is a Lancaster bomber. Staring out through the lace-trimmed hem, feeling as if she is inhabiting a cloth fishbowl, Lucilla spots his sturdy legs, kneecaps scabbed, circling the room. Zoom, zoom! She envisions her granddad upstairs dying, his skin nearly the same yellow as her granny's dress. She thinks that she might like to die now – only not slowly like him, but in the blink of an eye.

'What's that terrible smell?' exclaims her mother.

'Oh dear me, yes,' Aunt Enid affirms. 'How very nasty. What can it be?'

'I can't think.' This last is Granny's kind, crumbly tones. They sniff like a trio of bloodhounds. 'It's been unseasonably warm. Perhaps it's the bins.'

'Pooh, it stinks!' Frank squeals, bending down to stare at them through his splayed legs. His upside-down face, growing a deeper scarlet by the second, dangles into view.

After this comes an unbearable silence. Rachel's pale green eyes resting on hers are sympathetic, as if she would like to come to her aid

148

but is helpless. Lucilla's heart rattles in her chest, going faster and faster. Then her mother hikes up the tablecloth and hauls her out by the scruff of her neck. She shouts at her, and Frank cups his mouth, jabs his finger and yawps crudely. Rachel scrambles after her, shooting her a pitying look. Nevertheless, she backs away from her cousin, until she is standing by the windows that overlook the garden. She wants to distance herself from the uproar, Lucilla discerns sadly.

'You mucky beggar! When did you do this?' her mother demands, wrenching her arm so that it feels as if it will pop out of its socket, like her doll's is prone to do.

'Don't be so hard on her, Harriet,' her grandmother chips in, climbing to her feet. 'She's only a child after all.'

'When did you do this?' her mother shrieks again, her accusatory tone if anything becoming more piercing.

'At school,' Lucilla whispers remembering the devil, and lies, and what a dreadful fate awaits children who tell them. 'I couldn't help . . . help it.'

But the truth seems to incite her mother into still more of a frenzy. 'Of course you could help it. Your first day and you dirty your knickers.'

Frank roars with mirth at the rude word, and his sticking out ears redden. 'Dirty knickers! Dirty knickers!' he sputters through his claps of laughter.

'That's quite enough, Frank,' her aunt Enid chides, rising and half-heartedly attempting to swat her son with a napkin.

'How dare you show me up like this? What the teacher must have thought of me, I don't know. Get upstairs to the bathroom right now, missy,' her mother orders.

At the door, Lucilla wheels back, to see Frank stuff a whole lemon tart into his mouth when no one is looking. He pulls a face at her and a dribble of lemon curd snakes down his pointed chin.

'Rachel can lend her a clean pair of pants,' her aunt Enid offers with a superior smile. 'No real harm done.'

'Thank you, Enid, but really I shouldn't be having to cope with this sort of pantomime,' her mother carps. 'She's five years old! Five! After all the trouble you've been to, Mother, with the preparations for tea. I am *so* humiliated. She's such a naughty girl.' Then, under her breath, 'Goodness knows where she gets it from.' She exchanges a meaningful look with her sister-in-law, a look that is not lost on Lucilla.

'Gracious, Harriet, what a fuss about nothing.' Her grandmother is dismissive. 'You'll give the girl a complex if you keep on at her. It was all new to her today and she was probably nervous. It's understandable that she's had a small mishap.'

'You don't know what I have to contend with,' her mother rejoins tetchily, her eyes, magnified eerily by their lenses, fastening on her adopted daughter with distaste.

Frank, pastry crumbs around his mouth, pinches his nose. 'Stinky Lucilla! Stinky Lucilla!' he taunts. 'Only babies pooh their pants.'

'Frank, stop that this minute!' Aunt Enid reprimands him in a tone of well-diluted vexation, sliding her hairband off and on again.

'He's telling the truth, Enid. This sort of disgusting behaviour should be long gone,' her mother interjects.

'Don't go upsetting yourself, Harriet. If you've tried your best with her it's not worth it.' Aunt Enid turns to Frank and Rachel. 'Go and play in the garden, there's good children,' she says, surveying her own wholesome brood. Frank runs off, his aeroplane in full flight again, his lips flapping as he reproduces the 'broom' of the engine. Rachel, resigned, follows obediently.

'Get upstairs, Lucilla,' her mother commands again, hat off and head down like a mad rhino, her timbre vitriolic. And, as she charges after Lucilla, she adds in a vicious hiss, audible to all, including the dying man overhead, 'You ruin everything.'

In time, Lucilla learns to negotiate the school maze, and nicest of all, an art teacher, Mr Westwell, is appointed. Meanwhile, at home a bewitching object is installed – a television! And it is so thrilling because barely anyone in their road possesses the amazing modern invention. Her grandmother, her aunt Enid, her cousins Frank and Rachel, and their neighbours the Friedmans, are all invited to their house to watch the coronation of Queen Elizabeth on their brand-new television. Her grandfather has finally passed, so he cannot join them. Fraught and expectant, her mother keeps dashing to the front windows, snatching at the curtains and saying, 'When will all the folks come. I hope they're not late. We'll miss it if they're late.' But thankfully they are not delayed, the relations descending first.

'What a shame Grandpa can't be with us,' Lucilla's granny says, wet-eyed behind her spectacle lenses.

'But he is here in spirit,' consoles Aunt Enid, raking the ceiling with her shrewd blue eyes.

'Shall I lay a place for Grandpa then?' Lucilla asks, only to have her head bitten off by her mother.

'Don't be so stupid. He's dead!' she scorns, colander in one hand, saucepan lid in the other.

'But I thought –' Lucilla begins.

'Oh do be quiet, Lucilla. You're giving me one of my sick headaches,' snaps her mother.

Frank rocks with laughter and draws a gun from the holster buckled on his hips. He fires off a cap, which feeds through from a roll in the barrel of his silver Colt. The report makes her wince and he yells delightedly. She can smell the burned powder and determines not to cry. 'You're as dead as Grandpa now,' he guffaws.

'Don't be such brute, Frank.' Rachel comes to her defence.

'I'm not dead,' insists Lucilla, picturing her grandpa laid out on his bed.

'Of course you're not,' comforts Rachel.

Lucilla recalls that she could not be persuaded to kiss his waxy cheek, no matter how many times they entreated her. For a moment though she did clasp his hand, and the skin was like rubber to the touch, frigid and intractable. Now Rachel pats her arm and says that she shouldn't listen to her brother, that he is just a show-off. A ceasefire is called by Aunt Enid as Mr and Mrs Friedman, their Jewish neighbours, arrive. They bring a big bowl of pretzels and some dips. Mrs Fortinbrass is the last guest, tiptoeing downstairs. It feels odd to have her in their midst. She is an upstairs resident who isn't meant to venture to ground level, Lucilla worries. Her mother has incinerated a huge feast. Granny and Aunt Enid hurry to and fro from the kitchen to the dining room with smoking serving bowls and platters.

Then they all stand solemnly behind their chairs as her father switches on the television. While the valves are warming up, they take their seats as if at a theatre, and start eating. Her father spends a quarter of an hour adjusting the focus, fiddling with the knobs to get the sound and contrast exact. When he is content, he sidesteps like a matador, revealing an animated photograph. 'Ta-rah!' he cries with a flourish. Frank crows and, brandishing it high in the air, fires his cap gun, previously secreted under his napkin. Aunt Enid immediately chastises him and confiscates it.

'Will you look at that,' comments awestruck Mr Friedman, patting his paunch and nodding at the programme.

'Such crowds all waving flags,' admires Mrs Friedman impressed, shaking her brassy poodle curls.

'I expect it was very expensive,' Mrs Fortinbrass chirps up querulously, nibbling on a piece of bread and margarine.

Her father pauses in carving a cold joint of burned ham. 'When it comes to royal occasions we lead the world, you know,' he aggrandises. 'British standards. Something for these coloured chaps to aspire to.'

He looks pleased with himself, as if single-handedly he is co-ordinating the coronation ceremony. 'Another slice of ham, Mother?' Both his mother and his wife look up, the former assenting graciously with royal nod, the latter scowling blackly at the sobriquet. Granny chews carefully, mindful of her false teeth. Frank spears a boiled potato and rams it in his wide mouth, quick as a lizard licks up a fly. He seems unconcerned by the unappetising greyish hue the King Edwards have taken on, as a result of the pan boiling dry. 'We have the Commonwealth to consider,' her father continues. He hesitates, probing two prominent discoloured molars with his pinkie, platinum grey in hue, between which a treacle-brown stringy particle of ham has lodged. 'Need to set an example, show them how to do things correctly.'

Lucilla is mesmerised by the footage of the state occasion. It is such a splendid sight, the very image she has of Cinderella's fairy-tale carriage. The horses are all decorated in finery, tossing their manes and prancing. They pull the young queen in her coach all the way to Westminster Abbey. And she waves regally at the waiting crowds from the glittering window. Entranced, Lucilla makes acute observations of the monochrome spectacle, the thoroughbred horses particularly. She will sketch them later, she decides.

But once the young Elizabeth sweeps into the abbey, it all falls flat. There are lots of boring speeches that drone on for what seems like hours. Lucilla pushes a lump of cold lamb around her plate. It has veins of yellowy fat in it that make her feel queasy. If she had a dog, while they were all hypnotised by the television, she could conceal the meat in the palm of her hand, lower it discreetly to her lap and dispose of it. Lacking a real pet, she invents one, sausage-shaped and shaggy, with a wet black nose. She sneaks the fatty meat off her plate and drops it clandestinely onto the floor, and her make-believe dog woofs it down in a gulp. The grey screen seems tiresomely dreary now. If she could instil a bit of colour into it she would make Queen Elizabeth's beautiful dress bright orange. And the horses would be purple with yellow manes and red tails. She would shade the carriage in hydrangea pink. She sighs quietly, her previous curiosity wholly dulled.

'I've finished. Please may I get down?' she pleads. Her mother looks annoyed at the interruption, but her father humours her, nodding in assent. So she climbs down, giving her imaginary dog a secretive wink. If you can't hitch up your fancy wedding dress and vault into the saddle for a gallop on your horses, there doesn't seem much advantage in being a queen. Suddenly, everyone at the table cheers. Then they clamber to their feet to sing the national anthem in hearty voices. And her father slaps Frank on the back, causing him to choke on the mouthful he is guzzling. Aunt Enid administers a glass of water with an annoyed frown.

'Long live Queen Elizabeth the Second,' bellows her father, and they all take up the shout. Now that she is crowned queen at last, Lucilla wonders if there will be another ride in the carriage, another opportunity to stare spellbound at those mystical white horses? If not, she will ask if she can go outside to play. She dearly wants to track the bumblebees crawling inside the yellow and pink thimbles of snapdragons.

Chapter 15

Bethan, 1953

We don't have a television. They're far too expensive. Only a wireless. But we listened to it on the wireless. What am I blathering on about? What is on everyone's lips? Why the coronation of Queen Elizabeth, of course. In fact, I'm glad we didn't see it on a television. No, honestly I am. Sometimes I think your sense of sight limits you. As it was, I could close my eyes and listen to the commentary, visualising the spectacle. Not camera shot by camera shot, but the whole thing, as if I was sitting in the sky gazing down over the edge of a cloud. The golden coach and horses, the radiant Queen's face framed in the window, the joyful crowds lining the streets, her dress when she stepped out sparkling in the sunshine, the crown being solemnly lowered onto her head. Oooh, it makes me shiver now to replay the pageant of it.

Actually we have a lot in common, me and the Queen. Ah, you wouldn't think it I know. Me, Welsh, a farmer's wife, busy at milking cows and churning butter all day, my complexion boiled with all the steaming pots on my stove. And she, a queen of the realm, covered head to foot in jewels and rich gowns, and showered with presents. Everyone bowing and curtseying to her and calling her Your Majesty. Her days are spent ruling Britain. Mine are occupied running the farm, and feeding great hulking men with bottomless stomachs.

I've anticipated what you're going to say. There's chalk in Wales and cheese in England. Not that I'm suggesting the Queen is a wheel of cheese, you understand. But if you think there's no comparison to be made, I suggest that you're being premature. You're ignoring some key similarities. For openers, we're both mothers. And I hear tell Queen Elizabeth takes motherhood very seriously. Second, we both gave birth to our first child in 1948. Granted, my time was before hers, but it was in the same year, mind. She was delivered of a son, a prince, Prince Charles. And I was delivered of a daughter, a princess, who I called Lucilla for want of a better name – my gift baby. And now the coincidences become uncanny. They do, really. Serendipity, that's what it's called.

In 1950, she gave birth again, this time to a daughter, Anne. And barely a year later so did I. My second child. My echo baby, Lowrie. Of course, you would be right to highlight the significant departures in the way our fates are unravelling. See, I had to give my gift baby away. She is five now, Lucilla. Fancy that. She'll be talking, walking, playing, laughing . . . crying. Calling another woman her mam. She'll have had her first day at school. I wonder how it went? Did she take to it like an intrepid duckling splashing into a pond, or were her reactions similar to her mother's, her true mother's . . . to me. I was impatient to be gone, gasping for want of fresh air. Although you don't get an abundance of that in London. A stew of smoke and smog and exhaust fumes there, if my remembrance serves me well.

The two tiny photographs of Lucilla that Valeria Mulholland, the secretary from the Church Adoption Society, sent me after the adoption are falling to pieces. I've kissed them so often, slept so many times with them under my pillow, or clutched to my heart, that it's hardly surprising. But when they do, disintegrate entirely I mean, I'll still treasure them. She was around six months in the pictures, lying in a cot and in a pram, gazing up at her. Of course by now she'd have changed so much. I spend hours trying to visualise her face, sculpting the alterations. Her strawberry-blonde hair growing long, her cheeks thinning down, shedding their chubbiness, the intelligence in her turquoise eyes deepening. I see it in the suds lying on the surface of the dishwater in the sink, in the crusty bark of an oak tree, in the ripples of a stream, in the wood grain of our dining table. Honestly, it's as though her baby face is stamped on the table. And when I touch it, let my fingers trace the lines of the silky wood, it is as though I am touching her skin, her lips, her hair. Don't laugh. It isn't a joke. It's a bit like one of those visions of Mary, Mother of Jesus, the ones that cause mass hysteria. You know, the way someone ordinary sees her features imprinted on a lump of stone, and the faithful flock for miles to glimpse it and pray for miracles. True, the circumstances differ, I suppose, because there's only me. No other pilgrims staring at the apparition, astonished, mumbling under their breaths, 'Don't you see? Don't you see her there in that line, and there in the curve. And look there, her eyes gazing out at you. That sunbeam striking the water. The luminous shade of turquoise. It's her eyes, I swear it. I'd recognise them anywhere.'

I have established shrines now, places I go and pay my respects. Leslie is an atheist in this, blind to sightings of the blessed Lucilla. For him she is merely theoretical, a name on a certificate of adoption. He's not a man with imagination. He doesn't dissect the past, doesn't fret about the future. The present is more than sufficient for him. Not for me though. He doesn't ask questions either, and that suits me very well. So the other day when I encountered him in the barn chopping up the old dining table for firewood, when I got hysterical, he was genuinely confounded.

'Whatever's the matter, Bethan?' I was yanking his arm, the one wielding the axe. I could feel his muscles bunched and unyielding, could see the pulsing raised veins. I thought about the blood pumping through them.

'Just stop,' I begged. 'Stop what you're doing. Don't destroy the table! Don't!'

'But, love, I've bought you another one. It was going to be a surprise. It's on the back of my truck. Solid yew. And a bit of carving on it too.'

'I don't want it. I tell you, I don't want it.' He'd only chipped a bit out of a sturdy leg, and now I threw myself over the table top, sobbing. 'Please, Leslie, please. I want to keep this table. I'm used to it.' I caressed the corner where her face was, fingered the imprint as if it was her supple skin I touched and not resisting wood.

'If it means that much to you, I'll repair it,' he conceded. No fight, no argument, simply total bafflement.

'Oh it does, it does, Leslie. Please can you mend it for me?' I slid off the table and hugged him tight till my arms throbbed.

'I'll never fathom women,' he muttered setting down the axe, his hand on my head, lifting a tress of my hair. 'I'll fix it so you won't know it's been hacked about by a farmer wanting to surprise his wife with a grand new dining table.'

I pulled back and studied his face. He was a kind man, a generous man. Some men beat their wives, I know. People talk. On market days you see the gaps, who isn't there, and you hear gossip. Leslie doesn't hit me. I don't believe that he has it in him. 'And it *was* a lovely thought,' I said at last, remembering myself. 'We will use it in the dining room. Let's put this battered thing in the scullery. It may be wounded but it's still useful.' I forced a smile, attempted too late to conceal how much it mattered. He had the final word and so I waited.

'Very well. Give me half an hour and I'll bring it in.'

I kissed him on the cheek at that. It was late afternoon and he'd be wanting his tea any moment. So I hurried indoors and chopped and sliced and peeled and fried, counting off the minutes. On the dot of half past five he appeared with my table, and together we manoeuvred it through the back door and into the scullery.

'No more tears now, *cariad*,' he said, standing back to survey his handiwork. I shook my head. He stepped up to me and encircled me in his broad, strong embrace. He pulled me close. And it was a comfort, I won't deny it. But in the way that a lesser comfort reminds you of what you really desire. With a nod of his head, he indicated a pile of tablecloths, freshly ironed, sitting in a wicker basket on the stone floor. 'You put a pretty cloth on it and we'll none of us know how scratched and chopped it is underneath.'

But I didn't even want to do that. It would have been like covering her up, like a winding sheet, like . . . like an omen, like she was dead. When I began objecting again, he turned on his heels and went quietly outside. I saw him through the window striding manfully across the fields, his Welsh Springer, Red, at his heels. He wouldn't give the dog a human name, said that was sentimental tosh.

'We're all God's creation,' I had challenged fondling the puppy. 'Can't we give her a more personal name?'

'Dogs are dogs,' he declared unequivocally. 'They have their place. Not to be confused with human beings. Red's a fine name for a working dog, a gun dog.' The puppy's ears twitched upwards. 'There, the bitch recognises it already.'

That is Leslie. The land is the ground under your feet. The fields are there to be carved up, to plough, to sow, to crop, to be harvested. The sheep are supplied for us, their wool to keep us warm, their meat to feed us. A dog earns its keep tracking, retrieving, hunting, herding. And when the animal fails, when age or disease catches up with him, the humane thing to do is dispatch him with a single shot to the head.

And a woman? Ah Leslie, the riddle of a woman. He faces the woman he has married with a complete lack of comprehension. I know he can't solve the riddle of me. His wife is a tangle, a knot that will not loosen. But that is his folly. If he takes a moment in his day to chew on a straw and meditate, he will have an epiphany every bit as powerful as God appearing to Moses in the burning bush. He will peer into the flames that are consuming his wife, and see that she is foremost a mother, and only afterwards . . . a woman. 'The farmer wants a wife, the farmer wants a wife, E-I-E-I-O, the farmer wants a wife.' But the problem, oh, the problem is that the wife doesn't want a farmer, she wants a child, her child. She is Modron. Earth mother. It is a mother he took to his bed, not a wife. And her heart is destined to be eternally elsewhere.

I'm sorry for him, that I can't be his helpmate. For my part he's become familiar, like a pot I cook with regular, or a cardigan I wear all the time, or shoe leather that has been worn to the mould of my feet with constant use. They say you can get accustomed to anything. And as such I'd miss him, I'd reach for him if he was gone. But no more than that. Besides, you can easily replace a pot, knit another cardigan, go to the shoe shop and purchase supple boots. The only faults I can level at him are that his hands are inclined to be clammy, that his breath can be a touch sour. But that's all. Not so dreadful when you consider what women have endured throughout history. I wanted him to give me a boy, like Charles, like Prince Charles. I prayed for a boy. It wasn't much to ask, all told. I could have forgiven him the rest if he'd managed that.

'Don't you think it's a boy?' I said to Leslie patting my mound, my anxiety doubling then trembling as my time fast approached.

'Ah I don't know about such things, Bethan. To me it's what it is, a boy or a girl. No earthly reason to get yourself all worked up about it. I'll be happy with either. Besides, we can have another go if it's a girl.'

Poor Leslie! He doesn't know that this is going to be my last, this echo baby. I'll have no others, no more counterfeits. After this I'm done with the business of procreation, or it's done with me. It depends how you want to look at it. Almost as much as I think of my gift baby, Thorston occupies my thoughts. I recall the letter, the second letter. I know there was a second letter. I saw it in my father's turquoise eyes, the darkening of them. Was it from him? Had he written with his address, so I could run away and find him? I wonder if he's met someone else by now? If he's married? If when he makes love his memory transports him to the war that brought us together, to Bedwyr Farm in Wales? If he sees my face in ecstasy overlaying hers? I wonder if there are days when he travels back to the bitter winter of 1947, to the walls of snow hemming us in, to the shed, battered and bashed by the moaning, mewling wind? I wonder does he recall our cold flesh meeting, the friction of it, the matches of our bodies striking against each other, and the fire we made heating our blood? I wonder does he also have another child? Girl or boy? He didn't know what we had, so it probably doesn't torment him so much.

But for me during my second pregnancy it became an obsession. I wanted a son. I willed it to be a boy. Oh, not because men hanker after an heir to bear their family name, a lad about the place to train to the labour, someone to hand the farm on to. Leslie wasn't troubled either way. It was no sham. He harboured no private longings, no secrets at all. He was a plain man, a predictable story. It was me who cared. I didn't want a girl. I'd had a girl, see, and she was flawless, the most perfect in all creation. You couldn't improve on her. No one could replace her. When my apprehension festered, I read old wives' tales about what you should and shouldn't eat if you wanted a boy child. My mam said to have lots of grain and meat to make a son. 'I did when I had Brice,' she confided with a wistful smile. 'And for a girl it's dairy products, cheese and milk and butter.' So I put myself on a strict diet, something that's not straightforward on a farm. I plucked a hair from my scalp, knotted my wedding ring into it, and dangled it over my belly to see if it would go back and forth for a boy. And when it began to circle I lied to myself.

Lowrie was born at 3.35 am, at home here on Carwyn Farm. And when they told me it was a girl, I was as disappointed as I imagine Anne Boleyn was when she gave birth to Elizabeth. I didn't have a King Henry strutting about expecting a prince. Only me. Well, what was left of me, like Swansea after they bombed it. I wanted a departure from my yesterdays. A boy to carry me into the future on his sturdy back. We learned about Anne Boleyn in school. When was that? Oh a million years ago now it seems. In that far off schoolroom the teacher said that if the baby had been a boy, Queen Anne might not have had her head chopped off. Ironically that stands for me as well. Since her birth, Lowrie's birth, my head's toppled off entirely. I don't recognise the one sitting on my shoulders. It has a shrewish tongue in it that isn't mine.

What did I feel when they put the baby in my arms, when my husband came in all glowing with pride and exultant, when my mam looked serene and top heavy with tenderness? Ah, I braced myself for the avalanche of love that had come when my gift baby was born. Nothing. Not so much as a snowball to unseat me. I looked deep into her eyes, brown like her father's, the brown of the upturned earth at plough time, and I felt . . . angry. No more than a handful of breaths and already she had let me down. Where were the turquoise eyes of my gift baby? What right had this imposter to show up and shove her shadow out of the crib? If I was worth anything as a mother I must fight to keep her space free, vacant, ready for her to return to me.

'Can you take her now, Mam,' I said, thrusting her away from me.

'But she's still hungry, Bethan,' she protested, as the tiny mouth rooted for milk. 'A few minutes more, surely.'

'I'm tired, Mam. And I'm not sure that I want to breastfeed. After all, I didn't breastfeed before.'

'But you can now. Nothing stopping you,' my mam whispered when Leslie had tactfully left us alone together.

'I know I can, Mam,' I retorted. 'But I don't care to.'

Her brow crinkled. She was confounded, uncertain how to react to this recalcitrant mother. 'It's good for the baby. When the first milk comes in it's full of antibodies. It'll protect her. You know that. It's why . . . why . . .' She broke off and dropped her voice still lower before continuing. 'It's why the other baby got sick.'

'The other baby?' I queried, heaving myself up on my pillows.

'Lucilla,' she mouthed.

'Oh well, she recovered all right didn't she, Mam?' I presented my case reasonably. 'She was in prime condition when I gave her away.'

My mam had the decency to blush, and hastened off with my legitimate baby to heat up some milk.

Lowrie was two years old last week. She's a pleasant disposition. I can't complain. Good-natured. Leslie adores her. He is devoted to his daughter, spending hour after hour playing with her, or merely sitting her on his lap before a cosy fire crooning Welsh ballads. I see her as his daughter, my husband's daughter. And not mine. Besides, she has more the look of him. I expect the Queen will go on to have more babies. Why not? She has the staff to help her, nannies and so on. The other night when Leslie came to bed (I generally go up before him), he lifted my nightgown and spoke, his large hands dividing up my body.

'Shall we try for another?' His tone was all husky with lust. I let him have his way. But I saw to it that he withdrew early. I use a diaphragm but I don't trust it fully. When he's big inside me I feel bunged up, blocked. I want to clench my muscles and push him out. I stroked his lined brow in the velvet of the night, tried to smooth the truth from it. 'A companion for Lowrie? What do you say, Bethan?'

'We'll see,' I replied, forecasting silently that there would be no more babies.

Chapter 16

Harriet, 1956

Isee this house, our home, as a fourth person in our *family*, one that left to its own devices would be as dissolute as the fathers in Bermondsey who drink their wages weekly. Each day I set about knocking some order into it. And each day the house does all it can to thwart me in my pursuits. The society, the Sons of Temperance, has become our second home, our home away from home. My father would have been pleased at our involvement, pleased as well that Enid, my sister-in-law and her children, Frank and Rachel, number in the ranks of our brethren.

Have no delusions, the destructive power of drink is awesome. It should on no account be underestimated. It splits families asunder. It corrupts the mind and ruins the health of strong men. It undermines the morality of women. And it lures children into petty crime. The dismal sights that meet our eyes when we tramp the streets are a constant reminder to me. We march frequently, give out leaflets, spread the word, welcome with open arms our suffering brothers and sisters who are called to sign the pledge of lifelong abstinence: 'We, the undersigned, vow to abstain from all liquors of an intoxicating quality whether ale, porter, wine or ardent spirits, except as medicine.'

We took Lucilla on the last march. That was an education for the girl, let me tell you. We held our banners high and paraded through the slums of Bermondsey, inviting the damned to swell our numbers and renounce the demon drink. Enid and I, spearheading our valiant troop, took turns displaying the finest of them all. Saint George painted on a fringed silk canvas. His sword and shield are at the ready. His cloak of temperance billows behind his plumed helmet. Under his conquering feet lies the slain dragon. His scaly body is beribboned by the horrors unleashed by drink.

'Disease, Pauperism, Death, It Biteth Like a Serpent, Drink, Lust and Drunkenness.' In the left-hand corner a rose bush blooms among the words, 'Virtue, Peace and Love' – the rewards for those that wrestle alcohol and, like Saint George, prevail. Frank, my dear nephew, nags me constantly, wanting to know when he will be tall enough to carry it.

'It's the most the brilliant of all the banners, Aunt Harriet. With Saint George stabbing the odious dragon, and the monster writhing in agony.' That boy is going to grow up into a fine young man, a man who will amount to something. Rachel, my niece, shy girl that she is, has no aspirations to head up the processions. She claims the scenes depicted on the banners give her nightmares – such a homely, sensitive nature.

Merfyn's immense contribution to the cause is common knowledge. His rise in the ranks has been meteoric. Already chairman, only last year, he was voted in as Intergroup Treasurer, looking after the savings of countless families who do not fritter away their money on gin, ale and whisky. It is a highly trusted position that only a celebrated few attain. When funds in the kitty are plentiful, we Sons and Daughters of Temperance holiday together, or arrange a day of field games, or an interesting and informative outing, or indeed attend an intergroup conference. In addition some members save for personal items, or budget for Christmas. On the marches, my husband cuts a dashing figure, as magnificent as the Lord Mayor of London, I like to think. His heavy gold chain of office is draped over his shoulders, the medallion with its enamel triangle at its heart, his badge of office, lying against his chest. To focus the group, we hold a prayer meeting before we set off.

"'Look not thou upon the wine when it is red, when it giveth his colour in the cup, when it moveth itself aright. At the last it biteth like a serpent, and stingeth like an adder. Proverbs twenty-three, verses thirty-one to thirty-two,'" Merfyn intones sonorously.

"'At the last it biteth like a serpent, and stingeth like an adder,'" we faithful disciples chorus, speaking out with one tongue against the devil's beverage.

And then we are off to scour the streets for new recruits. 'Give up the evils of drink!' we shout. 'Join us!' I let Lucilla give out leaflets. Her eyes were wide as saucers as she witnessed the poverty and misery, the ragged sickly children coughing and limping, the comatose mothers tippling on bathtub gin, the insensible, bleary-eyed men lying in the gutters babbling, their senses numbed with drink, the dogs licking their sores, and the piles of stinking rubbish attended by buzzing masses of blowflies.

'This is what alcohol does to a man, Lucilla,' I schooled, as a drunk made a grab for her with a shaky hand, mumbling unintelligibly. Sometimes they jeer us, as they jeered the Messiah. We embrace our martyrdom. It is their folly that separates them from God's grace. And it is our duty to prise open their blind eyes. After this experience, Merfyn and I decide Lucilla is ready to attend meetings. I anticipate a show of thanks at the honour we are bestowing upon her. What I get is a mule, hoofs planted stubbornly.

'I am perfectly happy staying home here with Mrs Fortinbrass,' she demurs.

'This is like school, Lucilla. When you were five you went to school. Now you are eight you will attend the temperance meetings.'

She tucks a straggle of hair behind her ears and her brow puckers. 'Must I go?' she asks, downcast.

'Yes you must,' I retort crossly. 'We take the trolley bus from East Finchley to Archway, to the chapel hall. There are special groups for children. Aunt Enid will be there, and your cousins, Frank and Rachel. There are games and competitions and dances. And you'll make dozens of friends. Nice children from nice families.'

'Are we a nice family?' she wants to know.

'Of course we are. The nonsensical questions you do ask, Lucilla! Why, it makes my head pound.'

Her father cajoles the little madam with a promise. If she does as she is told, he will give serious consideration to her requests for a pet, a dog. I glare at this, because it is obvious who will have to feed it and clear up after it. Still, her eyes brighten and she skips docilely out of the house. Unfortunately, it is soon apparent that Lucilla is as burdensome at the meetings as she is at home, and doubtless at school also. I have now lost count of the amount of times she has been sent to stand outside the chapel doors for her mischief. Frank reports her having shameful tantrums in our absence. Rachel loyally sticks up for her, but then she is generous and willing to forgive anything. When I discuss these aberrant passions of hers with my husband, he disregards them saying she is certain to get into the swing of things eventually. We are in two minds on this, but we shall see.

Lucilla is constantly under my feet, asking me *why* for goodness' sake. What kind of question is that? Why?

'I don't know!' I tell her, when she demands to know why Monday is wash day. 'Because Tuesday is drying day. And Wednesday is my day for ironing. While Thursday is earmarked for shopping. And Friday is when I give the house a thorough clean, top and tail.'

'But why do you do it all day?' she flutes. She does not keep still when she talks to me, and I dislike this habit of continuous purposeless motion. To me it indicates a lack of respect. She is hopping about first on one foot then the other, for no good reason at all that I can divine. 'Can't you do it for a short while and then go out to play?' she pesters me.

'No. I do it all day because it takes all day,' I rejoin, a sensation of pressure along my hairline giving warning of an approaching migraine. 'Clothes don't wash themselves, Miss Mousey.'

'I don't care whether my clothes are clean or ironed,' she toots back undaunted. 'You can leave mine out, Mother, if that makes less work for you.' Can you believe it!

'Do have some common sense, Lucilla,' I mutter under my breath. 'What would people think if I sent you out looking as grimy as a guttersnipe?'

She shrugs her narrow shoulders. 'Why does it matter what people think?'

That wretched word again. We are in the basement. The sheets are boiling in the copper with the Sunlight Flakes. The washboard is out. The tin bath is filled to the brim ready for rinsing. I tip in the Dolly Blue. We bought Lucilla a miniature wooden washboard and a small plastic tub. I have run water into it, added a few flakes and lathered it up. I dip my tongs into the copper and stir the linen sheets in the scalding water.

'Aren't you going to wash your dolly's clothes?' I ask, indicating her stubbornly unnamed doll, stoically bearing the indignity of being dangled by her hair.

'They're not dirty,' she cheeks me back. A sudden change of mood. She is as inconstant as the weather, this child. 'Can I turn the mangle handle?' she petitions her face all pleading now, her doll abandoned in a dingy corner.

I stare through the steam at my Harris table mangle. 'Perhaps. When we're ready.' The air is humid as a jungle, marbled with soapy vapours. And Lucilla's pixie face swims in and out of the steam. Apart from the slits in the wooden hatch of the coal shoot that afford a few needles of daylight, the only other source of illumination is an unshielded light bulb suspended from the ceiling.

'I like squishing out the water and seeing the sheets sliding through thin as paper,' Lucilla rhapsodises prodding at the handle.

My nose tickles in the poached air and I sneeze. 'I think your doll *does* want you to wash her clothes.' Her prolonged inactivity is beginning to grate on me.

'No, she doesn't,' she counters perkily. 'She told me. Besides, she can't stand her pink dress. She thinks it's ugly. She wants me to rip it up.'

'What an awful thing to say,' I growl, irritability now taking hold. 'It's a lovely dress and your dolly should be grateful that she has it.'

'Well, she isn't,' sings back Lucilla, her disposition bright as the noonday sun. She darts into the corner for a speedy conference with her doll. Lifting it up to her ear, she throttles it and nods.

'Yes . . . yes . . . mm . . . oh you do? OK, I'll tell her.' Those disturbing turquoise eyes come to rest unflinchingly on me. 'Dolly says she would prefer to wear trousers, like the ones Daddy has.'

'Well then, dolly is very silly with no brains at all,' I snipe, jabbing at the sheets with my tongs as if they are a harpoon and I am trying to lance a seal. 'If your doll was smart she'd know that girls wear dresses and only boys wear trousers.'

'But that's not true. I've seen girls wearing trousers,' Lucilla impugns. She drops her doll again and crosses her arms over her chest. 'Anyway I agree with her. I want to wear trousers too. All the time. Not stupid skirts and fancy frocks. You can't do anything in dresses. And they're draughty as well.'

I sometimes think I know less about her now, than when we rode home with her on the bus that spring day in 1948. 'Lucilla, I am not going to quarrel with you about this. I've told you, no daughter of mine is going to wear trousers.'

She turns her back on me, folds herself in half and spies on me through her open legs. 'You're upside down, Mother, standing on your head on the ceiling,' she observes merrily.

I did make a concession to our dress code. Blue needlecord, that's what I purchased. Three and a half yards, a fresh light blue. I made her some shorts and a shirt to match, on the proviso that she must obtain my express permission to wear them. You'd have thought the clothes were her second skin she was in them so much. But the material faded. And last weekend I noticed a tear on a sleeve, and another on the seat of the shorts. 'There is nothing for it,' I explained, 'but that the outfit will have to go to the ragbag.' What I had on my hands following this timely announcement was no less than a mutiny. I held firm and the house resounded with her petulant sobbing. But eventually she gave in and handed them over. With a sense of relief, I shovelled the boyish outfit into the bag, and consigned it to be recycled as patchwork.

I am constantly trying to engage Lucilla's interest in sewing, to demonstrate how my treadle sewing machine works. I want to teach her all the skills I mastered at the clothes factory where I was employed. But she does not seem to appreciate the opportunity afforded her. She is an unwilling pupil. To my chagrin, she makes herself scarce whenever I get out my sewing box. I purchased her a French knitting doll as a last resort. And to be fair crocheting woollen ropes diverts her for a few minutes before she starts to fidget. What frustrates me is that there is no appetite for more, no drive to learn the craft of knitting, of embroidery, to tackle the multitude of stitches.

'Wouldn't you like to have a go at basket weave? Single chevron? Windmill? Mock cable then? How about close checks? Very well, two by two rib,' I coax as she shakes her head. I persevere casting a few stitches on her stumpy plastic needles. And lo and behold that infuriatingly dreamy look screens her eyes. I may as well be communicating with a mannequin in a shop window. 'Well, wouldn't you, Lucilla?'

'They look fiddly. I've got a new book from the library,' she tells me on a sigh, bouncing on the stool by the side of my chair. '*Heidi*. The librarian says it's all about a little girl who is orphaned, and goes to live in the Swiss mountains with her grandfather.'

'Oh, I see.' Her previous disinterest is contagious. Prattling about her wearisome books has much the same effect on me as the mention of sewing does on her. I yawn and twist the hornet-yellow three-ply so tightly about my index finger that I cut off the circulation and it throbs. And that is another irksome thing. Constantly loitering in the library on her way home from school, when she has homework and chores to do. Books and drawing, that's all she seems devoted to. She's at her scribbles day and night. It has been known for me to come upon her sitting up in bed painting, her paintbox open, a jam jar of dirty water propped up against her pillow if you please!

'Lucilla! You do not paint in bed!' I said, seizing the lot. I commandeered it for a month. I would have liked to throw it in the bin.

Now she continues chattering about *Heidi*, this book that she finds so much more enticing than an hour's sewing instruction with her mother. 'Heidi's mummy and daddy are dead,' she says blithely. 'But it isn't a bit sad, because her grandfather looks after her. And he's ever so kind – although he pretends to be gruff. And he makes her toasted cheese and she sleeps on a bed of straw.' A pause, then, 'I'd like to go and live in the mountains with goats,' she adds shiny-eyed, tap-dancing her feet.

'Well, you don't live there now,' I riposte, unwinding the wool from my fingers. 'You live in London.'

She sucks in her lips, considering. 'I don't like London terribly much. When I grow up I shall live on a mountain.'

I give a sarcastic laugh, unable to resist baiting her. 'And exactly where will you live on your mountain? In a cave?' I rewind the ball of wool, snatch the knitting needles from her hands and ram them in my sewing bag.

'Maybe,' she says a little doubtfully.

'There are bats in caves,' I point out, smothering a smile. Your play now, missy. Fear fogs the blue of her eyes fleetingly. 'What about doing your embroidery?' We last attempted lazy daisy and stem stitch.

'Will Daddy be home soon?' she asks, changing the subject and glancing at the mantel clock.

'He's going to be late tonight,' I tell her. 'Now what about your sampler?'

'Oh, please can I go and read my book?' She looks hopeful and frankly my enthusiasm has drained away.

'Very well.' I get up suddenly and she shies away from me, falling off her stool. 'I'll see to tea.' We are having salad. In the kitchen, peeling the shells off the eggs, I realise that distracted by Lucilla I've overboiled them. The whites are stained a dark greyish green.

Chapter 17

Lucilla, 1959

When she was eight, Lucilla had a nightmare. She only had it that once but it stayed with her, repeated on her like the indigestible meals her mother dished up. In it there was a ghoul with shreds of silvered skin hanging down from its squat, voluptuous, pallid body. They were pinned to its torso, and the pinheads glinted fiendishly in a grid of moonlight. They rippled and undulated. But the pins anchored them securely in position. Some of the shreds had paper casings under them that rustled. But the scariest thing about the ghost was that it had no head and no arms, and a single crutch instead of legs. Where the head and arms should have been attached was nothing, only the vacuous night. The shock of seeing this decapitated spectre made her heart contract violently, and when she sucked in a breath she had a painful stitch in her side.

The head was the seat of nearly all the senses, eyes and sight, tongue and taste, ears and hearing, nose and smell. The sense of touch was there, as well, but then it was scattered all over your body. This decapitated fiend, though devoid of reason, its pearly epidermis all slashed to ribbons, pulsed with life. It reared up in front of Lucilla. She couldn't dodge the wadded bulk of it. What petrified her most was that it was her reflection. Most days she felt headless, armless, voiceless.

Where her brain should be, where an identity was normally planted in memory and knowledge, was a vacuum.

That was when she started screaming. The piercing shrieks didn't seem to be emanating from her, but from another girl sleepwalking on the landing. She was still screaming when the light made her squint, screaming too when her father loomed over her in his striped pyjamas, blue and maroon, and his brown wool dressing gown, screaming too when Mrs Fortinbrass's door opened a few inches and her diminutive face popped out of the gap. She alone was welcome, the North Star to a lost mariner. A lady in lavender. A lavender nightgown. A lavender knitted bed jacket. Even a lavender hairnet with her grey hair neatly coiled under it. Her smile was a damp scented flannel on a hot fevered brow.

'There, there,' she cooed. 'There, there.' And hearing this, Lucilla wanted to slip into the bony envelope of Mrs Fortinbrass. She wanted to have her mix up a mug of hot Ribena, and butter a Rich Tea biscuit then sprinkle it with sugar, and sit with her while she drank and ate. But when her mother gained the stairs, panting and beetroot-faced, she curled up in a ball like a hedgehog. She envied the prickles. Because she didn't have any her father kept patting her back. He said, 'You had a bad dream, Lucilla. It's all right now. Pull yourself together. We're here.'

And Mrs Fortinbrass said, 'Poor love. Oh, poor mite! Oh, poor little love!'

And her mother said, 'For heaven's sake! It's only my dressmaker's dummy! Whatever's the matter with you?' But when Lucilla answered her speech was all minced up with sobs. She gibbered about the strips of pasty skin, how they were peeling off her, how raw she was underneath them, how some days the pins felt like nails driven into her flesh and how her heart was trapped in the bony cage of her chest. 'That's the ivory satin gown I'm making for the temperance summer dance,' her mother interjected irritably. By then Lucilla had uncurled herself. She blinked at her mother, at her nightwear. Blink – a purple dressing gown baggy as a bedspread. Blink – beige knitted bedsocks. Blink – toilet-brush hair standing on end. Blink – wrinkles flecked with cold cream. Blink – knobbly nose with nostrils flaring. Blink – eyes pelting her like hailstones.

'Well, if you have it all under control, I'll say goodnight,' Mrs Fortinbrass twittered, giving a timid wave to Lucilla. Her parents apologised to their lodger for the upset, apologised for their daughter's deranged exhibition, but Mrs Fortinbrass insisted that she had not been able to sleep anyway, and that she had been reading the *People's Friend* to combat her insomnia. Then she closed her door with a click. Lucilla's father escorted her back to bed. He said that he was going to cover the dressmaker's dummy with a blanket so it couldn't frighten her again. And he said that he would leave the light on, although her mother already stomping downstairs was grumbling about the electricity bill. But despite this, after he left Lucilla thought that she could still hear the crackle of the paper as the tattered skin slip-slithered.

Scamp was the glue that stuck her back together. They got him four months after her eighth birthday. She told her father when he asked that she would like a spaniel, her turquoise eyes putting the stars to shame. Her hands were clasped in front of her and she very nearly dropped to her knees. It was a Saturday in May, a clear day. Her father was toiling at his bureau, balancing the books for the Sons of Temperance. His brow mapped with contour lines and he laid down his pen, so that for a dreadful moment she supposed he had changed his mind.

He shook his head and back and forth solemnly. He had on the mask he wore when the figures did not tally. Fixing her through his glasses from under the thicket of his dark eyebrows, he made an observation. 'Spaniels are pedigrees and prohibitively expensive. I don't think we can afford a spaniel.' Lucilla looked downcast, bereft. The dog that almost was had begun to evaporate before it had even been brought home. But then her father continued, saying that the following weekend, when Frank and Rachel were over, they would all go to the market to look at the pet stall.

Saturday, and she woke early, giddy with excitement. They were to set off mid-morning. At 9 am she was sitting at the bottom of the stairs in her Robin Hood outfit. Her mother made it for her entry into the temperance Christmas fancy dress competition. She planned for Lucilla to go as Sleeping Beauty, or Cinderella or Little Red Riding Hood. She showed her lots of tempting material: buttercup silk, apricot satin, velvet as red as cranberries. But Lucilla was perverse, insisting that she that if she couldn't be Robin Hood she would not enter. Her mother caved in, and then ranted bitterly when she did not win any of the prizes. Still, Lucilla, riding through the glen in the Sherwood Forest of her imagination, didn't care a fig, for she was Robin Hood, who robbed from the rich and gave to the poor.

She did have to admit though that the avocado-green nylon tights were rather itchy, and that the leatherette tunic with the crenulated hem was subject to chilly updrafts, which caught you unawares in the brisk May air. Her boots, also made in the leatherette fabric, had pointed curling toes and fringed tops that sat snugly over her calves. She tugged down the brim of her pointed cap and plucked impatiently at her bow. She had three rubber-capped arrows in her quiver. She was scheming to shoot Frank when he turned up, to score a bulls eye on the board of his fat head. At five minutes past, her cousins trotted in, Frank, a pack horse with saddlebags jammed with his stamp albums and his book matchboxes. She followed them into the front room where glasses of milk and a plate of Nice biscuits awaited.

'Do you want to be in my band of merry men?' Lucilla enlisted precipitously, as Frank spread his albums on her father's desk. Rachel, her manners impeccable, asked her aunt if she might sit down on the settee.

'Of course, dear. And may I say how charming you look in that matching two-piece. I do like the peach knit. Polyester is such an easy-wear fabric. Help yourself to a biscuit, dear,' her mother said. She gestured dramatically at the plate, as if she was a hostess in a Noël Coward play offering tempting hors d'oeuvres to her guests. Then, back down to earth with a thump, 'Lucilla, get off the back of the settee! You're scuffing the cover with your dirty boots!'

Lucilla dismounted reluctantly. 'Well, if you don't want to be a merry man, how about Friar Tuck, Frank? Then we can fight with long sticks and bash each other up.'

Her mother's high giggle sounded like a dentist's drill. 'Hehehehe! Really! Do you have to be so unladylike, Lucilla?' Her daughter adjusted the strap of her quiver and undeterred looked questioningly at her selected recruit.

'No fear,' Frank sneered. Now eleven and grown tall and reedy, her cousin's boast was that he was an expert philatelist and phillumenist – far too busy to play with foolish little girls. 'I've brought along my collection of book matches, the cigarette brands for Uncle Merfyn to peruse. Since he last went through them there have been some rare finds.' His horn-blowing was wasted on his cousin.

'What about the evil Sheriff of Nottingham then,' Lucilla persisted, cunning in her voice. If he were the enemy she would be entirely justified in using him for target practice.

'Lucilla, stop harassing your cousin,' her mother interpolated. She had on the mustard frock with the cowl collar she only completed a few days ago. She swirled her skirt and had a go at plumping up her resistant lacquered hair.

'You look spiffing, Aunt Harriet,' Frank said through an obsequious smile.

'Why thank you, kind sir,' her mother acknowledged bobbing a curtsey. 'Frank is a young gentleman now and doesn't want to be bothered with your childish pranks, Lucilla. Have another Nice biscuit, Frank dear.' Frank needed no further persuasion to post a biscuit, his fourth, entire, like a letter into his slit mouth.

'Aunt Harriet, I have a Matinée, De Luxe Tipped, Lambert and Butler of Drury Lane. "The kindly smoke",' he gloated through crumbs and sugar grains.

'Do you, dear?' Her mother managed a look that was a blend of blank and overawed. 'Jolly well done!'

'And that's not all,' ran on Frank sensing the limelight, 'I have Craven "A", "Cork-tipped for cool clean smoking".' As he bragged, he pulled book matchboxes out of his bag and wafted them under her mother's nose. 'And Wills Whiffs, "The little cigar with the big reputation". And . . . and Baron's, "Deeply Satisfying Baron! Because you get all the lift of deeply satisfying tobacco through Baron's unique easy draw filter".'

Lucilla, brain-bludgeoned into a condition of near-terminal tedium gave a kitty-cat yawn, despairing of Frank's credentials ever to join her valorous men in avocado green, in place of the usual Lincoln. Turning her attention elsewhere, she tugged on Rachel's jacket sleeve, desperate to be off to the garden and up the apple tree.

'Did you learn all that by heart, Frank?' her mother delved, her tone hushed, eyelids fluttering as if she had a speck of dust irritating her vision. Frank nodded, basking in his scholarly attributes.

Rachel courteously declined her mother's suggestion that she might like to cut hexagon shapes from the fabric scraps in the ragbag. 'But it'll be such a lark, Rachel dear. And I can show you how the patchwork quilt is coming on.'

'Thank you so much, Aunt Harriet, but perhaps I can do that this afternoon, after we've been to the market. You see I told Lucilla I'd be Maid Marian,' she forestalled ingeniously.

Her mother's features gave the optical illusion that they were edging closer to each other in umbrage. 'Oh very well,' she accepted defeat with poor grace.

Needing no further encouragement, the girls clattered outside. Minus Frank, they soon tired of being merry, so Lucilla switched allegiance to the Swiss.

'I'm William Tell now,' she informed Rachel, handing her an apple. 'Balance this on your head and I'll shoot it off.' She answered the look of alarm that dimmed Rachel's normally serene face with fulsome assurances. 'My aim is true. I never miss. If I can split the apple on my son's head, you've nothing to worry about.' They played for a further hour, then at her mother's bidding came indoors to ready themselves for their thrilling outing. Rachel had the scarlet imprint of three penny-sized misses, two on her forehead and one on her cheek. But she was stout-hearted as the victim of Lucilla's dismal aim, pleased to have survived the encounter rather than bearing her cousin grudges. When her aunt interrogated her, she claimed that she gained the marks by accident, tripping over a flowerpot. Without being told, Lucilla stripped off her Robin Hood costume, folded it carefully and slipped on the shell pink and light green seersucker dress her mother had selected earlier. She surveyed the decorative smocking in her dressing-table mirror, and reflected how unflattering and frumpy the garment was.

'I look revolting,' she attested.

'No you don't,' said Rachel, brushing her cousin's hair and using hair slides to secure it from off her face. Lucilla pulled on her cardigan, and buttoned it all the way up. Although she felt garrotted by the tight collar, she knew her mother would approve. And the plus was that it concealed the intricate smocking. But all attempts at prettifying came to nought when seconds later she crashed down the stairs, Rachel in sedate pursuit. In the front room, Lucilla was dismayed to still see Frank and her father inspecting the stamp and matchbox collection, through a magnifying glass.

'I haven't any yet from French Guiana,' cousin Frank complained. 'Or from the Ivory Coast or Martinique. Abyssinia's missing too. And it would be brilliant to get some from the Chinese Expeditionary Force, and Puttialla, Rajpeepla and Sirmoor.'

Her father, puffing on his pipe, emitted sympathetic grunts. 'Can't promise to deliver on those, Frank, but I will try to get a book of Olivier matches for you.' They were both so preoccupied that it took Lucilla and Rachel a full ten minutes to bring their industrious philately to a close. They travelled on the bus to Pentonville Road market. By the time they ground to a stop, Lucilla's mind was a kennel crowded with dogs of every breed. The market was a rowdy warren of stalls trading to hoards of people. Everyone was shouting, all trying to outdo each other.

Lucilla's eyes devoured the hectic scene greedily, the colours and foreign sounds, the characters and their banter, the wares displayed to snag the cruising shopper. She whispered in Rachel's ear that she wanted to paint it all, later that evening when it was peaceful. She had no interest in the racks of dresses her mother lingered at, or in the bunches of plastic flowers, which Rachel said would not fade or die. But she would happily have stayed by the stall that sold pets all day and through the night as well. There were mewing kittens and cheeping budgies, and tortoises chewing mechanically on leaves. And, most fabulous of all, there were two large crates full of puppies.

'These are pedigree,' the beak-nosed stallholder reported, indicating the larger of the crates, and pulling at a few stray whiskers on his square chin. 'Cocker spaniels. The real deal.'

Frank glanced down disparagingly at the squirming bundles of fur. 'I expect they're overpriced, Uncle Merfyn. Beat him down,' he urged, his tone low and sly.

'How much?' her father hustled, opting for the direct approach, while the puppies licked Lucilla and Rachel to death. Lucilla was smitten by them all. If she could she would have shouldered the whole crate and kept the entire pack.

'One pound,' said the stallholder with a shift of his heavy-lidded eyes, lifting out a black and white bundle. 'Top condition. Win prizes in dog shows these ones. I guarantee it. Worth every penny.'

Her father and her mother exchanged appalled looks, and she heard Frank mutter that if they were not careful they would be robbed. She could strangle her cousin, she really could. Her father, too, was transparently unmoved, raising his eyebrows and squeezing his nose between thumb and forefinger. To Lucilla this shilly-shallying was inexplicable. Couldn't they see that if the stallholder said ten or twenty, or even thirty pounds, it would be worth it, money well spent? Her parents consulted briefly, with Frank conspicuously eavesdropping. Lucilla swayed, nearly passing out, Rachel's hand on her arm restoring her balance. 'And the other box?' her father probed at length his cadence measured, indicating the second box with a nod of his head.

'Mongrels. Ten shillings and sixpence,' the stallholder replied peremptorily. He gave the twisting mass of chocolate-brown puppies a derogatory stab with a grubby finger. 'Can't vouch for anything with them. Don't know what they'll turn into.'

'They look fine.' Frank volunteered his expert opinion, hands clinking some coins in his pocket. 'If you ask me –' and Lucilla reflected privately that no one had '– they're all much the same.'

The stallholder whipped his cap off and shook his head, eyes narrowing on Frank.

'Not to the trained eye, sonny,' he said glacially.

Her father bent to inspect the occupants of each box in turn. 'Hmm . . . yes, yes, we'll take one of those,' he murmured straightening up. He flapped a hand at the half-breeds, the stock that had a pinch of this and spoonful of that, a blood-shake of types pulsing through their canine veins.

'Very wise, Uncle Merfyn,' Frank remarked, looking smarmy.

'I should think so too,' her mother contributed, adjusting the diamanté beetle pinned to the parsley-green angora monstrosity atop her head. 'Twenty shillings for a dog! I never heard of such a thing. You'd think the pups were eighteen carat gold.'

'And that, Mother, is why we're going to buy a mongrel at half the price,' her father the economist asserted. Lucilla's heart gave a lurch, and she and Rachel clutched hands and skipped in a circle. She didn't care whether it was a pedigree or a mongrel, so long as she had her dog. 'Will you take ten,' her father bartered, looking down his nose at the substandard puppies. But by now the seller had become surly, and was not in the mood to give them a deal. They wrangled over the sixpence animatedly until he surrendered, relieved to be rid of such stingy customers. Frank made a prat of himself applauding his prudent uncle so loudly that they attracted an audience, then planting a wet kiss on his aunt's cheek. Rachel smirked at Lucilla and grinned. And her mother, her cheeks cherry pink with embarrassment, wandered off to finger some costume jewellery. 'Lucilla, you can select a brown puppy. The spaniels are quite beyond our budget,' her father ordained counting out the coins.

She did not waste a second. Not knowing what the puppy would develop into was a bonus as far as she was concerned. Hurriedly, she disentangled herself from the spaniels she was fondling, and directed her focus on the wiggling, yapping mongrels. They all had floppy ears, but the pooch she lifted out had an adorably quizzical face.

'Is it a dog or a bitch?' Frank quizzed, revelling in speaking the term for a female dog with all its derogative connotations.

The stallholder gave it a cursory examination while it was still in Lucilla's hands. 'A dog,' he sneered, still smarting. 'Be warned, you get what you pay for. Could have any temperament.' As her father recounted the money for the third time, Lucilla tucked the six-week-old puppy under her cardigan, by her madly beating heart. Feeling the package shiver, lodged there, was a foretaste of heaven, she concluded on the bus ride home. As they travelled, they discussed names, settling on Scamp. Lucilla pleaded if he might sleep in her bed, but her mother was unswerving in her resolve that he should stay in the kitchen. Though, she added acidly, if she were to have her way he'd be kept in a kennel, all weathers, outdoors.

After the cousins had gone home, Lucilla rummaged in the garden shed, chancing on an old wooden tea chest which had previously held tins of paint. She lined it with newspaper and a cosy blanket. She borrowed a book from the library and followed instructions on house-training, taking Scamp out to the lawn every couple of hours and telling him to 'get busy'. Her mother bought him cheap offcuts of meat from the butchers that they called 'melts'. And when she boiled them, the putrid smell pervaded the entire house. Lucilla walked him in Cherry Tree Wood and Coldfall Wood and on Hampstead Heath. He sat at her feet while she sketched the horse riders she saw cantering there. If they went away with the Sons of Temperance, he boarded with her grandmother.

Each week Lucilla goes to the meetings with her parents, to the shabby chapel hall with coffee-coloured walls in Archway. As they travel, her turquoise eyes feed on the darkening palette of the sky, and on the ghostly blue sparks flying from the overhead trolley bus cable. And her ears tune to the hum and crackle of electricity. The hall reeks permanently of stewed tea, as if the plaster has been injected with it from the huge urn they brew up in the evenings. Refreshments amount to this, cup after cup of it, and molehills of biscuits that have lost their crunch – custard creams, jam shortcakes, digestives and, on extra special nights, chocolate bourbons.

Upstairs is another room, equally drab. It is here that the children's activities are held. The building is damp and musty, with a rash of mildew patches on the walls and ceilings. The plug-in heaters hardly take the edge off the invasive chill. On arrival, her parents don velvet robes trimmed with gold braid. These are stored on hangers in a locked cupboard, the floor of its broad mouth stuffed with mothballs. Smelling as if they are preserved mummies, they process, then take their thrones at the centre of a wide trestle table standing to the rear of the hall. Special girls and boys, temperance monitors who have earned the privilege, are nominated each week to take down the minutes of the meeting.

Like knights of the round table, except that it is rectangular, the adults deliberate in loud monotones. As well as the night ahead, they discuss forthcoming socials, scheduled marches, section meetings and intergroup conventions. All the children who attend are saving their pocket money, including Lucilla, Frank and Rachel. Her father says that his nephew, who has to date saved more than any of the youngsters, is a wonderful example to them all of what may be accomplished if they are thrifty. Lucilla, who has seen her mother slipping Frank a silver coin every so often, doubts his parsimonious reputation. They line up when the meeting ends, and when their name is called they each step forwards and present her father with their money. He stows it in a metal cash box, and jots all the transactions down in their savings books and in another much larger book, his accountant's ledger.

When he has gathered in all the money, the children are given permission to withdraw upstairs with their group leaders. They play games, or sing hymns, or have craft workshops. But Lucilla spends the largest portion of these evenings freezing on the doorstep outside the hall. It is to here she is banished like clockwork for her unruliness. It doesn't really bother her, apart from her fingers and toes growing steadily more numb. In fact she rather enjoys watching the men drinking in the pub next door. She can spy on them through a window illuminated like a Christmas scene by golden-yellow light.

The intergroup Temperance Music Festival is held in Bermondsey, in an even vaster hall than their own. There are different categories for the various instruments children can play. Lucilla's parents enter her in the piano section. Trembling with nerves, head thrust down the toilet, she spews up the brick of steak and kidney pie they had for supper, with only minutes to go before it commences. The hall is crammed with children and their parents, all come to perform and watch. Frank is in the front row with Rachel and Aunt Enid and her mother. Later Rachel will be playing the tragic ballad 'Barbara Allen' on her recorder in the wind section. Lucilla knows that stage fright will not overcome *her*, and that her performance will proceed without a hitch. Her father is supervising from the side, and the four adjudicators are seated in a row behind a desk, set stage left on the rostrum.

Lucilla has been having piano lessons for some years now with Miss Garside, who lives at the end of their road. She knows her mother harbours reservations about her tutor's appearance though, having overheard her parents confer on the subject. But her father's only retort was that her rates were very reasonable. And it is true that Miss Garside wears evening dresses in the daytime and lots of jewellery. Yet she also has bristles shadowing her jaw, bristles that Lucilla suspects will grow into a beard if left untended. And she has hairy legs and hairy arms and huge hairy hands, and a bass foghorn voice. But amazingly she also has a light touch on the piano keys. Although her pupil finds it pleasant playing to the potted aspidistra in Miss Garside's front room, the prospect of performing in the Temperance Music Festival is about as appealing to her as tightrope walking between the spires of the Houses of Parliament.

'Lucilla Pritchard. Number nine.'

Cowering in her seat in the depths of the darkened hall, Lucilla cringes when she hears her name and number called out. Her heart gives a drum roll, and her ears have the sigh of the sea in them. Heads swing round. Eyes home in on her. The clop of her shoes on the parquet flooring is deafening. It seems to take years to reach the rostrum. Stepping into the floodlit space is like having all her clothes fall off in school. Seated on the stool, she stares straight ahead at her music. But there is no music! She glimpses downwards. Her lap is empty. With horror her thoughts condense into a single, incontrovertible fact – sitting on her music book, she has neglected to carry it with her. Now she is as rigid as if rigor mortis has set in. Breath whistles brokenly in and out of her. The clock on the wall ticks like a metronome.

'When you're ready, Miss Pritchard,' prompts one of the adjudicators. But she is not ready. How can she be without her music? Heads bump. Whispers sizzle like frying bacon along the rows. At the back of the hall, someone holds a music book aloft and waves it. The pages flap as though it is a white flag of surrender. The whispers swell to titters, the titters become giggles, and the giggles shrieks of laughter rebounding off the high walls and ceiling. Then close by, so close she is sure she can feel his breath on her, Frank begins honking like a goose. Others join in until there is a gaggle of them. Her name is banded about, the punchline of the joke. She springs up and sprints down the hall, grabbing the manuscript from a steward who has retrieved it. When next she slides onto the piano stool, her fingers feel as if they have been crudely carved out of wood. The adjudicator who spoke previously is going full throttle to restore order.

'Can we please have quiet! This competition will be cancelled unless the entrants can behave themselves.' Her father is strutting about in his velvet cape, gold chain flashing, calling for order like an irate schoolmaster. A brittle silence returns. She inhales deeply, sending a rush of blood to her head, fingers poised. She is certain that they will stay stiff as pipe cleaners, unable to strike the keys. But Miss Garside has been too good a teacher. In seconds the music has claimed her, Czerny's Studies, Opus 261, No. 22.

'This piece is all about rhythm and clarity,' Miss Garside's granulated man-voice resounds in her ear. 'You need to let it filter through to your fingertips.' Her whole body pulses with the beat, the recollected waft of her tutor's tobacco breath quelling her whirlpool of adrenalin: Her relief when it is over is palpable. No one is more astonished than her to find she has won the top prize, a book token for three shillings for the most accomplished pianist in her age group. Her father is ecstatic at this unlooked-for success and propels her about afterwards, showing her off to the Brothers and Sisters of Temperance like a polished trophy. Even her mother seems passably pleased, patting her on the head and muttering sotto voce, 'Thank the Lord you redeemed yourself.' Aunt Enid seconds this, raising her eyes to the rafters.

Frank pulls her hair and, when she spins around to see who did it, says, 'I'd part with some of my savings to see you mess up again. Nincompoop!'

'Well done, Lucilla,' congratulates Rachel, pushing her brother aside. She did not win, but she did play very prettily when it came to it and was commended by the judges. 'I knew you could do it.'

'Musical fingers, see,' her father says, seizing Lucilla's wooden-spoon hands and holding them up for all to ogle. 'She has a gift. Of course we have done all that we can to nurture it. She has private lessons with a very exclusive teacher.'

Lucilla summons a mental image of Miss Garside, with her five o'clock shadow, her hairy hands and a smile as enigmatic as the Mona Lisa's. But her parents' praise does not act like a drug on her, making her crave more. She relays the grim details to her music teacher at her next lesson. 'I hated it. I don't ever want to play the piano in public again.' Miss Garside nods and lights up one of her cigars. She sucks on it thoughtfully. Lounging on the windowsill, her white cat suddenly springs down and arches its back. It rubs itself against Lucilla's legs, then picks its way haughtily across the piano pedals. Lucilla plays a note and they both cock an ear while it reverberates.

Miss Garside places her cigar in an ashtray on the piano lid and plays a stirring piece of music. When she finishes, she keeps her fingers resting on the keys for seconds before withdrawing them. 'That sounded like lots of thunderstorms coming one after the other.' Lucilla gives her appraisal.

'Beethoven. His "*Appassionata*" sonata in F minor,' grinds out Miss Garside from her flat broad chest. 'Drowns out the white noise.'

Dawdling on the way home, a simple solution to her problem offers itself. If she plays badly, if she makes mistakes on purpose, but adroitly so no one guesses, then she will not qualify for future temperance music festivals. And if she does not qualify, she will not have to take that dreadful walk up to the rostrum with all those eyes trained on her. Her slide from winner to loser fills her parents with rancour. Her father stuffs the envelopes with Miss Garside's fee more and more resentfully. Then comes the decree that for the present at least her musicianship must take a back seat to her schoolwork. Lucilla greets it with equanimity. She will not miss the loathed piano. But Miss Garside, with her hairy hands and her bristly chin, and the *Appassionata* sonata that drowns out the white noise – oh, these she will pine for.

A rare treat for Lucilla are days out with her father. Her mother does not accompany them on these trips. 'I'm far too busy in the house to go off gadding about London,' she says, flicking her duster like the ruffled skirt of a flamenco dancer. 'Do you imagine the house looks after itself?'

Lucilla does. She imagines this very thing. She assumes that when they shut the front door and stroll down the road, the house heaves a sort of dusty sigh and relaxes into itself. She suspects that the house wearies of being scrubbed and wiped and swept and washed, that it probably delights in its own lethargic company. Most likely it relishes a spate of slovenliness. Lucilla would, given half the chance. 'Tea will be at five o'clock on the dot,' her mother decrees as they depart, hinting at dire consequences if they are so much as a minute late. If Lucilla asks about the menu, her mother's reply is invariably the same. 'Windy pie and airy pudding! Windy pie and airy pudding! That's what we're having.' Though Lucilla has yet to witness a dish as light as air, come floating out of her mother's kitchen.

Lucilla visits the bank with her father, weighed down with the savings from the Sons of Temperance. She likes the polished marble floors, the vaulted ceilings, the cool money-tainted air. She stares fascinated at the decorative mosaics. They go by bus, and walk along the Embankment when they arrive. She is fond of the mingled strong odours of silt and rubbish, of oil and smoke. 'Thames mud,' her father says, inhaling a lung full and smacking his lips together. 'Clay and sewage. Muck and the river.' They inspect the boats, and amble over bridges watching the sluggish eel of grey green swilling on by. They go to St Paul's and, panting, climb up to the Whispering Gallery. They visit Tower Bridge and ascend the carpeted steps, passing windows inset on each landing. Once, in Hampton Court maze she got lost. She would still have been running up and down green corridors at nightfall if she hadn't been rescued by a kind attendant. They take trips on the river all the way to Gravesend. They picnic on spam sandwiches and drink orange squash, then buy ice creams for afters.

She feels at home in the parks. St James's Park is the loveliest, she thinks. And, oh, how she adores London Zoo. She is enraptured by all of the animals. But it is Guy the gorilla who has her heart – those eyes of his, those melting brown eyes, so intense, so full of wisdom. The skin of his hands and face is like the leatherette material her Robin Hood outfit is cut from, only black, with a dull metallic sheen. Oh, to have those powerful arms wrapped round her, to feel the thud of his great ape heart through the dark shaggy hairs of his keg chest.

Now the tigers have another effect on her altogether. Their dangerous stripes make her tremble with dread. There is a savage magnetic beauty in those lithe giant cats. But the small pens they are caged in bother her. 'Why is it that my Scamp can run around woods, and all the tigers have is that small cage?' she needs to know.

They settle their gazes on the pacing tigers. 'Dogs are domesticated,' her father says to himself. Then to her, he says, 'These are deadly wild animals, Lucilla. If they opened the cages, if they were set free to roam in the woods they'd go on a rampage, a killing spree.' She feasts on the colours, the golden orange, the black, the magnificent markings. Her father fumbles in a pocket for his handkerchief and blows his nose with an elephant's trumpet. 'They may look like pussy cats but trust me, they're man-eaters.'

Lucilla imagines a keeper letting them all out, the entire zooful spilling onto the streets of London, zebras stopping the traffic crossing at zebra crossings, flamingos in the fountains at Trafalgar Square, buffalo grazing Buckingham Palace Gardens, toucans in the leafy branches of the trees bordering the Thames, monkeys rioting in the Houses of Parliament and swinging off the chandeliers. And she imagines the tigers hunting prey, their stomachs achingly empty, juices running over their glistening ivory fangs. She imagines a streak of them stalking cousin Frank, when he sets off from the house in Archway to go trainspotting. Shutting her eyes, she sees them ducking behind privet hedges when, sensing he is being followed, he darts a look over his hunched bony shoulders. And then, caught off guard as he turns a corner, they pounce, and set about bolting down his scrawny hide. When they are replete, they saunter off down the Mall to find a sunny spot for a snooze. An untidy heap of clawed stamp albums, book matchboxes and trainspotting notebooks fit for nothing but a bonfire – all that would be left of cousin Frank! She gives an ear-to-ear grin. London, she decides, glancing back at the tigers as they slink by, would be vastly improved with a zooful of beasts prowling the city jungle.

They travel in coaches all over England attending temperance conventions. Aunt Enid and her cousins come as well. Often they visit the seaside and stay in bed and breakfasts, or at inexpensive hotels. Lucilla hates the coach trips. Almost as soon as they depart she starts missing Scamp. And she is plagued by travel sickness. The boiled sweets her mother keeps plugging her salivating mouth with merely aggravate it. She slumps against the prickly upholstery of her seat staring glumly into brown paper bags, while her tummy does pancake flips, and a burning sourness ebbs up her throat. And sometimes the coach has to squeal to a halt in a lay-by, the motor turning over, while she rushes out to retch in the bushes. All the other passengers peer at her from their telly screen windows, and tap the glass, and clap their hands over their gaping mouths. And when it is over and she climbs back in feeling like a twisted tube, they all mumble to each other the way they did during the temperance music festival. When Frank accompanies them, the teasing about these queasy episodes is merciless.

'You smell worse than a stink bomb, cousin Lucilla. You're making the whole coach pong, stink bomb,' comes his pernicious undertone as he leers over her.

On route to Brighton they stop at Beachy Head for this very purpose. While Lucilla is vomiting, the driver, lighting up a Woodbine, suggests they all get out and stretch their legs. The lighthouse is Frank's idea. He is the one who wants to see it, the Belle Tout Lighthouse. 'The name means "beautiful headland". Did you know that?' says Frank. Her father perks up instantly. He shares his nephew's mania for acquiring information. 'Building began in eighteen thirty-two after fleets of ships were wrecked and thousands of sailors were drowned.'

'Well, I don't know about shipwrecks but this wind is playing havoc with my hairdo,' Aunt Enid remarks needled, anchoring her black straw breton with an extra hatpin she removes from the brim. She buttons up her jacket and rearranges her fox fur..

'The light from the thirty Argand lamps was thrown over twenty miles out to sea. That put a stop to it,' Frank says.

'Twenty miles, eh?' Her father is nodding. 'Nearly all the way to France then.'

'Fancy you knowing that, Frank,' says her mother in admiration. 'You are a clever boy.'

Frank responds to this flattery with a courtly bow and another fact. 'I read about it in the *Encyclopaedia Britannica*. The chalk cliffs are five hundred and thirty feet at their highest point. That's nearly one hundred and eighty yards.'

'Near enough a tenth of a mile then,' her father adds, determined not to be outdone, consulting the conversion table in his own head.

'And did you know it was evacuated during the Second World War? Canadian troops used it for target practice. Or at least they hit it by mistake. But it's still standing.' Frank seems to be building up a head of steam.

'Well I never,' comments Aunt Enid, not listening to a word. She is examining the stiletto heel of one of her shoes, perturbed that she may have stepped in something unsavoury.

'I think we should take a look,' Frank proposes.

'Might as well as we're here,' her father agrees. They splinter off from the main party, her parents, Aunt Enid, Frank and Rachel. Lucilla is nearly left behind, but Rachel, remembering her, turns back.

'You don't still feel dodgy?' she calls out. Lucilla shakes her head, though she can taste the bile. 'Come on then. We are going to the lighthouse, the Belle Tout Lighthouse.' Her thin voice is lacerated by the wind, her long brown hair like an elaborate headdress torn this way and that. 'Hurry up, Lucilla.' She is wearing a greyish-blue gabardine coat with a shoulder cape. The cape keeps blowing up and covering her face, and she peels it off giggling. It is a blustery day, the wind sweeping inland off the sea. Lucilla drinks down the bracing salty moisture, letting it rinse her mouth. She catches up with them circling Belle Tout. Heads thrown back they stare at the monument, their shouts stolen from their open mouths.

'Uncle Merfyn, let's take a look at the view!' This is Frank, nearly as tall as her father now, his face battered by the wind looking more middle-aged than teen.

Her father, her mother on one arm and Aunt Enid on the other, yells back, 'OK, but do be careful.' And they set themselves into the teeth of the blast, trudging up the steep gradient, making for the cliff edge. None of them, not even Rachel, seems aware of Lucilla any more, tussling after them. When they are no more than a couple of yards from the sheer chalky drop, her father lifts a hand and, as if at a signal from their commander, they all halt. Legs akimbo they pit themselves against the onslaught, digging out divots in the scrubby grass. They huddle shoulder to shoulder. Their trappings, flannel and herringbone, corduroy and dimity, worsted and nylon, in blues and russets and greens and creams, fan out like an inflating parachute. At a distance, her mother's black cloche hat looks like a full stop. Their voices, indiscernible, scribble on the whirling scrolls of the wind.

Lucilla is stupefied by the brutal power slapping her face, buffeting her body. She is weak-kneed at the glassy altitude, drawn ineluctably to the brink. She has been here before, poised on the chalky brim of her island home. Dreaming? Has she dreamed this place, wind-thrashed, grass-quashed, on high, the sky an arm's reach, the sea beckoning at the foot of the turret? Coming under their radar, she shuffles ahead to the very edge. When there are no more than a few feet between her and nothingness, the flying dream becomes the master puppeteer. She feels the tug of the strings on her feet, her hands, her knees, between her shoulder blades. He yanks up the crown of her head then he croons lovingly into her whistling ears.

'You can fly! You can fly! You can fly!' And so . . . and so she tips her weight over the balls of her feet, angling herself into the resistant force of the wind. Further and further she goes, giving up her territory inch by inch. At the last, the moment of flight, another force hooks the collar of her coat and yanks her back.

'For heaven's sake, Lucilla, are you insane? Anyone would think that you were trying to kill yourself. I can't trust you for a second.'

'But I was going to fly,' wails Lucilla. 'I was going to fly!' They have retreated into the lee of Belle Tout, the mother and her adopted daughter. The lighthouse towers impassively over the struggling pair. The sun strikes the glass eye and it bounces back a white-gold ray. 'Let me go! Let me go!' screams the girl, wanting to race back and hurl herself off Beachy Head, knowing that the wind will catch her, that she *will* fly.

'Now, Lucilla stop this,' barks her father, sliding like a shark into looming shadow of Belle Tout.

'What's the matter with her?' screeches Aunt Enid, hand on her askew hat, bumping into and out of the shade in a flap.

'Lucilla, I'm warning you,' bellows her mother, walloping at her gyrating form. But the strings are still attached. The puppeteer plucks them expertly, so that her arms windmill as she knees her mother in the stomach.

'She's crazed, a loony. She's gone hopping mad, Aunt Harriet,' is

Frank's verdict, skipping sideways outside the fighting ring, attempting to tackle his raving cousin if she makes a dash for the cliff face.

'Don't hurt her,' implores Rachel, hands blindfolding her eyes, ghosting Frank.

'Give me a hand, Frank,' snarls her father, making a grab for her hair. 'I've got her.' But he hasn't, only a fistful of wisps.

'Righto, sir.' Frank has his orders and needs no extra encouragement to pile into the fray. 'Drat it, keep still will you, Lucilla!'

'Somebody do something!' Aunt Enid's histrionics are muffled in her fox fur.

'Ouch! She bit me, the little tyke,' bellows her mother leaping backwards and toppling over, smack, onto her bottom, landing in an ungainly heap.

'Harriet? Harriet? Has she killed you?' This from Aunt Enid, rushing in, the both of them now gagged with the swinging fox pelt.

Her father has wrestled her to the ground and pinned her flaying arms down, and Frank is sitting astride her still kicking legs. Her mother is jabbering something about bad blood, and Hitler, and how both her stockings have been laddered by the SS. Aunt Enid, the most unlikely of Florence Nightingales, realising that her sister-in-law has not sustained life-threatening injuries, dives with the aplomb of a tipsy ballet dancer onto the next patient. Her daughter is weeping inconsolably. She mops up Rachel's tears with the fox's tail, causing her to have a sneezing fit. Frank's face is contorted as he tries to quell his laughter. Overhead, obscuring the sun like the undercarriage of a fighter plane, comes her father's plum face. He is hollering uncontrollably, spittle flying from his mouth 'LUCILLA, CALM DOWN! CALM DOWN!' And impish Ariel, well seasoned with sea salt, is frisking them all, every atom of their lashing bodies. Then the strings are cut and Lucilla's eyelids flicker and close. As if sedated, she goes suddenly limp.

It is shortly after this incident that she comes home to the bowl of blood. And it is strange in a way, because she has been thinking about blood that very afternoon, and about her mother shouting about bad blood on Beachy Head, when all she wanted to do was fly, fly away. Perhaps some blood was dirty, though that seemed a rather stupid idea to her. Surely if it was dirty, dirty inside you, well . . . you'd get sick. For a moment she turned her hand palm upwards and traced the delicately raised veins she could see on her wrists. What, she pondered with real interest, about her blood? Was it good or bad? And how did people tell? Perhaps there was a test and doctors performed it when people were criminals, murderers and thieves. Perhaps that was what they told the judges in court. His blood is good and so he is innocent. But her blood, Lucilla Pritchard's blood is very bad and she should be sent to prison for a long, long time, for her whole life in fact. Lucilla shivers.

Lost in her meditations, she fumbles for her own key tied on a ribbon about her neck these days. The house receives her in reverential silence, save for Scamp whose tail thumps on the tiled floor of the hallway. She listens for upstairs noises. Mrs Fortinbrass opening a can of beans? Lifting a saucepan out of the cupboard? Boiling a kettle? Nothing. Downstairs is as still as a morgue as well, no sounds of her mother bashing and banging utensils like cymbals, no smoke fumes overcoming her. 'Mother?' she cries, hesitantly. 'Mother?' She cannot recall ever being alone with the house. The atmosphere is not hostile, only a fraction stunned, as if it is being roused after an all-night shindig.

She creeps from room to room, feeling like a trespasser, Scamp on her heels. An investigation confirms that all are empty. Her mother may be resting? Unlikely, but possible, she deduces, hovering outside her parents' bedroom door. She gives a faltering tap. Waits. Chews the left then the right side of her bottom lip. Taps again. The house holds its breath in suspense and, as she edges the door open slowly, sighs it out. A speedy scan shows that the curtains are drawn, the beds made up and empty.

These beds were friends once, corner-to-corner mattresses, their sheets and blankets laundry buddies. Lucilla cannot pinpoint the exact day that she noticed a cooling in the temperature of their ticking, that there was a rift in their relationship, a trough forming between them. All she can recall is seeing them incrementally ease apart with the changing seasons. Had one developed bad mattress odour, or an infestation of bed mites? Or had they developed extreme dandruff due to decades of being bombarded by dead skin cells? Whatever, it seems implausible now that they ever tolerated their close proximity.

She scans the floor for clues, a good detective's strategy. For a moment she wonders if her mother has died, if she has expired in a paroxysm of zealous cleaning, Jeyes fluid pouring onto the lino from an upturned bottle. But no, it is clear. On closer scrutiny, however, as she expands her fingertip search, there is an odd object crying out to be investigated – a chipped white enamel bowl sitting incongruously on her mother's dressing table, next to the tin of medicated talcum powder. She approaches it with caution as if it is alive. One, two, three steps and she peers inside, gasps, jumps back. The bowl is full of blood, gouts of blood, tissues sodden in blood. And look, there are more bloody tissues on the dressing table. Has an unfortunate person been massacred? But if so where is the body? For minutes, she stands and stares at the blood, at the wattle redness of it puddling in the bowl. The air smells like a butcher's shop, fleshy and raw. Scamp butts her leg and snorts.

When her father arrives home the explanation is forthcoming. Her mother has been admitted to Whittington Hospital in Highgate. 'She has had a nosebleed, Lucilla. A severe nosebleed. Wouldn't stop.

Gushing out of her. Doctor said her blood pressure is far too high. They're going to keep her in for a few days, so we'll have to make do for supper. But not to worry, they're going to fix her up.'

Mrs Fortinbrass has arrived back with her shopping and condolences. She offers to make Welsh rarebit. Upstairs through and through, the crisis has lured her into nether regions of the house. While she is cooking, Lucilla's father disappears into the garden shed. Lucilla takes notice of this because it is not the first occasion on which he has done this. This is queer because her mother takes care of the garden, and her father seldom, if ever, goes near the shed. She has also detected subtle changes in his behaviour when he re-emerges from the gloomy interior. On the way in there is a purposeful expression on his frowning face, a determination in his heavy stride. On the way out, some half an hour later, he has adopted an ambling gait, and his face is a trifle flushed and set in a cheery mask. There is, as well, a faint but distinct odour on his breath. It is rather like petrol but different, thicker and sourer.

Tonight he has grown garrulous too, walking in through the back door as though arriving at a party. They eat supper at the dining room table watching the *Black and White Minstrel Show*. Men with black faces, mini-moon eyes and smiling crescent-moon mouths, dressed in sparkling white suits. Beautiful women with complexions dazzling as new-fallen snow, swathed in fur-trimmed gowns. They link arms. They show their blinding pearly-white teeth. They sing 'Polly Wolly Doodle', and they wave their hands and dance. Lucilla bites into the savoury creamy cheese sauce, and dwells meditatively on the bowl of her mother's blood that no one has dealt with yet.

After she has gone to bed, but not to sleep, Lucilla hears the taxi pull up. She slips out from under the blankets, tweaks the curtains and spies Aunt Enid alighting from the black cab. She looks smart in a fitted suit in French navy, the collar trimmed with cream mink, a tiny scalloped hat sitting snug on her head like a mauve flower, petals open. The street lights shimmer on her black leather gloves and on her beaded clutch bag. Her high heels click on the pavement. She raps assertively on the front door, and Lucilla, treading softly on the upstairs landing, freezes as it is opened. Her father greets her aunt expansively and welcomes her in. His voice rising up the stairs is pitched much more loudly than usual. Together with the dressmaker's dummy, Lucilla overhears their dialogue.

Aunt Enid has been to the hospital to visit Mother. She reports that her condition is much improved, that the operation has gone well, but that they will be keeping her in for a few weeks of complete bed rest. Lucilla is somewhat baffled by the mention of surgery. To operate on a nosebleed seems a particularly drastic treatment for a condition that normally dries up of its own accord. Why in the hot weather at school she has had a nosebleed herself. The teacher sat with her in the medical room, while she swabbed it with cotton wool and in minutes it stopped of its own volition. She is pondering if the surgeon put something in her mother's nose or took something out, as her father ushers Aunt Enid into the front room. He leaves the door ajar. They talk long into the night, mostly about Mother, and the stress she is under. 'The child's not without her problems,' says Aunt Enid. 'It's wearing for Harriet at her age.'

'Oh, things will settle down.' Her father's tone is insouciant, reassuring. 'We must remember she's only young.'

'I don't know about that. At eleven, she's certainly old enough to know right from wrong,' Aunt Enid rejoins with conviction. 'After all, look at my Rachel.' For a second, Lucilla wonders if Rachel, her cousin, is with her downstairs this second. And then she realises that her aunt is only speaking figuratively.

'Aye, she's a grand girl, Rachel is. There's no denying that,' her father says wishfully.

'That day on Beachy Head, by the lighthouse, well, quite honestly, I thought Lucilla was going to throw herself off. She was so het up, I doubted we'd be able to prevent it either. I'm sorry to have to tell you there are times when I think she's as barmy as a fruit bat. It's the bad blood. No diluting it.'

'No, Enid, no! You're overreacting,' her father mollifies. 'She is hypersensitive, highly strung, but no more.'

'I wish that was the extent of it, Merfyn. You thought you could manage it, but I'm not so sure these days. I told Harriet it'd reveal itself somehow.'

They continue to converse in this wise for several minutes. Lucilla, confused by the oblique references, lets the sentences glide over her head like cartoon speech bubbles. If the headless dummy is unmindful, why, so can she be. Aunt Enid makes tea, and her father tells her he is going to bank up the fire. Lucilla, sitting on the floor, drifts off. Blinking in the gloaming, her hand clasping the dummy's sole peg leg, she comes to with a start. She wonders if her aunt is still here, or if the taxi has come yet to take her home. Tiptoeing downstairs, skipping the two doddery steps that creak complainingly when you put your weight on them, she strains her ears. She can decipher their voices, though both are quelled now as if they have grown tired, intimate. The hall light is off. The front room standard lamp is on though. This and the glow from the hearth filter through the crack in the door. Holding her breath, she cranes her neck and peers around it.

Aunt Enid is on her feet riddling the fire with the poker. Facing away from Lucilla, she has taken her jacket off and wears an ecru blouse with tiny pearl buttons down the back. Her bottom is squished into her tight skirt and seems to be straining to split the seams. Her hat is off, and firelight is playing on her loose brown hair, singling out golden strands. It all happens so fast. Her father rises and, with a cry, grabs Aunt Enid by the waist from behind. She drops the poker and yelps as it skids on the tiled hearth. She struggles manically in his embrace. All the while her father mutters all sorts of soppy things, tightening his hold on her. 'Oh you glorious . . . your breasts . . . brbrbr . . .breasts are so, so . . . let me fondle your . . . your . . . oh, oh, the softness of . . . squa– squashy . . . the scent of your hair . . . like satin . . . I want to . . . to . . . to . . . Ooh!' He is kissing her jerking head, her wavy golden-brown hair, and then her white neck. She manages to corkscrew her body in his arms. He is squeezing her like a tube of toothpaste, and Lucilla is sure she will come all squirting out any moment. Then he kisses her full on the mouth. There are some slobbery, wet, smooching noises. Next, an almighty grunt as Aunt Enid brings her knee up into her father's groin. 'Arrgh!' He stumbles back, his steamed-up glasses slipping down his nose. She advances on him. Her hand with its manicured crimson fingernails flies through the air and strikes his cheek with a whack.

'How dare you!' hisses Aunt Enid. Her scarlet lipstick is all smeared over her swollen mouth. And it is smudged across Lucilla's father's lips and his huffing cheeks as well, so that he looks a bit like a black and white minstrel – only red. Her aunt seizes up the poker, shaking it at him and backing towards the door, behind which Lucilla is hiding. 'If my Gethin was alive he'd show you what for. You were never a patch on your brother. He was worth ten of you. He'd teach you a lesson, Gethin would! You filthy sex maniac!'

'I'm sorry. Oooh, Enid, I'm so sorry,' moans her father, the breath coming out of him as if he has several punctures. He collapses into an armchair. His mouth and chin are slick with saliva, making the smudged lipstick gleam wetly. He groans, his chest pumping, his face suffused with blood. And his nose, brow and cheekbones are spotted with fat droplets of sweat. When he speaks again, lips quavering, he sounds as if he has a heavy cold, his words furred and blurring into each other. 'But Enid, Eeenid! Oh, Enid, you must know that I need to . . . want to . . . your body . . . I thought it was . . . mutual. That you wanted . . . The way I feel about you, how much . . . much I need . . .'

'You stay back you pervert or I'll . . . I'll tell Harriet, so help me I will,' threatens Aunt Enid, poker held aloft like a magician's staff. 'How could you? How could you when your poor wife is recovering from a hysterectomy in hospital. She must have been suffering horribly with her womb riddled with fibroids. The agony of it and blowing up like a balloon. But did she complain? Did she complain? Hardly ever. She is a saint that woman, a veritable saint. And what do you do when she haemorrhages, collapses and nearly bleeds to death and they have to give her an emergency hysterectomy, poor darling, you try to seduce your sister in law. You are despicable.' She slashes at the air with the poker and Lucilla's father ducks, then jumps back out of reach. Lucilla does not know what a hysterectomy is, but there isn't time to dwell on this conundrum. The action in the front room is commanding all her attention.

'No, no, please don't. I beseech you. Enid, we could have so . . . so much . . . I could bring you to an ec– ec– ecst– ecsta–. Oh, oh, oh, oh!' Then spontaneously he bursts into noisy, snotty tears. 'Forgive me. Please forgive me. I thought perhaps you . . . you – But no, no of course you don't. How could you? It won't happen again, Enid. You have to believe me. I don't know –'

Lucilla does not linger to learn more. In the semi-darkness, she climbs the stairs as she descended them, soft-stepping, avoiding the loose-tongued boards. She scurries back to her bedroom, hesitating only for an instant to sidestep the headless dummy.

Chapter 18

Harriet, 1959

Barbara is staying for tea again. She is such a dear, dear girl. Eleven years old. The same age as Lucilla, but the two of them couldn't be less alike. Barbara is contented, such a nice stay-at-home child, so content, whereas Lucilla is as restless as the wind. Barbara is tall, with the most lustrous wavy hair and comely eyes – both shades of polished walnut. Lucilla's hair is so fine and straight. You can't do anything with it. It hangs there looking like a limp shower curtain. She loathes me styling it. I've a good mind to perm it one day, get a bit of body into it. And Barbara likes her food, isn't a picky eater either. As do I. A healthy lass, with a healthy appetite. Lucilla is so fussy, prodding and poking and chewing for ages. I think Barbara looks more my daughter than Lucilla ever will. Merfyn says the resemblance between us is uncanny.

'She might be your *real* daughter,' he said after she left last week. 'She's a bonny lass, Mother. And she loves your homely ways, cooking and sewing. It's a rare pleasure to see the two of you, industrious as beavers bustling about the house, visions of womanly serenity.'

He left me to make the tea and went back to his columns of figures humming a tuneful hymn, 'For All the Saints'. Lucilla was sitting hunched on the stairs when I came out with the tray. She was moping as usual. 'What are you sitting there for, face like the back of a bus?' I asked.

She shrugged and wrinkled her nose as if smelling something offensive. Then, 'Where does Barbara live?' she wanted to know.

'You didn't finish your tea,' I accused, sidetracking.

'I don't like macaroni cheese,' she mumbled. 'It's all stodgy.'

'I'm glad Barbara didn't hear you say that,' I told her, now thoroughly out of sorts. 'She made it herself. I thought it was extremely tasty. And wasn't the parsley sprinkled on top such a clever idea? She's going to be a wonderful cook. Why are you still wearing your school uniform?' In the rush I'd forgotten to send her upstairs to change when she got home from school.

'Sorry,' she said routinely.

'Sorry doesn't butter parsnips,' I retorted.

'I'll change in a minute. Where does Barbara live? Where's her mummy and daddy? She doesn't talk about them.' She was dogged. She shrugged her arms inside her grey school cardigan and flexed them.

'Don't do that. You'll stretch the sleeves out of shape. Let me give your father his tea and then I'll tell you.'

When I returned she was still sitting on the stairs in the same place. 'Barbara doesn't have a mummy or a daddy. She's not lucky like you. She lives in a children's home.'

Her expression lifted immediately and her hands reappeared at the ends of her cardigan sleeves. 'A home with nothing but children in it?' she said perkily. 'No adults? None at all?'

'Don't be stupid, Lucilla. Peter Pan and the Lost Boys only happen in those stories you keep filling your head with. Barbara lives at Saint Teresa's, the children's home. You know the one. Not more than a half-hour's walk. They have aunties there, nuns who look after lots of children. It is very difficult because she has to share the aunties. You're lucky. You have a mother all to yourself.'

'Oh.' It peeved me to see Lucilla taking her good fortune for granted like this. Almost as if she'd prefer not to have a mother. Ingratitude!

She personifies ingratitude some days. She has no concept of how favoured she has been, how *she* could have grown up in a home as well. We'll have to tell her the truth soon. Merfyn keeps prevaricating. But she ought to know. It seems to become tougher to talk about it as the years go by. And, of course, it will be a dreadful blow. She might take a while to recover from it. She will be distraught learning that I'm not her actual mother, that Merfyn isn't her actual father. We shan't tell her about the German. That really would be cruelty. But for the rest, ah yes, the day is coming.

'Barbara wants you to go and visit her some time. Play. You could take Rachel and Frank. Make an outing of it.'

'OK,' she said without much enthusiasm.

We could hear the dog's bowl sliding on the lino floor in the kitchen as he licked it hopefully. 'Do you think you could be friends, you and Barbara?'

'I s'ppose,' she said, sounding unconvinced.

Barbara will undoubtedly be a positive influence on Lucilla. She may even bring about the transformation that we have failed so blatantly to do thus far. Lead by example. 'I'd like you to be best friends, you and Barbara. She may come to live with us, you know.' She yanked on the collar of her grey and white checked shirt, uncertainty writ large on her transparent face. I worked harder to persuade her. 'She could be your sister.' She stood up and bit a fingernail uneasily. 'I've told you not to do that. I'll paint your fingers with that bitter medicine if I see it again!' She snatched her hand away from her mouth and I saw that it was ink-stained. One fawn knee-length sock was rumpled around her ankle. And the leather of her brown shoes looked scuffed and dull. She was sorry sight. Hands on hips, I sighed my frustration. She had her school beret in her hand and now she pulled it down over her head like a swimming hat. I felt my temper rising. 'Lucilla,' I prompted, 'what do you think of that? Of

Barbara coming to live here?' She shrugged indifferently. 'Oh, for goodness' sake, do take that thing off your head.' She obliged and the static in her hair caused it to rise up and then settle in snarls. Radio music reached us, Joe Loss with Betty Dale and the Blue Notes singing 'Boo Hoo'. Merfyn called me to pour the tea. 'You'd have to share a bedroom, mind,' I cautioned.

'I don't think I should like that,' she muttered, stonily.

'Well, you might have to settle to it,' I told her, thirsting for that cup of tea, and being glad of the excuse to end this unsatisfactory tête-à-tête. I brooded on things for most of the evening, crunching down in my tribulation on jagged pieces of slab toffee, and making such a rumpus that Merfyn complained. In plain, Barbara is everything Lucilla isn't. She is the daughter I have always wanted, I have always dreamed of having. Lucilla hasn't worked out after all. The trial, and believe me that's what it's been, a trial, is over. Maintaining the pretence that we are a happy family can be terribly wearing. Merfyn would be horrified if he knew how often I've fantasised about taking her back, dumping her unceremoniously on the doorstep of the Church Adoption Society, with a placard tied round her neck that read, 'This child was not as advertised. She has not come up to the standards promised. Please take her back from whence she came.' The nuisance of her seems to increase with every passing week.

And she isn't in the peak of health either, as they had us believe. We were duped. She has earaches constantly, earaches of such severity that she winds up in Great Ormond Street Hospital. She was five when she had the first attack. They sent us straight to St Bartholomew's. When the doctor said we had to take her to a hospital I was stunned. Such a palaver for an earache, for goodness' sake. Surely a few drops of oil of cloves would do the trick, I protested. But no, off we had to go. She was in there for three weeks. Three weeks! I mean to say, the inconvenience of it. But he insisted, saying it was very serious, that she needed these new fangled penicillin injections. They put her in a ladies ward and she made such a din, holding her head and crying and crying. She was giving me earache, let me tell you. I was so embarrassed. The nurse asked if there was a history of ear infections in either of our families. I was offended by the aspersion.

'No such thing,' I informed her vigorously. 'I have a very strong constitution and so does my husband.' Between us, Lucilla, the epitome of a sickly waif, howled her discomfort. This was the forerunner of many infections. She's been admitted to hospital four times. The doctor says she has a predilection for ear infections. A congenital weakness if you like. Well, I don't like it at all. I thought she was perfect. That's what they told us. Recommended for adoption. This is the very thing that gave me pause when Merfyn had his brainwave. He sold it to me, made it seem so attractive, the ideal solution to completing our childless marriage. Back then I was concerned. Now? Depressing is how I view the future.

I realise with her condition that I should exercise restraint when it comes to boxing her ears. But she so riles me I can't stop myself. I whipped her with the dog lead last week. I wasn't having any more of her backchat, so I thrashed her with it and locked her in the cellar. It must have done some good because after I let her out she was a veritable angel. Merfyn says we must keep trying with her, making an effort. But, the other day, I came upon her kissing a boy behind the hedge of her junior school. I was so ashamed. If she behaves like this at primary school, what are we going to have to deal with when she starts at the secondary modern in a few months? When I interrogated her, the excuse she offered was that she wanted to know what it felt like. How do you discipline a child who says such evil things? I clouted her and sent her to her room. But no punishment seems to have any effect. And this business of trousers, she won't give up on it. I don't believe I'll ever make a lady of her.

It's because of how she's turned out that I want to adopt Barbara. She's grown up properly, respectful, accommodating. She won't just slip into our lives, she'll augment them. She adores sewing besides. We are making a dress together, a project I thought would bring us closer. She said that she was happy for me to choose the fabric and pattern, that she trusted my taste. Well, I was so pleased. I chose a bombazine, the design, blue and green squares criss-crossed with fine red lines. And for the pattern, full-skirted, a fitted bodice and a wide lapel collar. It's all pinned in place and ready to cut out. Barbara says that she can't wait. I want her to come with us to a temperance meeting. I told her all about them and she said that she would love to, that she thought she'd like the activities. I don't foresee *her* spending most of the evening doing penance outside in the street.

She likes to make an effort with her appearance. We spend long hours brushing her hair. We tried braiding it with a pretty chiffon scarf the other day and, although it was fiddly, agreed that the effect was worthwhile. I am also teaching her all my recipes. We made a lemon drizzle cake that Merfyn couldn't stop praising. He very nearly finished it off at one sitting. She rolls up her sleeves and gives me a hand with the cleaning. She says she likes the smells: Mansion floor polish, Sunlight soap, Bluebell metal polish, Min cream, Kelso, even Shanks porcelain cleanser, bless her.

'I like bringing up the brass until it gleams like gold, Mrs Pritchard,' she says, buffing the polish off my round-top brass table. She washes the kitchen floor, puts the carpet sweeper over the rug, wipes down the fridge, gives the Mainamel cooker a scrub as if she's in utopia. She loves curling up with a *real* book, *Mrs Beeton's Book of Household Management*. Lucilla's barely glanced at it. It's not a story, she protested when I gave it to her. Strewth! We sit together doing embroidery, while Lucilla begs me to let her go haring about outside. There's only one snag. Barbara seems to have something of a phobia about dogs. When we told her that we had pet, a mongrel, the colour drained from her face and her pallor went a shade of milky green, an indicator of how queasy she felt.

'Oh, I don't like animals, Mrs Pritchard. Really I don't,' she said. She'll have to stop calling me Mrs Pritchard soon.

'Oh, but you won't mind our dog. He's called Scamp. We bought him for Lucilla from Pentonville Market,' Merfyn elaborated. 'You'll soon get used to him.'

'No. No, I won't! They make me come over all peculiar.' She shivered out the words. We were walking in the gated courtyard of the home. But then she halted and shrank away from us, as if somehow we carried the taint of Scamp on our clothes.

'Oh, he's terribly friendly. He hasn't bitten anyone.' As Merfyn spoke he laid a calming hand on her quaking shoulder. But he had said the wrong thing.

Barbara cringed. 'Nasty creatures. I can't stand to think of the dirty fur and sharp teeth.' She was breathing rapidly and we could both see that she wasn't putting it on. Unlikely as it is, the girl is petrified of dogs. We coaxed her over to a wooden bench and sat her down.

'Now don't go upsetting yourself,' I quietened her. 'It's easy enough for us to shut the dog up when you come to the house.'

'That's right, Mother,' placated Merfyn. 'We'll put him in the front room or in the garden.' Sandwiched between us she nodded, her expression grim.

'We'll tell Lucilla that you're scared of dogs. She'll understand,' I promised. It was autumn and the leaves were falling. The sky was a heavy battleship grey. Sitting there with the daughter who was perfect, all but for the phobia of dogs, I had a twinge, a misgiving.

Barbara raised her head and found my eyes, her own bleak, her complexion now pale and clammy. She smoothed back a pigtail. There were other children from the home playing skipping games and catch.

Their voices chimed together like a chorus of bells. Beyond the gates that gave the building, however grand the stucco facade, the atmosphere of a prison, traffic lumbered by. 'If I come though,' she uttered querulously when at last she could speak, 'if I come and stay, if I come and live in your home, you will get rid of it.' She licked her dry lips and inhaled unsteadily. 'You will get rid of the dog, send it away.'

I glanced from her to Merfyn. We both knew that no person on earth would persuade Lucilla to part with her dog. 'Well dear,' I consoled her patting her back, 'we can organise that later, can't we? Let's see how we go on?'

'Mother knows best,' Merfyn joked, weakly.

She scratched her eyebrow and I could tell that she was pondering our offer against the threat of the dog. 'All right,' she assented, timidly. She was wearing a smart button-over brown tweed coat. Her hand grappled for the belt buckle and she seemed to hang on to it.

'Well done,' said Merfyn, getting up and moving so that he faced her. 'That's my brave girl.'

'I'm not really, and I shan't ever be able to live in a house with a dog running free. But I'll come, if you swear I won't have to be near it.'

Merfyn nodded and gave her a hand up. And after that she did seem to rally somewhat. No, it was me who felt despondent as we walked back. I glanced over my shoulder once. Barbara had melted into a crowd of girls, each taking turns to jump the skipping rope two of them were swinging. I thought I spotted her head, taller than the rest, moving among the throng. In that brief glimpse I also saw a girl with gingery curls, and a thin girl, her blonde hair pulled back in a ponytail. I wondered about them as well, if they might be a safer bet, if they didn't mind dogs. Should we have another go? Tell Barbara it was we who had changed our minds. It could go on forever. Perhaps, I reflected, as we strolled up Leicester Road, I was being unduly pessimistic. Didn't matter what she said, she was only a child. She hadn't handled a dog, that was all. If Scamp was the only stumbling block I wouldn't have hesitated to rehome him – but for Lucilla.

'What if she doesn't get over it?' I said. 'What if the dog is a real problem?'

'Oh, Mother, don't be so negative. We're new to her, and she's new to us.' Merfyn linked his arm through mine. 'You like her, don't you?'

'Yes, of course I do.' I adjusted my hat. 'I want it to go well, for her to feel part of the family, that's all.'

'And it will,' Merfyn insisted. 'You know Barbara may be the very thing our family needs, Mother. A friend for Lucilla, especially now she's growing up, and a companion for you. She's a reliable down-to-earth sort, apart from the hitch with the dog. But, mark my words, a month or so down the line and she'll be walking Scamp with Lucilla, and rowing with her over who is going to scratch his tummy.'

I so wanted it to be a success. I wanted Barbara to be the right one, the one we should have got in first place. I'd work on her dress that evening and I'd have it ready for the next temperance meeting. I'd make sure that she was the star of it, that she was noticed. At least with her she was ready-made. We could see what we were getting. We had a lot in common. I felt a kinship and I had a hunch that she did too.

'This daughter, our Barbara, is going to be a tick in the credit column,' I told Merfyn with a proud smile. He held my eyes for a moment and then we both looked away. I knew what he was thinking, because I was thinking the same. Lucilla was a cross in the debit column.

Chapter 19

Lucilla, 1959

She is watching *Crackerjack* when the visitor calls, sitting at the dining table, which has been laid up for tea. On the lighted screen there are three children standing on a block of wood, while Eamonn Andrews quizzes them. The skinny boy with the sticking-up hair, who she thought was going to win, gives an incorrect answer. He is presented with a cabbage. Lucilla is having a fit of laughter when she hears the doorknocker.

'Folks coming for tea. Folks coming for tea,' her mother cheep-cheeps. She bustles from the kitchen, wiping her hands on her apron, keeping up the repetitive bird cry all the way to the front door. Although Eamonn Andrews has her ear, Lucilla does strain from the muffled voices that her parents are penning up Scamp in the front room. The guest, inexplicably, doesn't like dogs. It is the Barbara girl coming for tea again and she doesn't like dogs. How can anyone not like dogs? Lucilla conjectures, astonished. How can anyone not worship Scamp? Why, he is all wagging tail and licks and bounces. He is a crumpet-hot smile on four furry legs.

Then her mother and her father enter and stand with Barbara between them. She is done up like a birthday cake, Lucilla observes. She studies her dress critically. It is gathered at the waist and the frilly white petticoat can be glimpsed underneath the skirt. There are buttons that look like sugar icing flowers down the front of the bodice, which is trimmed with yards of lace. The collar and the bell sleeves are also adorned with lace. The fabric is a deep pink printed in coloured balloons. Lucilla imagines a hoop of birthday candles sticking out of Barbara's head, and thinks they would look like a matching accessory. Maddened that her programme is being interrupted, she is visited by a vision. Candles burning down and setting that abundant brown hair alight. The corners of her lips turn up. All this comes to her in a blink.

'Lucilla, Barbara's here.' Her parents speak in unison as though they have been rehearsing. 'Say hello.'

'Hello.' Robotically, Lucilla does as she is instructed, though her turquoise eyes are on the television that her mother is about to switch off.

'Hello,' returns Barbara. Her tone is neutral, her rectangular-shaped face devoid of any expression.

'Don't you look pretty in that charming frock, Barbara?' This is her mother, eyeing the creation the girl is dressed in with undisguised approbation.

'Thank you.' Barbara beams, twirling a bit so that her skirt and petticoat swish out.

'Did you put it on specially?' asks her father, his eyes round and glistening with veneration behind his smudged lenses.

'Yes,' says Barbara still twirling. 'I wanted to dress up for you.'

'How thoughtful,' her mother says with a nod. 'Appearances are most important. I might have a length of ribbon long enough to trim the hem. How about that?' she entices.

'Oh, that is frightfully kind of you,' says Barbara, her voice sugary and sticky as strawberry jam. Lucilla is of the opinion that if any more decoration is put on the frock, the guest will look as though she really is a birthday cake.

'Why don't you two go into the garden and play while I'm making the tea?' suggests her mother.

'But *Crackerjack* is on,' protests Lucilla. Her tone is full of entreaty. Her own shift in a plain teal cotton is cinched in at her slender waist with a thin cream belt. Up and down goes her mother's chest, indignant heave after indignant heave. Her father pulls on his ear lobe, then waggles a finger in his ear.

'You can see your programme another day,' her mother says, stoutly. She deliberately blocks the television screen as Eamonn Andrews fades away.

'Now don't be rude, Lucilla,' her father rebukes. 'Off you go into the garden, and Mother will call you when tea is served.'

'Are you sure you don't need any help preparing the meal?' asks Barbara, currying favour in the most sickly of fashions in Lucilla's view. Nevertheless she hopes that her mother does. But no, she says that it is quite all right. Another day. But how well mannered of Barbara to offer.

They go out into the garden. It is a fresh spring day, the sunshine filtering down through streaks of feathery grey cloud, providing pleasing intermittent warmth. They walk along the crazy-paving path her mother laid, the path that seems to meander but lead nowhere. 'Do you like *Crackerjack*?' Lucilla canvasses, still feeling the smart of deprivation.

'I don't watch much television,' Barbara returns primly.

'Oh!' Lucilla is stumped for a second, but then she recovers, sure they will root out a common enthusiasm. 'I love *Champion the Wonder Horse* and *The Lone Ranger*. When he shouts "Hi-yo, Silver! Away!" and when that magnificent horse rears up it gives me goosebumps.'

'Does it?' says Barbara, as if rearing horses are awfully boring. She yawns so that Lucilla can see a shiny metal filling in her teeth.

'Also *Tenderfoot* and *Bronco*.' Lucilla is feeling awkward. Besides, she doesn't really want to talk to this intruder. 'Did you see the film *Smiley*?' A look from Barbara that signifies she does not watch films either. Lucilla carries on staunchly. 'It's all about a man who buys a bike for his grandson. And he has these adventures on it, running up against criminals, selling drugs and things. It's very exciting.'

Barbara gives her a disdainful sidelong look. Lucilla squats down to examine a caterpillar making its way along a rose stem, having gorged itself on new mint-green leaves. 'You could come to the Saturday morning pictures with me if you fancy it,' Lucilla offers, her attention riveted on the rhythmic propulsion of the caterpillar. The creamy fat segments concertina and then expand. It is like a letter on the run from the alphabet, making a break for it. 'I could ask my cousins to come along too. Their names are Rachel, she's thirteen, and Frank, he's fourteen. You'll like Rachel. She's kind. Frank can be rather mean sometimes but I ignore him. What do you think?'

'I don't mind,' says Barbara, neutrally, walking toe to heel down the path.

Her mother is delighted when Lucilla announces that they have made plans to go the pictures together the following Saturday, that she will ask the cousins to join them.

'Oh, splendid. Getting to know the extended family. That's right,' she says.

There are three cinemas close by, the Rex in East Finchley, known as the Flea Pit, the Gaumont in North Finchley and the Odeon in Muswell Hill. They settle on the Odeon. Right up until the last minute Frank threatens to go trainspotting instead of joining them. This is fine with Lucilla who would prefer he didn't come. But thanks to her mother's appeals, to her insistence that she wants her nephew to meet super-duper Barbara, he is persuaded. Now she comes to think of it, Frank and her mother have been conspiring a lot recently. She has no idea what all their whispering is about, but she has felt her cousin's cold eyes lingering on her a lot of late. It as if he has a secret, that her mother has shared a secret with him.

They meet Barbara there. On the way, Lucilla generously uses all her pocket money to buy them sweets. And she pays for their tickets with the allowance her father has given her. They cost a staggering nine pence each. She shudders as she pays out the grand total of three shillings and sixpence to the box-office attendant. She is relieved to see that Barbara doesn't look quite so frilly today, trotting up to them in a serviceable blue dress with a russet-brown collar and cuffs. Frank stands apart from the party as they make their introductions, giving Barbara a lofty nod when she shyly glances his way. The cousins notice her blushing, and immediately start chuckling and casting lovesick looks at one another.

They sit in a middle row. Frank, then Barbara, who nips between him and Rachel, and lastly Lucilla, plumped in the end seat before the aisle. She divides up the sweets as they settle themselves into the worn velvet seats. They are surrounded by countless other munching children as the Saturday morning shows are popular. When the lights go down an expectant hush falls. The curtains draw back as the eerie glowing funnel finds the screen. In Lucilla's lap is her bag of sugary delights: sherbet dabs, pineapple cubes, rhubarb and custard sweets, chews and toffees. She has splashed out and they all have Tizer to drink, ensuring they have a hyped-up edge to their appreciation of the entertainment.

As the main feature, a Western, opens with some atmospheric twanging guitar chords, Lucilla wriggles her shoulders. She is quite overcome with the thrill of it all. She inhales the stale-tobacco air, tainted with the hundreds of thousands of cigarettes smoked by adults at the evening showings. It is almost too much for her, this intimate nebulous setting and the euphoria it induces, this glimpse into fabulous America in the days when men built railways and warred with Indians. She glances to her right at the blur of Rachel's profile. Her cousin's wide eyes are fixed on the silvery screen, her jaw rotating with the determination of a cement mixer. Beyond her, Barbara is an ice maiden, looking braced rather than wide-eyed with heady anticipation, as if she is about to undergo the extraction of a deep splinter with tweezers and a needle.

Throughout the film the youthful audience are spellbound, their sparkling eyes held by the giant flickering screen. Hands move from paper bags to mouths, from mouths to paper bags with a good deal of rustling. Ears prick to the tantalising hissy crackle of the spinning film reel. Galloping horses, their hammering hooves churning up the dust, cloudy snakes whittling out a passage across vast wastelands, prickly cactus rising from the desert like alien beings, cowboys' hats pulled low against the blistering sun, gravelly voices thrumming in dry parched throats, frolicking saloon girls with plunging cleavages and feathers woven in their bouffant hairdos, chairs kicked back in a moment of tension, gunfighters' arms akimbo itching to draw, the slide of metal from leather – too fast to see. And bang-bang! A man keels over, dead. Lucilla revels in the thrill of it, the life and death drama. It is, she decides, chomping busily, sublime.

But now there is an interval in which the operator must change the reel. The spell is broken and the children grow restive. They start to boo and call out. Someone blows a loud raspberry. Cackles of laughter ensue. 'Why are we waiting,' belts out one bold boy and others sing along, the chant swelling. Feet begin stamping, only a few to start with, and then more until the auditorium echoes with the human stampede.

'They're taking ages,' grumbles Lucilla, drumming her own feet.

'Don't be so impatient,' Frank reproves, his teenage voice breaking in the darkness.

'What are they doing?' Barbara is spooked, as if they have found a log's worth of splinters running the length of her arm and amputation is the only cure.

And while Frank launches into a detailed breakdown of what precisely is involved in changing a film reel, Rachel leans over Lucilla. Lips tickling her ear, she whispers, 'Barbara loves Frank.' The two cousins collapse into each other, helpless with mirth. The lights suddenly come up and the manager, Mr Babbage, materialises through the red velvet curtains of the main auditorium entrance. A short sweaty man in a creased suit, he trots down the aisle to face the troublemakers. Rays from the lamps reflects off his shining bald pate, and off the metallic grey polyester of his jacket.

Centre stage, he briskly claps his hands. 'Now just settle down. Do you hear me, settle down. We'll have none of this tomfoolery at the Odeon. I won't stand for it, d'you hear,' he remonstrates in high nasal notes, nose in the air. 'I'm the manager of this establishment and I won't put up with it.'

Who pitches the first sweet, a pineapple cube? Who has the sheer pluck? Who is the anarchist? It is Lucilla, who else. She is halfway up in her seat. There are hot spices in her blood and soldier ants on the march in her toes. In the arc of her arm is the energy of a flying cannonball. All that William Tell archery practice on cousin Rachel has paid off. Her aim is true. Plick! The sugar pellet strikes the baldhead and rebounds. The children hack out their laughs between wolf whistles. More boisterous singing. The manager gesticulates wildly. His short arms karate-chop the dimly lit, stifling air of cavernous theatre. The giant shadows of his stubby limbs leap on the ornately moulded walls.

'Pipe down. That's quite enough. You put a stop to this racket right now. Do you hear me, settle down. I am not having this sort of vandalism in the Odeon.' The children are hyenas, hacking with laughter. More missiles adroitly aimed by other rebels ping off him. He raises an arm to shield his face. He is being stoned with lumps of sugar. Lucilla feels a restraining hand on her elbow.

'Sit down and behave!' rasps Frank, on his feet and louring over her, gusting aniseed breath. 'You're a disgrace!' She wrenches herself away. 'Your parents will have something to say about this.'

'Not if you don't tell them,' Lucilla yells back.

'Oh but I shall,' he menaces.

'Telltale tit! Your tongue will split! And all the little birdies shall have a little bit!' taunts Lucilla, brazenly.

'Ouch! That's my toe, Frank,' squeaks Rachel. 'You stepped on me. Sit back down.'

Muttering angrily that he would rather be on the platform of Clapham Junction jotting down train numbers, Frank returns to his seat.

'I don't like this, really I don't,' whimpers Barbara, her remark ignored by all three of her companions.

'Now pay attention children,' Mr Babbage continues, plucky under fire. 'There will be no second half, no cartoons, no Mickey Mouse if you carry on like this. The show will finish right now.' More screams of hilarity and brandishing of fists in the air, peppered liberally with a few rude signs.

'Frank, I want to go home,' Barbara bleats. 'Take me home!'

'You don't have a home,' hoots Lucilla, gaily.

'Oh dry up you stupid cow!' Frank rebuffs, ungallantly, talking over Lucilla, his forbearance at an end.

'Oh how could you? How rude. I'm so . . . so miserable!' mewls Barbara, clinging tenaciously to his arm.

'I'm not having a ball either – so what!' snarls Frank, trying to shake her loose. 'Get off me.'

'Oh, oh, and you were so nice!' snivels Barbara. Though unused to callous teenage boys, she adheres to him as a shoreline limpet does to a rock.

'What's wrong?' asks Rachel, having lost track, distracted by the growing turmoil around her.

'There. Have my sweets and put a sock in it!' belts out Frank, thrusting his bag into Barbara's lap, and disentangling himself from her with a less than chivalrous shove.

Lucilla, the spirit of the revolution flowing through her blood, shouts at her guest. 'Don't be such a baby, Barbara!' Barbara crumples in a gush of ungainly tears. But Lucilla doesn't have time for sympathy. She is on a mission, off racing down the aisle, a sherbet fountain grasped threateningly in her hand. All around her come cries of encouragement. 'Go to it.' 'You get the stuck-up prig.' 'Give it to him.' Only yards from her prey, she crouches down. For a pin she pulls out the stick of liquorice, and carefully teases apart the paper seam of her sherbet grenade. She takes aim then hurls it with all her strength at Mr Babbage. She scores a direct hit. His mouth is open. The words flying from it are sent scurrying back on a flurry of lemon powder, generating a fit of fizzy coughing. It adheres to his sweat-slicked features, and it coats his suit jacket and his tie, as though he has been dipped in flour.

Amidst the uproar, he blinks, sights his attacker and gives chase. They circle the seats, their shoes pounding the carpet. He stumbles. She dashes down one of the rows. He clambers after her, over hurdles of instantly straightened legs. She thunders along paths rapidly cleared of obstructive limbs. Lucilla is panting, alive with the high voltage of pure adrenalin coursing through her. But he is closing on his quarry fast. When she is caught up by her collar and frog-marched out of the theatre she is not in the least cowed. She puffs her chest out, her ears burning with the many echoes of exuberant praise. She is a heroine to her fellow cinema-goers. She gulps in a breath, winded by the lightning speed of her rise to fame. Mr Babbage, flushed with his exertion and wheezing asthmatically, deposits her unceremoniously outside the doors of his establishment.

'You're banned from the Odeon,' he decrees. Arms up, he indicates that like Adam and Eve she is banished forever from the cinematic Eden, for she has tasted of the forbidden fruits of insubordination. 'Banned, you little thug. Banned! Got that, squirt,' he hollers, whisking hands dusting the sherbet off his clothes. He turns his back on the vagabond and pushes the heavy swing doors open. He is about to stride through them in belated and albeit sherbet-dusted victory, when the perpetrator of this dastardly crime jeers back.

'Don't care if I am! Don't care a jot! I'll go to the Rex instead. It's better than this crummy dump any day.'

He is robbed of speech, gaping at the insult as he wheels back on her. But, fleet of foot, she has scampered down the street. She mooches about for ten minutes, before she finds Rachel and Barbara taking cover in the sheltered doorway of a jeweller's. Her cousin is trying unsuccessfully to pacify Barbara. The orphan's cheeks are smudged with tears, and yellow pineapple and rosy rhubarb dribble.

'There you are, Lucilla,' says Rachel, thankfully. 'We came after you but you'd gone. You were brilliant. That odious manager looked a riot all covered in sherbet. Did the rotter do anything to you?'

'Nah, I was too quick for him,' Lucilla assures, cockily, outlaw blood still pumping in her veins. Then as an afterthought she adds with pride, 'Banned me from the Odeon.'

'Oh what bad luck!' says Rachel offering her a Black Jack from the few sweets she has left in her pocket.

'Thanks,' says Lucilla, aglow with pride. She unwraps it and pops it in her mouth.

'Frank's going to snitch,' Rachel adds dejectedly. 'I told him not to, but he said Aunt Harriet should know.' A pause while this blow sinks in. Barbara gives a dry sob. Temporarily forgotten they both glance at her, as does the jeweller shooing them away through the display window.

Lucilla gives him a Black and White Minstrel wave. 'Frightfully pretty rings,' she mouths through the glass. 'When I get engaged I'll come back.' She mimes putting one on her finger and admiring it, before returning her attention to her cousin. 'Oh well,' she sighs philosophically, 'Barbara would have blabbed anyway. Still, I'm in no hurry to go home,' she adds, grinning.

'What d'you . . . d'you have to go and do it for,' stutters shell-shocked Barbara, her breathing still rapid, her shoulders rocking with ugly emotions she has not previously experienced, closeted in the safe disciplined confines of Saint Teresa's.

'Aw, it was only a bit of fun,' yips Lucilla, giving her a mock punch. Barbara flinches. But Lucilla shrugs it off good-humouredly. Her heart is still throbbing with the delirious empowering joy of it. 'Did you see his face? Wow! He was steaming he was so mad.'

Barbara casts a mournful eye over a display of watches and wilts. 'But he threw you out. We didn't get to watch the cartoons. And that was the only bit I really wanted to see.'

'Didn't you enjoy the Western?' Lucilla wants to know, her cup definitely half full, her indomitable spirit busting to bestride this petty world. Her tongue by this time is stained from the Black Jack, and her lips are coated with dark saliva, giving her a gothic attraction.

'No, I was really fed up actually. Nothing but horses and guns.'

'How can you say that?' exclaims Lucilla, incredulous that anyone could not be a fan of Westerns. Horses and guns! And those incredible cactus, tall as prickly people. Could you honestly ask for more, she ruminates. 'Did either of you throw any of your sweets at him?' she inquires innocently, hoping to have led by example.

'Three Parma violets,' Rachel confesses shyly. 'And . . . and I'm almost certain one hit him.'

'Oh brilliant,' congratulates Lucilla, reflecting if she only achieved one convert then all is not in vain.

Barbara shakes the brown paper bag she is clutching by the neck. 'Of course not. It was a dreadful thing to do. And I've had a perfectly horrid morning.'

'Oh don't start up again, Barbara,' says Lucilla, her tone defiantly unrepentant, the bright sides of this unlooked for day revealing themselves to her like a many-faceted diamond. 'Because I had a blast. Though I'm still hungry. Typical, I dropped my sweets in the rush.' She has finished the Black Jack and wouldn't mind a second.

'You can have all of mine, so there.' Barbara shoves hers towards Lucilla. 'I'm not feeling well.'

'Pity.' Lucilla seizes the bag and rifles inside. 'You've still got your sherbet dip. That's fantastic.' Her happiness is complete. She fishes it out and proceeds to dip and suck contemplatively. 'Do you want some?' she says, offering round the chewed liquorice stick. A generous helping of sherbet is welded to it with her grey saliva. Rachel accepts with alacrity but Barbara's oatmeal complexion takes on a greenish tinge.

'No thanks. I truthfully do feel sick. I might chuck up any moment.'

'Oh how beastly. You better not do it here. Where shall we go now?' says Lucilla, sucking with relish. Her eyes rove about the busy street looking for inspiration.

'Nowhere.' Barbara pouts. 'My hands are all sticky and I can't wash them.' Her voice breaks with the ghastliness of it.

'Oh crumbs, don't go crying again,' pleads Lucilla. 'My hands are sticky, too. See.'

'So are mine,' says Rachel in solidarity with her cousin. They hold them up to prove it.

'Oh, that doesn't make me feel any better.' Barbara's face spasms, and her eyes well up.

'We could go to a park and look out for a pond to wash in.' To Lucilla the remedy seems logical, but Barbara is aghast.

'You're not allowed. Besides,' she hiccups tragically, 'the ponds are full of duck poo and diseases. It's very dangerous. I'm going back to the home.'

'Do you want us to come with you?' asks Lucilla, hoping that she doesn't, that they are about to offload the tedious and temperamental Barbara.

'No fear!' Barbara replies adamantly. 'I have to get back anyway. I'm going shopping with one of the nuns this afternoon.'

Neither of them make a move to impede her exit. In fact they both stand aside and make way.

'Do you want to come again next week?' Lucilla calls after her as she weaves her way through the weekend throng. But answer comes there none, only a backwards look generously sprinkled in malice. However, retribution is swift on her return home. Frank has lived up to his reputation and grassed her up. Her father, on a mission for the Ever Ready Company, is not present to moderate her mother's wrath. Punch drunk from the blows to her head, she sits on her bedroom floor, stroking Scamp. Her left ear is throbbing, and it feels as if someone is spearing her eardrum with a scalding fork. She drops her head, lifts one of Scamp's silky ear flaps, winces and whispers, 'But it was worth it, Scamp. Oh boy, was it worth it!'

Unfortunately though, being bounced from the Odeon does not put paid to Barbara's visits. As spring gives herself to summer and the flower beds of the London parks fill up with geraniums and marigolds, Barbara seems to snuggle ever closer into the Pritchards' family unit. Lucilla comes home at least twice a week to find Scamp tethered up like a criminal in the stocks, and Barbara and her mother busy with some domestic project that fills her with tedium. She now regularly attends all the temperance meetings with them and everyone loves her.

Barbara! Isn't she a boon, they all say. Such a willing, sociable girl, so tidy and comely. So mild in nature. Lucilla's parents parade about like farmers showing off a prize heifer. Her father holds his lapels and unzips his stained teeth in sickening smiles. Her mother picks up one of Barbara's thick plaits. She weighs it in her hand as if such is the fantastic quality of the hair she is considering selling it to a wigmaker.

Before long Barbara is a monitor on the high table, taking notes at the meetings. She starts to win the sewing competitions, and her fine embroidery work is admired by young and old. Frank, earlier in the year immune to her feminine wiles, is now definitely taking note of her. As the esteem in which the Brothers and Sisters of Temperance hold her grows, he deigns to engage her in conversation. Lucilla gauges the depth of his feeling by the access he gives Barbara to his stamp albums and numerous collections. The Saturday they set off train-spotting together she reckons her cousin is truly smitten.

Then one autumn day during a visit from Barbara, a day like any other Lucilla assumes, Scamp escapes. He is shut in the front room, reprieved from being tied up in the garden for once. Her mother and Barbara are washing up diligently, talking about scouring saucepans until you can see your face in them – though why you should want to Lucilla has no idea. She is pleased to have successfully absconded from what she deems a tiresome, repetitive task. Campfires, paper plates and cups, that's the way to go, she decides. Sitting at the kitchen table, her mind moves around an imaginary farmyard. The pencil in her hand slides smoothly, swiftly, as though it has been oiled. She is drawing farm animals, pigs with their slobbery snouts and a cockerel spruced up in splendid plumage. She wants to get out her paints and bring the rooster to life with reds and browns and ochre shades. But she knows it is too late in the evening for her mother to permit it.

Then comes the piercing scream, the kind of scream, identifies Lucilla, which you might give if you were being stabbed to death.

Wishful thinking, she decides, as she springs to her feet and runs into the kitchen. Jail-dog, Scamp, has snuck out of the front room. He made a *pad* for it while her father, in an abstraction of facts and figures, wandered into the hall to fetch his briefcase. On the scent of the new-person-in-his-territory, nostrils aquiver, he heads for the kitchen. Once there, discerning its source, he hurls himself at Barbara. Jumping up as he knows he mustn't, he cycles his front paws frantically in an attempt to conquer this challenging summit. Sniffing her panic sends his highly sensitive olfactory receptors into mayhem.

Arriving on the scene, Lucilla stares agog. There is a lunatic in their kitchen, one shriek following another as they ascend scale after scale, a choir's worth of panic-stricken arpeggios. Barbara's arms whip-crack about, striking anything within reach, including Lucilla's astounded mother, who recoils as her face is slapped. Barbara's pigtails thrash. Her limbs grow rigid then jerk violently and her mouth froths obscenely, as if, Lucilla hazards wishfully, she has swallowed poison. Her mother tries to grab the rabid girl, to contain her, only to be hit afresh, this time a clenched fist gonging against her breastbone. Lucilla rushes forwards and scoops up the bouncing dog.

'He's just a dog being friendly,' she lulls the crazed Barbara. 'Scamp only wants to say hello to you.' Her tone is all innocence as she offers the mass of paddling fur. But the devil bat, waiting in the wings of her life, has chosen this instant to claim her soul. 'You can pet him if you want,' she coaxes, thrusting the canine weapon into Barbara's gibbering face. The screaming becomes a stifled squawk and the arms slish-slash the air, doing petrified semaphore. 'Take it away! Take it away! Oh, oh, take it away!' Her father blunders in like a policeman from the Keystone Kops – without a truncheon but just as useless. And then the blood leaks out of Barbara's face as if she has just been juiced, her legs go from under her and she passes out, her body hitting the floor with a resounding bang.

Scamp, streaking about like a greyhound hare racing, is caught and fettered anew. Barbara is brought round with smelling salts, and smacks to the face, liberally supplied, Lucilla notes with a twinkle, by her mother. A cup of heavily sugared tea is drunk in a deafening silence. And then without more ado, and to be fair there has been plenty of ado already, her father takes her back to the home. As the bruises appear on her mother's face, like photo-sensitive paper washed in developing fluid, so Barbara, the imminent addition to the Pritchard household, is repatriated into St Teresa's Children's Home for good and all.

Chapter 20

Bethan, 1961

The woman standing on the doorstep was irate, florid of face, breathing at a furious pace, brandishing the torn pinafore in her hand like a sabre. 'Well? Well? What do you have to say about this, Mrs Sterry? That's what your daughter Lowrie got up to at school today. If you don't believe me, you call her down and ask her. Tell her, Rhiannon, tell Mrs Sterry what occurred.'

On cue, the girl with the freckled face and short pigtails stepped forwards. She delivered her speech in a singsong voice, as though she had been going over it all the way to the farm. 'I was standing in the lunch queue and suddenly Lowrie Sterry shoved me over. She said I pushed in, but I never. As I fell, I heard a rip. When I went to the toilet, I saw what she'd done to my uniform.' Performance completed, she took a deep breath and fell back. Her mother emphatically nodded her approval, the tight auburn curls springing against her wrinkled brow.

'What did I say? There you have it, Mrs Sterry. My Rhiannon doesn't tell lies. If she says that your Lowrie did it, it's true. What I want to know is what you're going to do about it. It was new this term, her pinafore was. And it cost a bob or two. I can't mend a big tear like this.' She folded her arms across her indignantly heaving bosom, her pretty headscarf fluttering in the autumnal breeze. Then she delivered her coup de grace. 'I want reparation.'

'Oh, Mrs Jenkins, won't you come in and have a cup of tea,' I appeased, opening the front door wider. 'It's so cold and I've just baked some scones. And I've a pot of home-made jam and a bit of newly churned butter.'

'No, I'm afraid I can't stay,' Mrs Jenkins said, ferreting in her cardigan sleeve for her hanky and blowing her nose contemptuously. 'The animals, I've an allergy you know.' Her daughter, who was teasing Red with a stick, obviously had not inherited her mother's susceptibility.

'I'm sorry to hear that, Mrs Jenkins. Another time maybe,' I offered, my heart pattering in anxiety.

'Your daughter has a temper on her, Mrs Sterry. It's not my affair, I know. And generally speaking I do not believe in interfering with the methods mothers use to discipline their children.' Red yelped as Rhiannon poked him. Distracted for a moment, Mrs Jenkins told her daughter to get into the car, a blue Ford Popular parked by the barn. 'You'll get all muddy larking about with that dog, never mind the fleas.' Rhiannon, shoulders slumped in disappointment at having her sport interrupted, slouched back to the car. Her mother watched her progress for a second then resumed, picking up where she left off. 'You really ought to make her behave. It's not right letting a child get away with such rages.' I sighed and gave a weak smile. I felt defeated, and I hadn't yet summoned Lowrie to hear her version of events. 'I shall be buying a new pinafore for Rhiannon, and sending you the bill.'

'That's perfectly fine,' I acquiesced without protest. 'I'll be glad to pay for any damage Lowrie's caused. And I really am very, very sorry.'

'Sorry! Sorry! I should think so too,' Mrs Jenkins said, casting the offending garment on the tiled porch. 'Though it's not much good you saying you're sorry. It's Lowrie who should be apologising. And I'm not the only one who has complained about her recently. That girl needs a lesson in manners. So she does.' Rhiannon honked the car horn. I smiled amenably and opened my hands, still floury from baking, in a gesture of reconcilement. 'If you don't take a firm line with her now you'll be storing up problems for the future. You take heed.' She re-knotted her headscarf and stared down at the crumpled navy pinafore. 'My bill will be in the post and I expect prompt settlement if you don't mind. Good day to you, Mrs Sterry.' I offered her a hand, which she glanced at in disdain, before stalking off to climb into her car and drive away in high dudgeon.

I stood for a lengthy moment, mentally girding up my loins for yet another wearying confrontation with Lowrie. Red padded over and snuffled the ruined garment with interest. I wiped my hands on my apron, and then with resignation I stooped and picked it up. I closed the door on Red. Stepping into the vestibule, I spied Lowrie crouching at the top of the stairs peering down at me through the banisters. 'Lowrie, were you listening to that exchange?' I asked. She shrugged, peering at me with her inscrutable brown eyes. 'You heard what Mrs Jenkins said?' Another shrug, this time more exaggerated. Her hair, dark, thick and unruly, fell across her face curtaining her sullen expression. She made no move to tuck it behind her ears. I crossed to the bottom of the stairs and held up the pinafore, sliding my hand into the slash as if I was pushing it into a wound. 'Did you do this?' I enquired trying to keep the accusatory note from my inflexion. A sulky silence. 'Lowrie, did you do this?' I repeated, losing the struggle to keep my tone level.

'So what if I did?' came the pouty reply. 'She deserved it. She stepped in front of me. Silly bitch!'

'Lowrie! You hush that tongue of yours or I'll tell your father.'

'Don't care if you do.'

'Did it mean that much?' I said, my spirit for this confrontation already flagging.

She tossed her head, released the banisters and pivoted on the step she was perched on so that she faced me. 'I told her to join the back of queue but she ignored me. Well, I wasn't having that and so I pushed her. I didn't plan to rip her stupid dress. It was an accident.' The rounds of her cheeks had darkened to a strawberry blush, and her expression was openly hostile.

'It was wrong. It was wrong to push her. Next time you see Rhiannon I want you to say sorry.'

She looked away from me with undisguised scorn. She was wearing a brown corduroy skirt that she pulled over her knees, humping them against the fabric. 'I shan't,' was all she said.

'I'm going to have to pay for a new pinafore to replace the one you ruined,' I told her. A sudden wave of exhaustion made me want to abandon this futile attempt at instilling some remorse into my daughter. Clearly she felt no regret for what she had done, no guilt. She would undoubtedly do it again if Rhiannon, or anyone else, antagonised her. 'School uniform is awfully pricey,' I disclosed, tears filling my eyes. Lowrie climbed to her feet and deliberately snubbed me, showing me her back. 'I haven't finished, damn you!' I hollered, striking a pathetic chord though I say so myself.

'I've got homework,' came her unlikely excuse, mumbled over her shoulder through her mass of hair.

'You can blinking well use your pocket money to pay half of it.' Her pained sigh was audible. 'And I don't care how many months it takes,' I added with a touch more conviction. But my daughter was already stomping off in the direction of her bedroom. A moment later and her door slammed. I trailed disconsolately into the scullery room, sank into a chair and, elbows propped on the table, rested my throbbing forehead in the palms of my hands. My ears were singing, the precursor to a full blown earache. To think once I had fretted that Lowrie, a self-contained infant, would not venture out of her shell. It seemed she had been biding her time, storing up her resentments.

Her father could see no fault in his daughter. And indeed in his company you might be forgiven for assuming that here was a loving devoted child, who would, as she matured into a woman, prioritise her filial duties. But it was me who was burned by Lowrie's fireworks, me who was called to school because our daughter had bitten another child, and, the teacher told me, shaken, had actually drawn blood. It was me who picked up the pieces of the Wedgwood vase, a rare treasure my mother had given me on my wedding day. Something blue, see. My daughter had thrown it in a temper. I had concealed the breakage from Leslie, hiding the pieces under old newspapers in the rubbish bin. And it was me who played the part of a martyr, clearing up the mess she left her room in after one of her turns. I was called when she had an argument in an art class and hurled a pot of black paint over a friend's painting. I collected her from parties only to be told she was having a tantrum because she hadn't won a prize.

Most distressing of all, her teacher, Miss Duggan, had asked to see me on three occasions in the spring and summer terms. She wanted to discuss Lowrie bullying a new girl who had recently joined the class. She reported to me that my daughter's loutish displays had progressed through name-calling, to pinching, graduating to tripping the child up and sending her flying down a flight of stairs. 'Lowrie was lucky she didn't seriously injure her,' she told me when I arrived to pick the reprobate up from school, clearly shocked by the incident. For this abhorrent act she was justly punished. Miss Duggan made her learn by heart several passages from the Bible, as well as filling a notebook with the line, 'I must be kinder to my classmates and help my friends.'

'Is there something wrong at home?' Mrs Crunn, the headmistress, a wiry astute woman, had put the question solicitously, even tactfully. But I had seen the sharpness in her green eyes. 'Something that might be causing Lowrie distress?' I blinked rapidly and made an effort to look confused, as if I was hurriedly sifting through a file of benign family memories. We stood uncomfortably surveying my daughter wandering the playground kicking at stones. School was finished for the day, but I had been kept behind, an increasingly frequent occurrence, to discuss my Lowrie's latest offence. This time there had been no living casualties. The victim was school property. She had stabbed the nib of her pen into her desk, carved her name into it, leaving the wooden surface permanently scarred. 'Has something upset her? The death of a pet maybe?' she jogged me, eyebrows raised quizzically.

'No,' I replied, eyes avoiding hers. But then, seeing the opportunity for a reprieve I added, 'But living on a farm, I suppose she might have seen something that bothered her.'

'It's just the child seems so angry. There's such a lot of pent-up emotion there. And although I've tried, she refuses to open up.'

'I'll talk to her,' I promised.

'See that you do that, Mrs Sterry,' Mrs Crunn advised sternly. 'It would be a shame if she started secondary school with such a bad attitude. And I have to tell you they may not be as patient or as tolerant as we have been.' I nodded knowing she was speaking the plain truth. Then I went to claim my mutant child, feeling as bleak as the day was.

Now, sitting at the kitchen table, the torn pinafore slung over the back of my chair, I grew aware that my brow was no longer cradled in my hands. Unconsciously, I was drawing the features of her face on the polished veneer with an index finger, Lucilla's face, the face of my gift baby, of my firstborn, the child I had given away. In London that couple have Lucilla. A girl with my blood in her veins, and the imprint of me and of her father, Thorston, tattooed on her very soul. I wondered . . . no, wondered was an inadequate description of my obsession. *Wondered* suggested unsteady vague concepts, flyaway thoughts light as spider's silk. I did not wonder, I agonised over what my daughter looked like today, because today, 14 January, was her thirteenth birthday. Was her hair long or short? How did she like to wear it? Was she a fan of the new fads in music? What was her favourite colour, her favourite food? Did she have any hobbies? What was her best subject at school? How did she dress? Did she follow fashion? Had the signs of puberty started, the stirrings within that would change her from a girl into a woman? And what of the parents I had presented her to? They seemed so old to me back then. Thirteen more years would be ingrained on their lined cautious faces today.

Part of me despised her, my throwaway daughter. Lucilla was like a cloud over my vision, a cataract that greyed any life, leaching the light from my days. And, like the shadow of a bird of prey falling on a mouse as it scurries across a field, I wanted to flee it, to escape. But there was no escape. My own life, the hollowness of it, fenced me in. It was as if all the savour was gone from the meal of it, as if hour by hour I was supping on dry oats. I stiffened in my seat and placed my hands solemnly over Lucilla's imagined face. I still had the snapshots of her as a baby, but they'd worn away to ghosts now. I hid them behind the mirror of my dressing table. The damp had got to them. It's dreadful damp in Wales. You couldn't even see her face any more.

Because of her I could not give myself to my echo baby. I could not love her unconditionally as I knew a mother should. Maternal love should be passionate, and willing to combat destiny if necessary for the sake of a child. But I felt none of it. I realised the gargantuan emotions I ought to feel for Lowrie, because habitually each daybreak I was swamped by the love I had for Lucilla. I had followed the rules but the discipline was wasted pitted against such a force of nature. I might carry her, but then I must not gaze into her eyes. Or I might gaze into her eyes, but then I must not touch her. It was almost a superstition with me in those sorry days that followed her birth. I would swim in those turquoise eyes that reflected my own, my arms straight as rulers at my side. Or I would hold her close, drinking in the sweet tender smell of her, willing myself to be blind. A communion of eyes and flesh would have knitted us together for life. It would have meant that a parting, a severing of that umbilical cord was inconceivable.

I was lying to Mrs Crunn when I said I couldn't think of a reason for my daughter's outbursts. Lowrie was not, as I had initially thought, a dullard. She was introspective, but that was not the same thing at all. She was also intelligent, certainly intelligent enough to comprehend that there was something amiss in her life. One of her parents loved her without reservation, but one of her parents didn't. This fact had not gone unobserved. Her mother gave no sign of her indifference, no hint that she was not the daughter she had always wanted. Her mam did everything that good mothers do, was attentive to all her needs and wants, sometimes too attentive – as though she was trying to salve a pricking conscience. I would have said that no one else had noticed that I was a mother in deed, but not in thought. But then my own mother assembled herself in my mind's eye.

Lowrie stayed with her grandparents increasingly, especially during the long summer holidays. My mam's love for her granddaughter put my lukewarm fondness to shame. She doted as I could not. And Lowrie returned her love in equal measure, as children often do when they sense genuine affection. When I dropped her off on her last visit during the Christmas holidays, while she went off with her grandfather to feed the horses, I drank a cup of coffee with my mother. We talked for several minutes about the weather, as people do when they are skirting the sinking sands of veracity. We were sitting in the front room where I had sat all those years earlier with Dad and Leslie, squirming under my suitor's attentions. I thought my mother looked drained these days, the strain showing in the fine fretwork of crows' feet at the corner of her eyes, on the cracked paintwork of her skin. I asked her if she was having one of those headaches that had been troubling her of late.

'No dear,' she told me, fidgeting with her coffee cup, raising it to her lips and then lowering it again. She took a meditative breath, frowning before she spoke. 'I worry about you, Bethan.' I broke her searching gaze and my eyes roved the room. I might as well have been at Carwyn Farm the surroundings were so similar. A cottage suite, tapestry-covered cushions, wine-red curtains, a busy woven rug. My mother set down her cup and reached a hand towards my arm. At her touch I reared back. When I raised my head I saw she was hurt. 'Are you happy?'

I gave a sharp yell of laughter and her injured look intensified. The mantel clock ticked the seconds of my life away. 'Am I happy? What a strange question to ask me, Mam,' I commented. Then added, a rind of bitterness in my tone, 'After all these years.'

'It's not,' she said, defensively, pulling her myrtle-green cardigan tighter about her. 'You're married to a good man,' she went on, and now it was she who glanced away.

'Yes, Mam, he's a good man. I s'ppose I should feel obligated to him, indebted to my parents for arranging our marriage.' I set my own cup of coffee down in its saucer on the table between us. The taste galled.

'We tried to make it right. And you've a lovely daughter, don't forget that,' she reminded me. She rubbed her hands together and, as if feeling the chill, rose to put another coal on the fire.

'Which one?' I said under my breath and she spun round.

'Bethan don't,' she hissed looking beyond me, as if expecting Lowrie to come running through the open door. She moved swiftly and closed it.

'Why not?' I said, challenging her.

She took a step nearer to me. 'Because we made a pact to keep it secret. Think of the child.'

'A pact? Is that what it was, Mam?'

Her frown blackened. 'Does he bring it up? Does Leslie mention it?'

'No.'

'He doesn't condemn you for it?' I gave a small shake of the head. 'Then why must you condemn yourself?' she said brusquely, annoyance in her crisp diction.

'I'm not maligning myself,' I told her slowly, as if talking to a simpleton. 'I'm remembering.' I straightened my back, set my head at a proud angle, before twisting the knife with my next words, a suggestion of insolence in my cadence. 'Lest we forget. Have you forgotten your son? Have you forgotten Brice?' She winced and I felt glad.

'Of course not. But that's different. He was ours, born in wedlock, your brother, part . . . part of our lives. The . . . the . . .' She trailed off unequal to tonguing the truth.

'The baby,' I volunteered. 'Though of course she wouldn't be a baby now, would she, Mam? She'd be nearly thirteen, a teenager.'

'It was never meant to happen.'

'But it did happen,' I shot back, defiant.

'It's in the past. We saw to it that she was settled. She'll be happy with her own family. Why can't you be?' She plucked the loose skin at her neck and I thought how fragile she was looking, how worn out. Sixty-two years old and it was as though she was gradually blurring, all definition to her features gone.

'How do you know?' I asked.

'How do I know?' she mimicked, wrong-footed.

'How do you know that she's happy, that Lucilla's happy?' I said, rising and glaring at her.

'You must leave this behind you! You have Lowrie now,' she importuned. 'Can't you make the most of *her*, of the richness she brings to your life? You're in danger of alienating your own daughter.

If you don't make more of an effort you may lose her, too!' I gulped a breath that was half a sob. My mother sighed and closed her eyes, squeezing her eyelids as if she had a sick headache. When she reopened them, real anguish caused them to sparkle with unshed tears. 'I'm sorry. I didn't mean that. What I'm trying to say is that you're in danger of missing what you have with your family, here, now, by looking backwards.'

In the grate the fire caved into its hollow heart with a sputter and flurry of red sparks. I shook my head violently. 'If it were that simple, Mam, don't you imagine I'd do it. If I could I would set her down and move on without her. But I can't. I've tried, oh dear God, I've tried. What I would give to leave her in the past, to rid my life of her. But my baby is branded on my heart. She is with me every waking moment.' My pitch throughout this was repressed but urgent. As I gathered up the cups, we heard approaching footsteps. My mother placed a finger to her lips and mouthed, 'She must never know. Never!' The door flew open and Lowrie burst in, rushing up to her grandmother and throwing herself into her arms with greedy desperation.

Chapter 21

Lucilla, 1999

The fourteenth of February. Valentine's day. There is snow, lots of it, and it is bitterly cold. Rudolph-red-nose weather. Normally, I adore the snow, the stark uncompromising air of winter. But this winter I'm grieving. Merlin has passed away. They let me bury him in the grounds. It's a peaceful spot in the woods. I've covered his grave with rocks so I'm hopeful no fox will dig him up. He was sixteen, a veteran in dog years. I miss him like a raging toothache. Damn and blast! Why can't dogs have the lifespan of humans? Why can't they trundle beside you all your days? They've got a small pet cemetery at the rear of the house. A clutch of lollipop tombstones with the dearest inscriptions on them, enclosed with wrought-iron railings. There is a dinky gate that creaks loudly when you push it open, like a sound effect in a horror film. And there are tall conifers leaning over it protectively, perfuming the air with the resinous scent of their sap.

While he was still sprightly enough to inspect the grounds, I asked Merlin if he fancied being buried there. Of course he didn't give a direct answer. But he rolled his milky eye at me and there was such an expression of disdain on his face, snub nose held high, that I believe I interpreted it aright as aloofness. He was no common sort, my Merlin, my canine Anubis. Lie with other hounds of uncertain pedigrees for eternity? Not likely. He wanted a graveyard all to himself. And so I accommodated him. I think he's pleased with the site. Rabbits and squirrels galore, perfumed peace to keep his spectral nose twitching – an ideal resting place.

It was God-awful at the end. There is a footbridge on the estate and he was nosing around the stone balustrade. It had been raining, and he slipped and fell a good six feet onto the path below. Unbelievably, he didn't break anything. But in the weeks afterwards his rear end seemed gradually to become atrophied, until he was dragging it behind him like a withered limb. He was basket-bound in his final days. His breathing became laboured and he stopped eating. He would lap water out of my hand though. I liked the sensation of his tiny tongue rasping against my palm. I took him to the vet. Henry came. He held my hand in his and I held Merlin's paw. I had the strangest feeling of déjà vu recalling Scamp's death all those decades ago. We brought him home bundled up in my pearly-grey satin quilt. I shall miss Merlin when I lie on our bed and probe for his silky fur with my toes.

Enough of woe. The joyous tidings are that I have gained a puppy. Well, she is four months old, an English Springer spaniel, as flexible as a rubber band and as bouncy as a super ball. Her coat, liver and white, is like floss, and she has winsome brown eyes that plead a permanent state of malnutrition. How did I come to acquire this limpid-eyed, piston-legged addition to our family? I expect you have a shrewd idea and you would be correct. When Henry initially and with his trademark diffidence mooted the possibility of buying another dog, I dispensed it with a vehement diatribe.

'How can you have the insensitivity to assume that Merlin, my dear, dear Merlin, can be so easily replaced? Why you're no better than my adoptive mother who decided when I did not work out, that her and my adoptive father should shop around again, and come back with a ready-made faultless Barbara!' I screeched, wife to a whole ocean of fish. This last taunt was unforgivable and the instant the words had left my mouth, I wanted more than anything to take them back. But it was too late. The hurt in Henry's blue eyes was palpable. We were in the kitchen, me stirring a cheese sauce in a desultory fashion guaranteed to produce a lumpy inedible affair. Slowly, I shuffled about to make my abject apology, but Henry had disappeared.

'Going for shower. Digging the beds today ready for the summer planting. Bit grubby, my love,' I heard him call back to me, and then the thump of his footsteps receding on the stairs.

For minutes I stared miserably and repentantly at the scrubbed but stubborn spatter pattern on the magnolia emulsion, the backdrop chronicling far more appetising meals. When the distinct acrid odour permeated my nostrils, I glanced down to see that the sauce now resembled something my mother might have proudly dished up. As soon as it was sufficiently cool, I began scraping it into the bin. At this disheartening, guilt-ridden moment, Henry chose to re-enter the kitchen. He was beaming as if nothing untoward had happened, attired in fresh clothes that smelled angelically of fabric conditioner, his shaggy hair, beard and moustache still dripping from the shower. He shook himself as though he was a playful dog bounding out of the River Mole after a refreshing dip. No more was said that night as we ate our rolls and tinned minestrone, judiciously refraining from comment on the sudden change of menu.

However, come the weekend, Henry announced that he was taking me on a magical mystery tour in honour of a group whose music we did and do still idolise – the Beatles. We took a train to Guildford, and then we took a bus to Bramley, and then we walked a leafy lane and from thence trod a winding drive to a farm. I was intrigued. Henry marched purposefully up to the front door and rang the bell, as if this was the most ordinary thing to do when you arrive at house you have not visited before. In due course, it was opened by a tall woman of advanced years, with an authoritative hook nose, kind but firm grey eyes, a scarf tied at her chin, and wearing Wellington boots.

'Ah, Mr Ryan, Mrs Ryan, punctual I am pleased to see,' she said, shaking both our hands in a steel grip. 'Mrs Gregory,' she introduced herself, jabbing a none too clean thumb into her chest. She appeared unbothered by our arrival on her farm. 'Follow me,' she ordered in a military tone, striding past us in her jeans and sweater. She led the way in the bright spring sunshine to a barn, shoving wide the door and beckoning us through with a wave of her arm. Inside were some stalls currently empty of occupants, in the process of being mucked out by a young farm lad. She greeted him with a swift businesslike nod. 'The Ryans,' she said by way of explanation. He too nodded, his tufted light-brown hair shedding a straw or two as he did so. The half-door to the fifth stall was closed. We drew level and one by one peered over it. And there on a bed of fresh dry hay, reclining in maternal majesty, was a beautiful English Springer spaniel, while all about her tumbled six hyperactive puppies.

'Hello, Suzie,' Mrs Gregory said, her brisk manner replaced with one of unashamed adulation. We all three slipped inside the stall. While she embraced Suzie with an affection clearly reserved for those lacking human DNA, she directed us to select one, with the adjunct that the two biggest bitches were spoken for, but we could have our pick of the three dogs and the smallest bitch. Under attack by squirming licking puppies from every quarter, whose eyes beseeched and whose yelps entreated *take me, take me, take me,* it was the tiniest who demanded my immediate focus. This scrap, batted out of the way by its stronger healthier siblings, kept rolling and skidding into the sides of the stall, then rebounding like a furry ball.

I extricated myself from the tangle, and crossed to where the smallest puppy was readying herself for another assault. I bent and picked her up. She snuggled into my arms with a sigh of relief. 'I want her,' I declared, my steady voice belying the wobble of my heart and the clench of my stomach.

Mrs Gregory gave me a considered sidelong look. 'She is the runt,' she told me with candour. 'One of the bigger dogs might be a more sensible choice.'

'I know she's the runt,' I replied. 'And it's her I want,' I added obdurately.

'Jolly good,' retorted Mrs Gregory with practical acceptance. When the transaction was over, the papers exchanged, and we were just setting off with our new puppy on board, Mrs Gregory called out. 'Mrs Ryan!'

I spun round giggling as our puppy explored her carrier, with scrabbling legs and a wet inquisitive nose. 'Yes?'

'You've got a good bitch there,' Mrs Gregory imparted frankly. 'What she lacks in size, she'll make up for in other ways.'

So there we are. I tried to express my thanks on the bus ride home. But Henry brushed it off. I tried to apologise. But Henry stopped me with a kiss. 'You're a bit fresh, aren't you? Spots and leopards. Some men never change,' I said, and Henry gave me a confident smile that would have sat well on the lips of Casanova. And I still find that dashing scar on his cheek *très très* erotic!

We have called her Lola. Today she flushed out a pheasant and went berserk. It flew squawking away, a mass of indignant feathers. I shall have to watch that or the gamekeeper will reprimand me severely, and insist I keep her on a short lead. There is a bitter east wind blowing and the temperature is minus ten degrees. A seasonal helping of fog too, so the grounds looked all dank and eerie. The pussy willow is out and it is so soft and dainty. I don't know why but it makes me want to smile. It's like a feather tickling the nose. The moment I set eyes on it my mood lifts, a helium balloon bobbing skywards. This morning I made six jars of marmalade, so I think I can feel justly virtuous. I even decorated the labels I stuck on with drawings of oranges and orange blossom. And I cut out gingham hats with my pinking shears.

While Lola is sleeping, I grab the opportunity to write to Childlink. It has been on my mind ever since Merlin died. My life is also passing, and so must my mother's be. Haste is in order, haste or capitulation, I'm not sure which. I am stranded in purgatory, a crush of yesteryear's ghosts and today's demons. I tell Childlink everything. Well, not quite everything because I don't know everything, not yet. Still, I notice that as I accumulate documents my story is gaining fresh chapters, developing more elaborate layers of plot, more kinks and loops. My tale is expanding. It is metamorphosing from a paragraph into a short story, from a short story into a novella, from a novella into a full-blown novel. Who knows, before I finish I may have an epic on my hands.

As I strike the keys of our antique computer, and it clucks and whirs like a broody hen, I am keenly aware of my upgraded status. Now I am a member of Norcap, officially a seeker of my identity. I tap out my number with satisfaction and then survey it with a smile. I like to think it attaches a certain gravitas to my missive.

I was adopted through the Church Adoption Society, 4a Bloomsbury Square, London, WC1. From the information I received from Norcap, I was delighted to learn that Childlink hold the records of this particular society. Hopefully they will go back to 1948 when I was born.

I enclose copies of all the documents I have managed to collect so far, then bike into Dorking and post my letter. I check the mail each day and after a week I am rewarded with a reply, a summons. They send me an appointment for Tuesday, 9 March at 2.30 pm. There is a map enclosed with it.

*

I have a near terminal case of the jitters on the train ride to Waterloo. My condition is aggravated when, after this, I am shaken up like a martini on the underground to Clapham Common.

It only takes a few minutes to walk to Childlink's offices. I am ushered in by a kindly middle-aged woman, who introduces herself as Mrs Belfrage. Her woolly hair, a shade of antique gold, is caught up in a sort of sausage at the back of her neck. She has grey-blue eyes that rest on me inquisitively. Her black shirt is unbuttoned to reveal a lacy lemon camisole. And a dark-blue scarf is draped below her double chin. She invites me to take a seat, and we sit and face each other over an impersonal desk. On the desk is an A4-size envelope. I cannot tear my eyes from it. When Mrs Belfrage gives it to me, my hands are trembling as if I have the palsy.

'We uncovered quite a lot actually, Mrs Ryan,' Mrs Belfrage confides with satisfaction. 'You never can tell with old records. Things get wrongly categorised. Misfiled. Even discarded. It's a pity, but tragically it occurs.' She is well spoken and has a self-possessed manner, someone who is used to being listened to and obeyed. 'What I generally do is leave the client alone for a bit to absorb the information. And then if you like we can talk for a few minutes.' I thank her and tell her that, yes, I would appreciate some solitude. She rises and walks quietly from the room, closing the door softly behind her.

Things get wrongly categorised, I reflect. They get misfiled. Even discarded. I didn't have to be told this. I had been discarded. The sleuth in me comes to the fore as I slide the Church Adoption Society's inquiry sheet from the envelope. The rain that had just started falling when I arrived, tip-taps at the window as if wanting to be let in. I ignore the distraction, and turn my attention to the paper in my hand. Here again is confirmation of the hospital I was delivered in. But to my astonishment, I discover that I have been baptised. Yes, baptised on 6 February 1948, at an address in West End Lane, Hampstead.

Apparently I am C of E, part of the Church of England flock. It confirms what I gleaned from Cousin Frank's letters, that my father was a farmhand. But now I have a name. 'Thorston Engel.' I speak it aloud and it meets with my approval. 'Thorston Engel. My daddy.' But that is all there is contained in this box, no address, no date of birth, no additional information. They do not mention the fact that he was a POW, a prisoner of war. So he is still an enigma.

However to my surprise my mother's box is crammed with details. Bethan Modron Haverd lived on Bedwyr Farm, Newport, Pembrokeshire. And her date of birth is recorded too. I do the maths on my fingers. She would be seventy-one years old now. I was, it says, my mother's first born.

Why was I offered up for adoption? I speed read ahead, my heart racing as I brace myself to discover the cause. 'Mother unable to support baby.' The phrase is devastating in its brevity, incomprehensibly so. It sounds as random as choosing whether to buy a tin of sardines or a tin of baked beans for your tea. Shall I keep my baby? Or shall I pack her up and give her away. No more than a whim. Why was she unable? I burn to know. I cannot abide the possibility that she cast me off so easily. My eyes are watering as they run down the page. 'Can all the necessary consents be obtained to the adoption of the child?' And there is my answer in the adjacent box. 'Yes.' Just like that. No dilemma. No scenes. A tick and I was gone. Now you see me, now you don't. I glower at it, as if I have been short-changed by a shop assistant – and in manner of speaking I have. A lifetime pondering the question why. Why? Why? Why? To discover, 'Mother unable to support the child.' It is like one of those Japanese poems, haiku. A few choice lines. But oh so much, so very much squashed into them. You may say an entire life.

Next, I lift out a document of my medical particulars, which it specifies has to be filled in by a qualified doctor. It gives my name, my date of birth, my birth weight – 7lbs and 6oz. Then in brackets it says, '(normal)'. Normal! Well, well. I certainly do not feel normal. But now to more scientific observations made by the good physician . . .

'What do you consider the state of nutrition?' I score well here. 'Good,' says the doctor, no doubt looking at my chubby flailing limbs. There follows a list of questions to which the practitioner has almost without exception answered 'no'. 'Has the child any affection of bones, muscles or joints? Are there any evidences of paralysis? Are there any evidences of syphilis? Has the child had fits? Has the child any discharge from the ears, or any ear trouble, and is its hearing normal?' He slips up here I'm sorry to say, recalling my protracted medical history of ear infections, infections that still lay me low for weeks at a time. But we'll consider this a minor hiccup in an otherwise proficient assessment of my health. 'Is there any evidence of tuberculosis? Has the child been vaccinated? If a boy, do you consider circumcision necessary?' He deviates from the yes/no answers in this instance and scribbles '(girl)'. For which reprieve, envisioning what circumcision involves, I am awash with relief. 'Has the child normal control of bladder and bowels for its age?' He has given me a 'yes'. 'Has the child been immunised for diphtheria?' It appears not.

Then something that does gives me pause. 'What ailments, if any, has the child had?' Gastro-enteritis is listed here, the sickness so extreme that I was admitted to hospital. Immediately, I am curious. Perhaps I nearly died. Or did someone try to kill me? Was it my mother at her wits' end? Unable to support me and unable to locate adoptive parents who could support me, she ground up laburnum seeds like a witch and put them in my milk? Now I am just being self-indulgently macabre. Because she was unable to support me, because she gave me up for adoption, it does not mean that she wanted to murder me!

On the second and last page of this medical record, the relentless quizzing continues. 'Is its behaviour and speech normal for its age?' I imagine we broke off and had a brief conversation in this interlude, me in baby gaga, him in medical jargon, before he gave his affirmation that it was. 'Is the child's mental and physical condition normal for its age? Yes. If you cannot recommend the child for adoption now, do you consider that by good nursing and proper care, it would become suitable for adoption? Recommended.' This at least is decisive, a gold star, the British stamp that makes me worthy to be adopted. Hurrah!

My eyes travel on and I see I may have spoken too soon. 'Is the child British, or have you any reason to believe that there is an element of foreign heredity such as Latin, Jewish or any oriental race, or any other nationality?' I am prepared for this one. 'Father is German.' I am grateful that I cannot see the doctor glare while he fills in the blank. I am affiliated with the Third Reich. A Fräulein in the making. 'Is there any birthmark, slight physical deformity, facial irregularity or anything else about the child not mentioned above, which the proposing adopters would wish to know about? Small birthmark at top of scalp, of no consequence.' I reach up and comb my fingers through my hair feeling for the familiar tiny ridge. 'Would you recommend the case for adoption?' A resounding 'Yes' from the doctor. His signature is a bit tricky to read. I decipher it as Dr. F. V. Lawson of Finchley Road, Hampstead. It is dated 24 April 1948. I was three and half months old.

Next I draw from the psychic envelope a copy of my birth certificate, already provided me by Clarice Goss. I move on greedy for more. 'Notice of Application For An Adoption Order' follows. And then my adoptive parents and my birth mother's names and addresses, alongside the Church Adoption Society's. I guess the notice was served on the adoption society, that they kept the details confidential, only passing on to Bethan the facts she needed to know. All these years it has been hidden in some dusty file, eventually washing up in the archives of Childlink. This was the court appearance my mother had glossed over when she told me I was adopted, refusing to say more.

Now with an audible intake of breath I process the record realising that they were all there that day, we were all there, my birth mother, my adoptive parents and me. Clause three of the notice states, 'That the said application will be heard before the Juvenile Court sitting at Avenue House, Finchley, N.3. in the said county, on the 14th day of September 1948 at the hour of Ten in the Forenoon and that you are severally required to attend before the court (and in the case of Mr and Mrs Pritchard to produce the said infant before the court).' By then I would have been eight months old, having spent four months with the Pritchards. How must it have been for Bethan to have to attend the court in person, to see her baby again, to see me, to witness the adoption being made law before the final parting.

This is trumped by a copy of the Adoption of Children Act 1926, in which I discover that I was bought by the Pritchards for the princely sum of ten shillings – the same amount as they paid for Scamp, our mongrel puppy. That is to say that the Applicants, my adoptive father, the 'stock controller', and adoptive mother, the 'housewife', were ordered to pay costs of ten shillings. Here, too, is the whisper of scandal revealing that the birth mother, Bethan Modron Haverd, was unmarried. And last of all comes the adoption certificate, given at the General Register Office, Somerset House, London. The date of entry is 24 September 1948.

So there it is. My mother has a name and an address, though of course it is highly unlikely that she still resides there. Included are also a series of fascinating letters. Some are handwritten passing between my birth mother and Valeria Mulholland, Secretary for the Church Adoption Society. She is arranging for Bethan to come to London to finalise the adoption in court. Bethan appears reluctant to attend and virtually has to be ordered. Though she does write, and this is a dart to my heart, the pain of it both bitter and sweet, 'I only wish I could have kept her.' It is the gaps between the words that I fall through, the emotions omitted in the arrangement of letters. Bethan stresses that it is harvest time and they are very busy. The secretary proposes that she travel there and back in a day. Her father intervenes confirming she will attend and requesting that his daughter's expenses are covered. So my legal adoption was slotted into the harvest with barely a pause for thought. Peculiarly, it is fear and not joy that has me by throat.

Mrs Belfrage returns with a restorative cup of tea in her hands. She leans on the side of the desk while I sip it and we chat. Afterwards, I am unable to recall a single word we said. She sends me back to Norcap. They paw over my trove jealously, and tell me in hushed tones that it is time for me to lay claim to my past. They give me a list of researchers. And that is how I come to employ my very own private investigator, Rosemary Dixon.

Months later, I will recall Mrs Belfrage and her salutary augury, delivered like the fairy godmother waving Cinderella off to the ball. 'If you are successful, if you reach the rainbow's end where your mother currently lives, tell your researcher *not* to make contact. Return to Norcap and they will appoint an intermediary, an expert who will mediate on your behalf.'

All that registered on me at the time was the intoxicating prospect of a meeting with my real mother, the one who wished she could have kept me, the one who could tell me about my father, the one who had the power to gather up the pieces of my life and return them to me sewn together, a made-to-measure outfit. But the warning, like snippets of waste fabric, I binned.

Chapter 22

Lucilla, 1960

Lucilla had been shown around the grammar school where she had been destined to enrol. She took an instant dislike to the stuffy corseted Victorian building. She wanted more. She had viewed Hillside Secondary Modern, standing in all its glassy splendour towards Friern Barnet. She had fluffed her eleven-plus deliberately in order to be rejected by the former and accepted by the latter, becoming a Hillside girl. Mr Ireland was her art teacher, her mentor, her guru. He was a stout man with thinning black hair splayed on his skull like the teeth of a comb. His features – large Roman nose, close-set dark hazel eyes, thick-lipped small mouth – sat in a solid stern face. His glasses were similar to her father's, Lucilla noticed, though the frames seemed more flattering. And, like him, he smoked a pipe, the fragrance of it exuding from his skin as he stood behind her and surveyed her work. His praise came seldom, but when it did she swooped on it like a ravenous seagull. All other lessons paled into insignificance beside his. Anything might be endured so long as she could retreat to the art room, a space crammed with light, in which the inviting odours of paint and paper wafted.

Hillside's playground was a concrete country all of its own, with a dividing line marked in red, like the Berlin Wall, running through it. On one side the tribe of girls set up camp, while on the other the boys charged about romping rowdily, their eyes straying over the boundaries from whence the enticing aromas of feminine hormones emanated. Where the playground ended the fields began. Here sports, athletics, netball, rounders, football and cricket were fought to the death like medieval tournaments. Further exploration led to a singularly pungent destination – the sewage farms. In the winter, the frosty air deadened the miasma. But throughout the summer months, the stench overcame them until their eyes stung and welled with tears, and their breaths came shallowly like overheated dogs. The windows had to be secured no matter how sultry the day. While in September, Old-Testament style, a plague of leggy crane flies descended, until the atmosphere was choked with them. The boys caught the gangly insects in the palms of their hands, and the girls squealed as they pulled the spindly legs off and smeared them on their trousers.

Lucilla's desire to blend in was thwarted from the outset. The school uniform, the very thing guaranteed to give her anonymity, became an immediate source of contention. At the school outfitters her mother was disgruntled at the price of the plain blue jumper. It was an indiscriminate shade of navy, V-necked. And Lucilla wanted it to be baggy, hiding her narrow waist.

'I'm not paying that,' her mother complained. 'It's ridiculous when I can knit you another exactly like it for half the money.'

'But we're supposed to buy it here, all wear identical jumpers,' Lucilla attested, becoming increasingly upset.

'A blue pullover – that's all it says,' her mother asserted, studying the list with a contemptuous snort. 'No one will be able to tell the difference.'

But they could, all the children could. For a start the shade of blue was brighter, not really navy at all. And the stitches looked big in comparison to the neat machine stitching. As if this wasn't humiliation enough, her mother embellished the collar with a fawn trim. 'But you're not permitted to do this,' Lucilla imputed.

'It'll keep you snug and it looks smart. What more do they want?' came her mother's dissent, stubbornly pinning the pieces together. She would have it so and no one, no, not even the headmaster at Hillside would stop her. 'You're my daughter and I should have a say in what clothes you wear to school.'

Was she? Was she really her daughter? Lucilla questioned, setting off on the trek across the seemingly endless grey of the playground. She had only managed a few yards before her progress was impeded. 'That's not school uniform,' a girl with brown hair pulled into fat bunches heckled.

'You'll get in trouble coming to school in that,' another at her side contributed, turning up her nose desparagingly.

'Most probably you'll be sent home,' chimed in a third.

And so it went on as she trudged towards the main school doors.

It wasn't the headmaster but her form teacher, Miss Merrall, who tackled the break with dress code after register was taken. While the rest of the class were busy with a piece of English comprehension, she beckoned Lucilla to the front. 'Lucilla Pritchard, isn't it?' she asked evenly. Lucilla nodded uncomfortably. The wool of the jumper was irritating her neck, and she could hear a couple of girls whispering about her. 'Yes, Miss Merrall,' the teacher prompted her, adjusting glasses with lenses the shape of tulip petals.

'Yes, Miss Merrall,' Lucilla parroted, unable to quite believe that glasses, those sobering ugly aids to sight that her parents wore, could look so delicate and decorative.

'That jumper . . .' Miss Merrall opened thoughtfully and not unkindly, 'it's not school uniform.'

'I know,' said Lucilla, head hung low combating tears.

'You're at secondary school now. We insist on school uniform.'

'I know,' said Lucilla again, her cheeks roasting apples.

'You did receive a list in the post, didn't you?' Miss Merrall continued.

'Yes,' confessed Lucilla. Outside the window the crane flies hovered. And through the narrow opening, the stench of sewerage seeped, driving out the more wholesome smells of chalk and books.

'Then why don't you have the correct uniform on?' This was the voice of logic and common sense.

She had no answer for it. 'My mother knitted it,' she mumbled, lamely, under her breath.

'I beg your pardon?' said Miss Merrall, tidying the brown curls at the back of her neck.

'My mother knitted it.' She elevated her voice and heard it fracture with shame.

Giggles broke out in the front row of desks, and licked across the room like a fire consuming touchwood.

Instantly, Miss Merrall was on her feet clapping her hands. 'Be quiet! In a moment I am going to collect up your exercise books, and anyone who has not finished will be staying in at break time.' Silence descended with the agility of a falling axe. Miss Merrall stooped and spoke in a confidential tone. 'I'll write to your mother. See me at the end of school to collect the note. Understood?' Lucilla nodded. Privately, she reflected that no power on earth could persuade her mother to remove the offending jumper. But she was mistaken.

'What's this?' demanded her mother suspiciously, as she tore it open and read it. She was propped up against the dining-room table where tea was laid out by the time she had finished. She collapsed into a chair, as the intelligence of the communication penetrated. 'Well, I never! I can't believe it. A perfectly good jumper. No, a jumper that's a great deal better than those shop-bought, machine-made efforts. I've a good mind to go into your school and take this Miss Merrall to task.'

No, oh no, Lucilla standing close by quailed inwardly. And a shiver ran through Scamp's small body huddled by her feet.

However, that Saturday another trip was made to the shops. To Lucilla's amazement, a school jumper, roomy enough to conceal several narrow waists, was acquired. Her mother's neglect was also uncovered in the routine medical examinations that took place at Hillside. Lucilla had never had a dental check up, and like a crumbling sea wall it took eight fillings to shore up her teeth. Nor had she been immunised against any of the childhood diseases, causing the indignant nurse to make a pin cushion of her with frantic injections. When Miss Merrall took her mother to task on both counts, she had only simpered foolishly in reply, as if she had pulled off a splendid practical joke.

But Lucilla's relief at her form teacher's dominion over her mother was to be brief. The Christmas holidays came and she announced that she would be giving Lucilla's intractably straight hair a perm. 'Please, Mother, don't,' pleaded Lucilla. She was still pleading head over the sink, as she applied the brown liquid. Her scalp tingled and fumed rather worse than the sewerage plant was wont to do on midsummer days. The harsh chemicals worked savagely on her fine hair.

'You are going to look lovely, Lucilla,' her mother proclaimed, brooking no dispute. She separated out strands of damp hair and wound them with tissue paper around pink and blue rollers. After a couple of hours, during which Lucilla felt her scalp was going to split open like a hatching egg, it was time to rinse the vile concoction off. Head bent, spluttering with the scorched odour, she prayed for a speedy death. Flattening by a bus would do. A preferable fate to returning to Hillside. A minute later, lukewarm water streaming off her face, her eyes running because some of the perm solution had got into them, she was yanked up, as if from a ducking stool.

'I can't wait to see how it turns out. You might look like Barbara,' her mother declared with misplaced optimism. 'Do you recall her glorious wavy hair? Imagine, with the help of a perm and some dye you could be her twin.'

She did not want to imagine. For once she wanted her mind to be stagnant, incapable of projecting forwards or backwards any emotions or images at all. But the final rinse completed, Lucilla did make believe. She was a blind girl, her sight lost for ever in an inferno that torched both her father and her mother, though it spared Mrs Fortinbrass . . . and Scamp. She bore the deformity of her scars with fortitude. Half bald, the shreds of her fried hair patching her head, she thanked God for his infinite mercy. The loss of her vision meant that she would not have to find the valour to gaze in the mirror ever again. The daydream evaporated.

If her father was surprised by her appearance, he made little comment. 'Oh dear, Mother. I think you've overdone it. Never mind, it'll soon grow out.' *Et tu*, Father, Lucilla thought, betrayed.

On the Monday, she went unwillingly to school. Her hair, what was left of it, was a startling orangey-yellow, interspersed with pale green, so that her head from behind looked like a sucked mango pip. Her scalp was inflamed, itching torturously. And when she succumbed to the irresistible temptation with a fit of manic scratching, she shed hairs as though struck down with alopecia. She was mocked and jeered by the entire playground it seemed, as she ploughed through the welter of spiteful faces. Even the teachers on duty looked askance, watching her weave her sorry way to the comparative sanctuary of her classroom. I know what Jesus felt like with his crown of thorns, she reflected, mournfully, as she stuck her head gratefully into the hollow of her locker. But eventually she had to emerge. Miss Merrall took her in, her light-brown eyes so wide that their lashes brushed her fringe.

She was called to the now familiar front of the class, the stage for the unfolding theatrics she was the unwilling star in. With a tentative hand and the lightest of touches, Miss Merrall took a shrivelled lock of her hair and ran it through her fingertips. 'Who did this to you?' she probed gently.

'My mother,' said Lucilla, not daring to meet her gaze. The angry flare in Miss Merrall's complexion was quickly diluted. She left the class in no doubt that anyone found teasing the girl with the thatched head would be severely dealt with. Another note was scribbled. This her mother read alone in the confines of her bedroom. Its contents remained private, but when she came out Lucilla observed that her skin had a greasy pallor to it. Next day, Lucilla was kept home without explanation. In the afternoon, they visited a hairdresser who snipped and snipped with shiny scissors at the tangled mass. When she had finished, Lucilla surveyed herself with shy pleasure. She looked like Peter Pan. And although here and there her hair still resembled coconut fibres, it was survivable.

That night she dreamed again of flying, of standing on the precipice of Beachy Head at night, with the Belle Tout Lighthouse at her back. The great glass Cyclops revolved blinking dispassionately. On, off, on, off, on, off. Dazzled by the light coming and going, by the distant murmur of the restless sea, she keeled over into the wind, let it bear her up on beating wings. She might have cried out, 'I'm flying, flying off Beachy Head!' But no one came, so perhaps it was part of the dream.

As the sea gusts bore her away to distant lands, to another life, she glanced back in the moonlight and saw them, her father and her mother. Only they weren't, weren't her father and her mother. They looked like toy people standing there with Belle Tout towering over them, mouths agape as this child who was not theirs soared up into the silvered dusk. She didn't wave and neither did they. She was leaving them behind, jettisoning them. They were sure she would plummet and smash to bits. They had wanted to grab her back, to harness her, to keep her on a short rein plodding in step with this counterfeit family. But she hadn't crashed on the shingle far below. She tipped herself up and poured herself out into the salty wind. She slithered off her skin, her shredded skin, and let her liquid spirit go, swept high by the up current that scaled the chalky cliffs.

Bizarrely, the hair fiasco liberated her. Now she was shorn there were no more fantasies about Rapunzel. Besides she did not want to stay cooped up in this oppressive tower growing back her hair. She loved . . . what did she love? Her dog, her books and her roller skates. Oh, she did love her roller skates. With them strapped to her feet, she would alight from the bus while it was still moving, and hang on to the pole, letting it drag her the last few yards to her stop. Not the remarks of other passengers, 'Cheeky devil', 'What a saucy madam', 'Needs a good thrashing that one', not the bellowing of the furious bus conductor, not a telling-off from a local bobby made an ounce of difference.

The previous Christmas she'd been given a record player, a Dansette. She'd taken it over to the Friedmans to show it off. 'I got a record player,' she boasted. Then her smile fell. 'Mother says I don't deserve it because I am so wicked.'

Mr Friedman's brow settled into three deep pleats. 'Have a pretzel. You're not so bad, Lucilla. Why ever should your mother think that?' His octopus hands plumbed the air searching for a solution. Lucilla shrugged, unable to solve the riddle for him.

But change, like the nip of winter, was pinching. The year she became a teenager, the ground under her feet shifted. On Guy Fawkes Night, her father came home with a five-bob tin of Pains fireworks. He made a great to-do of setting them up in the garden. Afterwards, he spent a mysterious hour in the shed, before rejoining the preparations. And it struck Lucilla on his re-emergence, that the loose-limbed slap-dash approach he subsequently acquired was something of a liability around explosives. Mother tweaked the curtains and said that there were folks coming, that she had such a lot to do she didn't know where to begin. Shortly afterwards, the Friedmans arrived bearing sparklers and chicken soup. Then Aunt Enid and Rachel and Frank fetched up with a tray of toffee apples. Mrs Fortinbrass crept downstairs for while, but after sipping a cup of soup, she stole upstairs again, saying that the view was better from her window.

There were Catherine wheels that spun, bowling colours into the wintry night, and rockets that took off with a whiz exploding an instant later in a puff of light. There were jumping crackers that, once lit, zigzagged after you like sparking snakes. And there were Bengal bursters, whirl wheels, Italian streamers, jewelled fountains and humming spiders. Frank helped her father co-ordinate the display, shooing her and Rachel away, commanding them not to meddle for their own safety. He was frightfully grown up now, nearly an adult himself, studying for his O levels.

'Why don't you girls write your names in the dark with your sparklers?' suggested her father, with grin that continued stretching all the way across his face like elastic pastry thinned by a rolling pin. His deliberate almost fastidious style of speech was unsettling Lucilla. It was as though, as a result of some temporary mental aberration, this accomplishment, previously taken entirely for granted, had for some obscure reason morphed into a linguistic challenge. Lucilla hoped the guests, most especially Rachel and Frank, did not notice anything out of the ordinary about their Uncle Merfyn. Fortuitously, they both seemed otherwise occupied with the celebration. Rachel smiled at her and, gripping her sparkler like a pen, began signing her name. But Lucilla made no move to copy her. She grimaced down at her own sparkler, at the spitting luminous snowflake, and watched it die.

'Why didn't you do it?' Rachel wanted to know. 'Sign your name?'

'It's not my name,' divulged Lucilla. 'It's code for my real name.'

'Yes, it is,' said Frank haughtily, overhearing them. 'Like it or not, Lucilla Pritchard is your name.' He had a box of sparklers in his hand, and he prodded her between the shoulder blades with it. 'What tosh you do talk.'

'Well, I don't like it and it isn't my name, so there,' came Lucilla's riposte, dropping her dead sparkler in disgust. 'Anyway it's none of your bees' wax. You shouldn't be listening in.'

'Touchy!' teased Frank. 'Have another sparkler and try again,' he goaded. 'If you can't spell it, I'll tell you the letters.'

'Oh buzz off,' muttered Lucilla. Rachel raised her eyes to the night sky, used to this sparring between her brother and her cousin.

'Dear, dear, we have hit a raw nerve,' Frank sneered, sauntering off. Then changing key, his voice mellifluous as runny honey, 'Scrumptious food, Aunt Harriet. What a wizard cook you are.'

'Why don't you like your name?' asked Rachel, the question sincere and artless. 'I think it's rather pretty.'

'No, it's not,' Lucilla shot back, her assertive tone allowing no room for manoeuvre. 'It sounds like a scream, like someone's in pain.' Rachel tilted her head to the side, testing the validity of this. She pushed her lips together and fastened her eyes interrogatively on her cousin's. 'Well, the way my mother says it, it does. The way she speaks my name sounds . . . sounds . . .' She teetered on the brink of saying too much and pulled back. 'It just doesn't sound very nice, that's all,' she wound up with a mumble. 'Sparklers look so pretty when they're alight, but they are dreadfully ugly when they're dead,' she broadcast into the vast coldness.

'Mmm,' agreed Rachel, accepting Lucilla's exposition, and her cousin's reticence to say any more. She sucked her lip, an affectation that looked charming on her. Playing along she enquired, 'If your name isn't Lucilla, what is it then?'

'Laura,' Lucilla told her without hesitation. 'My true name is Laura.'

She had been inspired by Laura Ingalls Wilder, who wrote *Little House on the Prairie*.

'Do your parents know that you've changed it?'

Lucilla shook her head. 'It's top secret,' she said. 'Swear on your life not to tell.'

'I swear,' vowed Rachel gravely. Then she winked and mimed zipping her lips. 'I'll get a couple more sparklers from Frank, and then you can have a go at writing your real name behind the apple tree.'

But when she trotted back, lighted sparklers in both hands, Lucilla crossed her arms and shook her head. So Rachel drew abstract shapes instead and tied bows, and made a compass of her sparkler describing diminishing circles. Her mother gave them both burned hot dogs, and Lucilla crunched through hers feeling as if she was biting into a piece of coal. The stars above London were very large, like silver-white urchins spiking the black cave of the night. Scamp rushed about snapping at the fading sparks overhead, his eyes neon. A few days later, she woke to an apparition, Scamp, with all his fur lying the wrong way. His eyes had an unnatural sheen to them and he was limping. They took him to the vet and, when he prodded the swollen forepaw, Scamp yelped in pain. A fragment of a sparkler, an inch of fine metal wire had worked its way into his footpad. The vet administered a local anaesthetic and extracted it with tweezers. He prescribed a course of antibiotics.

'That dog has cost a fortune one way and another,' her father groused, sitting beside her on the bus as they rumbled home. He was jotting his calculations down in a small notebook. 'When some men don't earn enough to feed and clothe their families, we spend more than you would on a child to keep our dog.' Lucilla stroked Scamp as he lay in her lap, nursing his hurt paw. And as she did so a shadow moved across her sun, a premonition. She drew the warm body a little closer. The limp did become less pronounced as winter settled in, but it was not eradicated.

*

One Christmas, Mr Ireland paid them an unexpected visit. On recognising who had come calling, added to the normal concerns any student might have if a teacher of theirs appeared uninvited on their doorstep, was the fact that it coincided with an evening when her father had been to the shed. He did not go to the shed every evening, which made it all the more nerve-wracking. Still, it could not be helped. Mr Ireland, unaware that anything was amiss, sat in the front room and drank tea. Lucilla eavesdropped at the door. She heard him say, 'Your daughter is gifted. She is an artist. I want her to sit a scholarship for the Royal Academy. I think she'll get a place. And if she succeeds, her fees will be paid for.'

An interminable hiatus followed this. The clock struck seven before her father said, 'I see.' Then he said, 'It's int– inter– interesting that you think –' To Lucilla, rapt and drinking in every word, it was apparent that the belt of her father's diction had been loosened by his sojourn in the shed, though thankfully it had not quite become unbuckled.

'It's more than interesting,' interrupted Mr Ireland and his gritty voice became a rumble. 'Do you understand what I'm telling you? Lucilla has an ability that is out of the ordinary. Exceptional. We need to do all we can to nurture it.'

'Would you like a macaroon, Mr Ireland? They're home-made.' This, the high condescending voice of her mother, playing at being genteel.

'No, no thank you.' Mr Ireland sounded nonplussed. 'Look, Mr and Mrs Pritchard, may I speak plainly?'

'By all . . . means,' came her father's slack riposte.

'I have taught art for many years. In all of my career, I have not encountered another child with a talent like Lucilla's. When I describe her as exceptional, I mean it.'

The Adoption

Her mother gave a blocked-up nasal laugh. But it was her father who was their elected spokesperson. 'Once again, Mr Ireland, we are grateful to you for making the effort to come and see us, but ... but –' He appeared to lose his thread, and Lucilla was humiliated into a hot-cheeked blush.

Mr Ireland used her father's meandering syntax as the opportunity of a second interruption. Lucilla imagined her toes digging into the chalky scrub of Beachy Head, the salted wet wind slapping her face until she was quivering, her blunt senses awoken. Let it be, let it be, let it be, came her speechless invocation. She pressed her forehead into the hallway wall, inhaling the frowsty taint of antiquated wallpaper. To her right, she glimpsed a photograph of the Royal Family. The tiny Royals clustered around the skirts of the Queen, Her Majesty's face a mask of ordered maternal tenderness, the Duke looking masterfully on. An image of her own family barrelled in like an apocalyptic thundercloud, her father tottering out of the shed to juggle blurred numbers into the dead of the night, her mother's knitting needles clicking, slab toffee scraping the enamel off both of their browned teeth. And she thought of her art, how it shouted out to be expressed.

She came back to the muted conversation that was deciding her future. 'I'm sorry, Mr Ireland, but it's not really what ... what we want for our daughter.' Another plunge of the knife from Brutus.

'But, Mr Pritchard, surely this is about what Lucilla wants. She's growing up. She's nearly an adult. Soon she will be able to make choices for herself.'

'But not yet, Mr Ire– Ireland, not yet.' A cautionary flintiness in her father's tone, which made her flinch, arrives with a spray of spit beyond her sphere of vision. 'As her parents we must make choices for her.'

'Art for a hobby, maybe, but not a career, surely? You can't possibly expect us to sanction Lucilla chasing some hare-brained scheme to become a painter,' her mother twittered.

'Be sensible, Mr Ireland. There's no money in it, no security,' her father continued and so did the spit. 'We want Lucilla to have a stable life, one where she does not have . . . have anxieties over living expenses.'

'That's not necessarily true, you know.' Mr Ireland debated his corner with a terrier's tenacity. 'She might have to struggle to begin with. But I believe Lucilla's art is so unique that recognition would only be a matter of time.'

'But how much time? It could be years of hardship. And in the interim who would have to support her? Mr Ireland, I'm sorry. Our . . . ans– answer is no.' Her father was unyielding, a chord of childish perversity humming as the belt widened to hook a last tenuous notch.

'Do please take a few days to discuss this.' Mr Ireland's pitch hit a trough of dismay. It made her want to weep. Scamp rounded the bottom of the stairs and limped to her side, nosing her leg in empathy.

'We have considered it, Mr Ireland. And re– rejected it. We're sorry, but we would be grateful if you did not raise false hopes in our daughter.' Her father's breathing was audible in the short interim that the stand-off now afforded the trio. Then he cleared his throat as if signalling the meeting was concluded.

'Besides, Lucilla is bound to get married and have a family. And really, what more could any woman want than a home of her own and children?' Her mother expounded her ethos for a rewarding life. 'There's nothing stopping her doing a bit of painting now and then if she likes it.'

'She needs training! The artist has to hone their skill, develop it. If you don't let Lucilla sit the scholarship you will be stunting her growth.' Poor Mr Ireland was getting quite overwrought.

'I think we have had a reasonable exchange of views and that we, my wife and I, Lucilla's parents, have . . . have made our position clear. Now if you don't mind, we have things to do.'

The Adoption

Things to do? Back to the shed her father would go, surmised Lucilla, with a cynicism well in advance of her years. They were getting to their feet. It was done. The dice had been rolled and she had not won. Lucilla dashed to the understairs cupboard and hid in it, leaving the door ajar an inch or two. She heard their footfalls on the hallway tiles, felt the drop in temperature as the front door was opened.

'There is nothing I can say to make you reconsider?' A pause in which she guessed her mother's head was shaking resolutely, her father's rolling from shoulder to shoulder. 'Well then,' her art teacher said, with finality, 'well then, there is one last caution I must add. If you do this, if you stand between Lucilla and her art, she may react strongly.'

'Please don't tell us how to bring up our daughter. These are family matters, Mr Ireland, and you . . . you are interfere . . . interfering,' her father declared, biting his lazy lolling tongue so savagely it would bleed until a second dose of antiseptic might be sought from the shed. But he was numb to the sting.

Behind the cupboard door, Lucilla faintly heard a valiant grumble. 'But she may –'

'Good evening, Mr Ireland,' her father cut him off.

'Good evening,' her mother seconded with a raven's caw. Mr Ireland, having spent his words, having intervened for the sake of art, Lucilla's art, was now as mute as if he had merely been a signpost that a driver opted to disregard.

Lucilla woke the following morning to find blood in her bed, blood soaking the crotch of her pyjama bottoms. She realised what it was. Her periods had started. The girls at school spoke about them like a rite of passage. Her tummy felt swollen and there were dull cramping pains that came and went. She felt rather nauseous too. Overnight she had shucked off the cocoon of girlhood.

'You're late down.' Her mother was curt as she mooched into the dining room. 'I've made you porridge and it's been getting cold. Sit down and I'll fetch it.'

'I'm not hungry,' admitted Lucilla, sniffing scorched oats.

'You need something hot on a cold –'

'My periods have started,' Lucilla bugled, packing books into her schoolbag.

'Don't talk such rubbish.' Lucilla saw the blush rise to her mother's gaunt cheeks and reaped some small reward. 'How crude you are and what a liar.'

'They have,' she reinforced prosaically. 'Go and look if you don't believe me. My sheets have blood on them. My pyjamas as well.' Wagging her head as if some demented weevil was crawling around and around in it, her mother escaped to the kitchen and slammed the door.

At school, Lucilla made do with wads of toilet paper. Returning home in the afternoon, she found a belt and a packet of bulky sanitary towels on her bed. It was Friday. Unusually her father was home early. As a treat her mother said that she had made roast lamb.

Lucilla filled the kitchen doorway, fidgeting her thighs together. The bulky sanitary garment wedged between her legs made her waddle like a duck. She had spent five minutes fiddling with the damn contraption in the toilet. The sensation of her blood soaking into it was foreign, weakening. And as it flowed out so her animosity flowed in. She breathed in the smell of burned flesh and the queasiness that had been with her all day hit her with knee-buckling ferocity. I shall puke, she thought, puke my guts up, chuck up the lunch of sandwiches that had sat below her midriff undigested all the afternoon.

'Mint sauce,' piped up her mother merrily, holding out the jar. 'Pop it on the table will you.'

'No,' declined Lucilla. 'I want to sit the scholarship. I want to go to the Royal Academy. I want to be an artist.'

Her mother flung wide the oven door and smoke billowed out, making them both cough. 'Has that awful Mr Ireland been putting crazy ideas in your head?' Hands wadded in oven gloves, she hefted out the piping-hot metal dish bearing the overdone roast. The fat sizzled and smouldered and spat. She set it down on the sink's draining board with a bang, and fanned away the bluish-grey haze. 'I know it's rather . . . rather . . . rather chilly, but I think we'd better open a window,' she hacked.

'Why won't you let me go?' accosted Lucilla. Her mother bobbed her head, making Lucilla want to tear out a handful of her now page-boy styled hair. 'If I win a scholarship you won't have to pay any fees.'

With a patronising laugh her mother released the metal catch on the sash window. 'If only it were as easy as that, Lucilla.'

'But it is,' she argued. She felt suddenly woozy, vertiginous. And again the pull of Beachy Head was on her, that ineluctable force sucking her into its vortex. 'It is that simple. Just let me go!' She found that her voice had run up a scale, that she was screeching in a shrill falsetto.

'Don't you raise your voice to me, Miss Mousey,' her mother castigated, wearing an expression that suggested her daughter had changed overnight into a giant unwelcome rat. She swung her arms about as the cold air blasted in. Her glasses had fogged up, and the misty rings scanned for the insurgent in her midst. 'Must have, won't have. Gratitude, that's what you ought to feel towards us, gratitude. All we've done for you, and you're not even . . . not even . . .' She wheezed to a stop.

'Not even what? Not even what?' Lucilla yelled. 'That's all you ever do, find fault.'

The mist was clearing. As her mother's brown eyes came into focus, Lucilla recognised enmity in them. The kitchen had gone from a sauna to a freezer in a trice. Scamp yap-yapped and hobbled after his tail.

Lucilla could have sworn she detected a lump on his leg the other day, slight, but nevertheless sufficiently swollen to feel.

'Drain the sprouts, Lucilla.' Despite 'or else' being missing from this injunction, she realised it was an ultimatum.

'Oh stuff the bloody sprouts!' she threw back, hammering on the door frame with a fist. 'They stink, all waterlogged and stewed and smelly!'

'Don't you dare blaspheme. I don't know what's got into you these days.' An instant later the lips in her mother's puce face winched up into a slow knowing sneer.

'I want to be an artist!'

Her mother tipped the saucepan of steaming sprouts over the sink, into the metal colander. 'Tell your father dinner's ready.'

She went reluctantly, escorted by crippled Scamp. She relayed the message. 'Bit of a drama,' her father commented mildly, tipping out his pipe into the ashtray. She shrugged and he glanced at his watch. 'Mother's three minutes late today,' he observed, pinching his nostrils censoriously.

'Dad, please, I want to sit the scholarship. It's an honour to win a place at the Royal Academy. And I really think I could.'

'Ears burning, eh? Prying on adult conversations? Tut-tut!' Her father did not even look up. He ran a forefinger down a column and gave a nod. 'A place for everything and everything in its place,' he said. She moved like an automaton to the dining room, where the acrid smells of burned meat mingled with the soggy steam from the overboiled vegetables. Her parents filed in, paused behind their chairs, pulled them out and took their seats. But she remained obstinately upright.

'Sit down, Lucilla,' her father commanded, taking up his cudgels, the carving knife and steel. He began sharpening the knife. Lucilla gritted her teeth as the blade's edge ground rhythmically. Her father looked like a toy soldier beating on his drum. 'Roast lamb, Mother. Looks very tasty.'

She eyed the blackened leg sceptically, while her mother preened and patted her damaged hair. 'No it doesn't,' disputed Lucilla, with a suddenness that made both her parents start. 'It's burned. It's always burned, whatever she cooks.'

'Don't be so insolent, girl.' Her mother gnashed her teeth, a viper rearing up in her seat.

'You'll go to your room if you can't behave in a civil manner,' was the sentence of her father. Grist-grust went the knife and the steel. Grist-grust. Grist-grust. Grist-grust. Scamp began *wheeking* piteously, whether in pain, or in hunger, tormented by the smoky odours of cremated meat, who could tell. The ants that hatched in her toes that day at the cinema had infested her entire body, and she was alive with the itch of them.

'I want to go art school!' she bellowed, stamping both feet alternately.

'Well, you can't and that's that,' her mother barked crossly.

'Temper, temper! Lucilla, I will not have –' But quite what her father would not have remained unuttered. The ants marched up through her ankles, her calves, her thighs. They marched in fury around the menstruating core of her, and up through her aching stomach. They made her nipples stand erect through her cotton starter bra and the fine wool of her blouse. They marched down her arms and caused her hands to lift from her sides, to lift and seize the joint of lamb. By now dried out to the texture of a fibre mat, the skin and toughened meat parched to the charred bone, it was not actually scalding, only hot. Her parents, stunned into immobility, their mouths falling open to reveal rows of teeth ruined by slab toffee, among other sugary sins, stared in appalled fascination at their adopted daughter. She had it in both hands, a firm grip. Raising it above her head like a discus thrower, she circled twice with perfect poise and then let it fly.

It belted through the air and slammed into the French windows. There came a *crump* as the teeth of glass made a meal of it. Then it slouched on the floor leaving a stain behind on the broken pane, like a greasy exclamation mark. Seconds ticked by. No one had the gumption to break the impasse. Mongrel eyes swivelled from one human to another. Then Scamp took the initiative. He crept over to the battered joint, deftly took the bone in his mouth, and made as swift an exit as his limp afforded him.

The turquoise seas of Lucilla's eyes boiled. Her cheeks stained damson. 'Say something, Merfyn,' gasped her mother, falling back to fan herself with her handkerchief.

Her father made fish mouths.

'I'm not sorry,' spat out Lucilla, vengefully. 'Some things are more important than lousy legs of lamb and damn mint sauce.' Her father jumped in his seat and her mother emitted a squeak. 'And does it matter if your horrible meals are a minute late? It's not as if they'll spoil. You're a rotten cook anyway, and I hate your food. I wish I lived next door at the Friedmans' and ate pretzels every day. I wish that I lived anywhere but here!'

'Now, Lucilla,' began her father heaving himself out of his chair and trying to regain some vestige of control, 'you –'

'And you needn't tell me to go to my room because I'm on my way.' She strode to the door, the uncomfortable pad on the move inside her pants. Yanking the door open, she whirled back. With a jut of her chin and a smirk, she dared her mother to dash over and strike her. If you try it, she thought, I shall empty the dish of soggy sprouts over your head. I shall squash them into your nest of tired hair. But her parents' condition of semi-paralysis continued, so she strode off and left them to it. The incident was not mentioned again. However, when Lucilla arrived home from school on Monday, her mother ambushed her on the stairs.

'I'd like you to step into the dining room. I want a word with you if you don't mind,' she said, untying her apron. Lucilla shrugged listlessly and followed her. Nothing seemed to matter any more. 'Sit down, Lucilla,' her mother continued, gesturing towards a dining chair. The table was not yet laid. The polished oak surface looked like a glossy mirror. Lucilla didn't argue. She was fed up. All she wanted was to get this confrontation over with, so that she could go upstairs and read her library book, *Lord of the Flies*. She sat herself down, folded her arms and waited. Her mother stayed standing, transferring her weight from foot to foot. And now that Lucilla appraised her, her eyes skittering up and down, she became aware of her dishevelled appearance, her crumpled clothes, her unkempt hair, her bleary glasses. Something was awry, she sensed. Immediately her thoughts hopped to Scamp.

She sprang up. 'Is Scamp OK? Has he been ill?'

'No, no, he's fine.' Her mother sounded peeved that she had been upstaged by the dog. 'For goodness' sake do sit down.' Lucilla lowered herself once more into her seat, as gingerly as if she were a pilot about to be ejected without a parachute. 'The dog's perfectly well. This is about you, Lucilla.'

Several thoughts chased each other in her head. She was going to be punished for the other night, for being a discus hurler and chucking the joint of lamb against the windowpane. It was taped up now with cardboard, as if a huge sticking plaster had been applied to a cut. She sniffed the air tentatively and a rotten sulphurous odour invaded her nostrils. Eggs again, their whites cauterised to an unappetising slime green. Perhaps they had reconsidered the scholarship and done a U-turn? But this seemed unlikely, her heavy heart told her. Perhaps they had decided to send her to boarding school after all? She was too much trouble at home. Oh, she did hope so. Perhaps she could go to Switzerland and be a Chalet School girl? Or perhaps someone had died? Her mother broke into her reverie.

'Lucilla, I've something to tell you, something that really you ought to have known by now.' Her mother was wringing her hands and she was not clock-watching, counting down to the exact second that tea must be thumped onto the table. 'Your father promised that he would undertake this, but the years have slid by and . . . and . . . well, he just hasn't.' She harrumphed out a breath and stalled. Then she spread her hands on the table and braced her arms. She fixed Lucilla, her brown eyes stretched and bulging behind their round lenses. 'I'm afraid . . . I'm afraid that you're not our little girl. The truth is that you are adopted.'

Adopted. Adopted. Adopted. The word shrilled like a police siren. She stared up into the face of the woman she had instinctively known was not her mother. Her spontaneous reaction was immense relief. Exultant thoughts collided. Oh thank God, thank God! You are not my mother. There is no biological connection between us. That I am here in this house in East Finchley was not meant to be. Understanding that her spreading smile was not an appropriate reaction to this devastating announcement, she buried her face in her crooked arms, the smooth wood of the table cushioning her warm cheeks. 'Oh dear, oh dear, and I turned out to be so . . . so wicked!' came her muffled manufactured sobs. After what she estimated was a credible gap, she lifted her head, registering as she did so the reflection of her face in the table's polished wood grain. 'So you are not my mother?' she could not prevent herself from saying, dry-eyed, her tone fizzing like champagne. In reply, her adoptive mother drew out a chair and fell into it. Lucilla waited for an excruciating half-minute. Then, her impatience brimming over, she asked, 'Who were my real parents?'

'Your birth mother was Welsh,' her mother revealed tonelessly.

'Welsh?' Lucilla was gripped. Wasn't Wales the land of legends, of the myths of Arthur and his true love Guinevere?

'Yes, Welsh. But that's all I know.' The tone was churlish. Lucilla felt overwhelmed with disappointment. Surely there was more. She shot her mother, her adoptive mother, an imploring look. 'I did see her, once, at the Church Adoption Society when she gave you to us. Oh and we caught a brief glimpse of her in court when the adoption was made legal.' A disapproving chord thrummed in her speech. 'She seemed a . . . a pleasant young woman.' She picked over the adjective as if it was something nasty she had trodden in on the pavement. For her closing coda, she produced her hanky from a pocket and wiped her nose.

'But why did she give me away?' So soft was Lucilla's voice that it barely qualified as a whisper. They were shut in by wintry darkness. She threw a glance beyond the reflected light of the dining room windows, beyond the gaping injury in the French doors, beyond the bottom of the garden. There she saw the lights of other lives. She wondered what was occurring in their back rooms, what melodramas were being enacted. The windows of other houses similar to theirs blinked their yellow eyes at her dispassionately. 'She gave me away. Why would she do that?' Her mother proffered nothing further. 'Surely you were told more facts?' Lucilla persisted. 'My father – what about him? Was he Welsh?' Her mother shook her head and gave her a funny look. 'Well then, what was he? English?'

'I've explained it to you. They kept the rest from me.'

'But didn't you –'

'No, that's all! They don't like to tell the adoptive parents too much. Well, now you know.' She sighed as if the tedium of Lucilla's origin was beginning to pall on her. 'It's fact. Can't be changed. But we've done our best by you.' Had they? Had they really? Was this their best, this pitiful show of meagre pettiness, this barracks that substituted as a home. 'Off you go and wash up for dinner.'

She did not move. Her voice when she spoke faltered. 'You . . . you might recall more . . . more things about them that you've forgotten today.'

'No, I won't.' Harriet Pritchard flung the words at her.

'Oh! Do you have any . . . any papers, anything they gave you?'

'No, I told you. No, I don't. Sorry. Actually, now we've had this talk I think we should let it be. Make the most of it. Don't you agree?' She could dredge up no counterpoint to this. 'Well, if you don't now, I expect you'll see the sense of it in a few days when you're more yourself.'

More herself! The irony of this remark was inescapable. Lucilla heard the clock in the front room start to chime. That's all it took, five chimes, for the transformation to take place. The years of trying to make herself belong trooped before her like a cavalcade of circus acts. She had been grafted from another plant onto this one. She was a hybrid. Who am I? she asked herself. She had no idea. But I do know who I am *not*. She clung to this. I am not Lucilla Pritchard. From the cloudy sediment of non-being an 'I' surfaced.

Chapter 23

Lucilla, 1963

The snow is very deep, reaching above my knees as I tramp through it. A severe winter, that everyone is talking about. The houses all wear snowy periwigs. And the snow doesn't look white but blue, a blinding blue, like the sea shot through with sunlight. If you look at it for more than a minute your eyes start to hurt, and pinkish stars blot your vision. I'm wearing my school uniform. I shan't be wearing it for much longer now. Overall Hillside has been OK. Yes, OK. History was good. How things used to be. The wars that have altered the maps. The past is the future in the making. That's what I believe anyhow, the pattern from which tomorrows are shaped. Quite a challenge to unpick it and set about radically remaking it.

We had a stabbing in the school last summer. No one died, but we were all confined to our classrooms while the police investigated. The head made a speech about it in assembly. He said we had to crack down on this kind of antisocial behaviour. He said that young people today had no discipline, that they were running riot. He said that we must preserve family values at all costs. Sometimes I think I'd like to stab someone, take a stand, join a protest.

The chemistry teacher, Mr Wright, went on a Ban the Bomb march last year, 1962. He set out at Aldermaston and wound up in London. Ironic really, because chemistry is probably where all this split the atom business had its nativity. But we all thought it was fabulous. 'Nuclear War is an evil that will obliterate all of us and this beautiful planet besides.' It's so cool! That's what he told us before he went. I bought a badge, which I only put on outside the house, as a concession to my stuffy parents. It's black with a white peace sign on it. Mr Wright got into a skirmish and had to go to prison for a week, so overnight he became a celebrity.

Living without my art is like being the victim of a hit and run, suffering a blunt trauma that won't heal. I have an imaginary twin who is attending the Royal Academy, painting her days all the colours of her life. She is doing extremely well, thank you very much. Her name, the name she will sign all her masterpieces with, is Laura – simply Laura. I've kept up my pen and ink drawings. I like doing galleons especially. The rigging, the sails, the hull, the figures on the deck, the tossing seas. What it must have been for the sailors back then to go exploring, not knowing what was out there, or where they would end up, not knowing if they would plunge in a torrent of foaming waves off the world's rim.

My back is in agony. I'm shouldering a rucksack loaded down with newspapers, the *Daily Sketch*, *The Times*, the *Daily Mirror*, the *Telegraph*, the *Radio Times* – and a few comics besides, the *Dandy* and the *Beano*. I can feel the straps cutting into my shoulders. My shoes are frozen. So are my socks. And my kneecaps are like discs of ice. This is my paper round. A 6 am start at the newsagent's down the road, marking the papers up with the names and the addresses. I deliver to the shops on the High Street as well. I work every day and I pick up extra money for Sundays. Hampstead Garden Suburb. Bishops Avenue. Millionaires' Row. You should see those houses, like palaces they are.

I've gained something of a reputation at school for being a rebel. I'm in detention most afternoons. I skive when I fancy it, or don't fancy it rather. In my last report I was described as a problem student, unmanageable, aggressive. I told a teacher to get stuffed the other day. He stopped me in my tracks as I was charging down a flight of steps, late as always.

'You know not to run indoors, Lucilla.' Mr Pratley is his name. He has bad breath and spotty, cratered skin. And I've seen him picking his nose when he thinks no one is looking. He teaches maths. He gripped me by the arm as I tried to get my breath. All the kids stopped and stared at me, even though he told them to get to class. Calling me Lucilla pissed me off. I'm known to most, teachers included, as LP. LP. My initials. Isn't that wild? Like a long-playing record. I've grown fond of the nickname. I wrenched free of his grasp.

'Get stuffed, Prat!' I said, my volume up full for the benefit of my entourage. There were gasps and wolf whistles. I was infamous.

'What did you say?' snarled Pratley, smoking like the biscuits Mother makes.

'I said,' I repeated enunciating each syllable carefully, 'get stuffed, Prat!'

I was dragged to the headmaster for that and put into detention for a fortnight. So what? I prefer it to being at home. I don't care. For their wedding anniversary last autumn, I saved and saved and bought my mother, *my mother*, a pair of fluffy bath towels with big blowsy blue and purple flowers on them. I watched her face as she opened the box and lifted them out. She looked as staggered as if there was a cobra coiled in the tissue paper.

'What are these, Lucilla?' she asked, her mouth as tight as a cat's arse.

I thought it was obvious but I told her anyway. 'Towels. Bath towels. Don't you like them?'

'Oh, Lucilla, you must see that they are dreadfully vulgar. Bath towels should be plain, a plain colour, white or cream.'

You'd have thought I'd have got used to it by now – but no. In my head I added up how many mornings, the icy chill invading my bones, the dawn opening up in the sky like a headache, I had slogged round with that back-breaking sack of papers to scrimp for that gift. I vowed it would be my last present to them. I am full of 'won'ts' these days. They have been incubating for some years and now clutches of them hatch out daily. I won't play piano. I won't wear dresses. I won't eat fat. I won't stay indoors. I won't be a lady, whatever that is. I have two pairs of drainpipe jeans that I wear in strict rotation, and a jumper that nearly covers my knees. I've decided to be a beatnik. My hair's grown a bit, and I backcomb it so that it sits like a beehive above my head. I adore my record player. I am constantly saving up to buy records. At three shillings and sixpence they are expensive, but oh so worth it. I am a fan of the Beatles, Elvis Presley, the Rolling Stones and Mick Jagger. And Adam Faith is to die for. Jazz makes me wild, Acker Bilk, Kenny Ball. Father took me to the Royal Festival Hall to see Oscar Peterson play piano, which was amazing. I went to *West Side Story*, as well, three times. It was on at the Odeon in Muswell Hill. I've put the poster up in my room. It's red with big black letters printed on it. I lie in bed and pretend that I'm Natalie Wood starring as Maria, singing 'Tonight'. And I *do* feel pretty.

I had all but stopped going to the temperance meetings when our eyes met across a crowded room – Tony's and mine. I preferred to stay home and listen to my records. But they nagged me incessantly about the summer dance until, as much for a bit of peace as anything else, I said that I'd go. What I would be wearing became the hot topic of debate over the next week. I knew that I would have to go in a dress, that trousers would not do. My mother might believe bath towels with a garden of flowers printed on them are garish and common, but when it comes to posh frocks it is she who excels in the vulgar and not I. All my protests accomplished was a compromise on colour. Vanquished were the girly pinks. It would be blue or turquoise if I preferred.

I conjured the mental image of a cotton shift. But what my mother ran up on the sewing machine was a creation made of tulle and net, more suited to an extrovert fairy than a tomboy. It was turquoise, maxi-length, empire style, with a high neck stitched with gold sequins, and what felt like wings hanging from the drooping sleeves. Turquoise silk shoes to match, and enormous clip-on earrings that looked as if I had gleaming turquoise beetles fastened to my ears, and I was ready to go. My mother swept my hair up into a knot that kept unravelling. Even while it was happening I knew I was making a lifetime memory. As a toothless old hag of eighty I'll still be indulging in it, like a box of Mackintosh's Carnival Assortment. My production of *West Side Story* screening any time I want. I settle back to enjoy.

I am perched on a chair sipping flat lemonade, waiting to be asked to dance. I am catatonic and in need of a blood transfusion to wake me up. The hall has been cleared and decorated with paper streamers. At one end is the refreshments table. At the other end is my father, the chairman, in charge of the record player. Mostly he selects waltzes. The boys are lined up opposite us. They look timid as they muster the nerve to request a dance. You'll be pleased to know that I am not exclusively a wallflower. I have been asked twice so far, once by a boy called Christopher, who had a stutter and was so short he could hardly raise his head above the shelf of my small breasts. The second time with a tall, gangly youth whose ears waggled when he talked, and whose sweaty hands were pasted to me.

I am perspiring under the layers of my dress. I can still feel the cold sausage roll I have just swallowed moving like a bullet down my gullet. I want to go home. Scamp is not at all well. He was sick earlier in the evening. He is struggling to keep food down. I keep telling them to take him to the vet, but I think I shall have to do it. Across a forest of couples gliding to the one two three rhythm of a Strauss waltz, I notice a young man leaning indolently against the wall. I study him with interest, blond hair with a suggestion of light brown at the roots, fair complexion and a dashing scar across one cheek – until I realise that he is also studying me. The second before I drop my gaze, I feel his pastel-blue eyes sweeping over my ridiculous dress. Perhaps he thinks if he keeps tabs on me all evening I will eventually flap my wings, lift out of my seat and swoop around the ceiling. I try to glance about me casually, but my treacherous cheeks torch.

The music stops. Couples thank each other politely and make their way back to their respective positions to gossip about their partners. Out of the corner of my eye, I see the blond boy push off the wall. He is moving vaguely in my direction, but definitely in no hurry. Scouting for competition, I realise that I am not the only one who has been distracted by his striking good looks. A girl in a mauve two-piece on my right sits so far forwards on her seat that I think she may tumble off it onto the parquet floor. To my left, a much bolder play for his attention is under way. This hussy rises with a provocative wiggle, one hand on her bony hips, the other fussing with a paste necklace that glitters over her full bosom.

Accepting that I am outnumbered and outdone, I gather up my wings, bend from the waist and closet my pink face. He is talking now to the girl with the generous bosoms. 'Isn't this simply super?' she says in a refined voice – glaringly contrived. 'Have you tried the non-alcoholic punch? Gosh, it really is most refreshing. Oh look, I've finished mine.'

I've tried it and it's filthy stuff, I reflect with a grimace. It is dense, with chunks of floury apples and segments of pithy oranges, and has the consistency of syrup that does not slake a thirst, but engenders one. She continues to give her admirer the cue to rush off and top up her glass, but he might be bolted down so ineffective are her clumsy hints.

'I don't actually like it myself,' he comments lazily. His voice is smooth as swan's down and seems to purr in his chest. 'Far too sweet.'

My father is babbling about taking your partners for the next waltz. 'Oh, I do love to dance the waltz,' gushes the girl, breasts aquiver. If she is not careful they will bounce out of her low-cut bodice like emancipated jellies.

'Do you?' I look up and see that the young man is smiling, not at her but at me, down at my lowered head draped in turquoise tulle. He turns his back on Miss Plenty and extends a hand for me to take. 'Hello. My name's Henry.'

'I'm Lu– Lucilla . . .' I choke on the admittance.

'Would you like to dance with me?'

I am thrown by his direct gaze, the blue eyes resting unfaltering on mine, the invitation delivered with just a trace of impudence.

'I am not very good at dancing,' I admit, my head ducking beneath my plumage.

'Oh neither am I. That doesn't matter. So long as we have fun,' he counters lightly.

The first strains of the waltz vibrate on air that smacks of mildew. I set my lemonade on the floor, nudge the cup under my chair and get up hesitantly, treading on the overlong hem of my dress and falling. Instantly, his hands are there restoring my balance. His grip is sure and strong. He leads me onto the floor. He places one hand on the small of my back and with the other searches for my palm. Our fingers interlock. We do not spin and twirl gracefully about the floor, nor are we on fire pirouetting like Maria and Tony. My damned dress is constantly getting underfoot and threatening to topple me over. So, necessarily, our dance is made up of staccato steps, me pulling my hand from his intermittently to, oh so unladylike, hitch up my skirt.

'I hate this dress,' I hiss and he chuckles. 'Go on, be honest with me. I look like a hideous turquoise moth.'

'No such thing,' comes his gentlemanly reply. 'You look very . . . very turquoise . . . and feminine.'

I trip and lurch into him and we burst out laughing. 'Sorry,' I say, breathlessly, through my hilarity.

'I like it. Do it again,' he flirts. And I do, shamelessly staging overbalancing so he can catch me up in his arms again.

'I'm not, you know.'

'Not what?' he asks. He is taller than me, a comfortable height without dwarfing me so that I have to raise my voice.

'I'm not very feminine,' I own honestly. I inspect his face, sensitive to his reaction. 'Mostly I wear trousers,' I blurt out preparing to stomp off, rejected for being so butch.

'I think women in trousers are sexy.' Now he is whispering, and I hastily survey the hall to see if anyone has overheard his outrageous comment. But they seem blithely unaware of the flagrant flirtation we are enjoying, as he staggers around the floor with me. My father keeps glaring over at us, his face all of a scowl. Henry is either oblivious to his condemnation or unperturbed by it. He pulls me against his manly physique, and I feel the delectable hardness of it between yards and yards of tulle.

'So are your parents here? Are they members of the Temperance Society?' I glance about wondering if we are also earning their disapprobation.

'Nah. A friend asked me if I wanted to tag along. Thought it might be a laugh.'

'And is it?'

'Oh yes.' His eyes spark. 'That and a great deal more,' he adds suggestively. I thrill to his words.

'What about your parents?'

'I'm afraid so. Actually my father's the chairman,' I disclose angling my head subtly to indicate my fuming father.

'Oops!' Our eyes lock and our shoulders quake with repressed mirth.

'You look European. Swedish or German or something?'

'Sorry to disillusion you but I'm English to the core.'

'I don't mind. How . . . how did you get that scar?' I ask, breathing fast with all the exercise.

He leans over me and speaks into my ear, so that I can feel the flickering candle of his breath. 'I fell out of my pram.' This time when I pile into him I hear something rip. 'Oh dear,' he says and we abandon ourselves to another fit of childish hysteria. Heads turn at our raucous behaviour. I catch my father's horseshoe smile clanging to the floor.

'Are you lying – about the pram I mean?' The knot at the back of my hair gives up the ghost of sophistication, and tresses tumble down about my face.

'Better,' he says, approvingly. 'I'm telling the truth. If I'm lying let lightning strike me dead.'

'No, don't,' I remonstrate. 'That would be too awful.'

He gives a slow, sly grin. 'I slammed my cheek on one of steel knobs that hinge the canopy to the buggy,' he elucidates. 'Split it open. Why? Does it revolt you, my scar face?'

I crane my neck up to his ear. 'I find it . . . *très, très* erotic,' I say huskily, drunk on daring.

The waltz is ending. On the dying note he says, 'Come out with me next Friday. I'll take you to the pictures.'

'All right,' I agree. 'I'll have to check with my parents, but all right.' I give him my address and we arrange a time. For the remainder of the evening, I am an electric fire, all my bars lit up.

The memory I review next has a bitter flavour to it – my parents' less than enthusiastic reception of this would-be beau, Henry Ryan.

'He looks foreign,' Mother says sourly as we wait for him to collect me. 'German. Two world wars I've lived through.' Her eyes fill with mawkish sentiment. Then pouncing, she asks, 'Is he German?'

'No!' I retort emphatically. Then on a quarrelsome whim, I add, 'And so what if he was? There's nothing wrong with being German. I should think they're jolly nice people. Mr Beirmann who runs the café on the corner is anyhow. Besides, the war was years ago, and I rather imagine that the Germans think we British are pigs for what we did to them.'

My mother gapes, ready to have me tried for treason.

'Don't you dare speak to your mother like that,' my father trumpets in a rare show of marital effrontery. 'You can't begin to understand what we lived through.' I raise my eyes rudely to the ceiling, as my astounded father raises his eyebrows in synchronicity. Then his eyes narrow and he licks a speck of spit from the corner of his mouth. 'If you ask me he took liberties when you danced with him. He was far too close, pushing himself against you. It was nothing short of lewd.'

'Oh for goodness' sake, we were only dancing. Everyone else was doing the same,' I dispute, with the brand of teenage belligerence that is a flashpoint to adults.

'No they were not!' my father booms. 'They certainly were not!'

Fearing my date may be forbidden, which would be unthinkable, I adjust my attitude quickly. 'It was only that I kept tripping over my dress. It's too long. I think the hem needs redoing. He caught me to stop me falling and hurting myself.' Sewing. My mother grabs the lifeline and her breathing slows, just as well, because she has been hyperventilating. I smile guilelessly. 'Look,' I continue, sensing if not a window of opportunity certainly a diamond pane, 'Henry's as English as you or I. He's from Bowes Park.' Relief brings colour flooding back into my mother's pale complexion. But my father retains an air of suspicion, as if I am about to date a rapist. Privately, I muse that Henry could come from Timbuktu for all I care.

'I'm only going to the pictures and I'll be back by ten thirty. Promise. What harm can there be?'

My father studies his watch, as if it is a stopwatch and he is already counting down the seconds to my return.

'It's not proper, her wearing trousers to go out with a young man. It'll give him the wrong impression,' Mother mutters grim-lipped, but now on terra firma and heading for her sewing box set in a corner of the front room.

Inside my trousers, my body shivers expectantly, lusting for the adventure of sex, the prospect of going further than I did behind the bike shed at junior school. Henry had been wearing a suit and tie at the temperance summer dance, giving him a semblance of respectability. But, to my delight, he fetches up on our doorstep in a navy, three-quarter-length, double-breasted mackintosh. He looks like a spy, a Russian agent, or a French sailor. *Très, très* romantic! Mother's face falls as she appraises his outfit. And my father, drawn up to his full height, with the demeanour of my bodyguard, taps his watch, cautioning Henry proprietarily. As soon as the front door closes behind us, Henry takes my hand. The gesture seems entirely natural, and I like the feel of it in his grip.

'What are we going to see?' I fish, as we head for the bus stop. It is one of those sunny Sunday evenings when the city glitters as though it is gold-plated. Peaches and pinks and coral reds are unleashed by a sunset that I imagine rivals the tropics for drama. Even the exhaust fumes smell sea-scented.

'Do you like horror films?

'I think they're divine,' I admit, relishing the prospect of being terrified in the plush dark confines of a cinema with a man I fancy.

'*House of Usher*, Vincent Price.' He gives my hand a squeeze as the bus rolls up. In the seat on the upper deck, his arm curves around my shoulders, and he gives me a swift kiss.

'You're a bit fresh, aren't you?' I say, my lips warm, feeling his fingers caress my upper arm, a spill of liquid fire igniting the wanton in me.

He grins, unflustered. 'If you're scared in the film you can cuddle up to me all you want.'

I kill the blush that threatens, by looking determinedly out of the window at the London streets. 'I don't frighten easily, you know,' I toss back breezily over my shoulder.

'I can tell,' I hear him say, humour in his tone. This time, when the lights go down in the cinema, I am not sucking on sweets and readying myself to hurl a lemon sherbet grenade. The chords of haunting music reverberate through me in the concentrated blackness, making my heart quicken and the breath roar through me.

'Are you spooked?' asks Henry when we are well into the film. A sideways peek gives me his silhouette, the gleam of his eye, and the silver of his hair, the signature of his scar, the line of his mouth.

'Yes, oh yes!' I whisper explosively.

'For hundreds of years, foul thoughts and foul deeds have been committed within its walls,' rumbles Vincent Price, larger than life on the vast screen.

He knows, I recognise guiltily, he knows my dark desires. He has read my mind. Courage! Courage! In my head I speak the word with a French accent. Courage! Somehow it is more powerful than the traditional English pronunciation, and far, far sexier. I turn to face the man I am with. He turns to face me. Then we come together – his lips on mine, light, mine on his, pushing with increasing pressure. I open to him and our tongues meet, explore the sandpaper friction. Cast into delicious depths of spine-tingling horrors, my senses shaved and primed, I feel Henry's hand on my knee and then on my thigh. When it roosts between my legs, heaven teases me. He strokes my sex, his fingers lingering, torturously erotic. Oh that there was nothing between his hand and my flesh! Now my breaths speed in and out, in and out, my pleasure climbing in rhythmic waves, until the exquisite shudder claims the wet centre of me. At the precise moment when the heroine screams, I reach a climax of pure ecstasy. Every cell, every nerve ending is tantalisingly alive, tender with sensual rapture. I can see Henry's white teeth flashing as he smiles.

'My girl!' he says. 'My girl!' And his lips are ice on my scalding cheeks.

Henry accompanies me home on the bus, walks me up to my front door. 'Give me a kiss,' he begs, his voice an urgent rasp, drawing me into his arms. I glance back over my shoulder to make sure no one is spying on us. Lights are on in the front room but the curtains are tightly closed. 'I'll die if I have to go home without tasting you one last time tonight.' I study his face in the golden orange lamplight to see if he is mocking me – deadly serious is my interpretation. I decide to risk it and our lips brush, once, twice, then a ravenous return consuming each other with open-mouthed hunger, our tongues laced, our bodies melded together, racing hearts pumping as one. I feel his groin harden against me, and the desire to open myself up and pull him inside me is all consuming. It is Henry who ends our embrace with unpredictable abruptness, so that I am suddenly afraid that I have been too easy, showing him how my body craves his. But comprehension comes when he speaks softly into my hair.

'Your father, I saw him. He was . . . watching us, through a chink in the curtains. He had a funny look about him. Are you sure you'll be OK?'

I nod. 'But we'd better be more careful next time.'

'Next time?' He grins, his charm back in the saddle.

I nod again. 'Tomorrow, Cherry Tree Wood. Eleven o'clock. I'm walking the dog,' I say under my breath.

'Are you sure that's all you're doing?' he returns in kind, his tone so low and so sexy it gives me vertigo.

Not daring another word I spin round and rush into the house.

Since then Henry has introduced me to jazz clubs, and to a dance hall in Bowes Park. I continue with my two left feet, stepping on his toes while we jive, elbowing him in the ribs when we do the twist. Sometimes we play ping-pong or have a game of darts, and drink half-pints of cider each at a pub a safe distance from East Finchley. When I tell Henry that Scamp is ill he doesn't falter.

'I'll come to the vet with you,' he says.

Scamp's limp is so severe now that he can hardly walk. I know he is dying. The vet is very caring. He examines him thoroughly and confirms this to me. 'He's in pain. You can see that, Miss Pritchard, in agony. The kindest thing –'

'The kindest thing. Yes. I want you to do the kindest thing,' I anticipate. Scamp looks up at me with trusting dewy eyes. I turn to Henry and feel my resolve weaken. 'Henry, I can't.' It is less than a whisper, a pleading fragment.

He takes my shoulders in his confident hands. 'You can,' he reassures. He stays with me at the last. He holds my hand and I hold Scamp's paw. I have the strangest feeling as we do this, a certainty that in the future we will do this again. The opposite of déjà vu? *Vu jàdé* would this be? I am being capsized by devotion for my dog, my dog that I have to say goodbye to. And Henry is righting my boat. The loss is acute. I feel it pressing on my heart, the warm-blooded weight of him inside my cardigan as we walk away from the animal stall in the Pentonville marketplace.

On the way home light-headed with grief, I make a declaration. 'When I leave school, I want to be a vet.'

'Great idea,' comes Henry's resounding endorsement.

Chapter 24

Lucilla, 1968

The barge is a beaten-up rusty hulk wedged in the mud. It is as distant from what I envisaged as the Ritz is from a hostel. I eye it reproachfully, Gina in my arms, recognising that the sickness I feel is of the morning and not my usual sea variety. Regretfully, I demolish the idyllic river dwelling I have constructed in my head. I throw the tubs of crimson geraniums off the cabin roof into the green murky waters. I look on impotently as the fresh paintwork in reds and blues, yellows and purples, assaulted by decades of stormy weather and devilish currents, bubbles and peels and flakes off. I witness the shine on the brass fittings, polished to a blinding gold, tarnishing. Below my feet the varnished teak floorboards, fodder for woodworm, rot away perilously. Gina fidgets to be put down.

'No darling, it's not safe,' I say, depressed.

'Let's not be hasty,' Henry jumps in, with the spirit of a Blitz survivor. 'A bit of sanding, a lick of paint, replace a few planks and she'll be as good as new.'

I lift my eyebrows and give him an unbroken sardonic stare. No amount of dedicated elbow grease, and no amount of money, which incidentally we don't have anyway, can restore this ghost barge to its previous glory. The name alone, *Mistress Hope*, seems a cruel jibe at us, the prospective purchasers of this bashed about tin can. She is moored at Maldon on the Blackwater estuary in Essex. My plan was to buy her with the small legacy of £200 a distant aunt has left me. My father had handed over the money very reluctantly. He said he didn't approve of living on the water, that it wasn't the *done* thing. By then, what with me having an illegitimate baby and living in sin with Henry's family, my mother made it transparent she detested everything I had *done* and was doing. The barge was a blow from which she refused to recover.

'It's abnormal,' she griped. 'Bringing a kiddy up in a floating house.' Then after a couple of seconds she added, her voice a pessimistic snarl, 'There'll be repercussions. You wait and see.'

Of course, the more they condemned the plan, the more attractive it became, until now, as the damp inhospitable reality swayed drunkenly under me. 'We can't live here.' There was despair in my tone because I knew, what with the second baby on the way, that we could not go on depending on the good nature of Henry's relatives. We all live together not in a yellow submarine, *that*, put bluntly, might be more spacious, but in a Victorian end of terrace in Bowes Park. They took me in after I had Gina. It's a crowded house. His mother and father dwell on the ground floor, and Henry and I are upstairs with his Aunt Ethel. It was she who brought him up, because his mother was so sickly.

Aunt Ethel is a ruby, a large woman with a massive bosom. She is as generous in build as nature, her only vice a fag that droops all day from her broad, slack mouth. She has a bed-sitting room. We, that is, Henry, our daughter Gina, and myself, share a small bedroom. The Ryan household has been kind to me. When we do move on, I shall miss their easy inclusive love. Aunt Ethel declares that if we go she won't have to attempt any more healthy eating regimes. 'I'll be able to give up dieting for ever, love,' she says, lighting up another cigarette, while she still has one, lipstick-stained, wagging on her lips. 'I'll waste away to nothing. You see if I don't. Without our Gina to cuddle, I'll be all bone, never mind the skin.'

While Henry was out at work as an electrician for a company in Southgate, I spent the afternoons walking in Broomfield Park. It gave his parents a break. It's a treat, the park, with its flowering borders, the vistas of mowed green grass, the splendid trees and the playground with swings and a slide. There's a grand old house as well, Broomfield House, set in the grounds. Parts of it are open to the public. Whoever owned it must have had a weakness for taxidermy. Stuffed animals and birds cram the rooms, their glassy eyes eerily tracking you, their pelts looking scruffy and moth-eaten. And the birds, varieties from far overseas, are spectres of their former selves, their feathers dowdy, their calls a distant memory. Gina and I prefer the aviary for the living. We spend hours entertained by hopping budgies and singing canaries. My habit is to order a milky coffee at the picturesque veranda café and while away the hours with my daughter. If it weren't for the high walls and the din of traffic, it would be perfect. I want to move to the country. The river had seemed a compromise, but it was impractical in the extreme. I realise this now.

If I had been able to take the job I was offered as a veterinary nurse with a practice in Mill Hill, it might all have been different. But no, my adoptive parents were adamant, refusing to sign the forms. Tending to sick animals was most assuredly not an arena for a young lady to work in.

'It's not suitable, Lucilla. Risky too,' my father disparaged.

'Who knows what germs the creatures may be carrying,' my mother added. And suddenly I was heartily sick of it all.

'Oh hang you both,' I burst out before dashing off to my room. But there was no way round it. I was a minor and until I was twenty-one had to submit to my adoptive parents' will. My father's ambitions for me did not extend beyond a nice office job. My mother's lay in a smart department store. 'John Lewis!' It was a reverential exclamation that made the hairs on my neck stand to attention with dread. 'You'd like that. You know you would.'

'No, no, I wouldn't,' I declared flatly. 'I don't want to be a shop girl.'

But the following day I was made to enlist with a crowd of others, more willing than myself. Near comatose, I listened as we were assigned to our various departments. My eyes flicked over the headings on the board ahead and stuck on haberdashery. If there was any mercy in the universe let me be saved from haberdashery, I prayed.

'Lucilla Pritchard,' sang out the supervisor with equanimity minutes later. 'You will be in haberdashery.' I opened my mouth to protest, but he had moved rapidly on. My fate was bound up in yards and yards of lace. My mother gave me a beatific smile. I weathered day one, training, as I might a winter hailstorm, hunched into the collar of my white uniform shirt, monosyllabic. Day two and it was all I could do to survive an hour on the shop floor. I examined my wristwatch in microscopic detail, as time crawled forwards like an encumbered stag beetle. At 10.05 am precisely, I made up my mind to give in my notice. I told my head of department and she gawked at me. 'That won't do, Miss Pritchard. You can't quit, you've hardly started.'

'Oh yes I can,' I snorted, ignoring the pleas of some dratted customer for darning wool. 'I cannot work here.'

I was duly sent to the manager's office. 'What's all this I hear?' he impeached, elbows splayed on his desk, fisted hands knocking together.

'I'm leaving,' I said.

'You can't do that. Why . . . why you've only just arrived,' he blustered. 'All our trainees complete their probationary period. It is unheard of.'

'Then I'll be kicking off a new trend,' I fired back, rudely. And, without waiting for his reaction, I swept out into the sunshine and strutted proudly down the Tottenham Court Road. But the exultant inner cry of 'I'm free' was soused after a few reckless minutes with a more sobering thought. What the hell was I going to do, because when my mother learned of my defection she would kill me. Still, head high, I wandered on. Arriving in Leicester Square, I found myself staring in at the window of Foyle's Bookshop, at the display of tempting novels. And then out of the corner of my eye I saw a notice headed VACANCIES. What had I to lose?

I went in and wrote my name on the list of applicants, all patiently waiting to see the great Christina Foyle. I was told that she would be interviewing prospective staff personally. Although there was a whole row of people who had more than likely been queuing for hours, before the ink was dry on my application form my name was called. I was ushered to an upstairs office, and invited by the lady herself to take a seat opposite her desk. She was an elegant woman with a wide, heart-shaped face and fine bone structure. She had cropped wavy dark hair, parted at the side and tucked behind her ears. When they rested on me, her greyish blue eyes brimmed with intelligence under their carefully shaped eyebrows. She leaned forwards and shook my hand.

'I am Christina Foyle. This is my bookshop. And you are Lucilla Pritchard?' I nodded glumly. Hearing my name spoken out loud invariably shattered my confidence. 'Do you like books, Lucilla?'

I did not have to consider my reply. 'Oh I love them,' I gushed. She gave a smile that began and ended in her perceptive eyes.

She glanced down at my form, which I now saw somewhat self-consciously was on the top of the pile set in front of her. 'You've only recently left school?' I nodded and waited.

'John Lewis.' The name fell like a boulder between us. 'What happened in John Lewis, Lucilla? You seem to have had one of the shortest careers in history with the prestigious firm.' I fixed her edgily, but the sparkle I saw in her eyes reassured me.

I considered that it might be prudent to lie, but settled for honesty in all its bold simplicity. 'I didn't want to work there. My mother forced me to go,' I blurted out. 'They assigned me to the haberdashery department. Haberdashery! I hate ribbons and bows and buttons, and all that sewing clobber. I couldn't stick it, not even for a day.'

'I see,' said Christina Foyle, and apparently she did because she hired me on the spot. I was to work in her book club. She had extensive offices from which she operated book clubs, she explained. And it would be my job to order and pack up all the books. I told my parents airily that being a shop assistant was not my style, that I had a vocation for literature. If not exactly relished, this deviation was palatable to them.

All this while, the romance between Henry and me continued . . . and flourished. My adoptive parents' dislike of him had also burgeoned. By now they had abandoned all attempts at concealing how much they despised him. Our relationship was becoming as tricky to conduct as if I had been a Capulet, and he a Montague. One night my father came to my bedroom after I had gone to bed. Up reading, I was startled by his sudden entrance. Closing the door behind him, he made his way unsteadily to my bedside and sat down facing me. He was wearing his dressing gown. His face without his glasses looked strangely bare, like a wall blotted with rectangles of lighter paintwork where the pictures have been removed. He hardly ever left them off. He was leering at me oddly. His face had the hue of a steamed lobster, his hair was messed up and a sour taint hung on his breath, which I now recognised as whisky. My father had come hot foot from the shed.

I wondered if my supposedly teetotal father, chairman of the Sons of Temperance, was inebriated at some of the meetings he and my mother attended? Or was he living a double life? Dissolute at home; a paragon of virtue with the Sons of Temperance. If my mother had detected the not so subtle changes in the climate of my father's demeanour, she was playing blind, deaf and dumb. What was that wartime phrase I had come across at school. Ah yes, I had it then, 'Keep calm and carry on.' That was exactly what my mother was doing. Keeping calm and carrying on. My father was just carrying on!

'Dad, are . . . are you all right?' I queried tentatively, setting my book aside.

He blinked slowly at me, owlishly. 'Oh ye– yesss,' he slurred. 'I only came to say goodnight.' His disposition of late had been markedly erratic. Now his eyes seemed to spider over me, scrutinising every plane and bump on view.

'Good– goodnight?' I tested. It was not a ritual I was used to.

'Can't a man come and kiss his daughter goodnight?' he asked, his diction smeary as peanut butter. He winked at me lasciviously, and shuffled higher up the bed until I was within arms' reach.

'Of course you can,' I said uncertainly, made uneasy by his proximity. My cotton pyjamas suddenly felt terribly flimsy.

He began to stroke my hair. 'I know things have been a bit awkward lately, what with you being such a big . . . big girl now. And going out with your young man.' He took hold of a few strands and lifted them, then sifted them through his fingers. 'You're a woman. A wooomaaan!' He extended the vowels in a wet embarrassing croon.

'Henry, his name's Henry,' I clarified, fighting the impulse to slap his hand away.

'Henry. Yes, Henry.' A volley of spittle landed on his chin and my cheek. His thigh was pressing on mine so I curled my legs away from him, underneath me. 'You've changed, Lucilla.' He ogled me blatantly, slewing words out of the corner of his mouth. I shrank back, pulling the blanket up over my breasts.

After that day when my mother sat me down at the kitchen table and proclaimed that she was not my mother, and that my father was not my father either, nothing had been mentioned again. Looking at my adoptive father, at the hollows and wrinkles in his face exaggerated in the twilight, it dawned on me quite how old he was. His entire hairline had receded so that it was level with his ears, like a wig that had slipped. There was grey steeling his crinkly hair. His brow looked like a rutted lane. And his complexion was all flab and pouches.

'My daughter,' he mumbled thickly. 'My daughter.' His hand had left off toying with my hair. It had slipped and now he was fingering my face.

I gave a pantomime yawn. 'I should get some sleep now. Work tomorrow,' I chirped up, willing him to go. I could smell his sweat, like the feral odour of tomcats.

'Well, give your father a hug and turn in then,' he said. Uncomfortably, I leaned forwards, put my arms under his and laid my head lightly on his chest. His heart was racketing.

'Goodnight, Dad.' But when I pulled back, his arms tightened around me, an effective straitjacket.

'This is pleasant, isn't it?' mumbled the father who wasn't my father.

'Mmm.' Again I wriggled, wanting to extricate myself, when I felt his hands moving up and down my back. Then his hand dived beneath my pyjama top and his fingers started to knead my flesh. 'Dad!' I tried to shove him away but I couldn't.

'Just . . . stay . . . stay . . . still for . . . a minute,' he puffed like a steam train climbing a steep hill. 'Just let me . . . let me . . . let me . . .' His wet lips mouthed my ear and, still pinioning me in position with one hand, the other burrowed into my belly, then higher and higher, until it was squirming between my breasts. I fought him off the way I would an attacker in the street, scratching aside his dressing gown, and clawing at his chest through the material of his pyjama top. With a gurgle, he fell back, then rose unsteadily. Reaching in his dressing gown pocket, he withdrew a hip flask. His roseate face was pimpled with perspiration. He fumbled clumsily with the screw top as he lumbered from the room. Within a quarter of an hour, I had barricaded my door. My wardrobe, my chest of drawers, my bedside table, all stacked up behind it, and standing sentry, Sammy, my balding Steiff teddy bear.

Not long afterwards, I left Foyle's and changed jobs. As much as I loved books, I missed the outdoors and fresh air. I was taken on by Barnet Council as a gardener, working in their nurseries. My adoptive parents were predictably appalled and did all they could to dissuade me. 'An *outside* job!' my mother exclaimed, as if I would be labouring in among the naked writhing bodies of Satan's fiery furnace. 'An *outside* job gardening with men.' In an armchair fortuitously, she did not fall down, but fell to fanning herself with her sewing.

'We don't like this business of you digging about in the land, ferreting around among grubs and worms and wiggling dirty things.' Other wiggling dirty things popped irreverently into my head and I suppressed a smile. 'Bending down and so forth, giving men ideas. Men can be filthy beasts, their minds cesspits of obscene images,' my father warned me sternly, apparently unfamiliar with the concept of being a hypocrite. 'You mind you cover yourself up, head to toe. And keep yourself to yourself,' was his paternal advice. Reviewing his recent behaviour, I was sorely tempted to return this to sender, where it might be of more benefit.

My parents continued their daily diatribe against my chosen occupation, even after I had been gainfully employed in the fresh air for over a year. I came to dearly wish that I was Virginia McKenna in *Born Free*. I went to jumble sales and kitted myself out in desert boots and a safari jacket. I imagined how fabulous it would be to live in the African bush with an orphaned lioness called Elsa, how it must have felt to release her into the wilds of Kenya. I wanted someone to release me.

I was grateful therefore when attention shifted from my woeful shortcomings to my cousin Rachel, an undoubted success. She had met and fallen in love with a city banker, with everyone's euphoric blessing. We had all attended the wedding at which Rachel Pritchard said I do and became Rachel Kirby. And we had all put on our glad rags, some of which I have to say, considering the ghastly dress I was made wear, were notably gladder than others. And we had all taken exorbitantly costly taxis to the glittering reception in a posh London hotel. Older than herself by ten years, her husband already owned a basement flat in Fulham.

'Oh, Lucilla, I'm in paradise,' Rachel had gushed at me through layers of lace, which created the impression that she was large fish caught in a substantial net. 'Shall I tell you a secret?' she had added in a mouse's squeak, before being hauled into the white limousine and ferried away.

'If you like,' I'd returned, fairly unreceptively I have to admit. My own dress also boasted some lace, Mother not wishing to be shown up or outdone, that was rubbing my underarms raw as a prime cut.

'Quentin wants us to start a family immediately.' She examined my face for an amazed joyous reaction, studied my lips to see if they would emit a jubilant whoop.

'That's lovely,' I managed, wanting to scratch like an ape.

'We're going to start trying for a son . . . well . . .' She emitted a shy giggle and cast her eyes downwards. 'Well . . . tonight.'

'Oh!' I exclaimed, not sure quite what spin to put on my response to this.

'Well?' Her shiny pink lips smacked on a petulant pout.

'That's . . . that's smashing. Good news soon . . . soon then,' I stammered.

'Yes, and you'll be the first to know,' she told me, as if pitching her bridal bouquet directly at me.

'Great!' I succumbed to a fit of violent underarm scratching that would have won me a leading role in *Tarzan* – as a gorilla!

The baby was now due in six months, though with the fuss Rachel was creating you would have thought it was five days. My mother embarked on a campaign of aggressive knitting in preparation (possible I promise you), the click, click, clicketty-click, as grating as grinding teeth. Though now I come to think of it, Mother's teeth could not be relied upon to grate vindictively, slab toffee had seen to that. I resisted repeated attempts to tutor me afresh in the joys of needlecraft in honour of my cousin's condition, lingering at work until I was forcibly evicted. The giant greenhouses were situated beside a sewage plant, the same plant that had so offended my schoolgirl sensibilities at Hillside. Henry quipped that I was back where I belonged. Ginger Tom was our tall lanky foreman. I worked with Louis, who, despite chronic rheumatism, sped to and from our glass Eden on a scooter. He became my teacher, growing the most gorgeous carnations I think I have ever seen.

I tinkered about hardening off primulas, and coaxing the closed butterfly wings of pansy buds into flower. I strolled through labyrinths of feathery green ferns. I dawdled in the altogether steamier microclimate of the exotic palms. I sprinkled seeds, pricked out spindly cuttings and tended the bulbs that bugled the end of winter. And I kept my dipsomaniacs well watered with the hosepipe and huge silver watering cans provided. At lunch we all came together outdoors sitting on plastic tubs of fertiliser. We munched our sandwiches companionably, sniffed the acrid sewage and beamed amiably at one another. Life was full of shit and I was content – even if I was only earning the princely sum of £8 weekly.

But it seemed that toiling among all that fecundity carried its risks. As I concentrated on nurturing seeds in their tiny pots, a seed of another kind was taking root within me. While my parents had attended a temperance meeting, Henry and I had given a demonstration of intemperance up against the apple tree in the back garden. Ginger Tom was the first to notice.

'Think p'raps you should go and see a doctor, Lucilla,' he advised in a low growl one Monday lunchtime.

'And why should I do that?' I retorted bemused, blithely unaware of the changes that my green-fingered colleagues had detected.

Louis chewed and spat. Cogitating, he stared into the heart of a modest blushing carnation. 'Might be prudent,' he said, adding his vote in his violin squeak.

I gave a chuckle at their joshing. 'I don't need to see a doctor. I'm perfectly well.'

Ginger Tom exchanged a charged look with Louis. 'Your baby might disagree with that,' was his only remark, nearly causing me to tumble off my tub.

'I can't be pregnant,' I protested, still chuckling but hollowly now.

''Course you can't,' agreed Ginger Tom with a sarcastic wink. 'You're another Virgin Mary.'

Louis gave his chopped-teeth grin. 'Immaculate conception?' He glanced at Ginger Tom for his input, and they both nodded sagely.

'Happens every day,' affirmed Ginger Tom, as he tapped out a cigarette with nicotine stained fingers.

I snorted. 'Think you're the two wise men of Finchley, do you?' The mayonnaise in my sandwich was making me feel sick so I set it aside with a sigh, and sipped my bottle of water decorously. As the weeks drifted by, I had to concede that Ginger Tom's hunch had been correct. I was pregnant. A double irony. As my mother had conceived me out of wedlock, so too had I conceived this baby, boy or girl, daughter or son. Although not reckless, unprotected sex between Henry and myself had taken place. Only seldom mind, as we usually managed to skirt the main event. However, full rapturous intercourse had taken place three times: once in Coldfall Wood, once in Cherry Tree Wood and once up against the apple tree in our garden. This I suspected might have been our Waterloo. The temptation of the apple tree. After all it did for Adam and Eve.

It had been, I recalled, a disquieting night because we were given to believe that my parents were at a temperance meeting and would not return home until after 11 pm. And yet post that delicious night a peculiar little note was slipped under my door.

> *Dear Lucilla,*
>
> *You may have been spied on the other night, you and Henry, in garden, under the apple tree. Your father didn't go to the temperance meeting after all. Your mother went alone. I spotted him going into the shed before you arrived. I wanted to warn you but I didn't know how. I'm sorry. Be careful.*
>
> *Your friend from across the landing.*
>
> *Mrs Fortinbrass*

It was upstairs Mrs Fortinbrass, bless her. A true friend. To have a peeping Tom was upsetting, but to having a peeping father was far more dire. However he said nothing, so I assumed that he was too embarrassed by his own voyeurism to confront me. Nevertheless, it gave me pause, and we avoided the lovely fruitful apple tree following this, and became far less promiscuous. Unfortunately, the damage was done by then, the apple proving far too luscious for us both. Now it seemed banishment might lie in wait. Leaving my adoptive parents would be the attainment of a lifelong ambition. But society too might banish us, and what then? Frequently during this period, I considered the parallels between my birth mother's life and mine. For whatever reason she was not tough enough to outface fortune. Was I?

It was autumn. I had a definite bump now, though small and neat enough to be easily disguised. Actually it was a triple irony, because about this time Rachel went into early labour giving birth in a toilet in Selfridges. Saddest of all, the baby, a scrap of only six months' gestation, lived for just a few days. I went to see her in hospital. She was pale as a peeled onion, speaking in a hushed frenzied tickle of disjointed sentences about how she would take her son home. They were to call him Russell. They were planning an enormous christening party and would I come. She had so much to do, so much to buy for Russell. She had to get organised. I leaned over and kissed her lightly on her sweat-slicked forehead, and that was when I saw the eerie glint of madness in her chalk-green eyes. Naturally I said nothing of my own pregnancy, and the nagging swelling problem of my inconvenient conception.

As my winter-flowering pansies blossomed in an array of oranges and purples and yellows and blues, I did the very thing I suspect my own true mother did all those years ago on the farm. I made believe nothing was happening, *nothing*, that I wasn't pregnant, that all I had to do was tread water till the rough seas calmed.

Come Christmas my neat bump had become a barrel, a barrel that my Mary Quant miniskirt was woefully inadequate at concealing. I told Henry. I rehearsed several times how I might gently apprise him of the fact that our lives were about to change beyond all recognition. I would say, I informed my director the moon, sitting on the windowsill in the middle of the night, 'Henry, my love, I am with child.' This muted truth had a biblical ring to it. The words inferred that the child was in tow, trotting happily and neatly behind me, rather than invading my body with symptoms that, like the rules of engagement, were becoming increasingly brutal.

In the end, however, I opened my mouth and let a tiger not a cat out of the bag: 'Henry I'm pregnant.'

We were shivering in the graveyard of a nearby church, the moon again providing sympathetic lighting, gentle illumination I was grateful for, considering the shock that registered on Henry's face. 'You mean you're going to have a baby?' said Henry rather stupidly, propping himself up on the grave of Lance Traherne, whose life spanned 1838–1873, the epitaph reading, 'In loving memory of a selfless father'. As Henry's eyes flicked over the inscription, I saw him calculating the lifespan of poor Lance, and wondering if fatherhood was the very thing that had finished him off.

'Yes, I am Henry. I'm going to have a baby.' In the same forthright style much to the moon's horror (she would have far preferred the lyrical poetic approach), I went on. 'Are you going to stick by me or ditch me?'

'Ditch you?' Henry echoed.

'Oh for goodness' sake, Henry, it's a simple question requiring a simple answer.' Actually I was so scared, so fearful that my Henry would turn his back on me and walk away that I was trembling, my shoulders locked with tension, my quick breaths misting on the cold air. The wind rustled the trees, and the lights of habitation pried over the heads of the gravestones eyeing our performance. A faint backing soundtrack was also discernible consisting mainly of London traffic. It had a *party's over* theme running through it.

'Are you going to keep me in suspense for ever?' I cried, with more combativeness than I felt.

Henry clutched the gravestone cogitating, possibly on the fate of Lance. Then, like a man who determinedly casts off his crutches and takes his first tentative steps, he pushed himself off his stony prop. His face lifted in a slow easy smile and his chest puffed out. Another two steps and he seized hold of my icy hands and dragged me close, closer, closest.

'We're going to have a baby!' he bayed at the moon.

'Henry, for goodness' sake!' I hissed, my head swinging around to check for other seekers of privacy in the ceaseless churn of the city.

'I don't care,' Henry reinforced at the top of his voice. 'I want to tell the world!'

I was moved, but reality was that the world could be a less than sympathetic listener. 'Well, eventually,' I said guardedly. 'But perhaps we should start with my parents.'

That thought sobered us both in a second. 'We'll do it tomorrow,' I shillied as we neared my home.

'Good idea,' Henry shallied. A sigh of relief whooshed out of him like the fast release of air from the open valve of a fully inflated bike tyre.

Over tea and rock cakes that lived up to their names, we broke the news the next afternoon to my parents that their grandchild was on the way.

'Mother, Father, I'm pregnant,' I said, hoping my candour might enlist the same belated jubilation as it had in Henry. My mother, half an eye on the knitting in her hand – a tank top that she was making for my father – choked on a raisin. She set her craft aside on the arm of her chair and beat her chest. The increasing agitation of her movements made me fear that if uninterrupted she would progress to rending her garments, wailing and gnashing the few teeth she had left that were up to the job. However, after a good deal of wheezing and spluttering, the raisin suddenly shot out of one of her flared nostrils. Following this party trick, she was seized by an apoplexy of coughing.

'I'm going to do the proper thing and marry her, sir,' Henry said to my father over the din.

My father's face flushed a dark grape, and his Adam's apple bobbed as he swallowed with increasing effort. 'You will do no such thing,' he stormed, rising slowly and menacingly to his feet like an anvil cloud.

We scrambled up too. Henry combed and combed back his blond fringe with spread fingers, a nervous habit of his when stressed. 'But, sir,' he importuned, 'I love your daughter.' He fingered his facial scar, another sign that he was wound up tighter than a reel of cotton. 'I'm going to stand by her.'

'Not if I can help it, you're not,' my father fumed, fists clenched and raised ready to punch Henry on the nose. My mother, finally recovered, kept on adding sugar lumps to her tea, until you could see the beige crystals cresting the brown fluid. 'Our Lucilla is class. Do you think for one second I'm going to let her marry someone like you?' Henry reeled back as if he had been physically struck by the insult. 'You're a worm, not a man. You won't amount to anything. You might as well give up now, because nothing you say will persuade me to consent to this match.'

I could see that Henry was stymied. I was weeks off turning nineteen. Without my father's consent we could not marry until I was twenty-one. 'It won't make any difference if you stop us now,' I defied him with all the hauteur I could muster. 'Henry will wait for me, won't you, Henry?' Henry nodded diffidently, his ear lobes and the tip of his nose pinking in his humiliation. Then I let fly my spleen. 'Why are you doing this? I shouted, tears of wrath spilling from my eyes. 'Why won't you let us be happy?'

'Perhaps we shouldn't be too hasty,' my mother croaked, putting in a word for me. 'She's in this . . . this predicament. Nothing to be done. Perhaps the most sensible thing would be to marry her off to this . . . this . . . this chap as soon as possible.'

We both looked pleased and surprised that support for our union should come from this unlikely quarter. But then, fastening my eyes on my mother's, on the truth encapsulated in that expression of panic, I understood. It was the prospect of her being landed with both me and the baby – a double maternal curse for evermore – that was prompting her to agree readily to our speedy marriage. The prospective husband could even be German for all she cared, so long as he took me and the baby to a distant land from where, henceforth, I would cease to be the loose thread in the fabric of her existence.

My father had another agenda. 'Don't be ridiculous, Mother. Lucilla will stay with us and we'll bring the baby up as if she was ours. Yours and mine, Harriet. Boy or girl, it will be Lucilla's little brother or sister.'

My mother looked poleaxed. 'But how . . . how could it be,' she faltered. 'How could the baby be ours? I'm too old, too old to have a baby. Folks won't believe it.' She pulled at a greyed curl, tugged the thinning hair in her fisted hand, taking the spring out of it. 'Besides, I've had a . . . a . . . I can't have a baby. At the hospital they took my . . . my . . . well, you know . . .' She widened her eyes until they were almost as big as the lenses of her glasses, willing conveyance of her delicate meaning. I guessed she was referring to her hysterectomy, the operation given out to be a lethal nosebleed. I had discovered the truth later with the assistance of a biology teacher at school.

'Nobody knows about that,' my father interjected obdurately.

'Yes they do,' countered my mother. 'They all know. Mother and Enid and Frank and Rachel.'

'Oh Enid,' my father gave out in a hoarse whisper, adding, 'Enid can keep secrets.' My mother was confounded, brow crinkling and recrinkling as if trying to outdo snowflakes with the originality of each fresh expression. 'And family will keep this buried. We've done it before, we can do it again,' my father revealed didactically, leaving me to wonder what my parents had previously interred. He snorted, raised his elbows and drew them back, as if following some prescribed exercise regime. 'Friends and neighbours will soon grow to accept the baby as ours.'

Henry and I listened in disbelief, so floored that neither of us could summon our wits to produce the outrage such outlandish schemes warranted.

My mother abandoned her curl and, reincarnated as a limp straggle, it sliced across her pleated brow partially obscuring her left eye. She spoke as though in her own world, her tone self preoccupied and rambling. 'I suppose . . . I suppose,' she said, reasoning aloud. She paused to take up her knitting once more, grasped the needles and hooked the wool around her index finger. 'I suppose we could palm it off as Rachel's. That might work what with her losing the baby and all.'

This was too much, her plan making me jump as though I'd had an electric shock. 'You're not giving our baby to Rachel,' I said, a dangerous stillness in my voice. 'I'd rather die than let you do that.'

'Hear! Hear!' muttered my Henry, with a jerky series of nods that a doctor would have diagnosed as a nervous disorder. I took his hand in mine and, raising both triumphantly, gave his a squeeze, before releasing it.

'Dying! Dying!' declaimed my father with the hectic loquacity of the shed upon him. 'Who said anything about dying? It's birth we're talking about.' He gestured vaguely in my direction with snaking hands, as if he intended to conjure the infant out of my womb then and there. 'There's no call for any of this fuss and no question of Rachel taking the baby, Harriet. It's ours, family, kith and kin.' Distractedly, my mother slid the knitting needles from the row of stitches, took hold of the strand of grey wool, pinching it between thumb and forefinger, and pulled, slowly but surely unravelling the nigh on completed back to her pattern. 'Put your mind at rest, Lucilla. But I won't have my daughter married to a man who does . . . does what he has done to you before marriage.' He fumbled in his pocket, drew out a handkerchief and mopped his brow. 'If he . . . forces her to do the . . . the act before they are married, what deviant behaviour, what vile perversions can we expect him to make our daughter perform to assuage his gross appetite after they are married?'

My mother subsided, a good two thirds of her knitting piled up like spaghetti in her lap, her breaths coming in tiny pops as she worked her lips. The candy pink of Henry's ear lobes and nose tip now suffused his whole face.

My father then ordered Henry from the house. I wanted to go with him – but where? He lived at home, and his parents knew nothing about the baby yet. If I wasn't working we couldn't afford rent even for a bedsit. Henry threw me a doleful look. Then he backed awkwardly from the room bumping into my father's desk, and knocking some of the temperance society's accounts onto the floor. I was prevented from showing him to the door by my father. He intercepted me and stomped after dear Henry, yelling abuse. When my father returned, my mother and I were eyeing each other like territorial cats.

He approached me, a conciliatory expression on his sanguine face. A pace between us, he paused and opened out his arms. I flinched backwards, almost tripping over the fire surround. 'Lucilla, you're going to be fine. We'll look after you and the baby.' A small strangulated mew emitted from my mother's blue-tinged lips. My father dismissed it and adjusted his glasses. 'You're best off home here with us,' he said.

The child in my belly kicked in displeasure and, glancing down, I realised that I still had a rock cake grasped in my hand. I dodged my father and made for the door, kicking at the accounts scattered over the floor en route. The theme tune of *Champion the Wonder Horse* blared out from the television in the dining room. Just where was that rearing stallion when you needed him? At the door, I whirled around, raised my fist and hurled the rock cake, scoring a tidy hit on the dome of my father's forehead.

As I neared the due date my father repeated his advances. It had been a hellish month. On a dim rainy day, I visited our doctor for a prohibitively late antenatal check. He harangued me, saying that I had been no end of a burden to my harassed mother. Which one? I had been tempted to reply. Which mother? The one in Wales who had carried me, or the one in London who had ruined me. 'It is no wonder that your poor mother has been so ill with tension,' he scolded, wagging his stethoscope at me. Lying on the examination table, my vast belly exposed, I felt at a distinct disadvantage. When I emerged, tears were coursing down my inflamed cheeks. A few days later, Henry paid my parents a second visit. This time he had his father in tow, an affable soft-spoken man with the friendly battered look of a favourite armchair about him. If Henry opened with a tone of reasonable discourse, he was hollering and scarlet with frustration by the time he closed. My father would not budge. Our marriage was outlawed. I was sent upstairs to stew in my room as if I was five. I heard the door slam on our unwelcome guests, when only a few minutes later they left.

The following morning, my mother confronted me on the stairs, demanding what the neighbours would think. 'What have you done? Oh what have you done, Lucilla?' she wailed. 'You bad, bad girl. The shame of it, the everlasting shame. How will I ever withstand the shame? What were you thinking of?' I really did want her to stop asking rhetorical questions or I might just surprise her with an answer. What was I thinking of, with the knobbly spine of the tree digging into my back, and the aroma of overly ripe apples filling my lungs? My knickers wound about one ankle, Henry's trousers rumpled around his knees, us groaning in chorus with each delectable thrust, and the apples thudding sweetly on the lush grass. Mostly that it was glorious, sensual and enthralling, and I wanted it to last forever. But I spared her the graphic image. Patting my Humpty Dumpty girth I japed back, 'I'd say that was obvious, Mother.'

My aunt Enid was equally galled, and only just stopped short of chucking stones at me. 'You're a harlot, Lucilla, a slut. I might have guessed. Cheapening yourself with that Henry fellow.' Frank added his penny's worth, telling me that I was no better than a dog. I rather liked this. Truthfully, I would have preferred to have four legs and fur, and nothing to worry about but a bone. And Rachel, who by now had suffered a second early miscarriage, ostracised me with cold resentment, saying only, 'There is no justice in this world when whoring is rewarded with pregnancy, and respectable wedlock with miscarriage.'

A Friday night with D day imminent. My father waylaid me when I went to bed. As I closed the door behind me, I saw him lurking in a corner by my chest of drawers.

'Did I . . . st– startle . . . you? I'm sorry, my dear,' he said.

I saw that yet again he was inebriated. 'Go away.'

As I went to open the door, he moved speedily to block me. 'I only wanted to say goodnight,' he slurred.

I took a few paces back. 'I'm tired,' I said.

'Of course you are, Lucilla. There's two of you now.' He came closer on a whiff of whisky.

'I shall scream,' I informed him, calmly.

'Let me look. Just . . . just let me look at you. That's . . . all,' he whispered feverishly, diving at my buttons with trembling hands.

My teddy bear was off-duty on my bed. I seized him by his mohair legs. A hop, skip and a jump and I was at my father, whacking him hard across his face with it. Momentarily stunned, he cowered, his glasses fogged, his hand rubbing his sore head. I made as rapid an exit as my cumbersome shape permitted. Mrs Fortinbrass, her door open a few inches, peeped out, giving me a timorous victory sign as I shot by. I was on the landing when I had the sudden urgent impulse to empty my bladder. Seconds later and there was a puddle at my feet. My waters had broken.

I'm not sure why, certainly not to deliver tea and sympathy, but my mother came with me in the ambulance. You'd have thought out of decency my father would have made himself scarce, but not a bit of it. Swaying precariously, he saw us off waving his grubby, spotted hanky proprietorially, promising to get to the hospital as soon as he could. It was as though he believed in his stupor that I was not his adopted daughter but his wife, that the baby I was about to have was not Henry's but his.

My mother appeared dazed on the journey to Barnet General Hospital. As I huffed and panted and moaned, arching my back and rocking my pelvis, she sat inspecting me curiously. It was as if she expected, *hey presto*, a pristine powdered baby to bounce out of me and into the medic's waiting arms. At the hospital, a nurse took me into a bathroom, leaving my mother waiting outside. When we came out, me now in the throes of strong labour pains, my mother leaped to her feet.

'Where's the baby?' she asked.

'The baby?' The nurse, Irish and as broad as she was wide, perused my mother from her feet upwards. When she reached the ridiculous hat with its spray of moulting black and white ostrich feathers, her expression was pitying. 'We've only had a bath, a shave and an enema to make room for baby to come out.' Hearing this, and feeling somewhat like a plucked chicken, I thought, oh my God, a bomb is going to drop out of my arse. A second later and I was groaning with another contraction.

'So she hasn't had it?' my mother assayed, staring idiotically at the tub of me gyrating under the hospital gown.

'Good gracious no! It's the early stages altogether, Mrs Pritchard. It could take all night. Probably will what with it being a breech birth.' Swimming in and out of seismic spasms of pain, my mother's face flashed before me, a vision of bewilderment. She'd no notion what a breech birth was. It might have been laughable if it wasn't so tragic. 'Why not go home and get some sleep, so? Your daughter will be fine with us,' came the nurse's practical suggestion.

My mother needed no second prompting. 'Get a message to Henry,'

I gasped, as she set off down the corridor, though I doubted she would. My daughter was born in the early hours of the morning. She was unquestionably the most beautiful infant I have ever seen, with ten tiny fingers and ten tiny toes, blue eyes and a golden down of hair. She was 7 lb 9 oz, a good weight the midwife said, as she was wheeled away to the nursery.

Dropping in and out of sleep, I started at my first visitor. It was not Henry, as I had hoped, come to clap eyes on the wonder of our baby, but my father. He was sitting in a chair staring at me through the large lenses of his glasses. He looked a sorry sight, eyes bloodshot, clothes and hair in disarray, as if his batteries had finally run down. I didn't think he had changed or slept since the previous night. He was prattling. As I rose through the confusion of slumber, I was able to extract his meaning, why he was there.

'Clever, clever, Lucilla. I've been to see her. Our daughter. The nurse pointed her out. I'm thrilled we've had a girl. Thrilled! I was wondering about a Welsh name for her. What about Gwyneth? Gwyneth is a good name, a name to be proud of. I've run it by Mother. She didn't say much but I think she likes it. Oh she'll be along this afternoon after she's done her bits and bobs. You know how she is. I can't wait to take you both home. I've been looking at cots. I've a bit of money put by. How do you fancy going shopping for Gwyneth? When you're rested, of course, and you're fit enough to be up and about.' He licked his lips and stood, running the rim of his trilby hat through his hands. 'We're going to be a proper family now, you and me and Gwyneth. Mend everything.'

Awkwardly, I pushed myself up in the bed, ignoring the discomfort. 'Her name's Gina,' I said painstakingly. 'She's not Welsh. And she's not yours. She's mine, my daughter.' The name had grabbed me instantly only weeks earlier. It was from a newspaper article about an artist. As I spoke my visitor seemed to close up like a book. He was not my father, not the chairman of the Sons of Temperance either. He was one of the shadow men, the shabby tramps crumpled in doorways swigging from their bottles, the fallen we prayed for on our crusades in Bermondsey. I took a breath. I was so tired and wanted desperately to rest, but this had to be dealt with before sleep. I was in a ward with other beds, where other mothers lay reconfiguring their lives, wrestling with the epiphany that they were unutterably altered.

'Lucilla, you're exhausted and –'

'I am not coming back to the house with you and Mother,' I said.

'Don't be silly. Where would you go, you and our baby?' My adoptive father scratched his forehead, as if this conundrum was too much for his befuddled brain to take in.

'Henry is going to look after us,' I said, trying to convince myself.

'Henry! Henry! Why the lad has no security. You're coming home with us and that's that.'

I didn't buckle. Henry came next. He had called at the house and Mother had told him. I watched him cradle our daughter in his arms, smitten with paternal love. As he gazed into her pinched tiny face, holding her as if she was constructed of glass not flesh and bones, I told him we were returning home with him. 'We will all live together in your parents' house,' I said. He nodded absently, adrift with our bundle. 'Promise to ask your parents,' I exacted.

'She's adorable,' he sighed.

'Her name's Gina.'

He smiled. 'Gina. Hello Gina.'

'Promise?'

'I promise,' he agreed.

My mother didn't visit me in hospital. She sent her emissary instead. When I'd been in hospital for a couple of days, a woman from the social services came to see me. Her name was Margo Keir. She was tall, her shoulder-length rusty brown hair swept back off her forehead and worn loose. She had a horsy look to her face. Her large but unappealing brown eyes homed intrusively in on me as I nursed Gina.

'Good morning,' she opened assertively. 'I thought I'd get in quickly before the lunch rounds begin. I'm Margo Keir and I work for Barnet Council Social Services. Your mother got in touch with me. She's very worried about you.' I flinched and Gina gave a reflexive little jump. Then she fell immediately asleep, her wee face a portrait of tranquillity. I tidied my pyjama top, and fastened a few buttons. I did not return the greeting. I had taken an instant dislike to this woman, and I was to discover that my intuition was sound. 'You are Lucilla Pritchard, and this is your enchanting baby daughter?' She paused and I continued in silence, lips pressed together. 'The nurse pointed you out to me,' she added, as if in reply to her own question. She showed me her uneven teeth, pulling her lips back in an ingratiating smile. Her shade of lipstick was too bright, an orangey red. Glancing about her, she moved to draw the curtain around my bed, as if the subject of our conference demanded privacy.

Then Margo Keir pushed up the sleeves of her primrose-yellow cardigan, as if she had had enough of this dilly-dallying and now meant business. 'Why don't you let me hold the baby,' she said, arms reaching for Gina. I clasped my daughter more tightly to me and shook my head. Another pause as she judged how entrenched my uncooperative attitude was. Then she shrugged. 'As you like,' she said. Her voice was very dry, a voice with all the tone sucked out of it, a smoker's voice. 'As I say your mother rang me. She asked me to look in on you, to see how you are coping. Lucilla – oh you don't mind if I call you, Lucilla?'

'Actually I do,' I rejoined, a fingertip touching Gina's flushed cheek.

She gave a fleeting smile. 'Really?' Her tone was falsely upbeat. 'I always feel it's so much nicer to be on first-name terms when you're nattering.' She sat down on the end of my bed, neither asking, nor it seems requiring permission for this liberty.

'Are we nattering?' I queried coldly. She kept eyeing Gina, swaddled in her blanket.

'Oh yes, I think we are,' Margo Keir ordained. Her backcombed hair looked plastered in place, staying put when her head moved. She must have used a whole can of hairspray on it. The synthetic odour she exuded was making my stomach heave. '*Miss* Pritchard –' she stressed the '*Miss*' '– I understand that you are unmarried? Your mother and I are of the shared opinion that it can be very difficult in your circumstances. Setting up home in a respectable society with this kind of obstacle to inclusion can be such an ordeal.'

'Do you have children?' I threw back.

She was momentarily stumped for words then recovered herself, rosy sparks of anger spotting her cheeks. The colour stood out on bad skin unevenly layered with ivory foundation. 'Actually, no. But you must understand I deal with babies and unmarried mothers every day. It's . . . it's my job. And believe me I know the pitfalls.'

'I'm engaged,' I fired back defensively. 'His name's Henry. And we're going to be wed as soon as I'm twenty-one.'

'And you're nineteen now?'

'That's right.' The hum of the hospital had suddenly ceased, or I had grown deaf to it I was listening so intently.

Horseface worked her mouth. 'Two years is a very long time, don't you agree, dear?'

'Not that long.'

'Your mother tells me that although your father feels compelled to help, her health is so precarious that having you home to live with the baby is not an option.' She smoothed the crocodile skin of the handbag in her lap. 'So that means we have to sort something else out.' She swooped, her hawk eyes locating their prey. 'An alternative route that puts baby first. Although you are of equal importance to us. A young woman with her whole life ahead of her. Do you know much about adoption, Lucilla?'

I almost burst out laughing but restrained myself. 'A little,' I replied economically. 'I don't want to go home anyway. We won't live there, not ever.'

'Ah, and why might that be?' asked Margo Keir, smelling scandal.

As if I would ever tell her what my father had tried to do. She would label me a liar and my accusation rubbish, further proof of my unsuitability to be a mother. A respectable couple both holding senior positions in the temperance movement? The father teeming with incestuous desires? Oh yes, this predatory social worker would most certainly deem my tale delusional.

'Then what *are* you going to do?' she wanted to know, her brown eyes unblinking.

'I'm going to move in with Henry, with his family in their house in Bowes Park.'

'So your boyfriend still lives at home with his parents?' Gina stirred, sensing my unease. 'And they are happy to accommodate both you *and* the baby?'

'Yes,' I lied. 'Thrilled to pieces in fact.'

'Is it a large house? Detached? A garden?'

'End of terrace. Regular-sized but perfectly adequate.' A second lie and Margo Kier twitched her nose scenting it. There was no room for Henry there, let alone me and a baby. But by now, as the unappetising aroma of lunch infiltrated the stagnant air of the ward, sheer terror had seized hold.

'It's not ideal, is it, Miss Pritchard? All crowded together. If you don't mind my observing, you're very young. Your mother and I are most concerned.' I felt such rage I wanted to punch her, and had I not been clasping my baby protectively to me I might have. My mother's knowledge of motherhood and babies would fit on a grain of rice and have room to spare, I brooded savagely. But I kept my temper in check, because I had deduced that a scene from me would be a disaster at this stage. 'It all seems rather rushed,' she continued. 'If you will be guided by me, I would take a few days in hospital to seriously consider your future and that of the baby.' Her fingers, almost clumsy with their big knuckles, clawed at the crocodile skin, avidity in the gesture. 'Accidents can be remedied in my experience.'

'It wasn't an accident. We planned it, planned the baby.' My third glaring lie.

Margo Keir repressed a smug smile. 'Ah, you don't have to be coy. These things happen, Miss Pritchard. Two hot-blooded young people alone together. You can confide in me,' she purred. 'I'm a woman of the world, you know.' Gazing at her with her hoity-toity air, I calculated that she could not have been further removed from the world, from the dance of desire, from the fragrance of mellow apples grown violet in the warm dusk. She hesitated, frowned when it was clear I would have to be press-ganged into her scheme, then forged unwaveringly on. 'You made a mistake, went a little too far. Some might condemn you for it. But not us. We at Barnet Social Services pride ourselves on being progressive, modern thinkers. We deal with reality. Your baby is a reality, and we can assist you with making the decision that best protects her interests.'

'I am her mother,' I said. 'I'll protect her interests.'

'You have your entire life ahead of you. This mishap needn't be a disaster for you.' She leaned towards me, her eyes glittering refariously. 'Have her adopted, Miss Pritchard. I believe that is the way ahead for you, and for the baby. Your mother and I are sure that this is the most sensible course for everyone involved.' I wanted to scream, to tell her to get out, to tell her that my mother was many things, but an authority on motherhood was not one of them. I focused on my breathing, my baby and my breathing. 'I can organise everything. All you have to do is relax, recuperate and consider your future.'

I sat up very straight. I was defenceless confined to my bed, in a state of undress, a milk stain over my chest. 'Her name is Gina. She is my daughter, mine and Henry's. We are going to live together and, as soon as we can, we will marry,' I attested. 'I am not putting her up for adoption. I will never put her up for adoption. I am her mother!' With the force of my maternal instinct my register had deepened, and I had gathered up a fistful of blanket.

Margo Keir got up slowly, not a lacquered hair out of place. Languidly, she picked up her handbag and gave me the kind of smile that might, had I possessed a gun, have driven me to use it. 'Early days, Miss Pritchard, early days. You are naturally a fraction overwrought. Childbirth is traumatic enough without you having to decide this now. And what with all those hormones, you are bound to be feeling addled.' She smoothed her skirt and drew back the curtain in fits and starts. 'But we shall keep in contact. Trust me. Plenty of opportunity to change your mind.'

'I won't,' came my oath as Gina woke and blinked startled blue eyes up at me.

'Ah, there's the lunch trolley. Enjoy your meal, Miss Pritchard. You need to keep your strength up.' And off she went, her crocodile handbag hanging from her wrist, her broad bottom swinging unflatteringly. I realised, as gristly meat and potatoes and some sloppy dessert was set before me, that if I was determined not to go the way of my birth mother, this would be war.

Luckily, Henry's parents welcomed me and their granddaughter, Gina. Aunt Ethel smothered her great-niece with affection. She sang nursery rhymes I had never heard of to her, and bounced our enraptured baby on her plump arthritic knees. My mother- and father-in-law, Carrie and Bernard, proved a tolerant pair, bearing the disruption stoically. I had two more visits from Margo Keir. When Gina was six weeks old she hammered on the door one chilly afternoon. The hospital had given her my address. I was about to take Gina for her afternoon constitutional. Busy negotiating the brute of a pram we had purchased at a pawnshop through the narrow hallway, I had just knocked over the umbrella stand. Crouching down levering the brolly out of the spokes of a front wheel, I jumped at the knocking. My face must have dropped when I pulled open the door and set eyes on that dread mane of hair. It made her look like a hairdresser's mannequin, her face just as immobile.

'Hello, Miss Pritchard. Sorry to drop in without warning. I would have called if Mr and Mrs Ryan had a telephone. Your mother asked me to look in on you. She hasn't heard from you in some while. Her devotion is very moving. You're a lucky woman.'

'I'm afraid it's not convenient at present. As you can see, I'm about to take Gina for a walk.'

'A breath of fresh air. I'm all for that ordinarily, but don't you think it's a mite cold for a newborn today,' she observed critically, glancing over her shoulder at the pall of grey that hung over the street.

'She isn't a newborn,' I shot back, fussing over Gina in the pram. 'And you can see for yourself that she's well wrapped up.'

'Everything OK, Lucilla?' came Carrie's anxious voice from the front room.

I popped my head around the door and told her it was fine, only a friend come to see Gina. When I wheeled back, Margo was bent over my baby retying the bow of her knitted bonnet. 'I told you she's fine.' As I spoke, I elbowed her out of the way. But to my consternation she did not go and, dismissing my protests, she accompanied me on my walk. Gone were all vestiges of a relaxing stroll with my precious daughter. As I rushed along in the vain hope I would lose her, she drilled me with questions. Was I still breastfeeding? Oughtn't I to wean her now? What were the sleeping arrangements? Was Henry working? Was Gina sleeping through? How often did I feed her? Did I bathe her every day? Had she been examined by the doctor? Was she gaining weight? And how was I managing? How did I feel? Was I depressed? Tearful? Did I miss work? Had I made any friends in my unusual circumstances? Were Henry and I getting on? Was I still set on marriage? Had I had any more thoughts about her proposition? About adoption?

I replied with as much politeness as I could dredge up. My heart was thudding so loudly I was sure that she could hear it, that she was taking a sadistic pleasure in how frightened I evidently was. I wished, how I wished, that I had an enormous house full of convenient gadgets, and a nursery all for Gina, daubed in bright murals. I wished I had an expensive crib made up with hand-embroidered linen, and not a drawer laid on the lino floor with a folded blanket for a mattress. I wished I had a washing machine that whirred all day, so I didn't have to hand launder nappies in the bath. I wished I could go to the shops and buy expensive clothes for our daughter, instead of unpicking the few knitted garments she had, and asking Aunt Ethel to remake them in larger sizes. I wished that I had a gold band on my finger, not because I particularly wanted to be married, but because I wanted to strip them of their ammunition. Gina was mine, all mine. My birth mother, Bethan, might have bowed to private and public pressure, but I would not. I loved my baby and no one was taking her from me. Meanwhile her lists of questions seemed endless. More grievous still, she appeared dissatisfied with my answers. She would come again, she presaged at last.

'And don't forget what I said,' came her parting remark. 'Adoption may well be the ideal solution all round. I'll send you some of the forms to read through.'

'That won't be necessary,' I shot back.

'We'll see,' I heard her say under her breath as I closed the front door.

Gina was nine months when she next showed up, an armful. She was crawling and into everything. It was winter 1967. If she was thriving, I was not. I had dark crescents under my eyes and I had lost weight. My hair was unwashed and tangled, and I was having one of those ear infections that I was prone to, especially in periods of stress. The problem was not our darling Gina, or the strains of motherhood, or the pressures of living with Henry's parents and his aunt. It was Henry. The company he worked for was having to make staffing cuts to survive in the tough economy. Henry had been one of the casualties. He went conscientiously through the job ads each week, but so far he had not even been called for an interview. We were broke. We had nothing to live on but the shillings Aunt Ethel kept thrusting into our hands.

I don't know how she discovered that Henry was unemployed, but she did. Margo Keir blew in like a blizzard from Siberia. Aunt Ethel opened the front door, puffing on a cigarette. I was coming down the stairs with Gina in my arms. Henry was out, though he was far too congenial a man to stand up to that viper.

'Visitor for you,' called Aunt Ethel, her cigarette wagging. 'What did you say your name was?'

'Margo Keir. Social Services,' said the blizzard, howling past her and positioning herself at the bottom of the stairs, as if ready to catch Gina when she clinched the deal.

'Thank you, Aunty. You get back to your tea with Mum. I'll look after the guest.'

Aunt Ethel shuffled off, casting a sour look in the direction of Margo Keir's back. She was nobody's fool. I might not have told her who this lady was, but judging by her expression I'd have said she had a shrewd idea. I made the witch a cup of tea. She took it weak without sugar. She perched on the edge of a chair at the kitchen table, as if she thought the seat was grimy.

'Do you think the baby ought really to crawl on the kitchen floor? Hygiene is very important when they're so little.' She hurried on not pausing for my reply. 'Tiny ones do put everything into their mouths, don't they?'

I put the mug of tea in front of her, scooped up Gina and sat down at the chair furthest from her. She took a sip of tea, swallowed, and her brow lifted and lined. 'Miss Pritchard, it has come to my attention that your fiancé is unemployed.'

'It's only temporary.' I returned service without breathing, frantically wondering which department she had foraged this information from.

'I'm sure you'd like it to be, but that's not the reality of the situation, is it, dear?'

My eyes narrowed at the condescending liberty. 'He's looking for work. Something's bound to crop up.' Gina, studying my mouth, ran her fingers over it, chuckling in delight when it moved under them.

Margo Keir sighed and fingered her hair, which lay unyielding as a stair brush. 'It's tricky, I know. But the truth is that an awful lot of men are in the unenviable position of being unable to secure employment. It's tragic really. They simply can't support their families.'

'How sad,' I mumbled, as Gina pinched my cheek.

'Mmm. And how are you affording to live, Miss Pritchard?' She had set down her mug but now she picked it up again, her little finger crooked as if she was drinking Earl Grey out of a bone china cup. 'Babies are expensive.'

'We're getting by,' I hedged.

'This tea is lovely by the way. So few people make it exactly how I like it.' I made no response to this, wanting very much to pour scalding fluid over her head to deflate her reinforced hairdo. 'Miss Pritchard, I hope you don't mind my saying, but you look rather weary. Are you getting sufficient rest?'

'I've had a cold,' I said, pathetically.

'Oh dear.'

'But I'm recovered now. Would you like a biscuit?' I tried to divert her with a garibaldi. I should have known better.

'No, thank you. Watching my figure, you know.' She pushed her cup aside. 'It is my job to find out how you are supporting the baby. Mr Ryan is no longer bringing in a wage. I'm afraid you have to satisfy us that you are not impoverished. Our overriding priority is the well-being of the baby, you understand.' Then as an afterthought, delivered so unctuously you could skid on it: 'And yourself, of course. We are also worried about you. As the baby grows, her needs will be many, and I have to be persuaded that you will be able to afford to keep her.'

Keep! The word was like a rapier stabbing my heart. If I couldn't come up with a convincing story for this dratted woman, she would scuttle back to her council offices and write a damning report. She would say that I was an unfit mother and that Henry was an unfit father. And soon they would all be buzzing around, petitioning some judge for an order to take Gina into care, to have our daughter adopted. 'I have money,' I said, a dreadful serenity stealing over me. 'We are perfectly comfortable.' I smiled amicably at her. The life of my child depended on this performance and I did not intend to fail her.

'And how is that?' There was a residue of vexation in her tone that gave me hope.

'Oh, didn't I say? My father sends me money,' I said as matter-of-factly as I could.

'Does he?' A doubtful upwards inflexion.

'Oh yes. He's been doing it for ages. He likes to make a contribution to his granddaughter's upkeep. As you told me yourself he feels *compelled* to help. Actually we're very fortunate.' Gina had hold of the beads that encircled my neck. They were nothing special, clear glass I'd picked up from Oxfam, but she was fascinated by them. 'I do feel sorry for young couples who don't have such a supportive family.' I scarcely breathed. Would she believe me? Would she interrogate me wanting further details, and in doing so uproot my lie? In that second I knew how a gambler feels when everything he holds dear is riding on a single number.

'I see.' She sounded annoyed. She might have been singing 'Land of Hope and Glory' I felt so uplifted. If she was needled she had believed my excuse.

On the doorstep she said, 'Well, what a relief that Gina is being so well cared for. But if circumstances alter please do get in touch. It's never too late.' She gave me a card with her number on it, and I assured her that I would. After she had gone, I stood with my head resting against the door. When my daughter yanked my necklace and it broke, crystal beads scattering over the tiled hall, I was sobbing so hard I paid no attention at all.

We gradually hauled ourselves out of the quagmire. From time to time, I heard from Rachel, bitter phone calls in which she ranted down the line about trying to conceive or her last miscarriage. They had run some test and discovered that, like my mother, she had been suffering from endometriosis and fibroids, and that consequently her doctor doubted she would ever carry to term.

'And yet you, still living in sin, have become pregnant with a second baby just like an alley cat. People with no morals should be banned from bringing up children.'

I forgave Rachel the nasty things she accused me of, because I felt sorry for her. To be consumed by frustrated maternal longings, an instinct so strong that the human race would perish without it, must be very dreadful. But after our grandmother died I felt as if the only real connection between us was severed. Some months before my twenty-first birthday, I came into my small legacy. And although it was not enough to buy my dream house, well, in honesty, any house at all, it was a stopgap. Then post *Mistress Hope*, as if the name of the rusting tub had been a charm after all, an advertisement in the newspaper caught my eye: 'Head Gardener Wanted for Private Estate in Dorking. Cottage provided for successful applicant.' Just as well, because without Henry working we had soon used up all the money.

'But I don't know much about gardening,' Henry prevaricated when I said he should apply.

'I'll teach you,' I told him undeterred. 'I'll go to the library and get lots of books for you to swat up on. We'll revise together.'

We crammed as if our lives depended on passing an exam, and perhaps they did. He went alone to the initial interview. We married at the registry office the following week. I travelled with him to the second interview and strolled around the estate. The grass was without railings fencing it in. The trees were without pavements making them line up. The sky was without buildings blocking out the light. It was a homecoming, a mellow spring pageant of youthful greens. I was entranced. But it was the copper beech, pinkish bronze leaves like varnished nails on hundreds of twiggy fingers beckoning me on, that engaged my imagination. Flaunting itself among the other green guards bordering the drive, it proclaimed the message to me that here differences were celebrated. In this haven we would be safe.

That same day they telephoned to offer Henry the job. He accepted it. We hired a small van and packed up our few possessions. By sundown of that day we had moved into Pear Tree Cottage – the home where we would bring up our children.

We kept in close touch with Henry's family though. However, trips to Bowes Park were sadly curtailed when the children were still young, as both his parents died within a year of one another. Aunt Ethel, diagnosed with lung cancer shortly afterwards, soon followed her sister and brother-in-law. As the property was rented and their chattels sparse, their lives were tidied away with the minimum of fuss. As for my adoptive parents, we had one catastrophic rendezvous at the house in East Finchley. We went for tea, blackened fish fingers, burned beans and charcoal chips. Gina was three and Tim was one. Father had been in the shed, all day judging by his condition, and had problems guiding his fork into his mouth. Tim had a temperature and a runny nose, and cried constantly in Henry's loving patient arms, earning my mother's censure. Gina, with the honesty of children, refused to eat anything because as she told her grandmother plaintively, 'It's horrid and all burnty up!' When Mother rebuked her, she too burst into tears, climbed down from the table and promptly wet herself. While Mother was frantically scrubbing at the puddle that soaked into the new carpet, Father passed out, his cheek resting on the pillow of midnight black beans on his plate. Mother sprang up, screaming at me to telephone an ambulance.

'Oh, oh, oh, he's had a heart attack! Hurry, hurry, Lucilla, or he'll die!'

Able to detect the whisky fumes from the open doorway to the hall, where I was providing solace to Gina, I pointed out the good news, that he was in fact blind drunk and had merely passed out. However, far from being relieved that treating his symptoms would not involve medical intervention, only several hours of sleep, during which glasses of water might wisely be administered, my mother was irate.

'Don't tell lies! Oh you wicked, wicked girl! You'll never change!' She flapped her arms towards her recumbent husband. 'Your father's signed the pledge! He never touches a drop! You know we're both teetotal!'

We left my father snoring and my mother wielding a bucket. After that we met rarely, and only outdoors, all the better to make a quick getaway should such be necessary. Although rare, these engagements proved so unpopular with the children and adults alike, that they were soon phased out. When Gina was ten and Tim was eight, I told them about my adoption. After this revelation neither of them could be coaxed into any interaction with Granny and Grandpa Pritchard over and above a formal thank you letter for small gifts of money on their birthdays and at Christmas.

It was a couple of years later that history repeated itself and my cousin Rachel was forced to have a hysterectomy. She was desperate to adopt but Quentin would not have it. A baby that was not his own was completely unacceptable to him. After all, he expounded, who could vouch for the breeding of a cast-off? By slow degrees, Rachel was worn down, giving up the battle for a baby and letting her husband trample her into submission. Her life became a round of trivia: cocktail parties, dinner parties, banking socials, holidays. She had a cleaner and a cook, plenty of money and a life as empty as a blown egg. We had nothing in common any more. I had to tread carefully in conversations with her, avoiding mention of the children and the joy they brought us. It seemed to me yet another dark chapter in the archives of that most complex of genres, the matriarch, the wellspring, the nurturing mother.

Chapter 25

Lucilla, 1999

I summoned every scrap of bravery I had and rang Rosemary Dixon one evening in September. She lives in Bognor Regis, West Sussex, my private sleuth. I felt guilty as if I was contacting a clairvoyant, someone with a hotline to the other side. She did not disappoint, speaking to me in beguilingly dulcet, sympathetic tones. She understood my rapacious need to locate Bethan Haverd, to establish a relationship with her. I wanted to roll back the years like a carpet, lay bare the floorboards of my life, to start over. I wanted the injustice of it all to be righted, the imbalance corrected. I wanted my suffering in this farce to be acknowledged. It was 1999. Bethan was seventy-one. I wanted her to gather me into her arms a lifetime too late. I was naive. The wheel of time spins inexorably forwards. It cannot go backwards. The past is quite simply that – past. But if I had an inherent understanding of this universal truth, I opted to be myopic. Rosemary Dixon was my fellow gravedigger. Her spade would be her assiduousness, and her assertion that, in step with Sherlock Holmes, the case of my identity was on the verge of being solved.

Henry stroked his whiskers, smoothed his sideburns and shook his head. But he knew that for good or ill this search must run its course. I wrote to Rosemary Dixon. The desperation I had quelled for so many years now resurfaced with a vengeance. I did not wish this to be a sedate pursuit, with me masquerading at nonchalance. I was in fifth gear and had my foot pressed down hard on life's accelerator. I intended to compress into weeks the passage of over half a century. I opened by thanking Rosemary for being interested in my personal quest, and confirming that I was enclosing a cheque for £200, together with photocopies of all the documents and letters in my possession.

Her reply fell on the mat on 7 November. It was dated Guy Fawkes Night. *Remember, remember the fifth of November, gunpowder, treason and plot.* I had woken early, had gone a-roaming in the dark with Lola. I like tapping my way with my hiking pole, guided by the owls' cries and those nocturnal birds, the black flitting shapes of bats overhead. The clocks have gone back, so I've gained an hour for my nebulous strolls. I saw what looked like a fire, a raging conflagration on the distant horizon. The tall pines stood out in relief against the lick of blood red flames. The field I was then crossing was soon bathed in streaks of butterscotch and blue grape. The sheep dotted about were backed with golden fleeces. It was dawn, an untamed inferno sweeping up the dregs of night. There was gale blowing as well, and the autumn leaves were being tossed and hurled about in a coppery tempest. The wind whistling through the treetops played the sea's song, the waves foaming and crashing on grassy knolls.

I expect Rosemary Dixon was penning her reply to me, while Henry and I, Gina and Nathan and little Lisa, and Tim were warming our hands over a token bonfire, munching on hotdogs, and lighting sparklers. The night jogged a memory. Rachel urging me to sign my name with my sputtering sparkler. But it wasn't my name. Henry and I read the letter together, upstairs in our bedroom. Lola lay sprawled under the window. We sat down beside her, leaning our backs against the wall. Her nose twitched to our distinctive scents and, without opening her eyes, her tailed thumped in taciturn greeting. In the dim illumination of a low-energy light bulb, my eye ran down the page as I read aloud.

> *Dear Lucilla,*
>
> *Hello! Thank you for providing your Norcap membership number, the cheque and all your paperwork. I am enclosing a copy of a birth certificate which I believe to be your birth mother's. Hopefully, there are not too many Bethan Modrun Haverds, who had fathers who were farmers, and mothers called Seren, and who lived on farms in Newport, Pembrokeshire. I am currently checking for possible marriage certificates, also for a death certificate for Seren Haverd. If a death entry is found she may have left a will, which could be a good lead.*
>
> *As soon as I know more I'll be in touch.*
>
> *Very best wishes,*
>
> *Rosemary*

We scanned the birth certificate together. The registration district was given as Cardigan. The birth itself took place in the sub-district of Newport, Pembroke, the date given 9 August 1928. '"Bethan Modrun, girl, born to father Ifan Haul Haverd and Seren Amser Haverd, formerly Kendrick. Occupation of the father – a farmer. Date of register, fourteenth of September, nineteen twenty-eight,"' Henry read.

'My mother would have been five weeks old,' I told Henry in disbelief. I saw the line stretching through the hazy annals of Welsh history. My mother, my mother's mother, my mother's mother's mother. Back and back it went through the world wars, the days of Empire, the Tudors, the Normans, the Vikings, to the maternal grunts of Neolithic mothers, their babies carried in fur papooses strapped to their backs. I interrupted that line. From order came the chaos of my birth.

Henry supplied the even tone of my reply, censoring my heightened emotions. '*Cave quid dicis, quando, et cui,*' he quoted.

'Queen's English, Henry, if you please?' I requested.

'Beware of what you say, when, and to whom,' Henry filled in prudently. We both knew how high the stakes were, that now was not the time to show our hand. So I signed off, wishing Rosemary a Happy Christmas, telling her to enjoy the festivities and take a rest from her intensive research. However, despite bluffing others, I could not save myself from my inner turmoil. The savour of my own holiday was gone. The mince pies were tasteless, the tinsel gaudy and cheap. I would have bartered my entire present for a solitary day from the past, a day spent with my real mother. My empathetic husband, like a loyal dog, suffered with me. But Rosemary, despite being unacquainted with our agony, did not delay. I next heard on 3 December. And what she sent me for a Christmas present was a copy of my birth mother's marriage certificate, and a request for further funds. I envisioned her as a Romany wise woman, with clinking bangles and gathered skirts, carrying baskets heaped with sprigs of white heather.

I took it on a walk with Henry, and we sat on a hillside bench, contemplating it reverently. It was still early, the sun just cresting the distant inky crowns of woods. Lola charged about overdosing on the piquant icy aromas. The frost-rimed slope looked as if barrels of diamonds had been emptied over it. I swung my booted feet and shuttered my eyes.

'What did she look like on her wedding day, Henry? Did my mother, Bethan, wear white or cream?' I whispered.

'Did her betrothed know that another man had gone before him?' Henry interjected. My eyes sprang open. 'Had he been told there was a baby, that a German prisoner-of-war had fathered a child with his young wife?' My husband looked so forlorn that I hugged him, then we held hands like a teenage couple.

'Was she happy? Was she in love when she said, "I do"? Or was this a marriage of another kind? Was she forced into it to give a semblance of virtue?'

Henry shook his head. 'So many questions.'

'So few answers,' I finished for him. I was temporarily blinded by the scintillating spiked frozen grass. Gradually, as my vision adjusted, I carried on scanning the certificate. 'After the banns were read, the marriage was solemnised on the thirteenth of May, nineteen fifty, in the parish of Nevern, county of Pembroke. In the Pritchard household in London I would have been two years old, standing in my cot shaking the bars.' I breathed in the frosty air, a memory tickling my nose, inhaling the astringent odours of cleaning products, polish, disinfectant, vinegar and lemon juice, while my mother clattered about. 'Did no one speak up for me? The first, the second, the third and final time of asking, did no parishioner climb to their feet, raise an arm, clear their throat and say, but what about baby you had, Bethan? What of Lucilla?'

Again Henry reminded me that it took two to make a baby. 'I wonder if the real father was told Bethan was getting married?'

'I shouldn't think so. If anyone knew, I expect their lips were gummed together,' I said, soberly. 'So it went ahead and Bethan married Leslie David Sterry, an agricultural contractor.' I tapped the paper with a finger. 'Look, there's even an address. Carwyn Farm, Hebron, Cardigan. Though I can't imagine she's still there.' The father of the groom was a farmer too, I saw. 'It seems that I come from agricultural stock.' The registration district was recorded as Haverfordwest. I gasped. In the tragedy of Lucilla Pritchard, this impacted on me as forcefully as Oedipus discovering that despite his every effort to escape his fate he had, after all, married his mother. 'Haverfordwest. My adoptive mother died in a hospital in Haverfordwest. Henry, do you realise they might have been living a cricket pitch from one another? They might have bumped into each other in the streets? They might have rubbed shoulders at the same market stall.'

'Well, I never, your adoptive mother and your real mother winding up in the same place. And nothing whatsoever in common, bar the baby handed over in nineteen forty-eight. Bar you!'

When my adoptive father retired, he returned to his childhood home. He and my adoptive mother moved to a pretty cottage in Pembrokeshire. I did not attend his funeral. I elected not to bow to convention and stand in a Welsh graveyard as his coffin was lowered into the earth. And when my adoptive mother rang me and asked if I would like to have his piano, I politely declined. The music died in me long ago.

I tucked the marriage certificate back in its envelope and into my coat pocket. The sun's rays could now be felt, and the frosty gems were melting and condensing into low-lying mist. We stood and set off ambling down the hill, listening appreciatively to the crunch of our boots on the still starched grass. Lola, tail wagging, lifted her head and loped after me. The air was delicious enough to eat. But my appetite was marred when Cousin Frank intruded on my reminiscing. I tallied the phone calls that I had taken from him over the years, his patronising visits, his hubris at the power he wielded when it came to his Aunt Harriet, the way in which he ingratiated himself with her. I also bookmarked with some satisfaction, juvenile though it might be, the arrival of Mr Whatmore, Alfred Whatmore. An allegory surely? My widowed mother met Mr Whatmore at her bridge club.

'Dropped in last weekend and that damned fellow was over again,' Frank repined down the line, unable to see me smiling through my responses.

'Is it such a bad thing, Frank? She's an elderly woman who'd benefit from a bit of company. You can't be there all the time.'

'You haven't met him, Lucilla. Tall, debonair, a slimy operator if you take my meaning. I'm telling you I know his type. A con man.' Takes one to know one, I thought acerbically as he continued. 'I don't like the way he goes about fingering her knick-knacks and curios.'

I yelped with laughter. 'There's a sentence loaded with innuendo if ever I heard one.'

'I'm being serious, Lucilla. This is not a matter to joke about. I suspect– Look, I don't want to alarm you but I suspect him.'

'You suspect him of what?' I asked. Would my adoptive mother be murdered in her bed by a suave bridge player? The ideal set-up for an Agatha Christie whodunnit. I'd heard it was a serious game, but I had no notion it was that deadly.

'She's been talking about selling the house. Scaling down, that's what she called it. She said that Alfred advised it was the sensible thing to do now that she's on her own. She says she's rattling around in the cottage.'

'Well, perhaps she is. Perhaps it would be an intelligent move. She might be more at home in a smaller place. A new beginning for her.'

'Lucilla, she's in her seventies. It's too late for new beginnings.'

'I don't know . . .' I returned, playing the advocate for Mr Satan, and enjoying it immensely.

'God, you don't think that she's going to marry him?' he erupted down the line.

'What if she did?' I said, continuing in the same vein.

'Don't you get it? He's a gold-digger. He's after her money. You might as well know that I'm executor and trustee of her will. She did consider you, but . . . but when it came down to it she wanted a man at the helm.'

'I know. Mother told me,' I returned frigidly, thinking that even when we were children I had disliked Frank. He was born of an age when male heirs were the height of fashion, de rigueur. He had been blown up like a bullfrog with self-importance as far back as I could remember.

'It's my responsibility to keep an eye on her estate. For her beneficiaries.' This discussion was becoming tiresome. Avarice has that effect on me. We live in a materialistic age. Frank was, and continues to be, the worst kind of glutton, estimating the worth of his aunt while she was still breathing. 'Whatmore took her to see some dismal terraced box on the Pembroke Dock Road. I shall do all I can to dissuade her, of course. But I'd be grateful if you'd have a timely word to reinforce my message,' Frank continued, his cadence doom laden.

'Frank, you of all people ought to know my opinion carries no weight with my mother.'

'Well, it can't hurt,' Frank nipped peevishly.

'Very well,' I sighed.

But as I had foretold my mother ignored my counsel. To Frank's chagrin she sold the cottage, and did indeed buy the poky terrace on the Pembroke Dock Road.

'God Almighty, she opens her front door onto the road, no less. Massive articulated lorries thundering past all hours of the day and the night. The noise and the stink! She says she doesn't mind, but I don't know how she puts up with it. That damn Alfred is still sniffing around her money. I'm doing what I can but she's putty with him, I tell you, putty.' It was hard to conceive of my adoptive mother as putty, light and malleable. I received this update of my cousin's with detachment. I did not care unduly about the money, or money in general. I am not mercenary, and truthfully am bewildered by an age where people's entire lives are spent in pursuit of the next best thing. Enough, *enough* matters to me. Food, shelter, walking my dog on a winter's morning and making love with Henry while Miles Davis plays jazz on the radio. It is an elegant sufficient, as my grandmother used to say. I wallowed for a second in the vision of Frank being deposed by the opportunist, the wily Alfred Whatmore.

At the bottom of the hill now, I leaned on a gate and asked Henry to go on ahead, said that I'd catch him up. He obliged without demur, sensing I needed a moment alone. I let my eyes lap up the wonder of the bright winter's morning. In her declining years, my adoptive mother's phone calls and letters became ever more pathetic. The last time my parents came to visit me was gruesome. They stayed for a few days. My mother cast disparaging eyes about Pear Tree Cottage. She pounced on cobwebs, on dusty windowsills, on grease spots on the hob, on corners where a few dog hairs gathered with a grain or two of soil.

'Your light bulbs need a wash,' she observed, with gimlet eyes. 'They're coated in dust.' It was October and the late afternoons had an autumnal bluish edge to them.

'Do they?' I said, tension tying itself in a constrictor knot around my stomach. I had been in a frenzy trying to knock our shabby homely cottage into shape, to make it fit for her inspection. I had failed and I didn't give a damn. In fact, I felt like whistling through the rooms like a tornado, restoring their lackadaisical air of dishevelled harmony. My father kept a low profile, making a fuss of Merlin, perhaps recalling Scamp, and the night of fireworks when he injured his paw. Did he want to atone for what he had done? But the responsibility of absolving him from blame was too much for me. I settled for suppression.

After their departure, I took six dinner plates out into the small cobbled courtyard. One by one I raised them high above my head and slammed them down. I watched them smash to smithereens, my scalp tingling with frustration. Staring at the shards among the cobblestones, the last thing I felt was remorse. Henry's whiskery visage swam into view at our kitchen window. 'I'll buy some more,' I placated when he came out with the dustpan and brush.

He shrugged. 'Not overly fond of the design anyway. Prefer to eat off plates without patterns all over them. Gives me indigestion.' I smiled and thought that some loves are like an onion, each year peeling back another pearly layer for you to gloat over.

In April 1992 my mother wrote us a letter in her shaky spidery hand. It was not very coherent because her thoughts were shaky and spidery as well, like dropped stitches.

> *Dear Lucilla and Henry,*
>
> *I expect you are wondering what I am writing for. I will be 80 in –* here a date that was illegible was scratched out *– I would like you and Henry to celebrate with me. Frank is coming. Not Rachel though. Please excuse my writing. I am sorry but I can't walk without my frame. Book to Pembrock, not Pembrock Dock. Hoping to see you both. Travel by coach.*
>
> *I had to put dear old Pip to sleep. I have got a toffee-coloured poodle now. Dandy. He is dear. I have meals on wheels and home help. My home help will be at the party. She will be washing up. I have asked her and she is quite willing. She reminds me of Barbara. You remember Barbara.*
>
> *Love to you all.*
>
> *Mother*
>
> P.S. *Go to Pembrock. Ask the driver and he will put you down at the bus stop.*

My mother was lonely, growing steadily more confused in her isolation. The loan of her daughter had come to an end with interest owing. Her husband had died. Her previous dog, a black Scottie, had been put to sleep. Even Alfred Whatmore had deserted her, his wallet fatter. Nowadays, no one cared how clean her house was. There was no one to join her for her meals on wheels. And it didn't really matter if the van was five or ten or fifteen minutes late. Her teeth were rotten, so she could no longer abandon herself to the lethal crunch of slab toffee. I was sorry for her, but we did not go. She rang me quite a few times in the handful of years she had left.

'Why don't you come and stay,' she mumbled, her voice sounding gritty through lack of use. 'Be my good girl and come.' But I wasn't her good girl.

'Why don't you sell up and move closer,' I suggested. 'If you were nearby I could help.'

'Yes, yes, I'll do that. I'll put the house on the market. I'll wait for the spring and then I'll get in touch with an estate agent.' But we both knew it wasn't to be. It was the poodle that was her downfall in the end. One morning, descending the stairs, she tripped up on it. She fell heavily and fractured her hip. No amount of rest improved her condition. She reported that walking had become unbearable. 'It's badly swollen and very tender,' she informed me tightly. The day after this exchange her doctor rang me and told me that she had been admitted to a nursing home to recuperate. A neighbour, who had coveted the mischievous Dandy, took the culprit in. I was going to do my duty and visit, but then I had another call. She had been transferred to a hospital in Haverfordwest. I should go there, her doctor said, in the sepulchral tones I guessed he reserved for life and death situations. A day later and I stood by her bed. I plumped up pillows and assisted her when she felt up to sipping a cup of tea. I brushed the crumbs from her lips as she tried to nibble on a biscuit.

'You are a good girl after all,' she muttered looking into the middle distance with her dead eyes. The nurse came and whispered in my ear that the consultant wanted to see me. I filed out of the ward after her, past other elderly women, who fixed me with rheumy vacant eyes, their jaws working on the cud of their yesterdays. I was ushered into a small room, where a trim middle-aged man who looked disconcertingly healthy and spry, shook my hand energetically. He introduced himself as Doctor Weddel.

'I'm sorry to be the bearer of bad news, but your mother has very little time to live. She has cancer of the pancreas you see,' he said without preamble, clearly having missed the training on acquiring a sympathetic bedside manner.

There was no desk in the room, only two easy chairs, the seats and backs upholstered in a synthetic lilac fabric. We both sat down. They were set ludicrously far apart at either end of the rectangular space. There were no windows, and it was unbearably hot and stuffy in there. I kept coughing and having to clear my throat. 'But she only tripped over the dog?' I said finally, disconcerted.

I was sitting upright, as if I was in school and the teacher had just walked in. The consultant, on the other hand, was reclining in his seat, as if he was resting after a relaxing swim. We eyeballed each other. It really was sweltering. The desert heat continued in the wards, to such a degree I was amazed the elderly patients did not expire from the roasting their poor sick bodies were subjected to.

'Ah yes, the dog,' the consultant murmured ruminatively. He steepled his fingers, his eyes behind their lenses lit with impersonal medical logic. 'Well, I'm afraid that was a bit of a red herring.'

'A red herring?' I repeated, stumped. I thought she had tripped on a dog not a fish. This was surreal.

He opened his arms out and rippled his fingers on the wooden arms of the chair. 'Yes. Oh, she'd hurt herself all right, though nothing that wouldn't mend given time. But what we soon found was that she wasn't eating and there were other, shall we say, more sinister signs pointing to cancer.'

'I see . . . see,' I faltered. I thought that I might faint, keel over in the chair and hit the carpet-tiled floor. Still, I supposed if I was going to collapse, here was where to do it.

At last his backbone seemed to prop him up. He adjusted his posture to accommodate it. 'I thought that perhaps you would like to tell her.'

'To tell her?' I echoed.

'To tell her how sick she really is.'

I felt weirdly protective over my adoptive mother. This shift was a stick of dynamite exploding in my reason. 'Does she have to be told?' I asked.

The consultant seemed taken aback. 'These days we feel . . . we feel that honesty is the best approach.'

'Do you?' I remarked. 'Who for?'

Now it was his turn to don feathers and squawk. 'Who for?'

'Yes, who for? I don't believe my mother will benefit from the knowledge that she is dying. If I tell her, or you tell her, she will be frightened, horribly frightened. There's no cause for that.' My tone had become matter of fact, and I felt like the parent and not the child.

'I wouldn't want to mislead a patient,' he returned, unsmilingly.

'God forbid.' There was a strain of sarcasm in my voice. The medical profession's take on the world seemed unnecessarily harsh to me at that moment. 'But,' I suborned, 'if you don't say anything and she doesn't ask, you wouldn't be doing that.'

'Granted,' he conceded reluctantly.

'So shall we just leave it? Make her . . . what is the word you physicians are so fond using? Oh yes, comfortable. Yes, make her comfortable. That will do.'

He nodded and began to rise. 'But if she questions me directly, I won't lie.'

'Fair enough.' We shook hands on the bargain.

And so my adoptive mother was ignorant that her moon was waning fast. I went four times in all. They called in the almoner. They said she needed new underwear and nightgowns and soap and talc.

They said, Frank . . . did I know Frank? That Frank Pritchard, her nephew had power of attorney and control over her pension, that they did not know what to do. I contacted Frank and got her pension turned over to me. I purchased all that she required and a few luxuries besides, sweets mostly. She couldn't eat but she could suck. And I could furnish this, let her sugar-coat the process of dying.

'You're a good girl, Lucilla,' she whispered faintly, patting my hand. The pressure was light as a feather. 'A good girl. Did I tell you that when you were small?'

'No.'

'Is it . . . too . . . too late?'

Yes, it was, far too late. But I said, no, and the flicker of a smile crossed her cracked lips. The hospital rang me on a Sunday night. My mother's condition was fast deteriorating and could I come. It was June. A lovely June day, the sky looking as if it had been swept clean, the blue floor of it floodlit by a bronze sun. I had packed an overnight bag. I was unsure what to expect. Henry said that he could make arrangements, take the day off, accompany me. But I wanted to go by myself. This goodbye was private. I took the train from Reading to Swansea, and then another train to Haverfordwest. I had been given the name of a kindly lady who lived adjacent to the hospital and put visitors up for the night. The taxi took me there. I rushed to the hospital. At reception, I said that I'd come to see Harriet Pritchard, that I was her daughter. A nurse materialised and took me to one side.

'Is she in the same ward?' I said.

'No, no. I am so sorry, Mrs Ryan. Your mother has passed. But . . . but if it's any comfort her going was peaceful. She's been moved. Moved to the mortuary.'

'Oh,' I said quietly. 'She's dead then?'

'Yes, I'm afraid so.' She clasped her hands under her neat bosom and assembled her face in an expression of commiseration. She looked oriental, and had attractive eyes actually, almond-shaped and very dark. 'Would you like . . . like to see her?'

'Yes, yes, I think that I would. I've come such long way you see.'

She nodded and led me down a seemingly endless corridor. Her shoes tapped smartly on the floor. The further we went the fewer doctors and nurses we saw, as if . . . as if we were walking purposefully out of life and into the domain of death, as if the hospital was layered. On the top floor were the beds of those who were making a full recovery, and who would be leaping about like Mexican jumping beans the second they were discharged. A few floors down and there were the *in-betweens*, the patients who fetched up somewhere in the middle of life and death, the crossroads. They might go up or alternatively they might go down. And then on the bottom floor was a tunnel that took you into the impenetrable blackness of death, into the ward where the patients lay down, never to get up again.

We went through flapping doors that gaped open as she pushed, exhaling an icy breath on us. They swung shut behind us, the jaws of death clamping closed on two warm-blooded mortals. It was dingy, the fluorescent ceiling lighting oppressive, the way it could be in some supermarkets. It made you long for natural light. More footsteps and then we came upon her, lying on a trolley, her eyes shut. I expected them to blink open, the greyish-blue mouth to poke apart in speech. *Who is that? Come closer. Lucilla? Ah, Lucilla. You're a good girl, Lucilla, coming to see me when I'm dead. Have you brought Barbara with you?* She was covered in a sheet up to her shoulders. She'd lost so much weight that her shoulder blades were like twin peaks.

'Would you like me to leave you for a while?' asked the nurse gently.

'Yes, if you could.'

'Take your time.' She tapped off, her heels sounding like a firing squad dispatching the condemned in the clinical vault.

I didn't cry. I didn't shed a single tear for the mother life had lent me. Instead a red-hot fist punched through me. From my mouth poured a lifetime's repressed anger. There was no gating this torrent of words. 'Well, Mum,' I spat out when I was almost spent, 'you've gone now and left me, finally left me with everything that's wrong! What a waste of life, of years! You were cruel to me! It could have been so different! You never gave me a chance!' I was dimly aware that I was shouting. 'And you haven't told me about my real self! You've held me back, held me back all my life!' Trembling all over, I reached a hand towards her face. 'Goodbye! Goodbye! Goodbye!' And with that jittery hand, I touched the mask that had haunted all my days and nights. I wanted to feel how cold she was. Coldish. Getting colder by the minute. Becoming more dead.

Head held high, I turned away and walked as sedately as I could to the swinging doors. I sidled out apologetically. It was just as well that I did not charge through them. I would have sent several nurses who were huddled there, eavesdropping on my farewell to my dead adoptive mother, flying like skittles. I must have looked the way I felt – whey faced and wrung out with emotions deep and wide as oceans.

'Mrs Ryan, are you all right?' It was the Chinese nurse who addressed me, peering anxiously into my face. 'Would you like to sit down, have a cup of tea?' I stared directly at her, saw my image in the twin mirrors of her dark almond-shaped eyes. Smothering a laugh, I decided that the apparition that gazed back at me was in worse condition than the corpse lying only feet from us. 'Mrs Ryan?'

I regained my composure. 'Oh yes, I'm fine now.'

'Are you sure?' She lowered her voice and drew me a few steps from her gawping colleagues. 'It's only that we could all hear you.'

I gave a huge sigh. I had been fighting for so long, and now like a soldier, the battle done, was stunned to find that I was still here. Swallowing hard, I managed, 'Yeah, yeah, I'm OK.' It was all I could do to put one foot in front of the other, walking down the corridor towards the main entrance. I felt their eyes drilling into me. But I wouldn't look back. I wouldn't swing round. I wouldn't thank the oriental nurse for her solicitude. They must have thought I was bonkers, a total screwball. Or perhaps my little death scene had been played out before them as often as there are cards in a deck. Was it rare, this squaring up to a dead relative, this hostile reckoning, this accounting delivered as a caustic denunciation? Could it be that the extravagances of grief that brought you to your knees as your dear departed took flight, were the rarity?

The corridor seemed to stretch for miles. It felt more as if I was crawling along a tunnel than negotiating a corridor, a busy hospital corridor. Faces bobbed by, nurses' outfits, orderlies pushing trolleys, visitors clutching flowers and squinting at signs, patients slumped in wheelchairs being steered around and around the maze. Life and death were vying for supremacy everywhere. I vowed that I would not end my days in an anonymous bleak mausoleum like this. I would prefer to lie down in a field of grass and let the rain soak into me, than slide into the eternal darkness here. I was vaguely aware of a source of light growing steadily brighter, sucking me in. Was this what a near-death experience was purported to be like? I mused wryly. The long tenebrous tunnel, the pinprick of light intensifying until it was a scream of brilliance.

And then I was loitering in a car park, shame at my outburst flaring on my cheeks. I dallied with the idea of going back, of tramping that long corridor in the other direction, leaving the light behind me. Should I apologise, offer some rudimentary explanation for my extraordinary behaviour? Should I wade through dozens of nurses until I encountered the one who had shown me the way to the morgue? Should I say, it's all right, she's not really my mother? We've only been pretending all these years. The whole thing was a hoax really, a sham.

But I had so much to sort out, her death certificate and my life. I hailed a taxi and told him that I needed an undertaker. He nodded as if this was a regular request on the road that ran past the hospital. As we drove, I decided that Haverfordwest, this town that had put my biological mother and my adopted mother on the same map, was rather pleasant. The undertaker, a bow-legged genial man who tried to smooth the incongruous dimples from his cheeks, took me to the registry office to fill out the certificate. Later, I rang Frank from my bed and breakfast.

'Frank?'

'Yes?'

'It's Lucilla. My mother has died.' I was candid. I felt drained of emotion and my tone was impassive.

'I thought she only had days in her. I'll come down immediately, sort everything out.'

'There's no need. I'm taking care of it.' I was perfectly capable of dealing with this. For once, Cousin Frank could take a back seat. 'You'll be attending the funeral?'

'Of course,' he replied, indignantly. 'I can make the arrangements if you like.'

'No, I've done it already. I've seen the undertaker.'

'Oh!' He sounded momentarily crushed.

'When I've finalised the details, I'll let you know.'

'Oh!' Now his downwards inflexion reeked of ill temper. My cousin Frank was quite out of humour. Then he reinflated, his breath voluble as a gust of north wind. 'Well then, I suppose I'll see you at the funeral?'

This I would savour. I too inflated, taking an unhurried lungful. 'No,' I said. 'I won't be attending.'

'You won't be attending?' he parroted back, elongating the words to exhibit his incredulity.

'Didn't you hear me? Have we got a faulty line?'

Oh, he was tetchy now and making no attempt at niceties. 'I heard you perfectly well. But you can't miss your own mother's funeral.'

I parried nimbly, mouthing my rejoinder. She was not my mother. Then my vocal chords vibrated. 'Yes, I can.' I felt in control, a novel sensation when dealing with dastardly Frank.

'I'm sorry, Lucilla, but your absence is out of the question. Being Aunt Harriet's executor comes with huge responsibilities. She would have expected you to be there, expected me to see to it. We have appearances to consider. Now I really would like –'

'Oh, just fuck off, Frank.' I dismissed him and hung up. It felt liberating, the expletive on my tongue. I only hoped that my landlady had not overheard her foul-mouthed lodger.

A few days later, back in Dorking, I wrote to the vicar and made my apologies.

I had spent my teens and begun my married life in the knowledge that I had two mothers; one was the genuine article, the original, and one was a fake, devoid of any maternal instinct. And now the fake was gone. Where she had been was a gap, a vacancy, an opening to be filled. My true mother, this figure of myth and legend, doubled in value overnight. She became a priceless commodity as the prized black tulips had once been. For if one mother could die, then why not two? What if I reached the end of my quest only to be told that she had perished as well, that the two of them, once neighbours, were now companions in death. I quelled my panic by reminding myself that my birth mother was young, well . . . at sixty-seven younger than my adoptive mother.

Hurrying after Henry, I reflected that, four years on, hope was reborn in the guise of Bethan's marriage certificate.

It did not take bloodhound Rosemary more than a month to find out that, on the death of her husband, Bethan had sold the farm. Hearing that a relative wanted to get in touch, the new owners were happy to supply a forwarding address in Haverfordwest. When

Rosemary updated me in a phone call, I strived to digest the meat of her communication.

'Lucilla, I am going to write a letter to her. I shall be careful, don't worry. Just confirm that she is who we think she is, and see how she reacts.'

A month later and I receive the reply sent from my mother, my real mother, still alive and living astonishingly in Haverfordwest, to Rosemary.

> *Dear Miss Dixon,*
>
> *Thank you for your letter. It was indeed a surprise to hear from you. And I am sorry but I have no idea who you are. My name is Bethan, Bethan Modrun and my maiden name was Haverd. I look forward to hearing from you. I hope that the news you bring will be exciting,*
>
> *Yours sincerely,*
> *Bethan Sterry*

I am suddenly out of breath and I have to sit down before my legs crumple under me. What hits me so powerfully is that she seems sincerely baffled that an apparent stranger is seeking her out. If she harbours any suspicion about the unexpected communication, it is that a distant relation has decided to bequeath her a great fortune. What she is not anticipating is a legacy of another kind. It is to come in the form of a daughter abandoned in the woods of time, a daughter who has at long last found her way home. I ring Rosemary Dixon the same evening. I say that at this juncture I would like to give the reins over to Norcap, let them initiate contact. But Rosemary insists that she is an expert when it comes to these delicate negotiations, and that I am being overly cautious.

'I think you should write to her now, Lucilla,' she instructs. 'Don't frighten her. Keep the tone casual, easygoing. Tell her about yourself, your life, your family.' This is not how such a precarious situation should be handled, my intelligence pleads. I should exercise restraint, and pay my detective no heed. But as I sit down to write to my real mother, it is my heart and not my head that dictates.

Chapter 26

Bethan, 2000

I am covered in sores like a leper, my skin split and bleeding. I have these episodes when all I can do is shut myself in my bedroom, with my curtains closed, shunning the light of day. I feel like a preserved mummy. Now there's a black witticism. Lowrie will be here soon with her briefcase. She will ask me how I am keeping. She will examine me. She will diagnose severe eczema. She will prescribe a cortisone cream and a course of steroids. She will say that eczema, like asthma, is exacerbated by stress, by anxiety . . . by contrition? I can tell her exactly what I am suffering from. A baby's worth of my skin has been peeled off me. She will say that eczema can be psychosomatic. Oh, she's clever my second daughter, my echo baby, my minder.

Finders, keepers, losers, weepers. Who am I? I am not a finder. That would be the adoptive parents. They went looking and found a baby, a daughter going spare, Lucilla. And Lowrie? Well she is the keeper. The baby who wasn't given away. The one who stayed put. Losers? Ah, this is more difficult. I have come to the realisation that we are all losers on this Monopoly board. I have lost my gift baby and there is no health in me. Lowrie? Well, she has lost her mother, her mother who from her birth has been residing elsewhere, her psyche trapped in a delivery room at New End Hospital. As a child, instinct told her that no matter how tightly she hugged her mother, she could not hold on to her.

349

I took Leslie's, my husband's, introverted character as an indication that he was emotionally stunted, retarded, that there was no passion in his male body. But then there were three of us in the bed. My husband could not compete with an absentee German POW, with Thorston, the man his wife was really in love with, the man who in remembrance had been elevated to the status of a god. Leslie is dead now. I am a widow. He died of a stroke, a last indignity that left him wheelchair bound, and a captive audience to his unloving and unlovely wife. But in retrospect I believe I can say that he, too, was a loser. His wife committed adultery in thought several times each day of their married life. So what of the weepers? Oh, this is a crowded category. Countless weepers, though I hold the record for mourning that well exceeds Penelope's as she wove her shroud for Odysseus.

Lowrie chose medicine as her career. It was a resourceful decision and I admire her for it. She couldn't tinker with our minds, heal our fevered brains, so she turned, pragmatically in my opinion, to an area where she might prescribe an efficacious remedy. She was midway through secondary school when she deduced her antisocial behaviour was serving no one, least of all herself. Overnight, our she-devil turned into a swot, her bedside lamp burning into small hours as she pored over textbooks. Leslie was overjoyed.

'I knew she was bright as a star,' he told me, as he surveyed glowing end-of-term reports. 'She needed to find something that she loved, something that fully engaged that busy head of hers.'

She needed to find something that she loved. I often mulled over those words when Lowrie was at school. And they boomerang back to me today. *She needed to find something that she loved.* Or did my second daughter need to find something, or more pertinently, *someone* who loved her back? In any case, once she had found her métier there was no restraining her. She became a slave to chemistry, physics and biology. She attended Cardiff University, embarking on a medical degree. I remember her relaying with glee the grisly details the day she dissected her first corpse. Some of the male students were clowning about, tugging on tendons, which made icy grey fingers twitch and bend. It sounded repulsive. Apparently, a few became queasy and had to leave the room. But not our Lowrie. She has a strong stomach. She did say that she was curious about him though, the man she dissected. She said it was sad to come to this at the close of your life, a corpse in all his discoloured grey splendour being sliced into segments by diligent, nauseous, medical students.

'He had tattoos. A mermaid on one bicep and the Eiffel Tower on another. I think he was a sailor. Roaming the seas and sailing back to this inglorious disposal of his body.' That was all she aired. But I suppose it was compassion of a kind. She spared him a thought.

I smoke twenty a day. I have done for years. I feel like a heaped ashtray inside. I have a smoker's hack and a smoker's husky voice. Lowrie has peered down my trachea and scrutinised my larynx. She says I have nodules and polyps on my vocal cords. She says I should have them properly checked out. I can't be bothered, though it's touching that she cares. And I'm not going to give up my fags however much she nags me.

'It's not good for you, Mother,' she berates each time I light up. 'It'll kill you, Mother.' Ah well, when you have known a fate more terrible than . . . Brice has become the most unlikely of companions lately. He shows up in the middle of the night when I can't sleep for ghosts. He brings a gun, and fires shots in the air until they have all gathered up their silverfish entrails and glided off. Leslie, Mother and Father, the dogs, Fflur, Gwil and Red, Thorston, and Jessy the horse, and, of all animals, the cow that got stuck in the mud that day. She ambles in still coated with brown sludge, smelling of dung, craning her neck and lowing mournfully. And I can see him now, my German lover, bare-chested, his skin prickling with the cold, pimpled with raindrops, the rope knotted about his hips as he scaled the bank. All of him, every nerve and atom, was bent on saving that cow, while my father looked on scornfully. The beast went to slaughter just the same though, but somehow that didn't diminish his feat. Still, Brice has no patience with all the animals.

'This place looks like a squalid farmyard,' he criticises, reaching for his gun. 'Your bedroom is turning into a pigsty, Bethan.' He sits on the end of my bed and rambles on about the war. His voice is like a sail full of regretful sighs. Some nights we share a cigarette.

'Was it hell?' I ask, and he draws his lips into that oh-so familiar groove. 'I was lucky really. Taken out before I had a chance to make friends with depravity.' I fix on the tip of his cigarette glowing like a firefly in the night.

'Only you could think that way, be philosophical about death, your own death,' I say, giving my raw skin a good scratch.

'Let's face it, Bethan, the war wasn't a breeze for you either.'

'The war was fine. Thorston was fine. The feel of his skin was fine. Lovemaking in a nest of snow was fine. Do I disgust you?'

'Disgust me?'

'Fraternising with the enemy.'

He shrugs. 'We were both young men fighting for our countries. We wore different uniforms – that's all.'

'I think it's generous of you not to condemn me.' I lower my voice so that it is barely perceptible. 'I want to wind back the years. I want to run into the Church Adoption Society and snatch my baby up from that lady's stiff arms.'

'I know you do, I know. But you can't, Bethan, *cariad*, any more than I can have back my youth.'

So because we cannot unmake the beds of our lives, I rest my head on his shoulder, feeling the rough wool of his uniform caressing my cheek. We play pass the cigarette. He tells me war stories of daring dos and daring don'ts. And gradually my skin irritation lessens and I sink into a fitful doze. In the morning he is gone.

'Mother, you look ghastly,' Lowrie says, studying me when she arrives. She has made me a nice cup of tea and a slice of toast. She has spread it with honey. She draws back the curtains and I wince. She strides across the room, the floorboards creaking under the pressure of her assertive steps. She sets down her briefcase, lifts my arms one by one, rolls back the sleeves of my winceyette nightgown, and snorts through her nose.

'You've been scratching again,' she says, her brow puckered with displeasure. 'I've told you not to scratch. It only aggravates the rash.'

'I can't help it,' I plead, pathetically.

'You make it spread.'

So here she stands, my grown-up echo daughter. She is tall like her father was, with a square plain face, homely – though to what she attributes this domestic slant I cannot say. Our home more closely resembled a war zone than a hearth to snuggle up to. She clicks open her case and rummages through it. She did make a tepid attempt at mastering psychology. She tackled it in her fourth year, the year in which they gain experience in hospitals treating living, breathing patients. But she said it was depressing. She practised medicine at Bangor, Wrexham, Swansea and Cardiff. She has elected to work in intensive care, resuscitating lives that are only a wavering candle flame. She likes to bring people back, she says. I wonder if they like it.

'I'm going to write you a prescription for another course of steroids. This time remember to take them,' she says, scribbling on a pad. Her dark hair is worn in two plaits coiled in fat circles at the sides of her head, like earmuffs. She wears transparent pink-rimmed glasses. The small rectangular lenses make her look dauntingly intelligent. And she is dressed in a trouser suit, grey pinstripes. She looks very commanding. 'And you are to rub this on three times a day,' she orders, producing a tub of ointment as large as a tankard. I nod meekly.

She is gay, my daughter, my second daughter. She thinks that I don't know. But I guessed when, in her twenties, no young men came to call. There was only a succession of women – one woman now. She has been with for her for some years. Glenice. They live together in a modern flat in Cardiff. I expect she thinks I would disapprove. Or perhaps she feels it's none of my business. She doesn't want children. She's told me that much. 'I haven't the patience,' she says. But I don't think it's that. It's a surplus of love she is missing. She daren't slosh it about. What she has she must guard wolfishly, for fear of depleting her already meagre supply. Besides, I do not hanker for grandchildren. Her choice does not rankle with me. In fact, I envy her – to be childless by design, to avoid the risk of having your heart steamrollered.

She has Glenice and is extremely private about their relationship. I won't pry. I haven't earned the right to share her secrets. I didn't share mine with her. With both my parents gone and Leslie as well, my secret will die with me. My mother had a form of dementia leading up to her death. Her short-term memory was irreversibly damaged, but past secrets surfaced with chilling frequency. That's how I learned about the letters. Thorston wrote to me three times. There *was* a second letter slipped behind mine to Thorston that day, and two more, which my father also destroyed. She told me he wanted me to go to him, to go to East Germany where he lived. She said he never stopped loving me, never stopped wondering about our baby. What I wish most of all is that she had died with that secret.

That is my only terror, Lowrie discovering that before her there was a gift baby, that she was the consolation prize. It would be over for us if that happened. The tenuous structure of our scaffolding lives would collapse under the burden of truth. She would comprehend all of it in a minute, that she was a substitute baby, that she did not make the grade, that as far as I was concerned she was only an echo of the real thing, an echo of my firstborn, an echo of Lucilla. I would prefer to die than that she has to come to terms with this. It may not be much but I can give her some peace of mind. At least let her have the pretence of her family intact. I have determined to take my gift baby with me to my grave.

I fumble for my cigarettes, for the packet on the bedside table, for my lighter. 'I wish you wouldn't,' says Lowrie as if scripted. 'It's not good for your heart.'

'But it's good for my soul,' I cackle in return, lighting up and inhaling deeply through dry lips. I have a bad heart by the way. When this was confirmed to me by some cardiac specialist in hospital, I'm afraid I laughed. He looked perplexed. 'I thought you were making a moral judgement,' I commented dryly. He didn't even smile. I have come to the conclusion that a sense of humour is a rare commodity in hospitals.

After Lowrie has gone, I reread my letter, a mysterious letter from a lady called Rosemary Dixon. It is all laid out very formally so I'm pondering if she is a solicitor – though there is no heading on the writing paper. And of all the people to enter my head, comes little Tilley Draper, our evacuee. The prospect that she may get in touch, that we may resume our friendship after all these years, is almost as enticing as finding out that I have inherited an indecent fortune. She was as fortifying as a tablespoon of tonic.

The following day, however, brings another letter. I inspect the envelope, the postmark. It is definitely another missive from Rosemary Dixon. I open it seated in my chair by the fire. It is summer, early summer, one of those days that begins cool as autumn, with the temperature climbing in the afternoon until it feels like cricketing weather. But it is not the afternoon yet and, as I button up my cardigan, I am aware of a coldness that seems to penetrate the marrow of my bones. Instantaneously, I am dyslexic, the words coming apart like the carriages of a derailed train. But her name is whole as my lips move to speak it. 'Lucilla!' It is not Tilley who has tumbled from the ragbag of the past but Lucilla, my gift daughter.

It must be a full fifteen minutes before the gist of Rosemary Dixon's manuscript penetrates. She is a private detective who has been seeking me out for her client, Lucilla Ryan. Ryan. Her married name I realise.

Lucilla, the daughter that you had in 1948, the baby who was adopted by Harriet and Merfyn Pritchard, and who grew up in London, has written to you. The letter is enclosed. I hope this will not be too much of a shock for you. But I assure you, Lucilla intends you nothing but goodwill.

It is nearly midnight when I drum up the courage to read it. I lock the front and back doors, the windows. I pull the curtains. I take pains to make sure that there aren't any gaps that a neighbour might peep through. I disconnect the telephone and turn off all the lights. I have a torch. I climb into bed fully dressed with it and hide under the duvet. And still I am paranoid that someone is out there spying on me from the darkness. I turtle-neck out my head, and the hand gripping the torch snakes. Lines of light dissect my room. I am looking for a little girl with flat brown eyes and an empty stare, a little girl with a plain solemn face and a lonely acceptance in the set of her mouth.

'Lowrie?' I whisper. 'Lowrie? Don't be scared. I must look a sight with all this cream slathered over my face. But see here and here, I haven't scratched. You'll be pleased to know I haven't scratched.' There she is crouching in the corner. The torch catches the gleam of her eyes. 'You mustn't be frightened. She's not coming. I won't let her come. I won't let her into our lives, your life. It's only a letter. After I've read it I'm going to tear it up.' But even as I say this I know I will not do it.

These few words I shall salvage, hide them at the bottom of my jewellery box. She is humming to herself, my echo daughter, some Welsh ballad her father will have sung her. 'You have my word on it.' In the cone of light, her eyes gaze back challengingly. 'But . . . but I have to hear what she has to say. I owe her that.'

I shift the bag of my bones under the cover again and spread the letter out on the mattress. The duvet capes me like a blanket of snow once did. I relive our lovemaking, the fire in my blood, her conception. Then Lucilla speaks to me.

Dear Bethan,

I shan't call you mother, although that is how I think of you, as my mother. Please don't be upset by my writing to you, by my wanting to know you. And please, please understand I mean you no harm. Over the years I have gathered information, papers, certificates, gradually building my history, your history. I have my birth certificate and copies of your birth and marriage certificates, and the letters exchanged between you and the Church Adoption Society. So many certificates, all testifying to who I am, where I came from. And so I know that my father was a German prisoner of war working on your farm, Thorston Engel. I've tried to imagine how it must have been, what you went through. But I like to think that you didn't forget me.

The Pritchards, my adoptive parents, . . . well, we got by. And I have a family of my own now. My husband is a gardener. His name is Henry. We live in a cottage in the grounds of a large country estate outside Dorking, Brightmore Hall. We were married in 1969 and we have two children, Gina and Tim. All grown up now, and Gina is married with a daughter of her own, Lisa – your great-granddaughter. I've built a good life for myself.

I hope that you've been happy, that you weren't scarred by events. I don't want anything from you. It would mean so much to me if we could correspond, be like pen pals, get to know each other through letters, send photographs. It would be wonderful if we could just be friends.

But I am running before we have taken our first steps, our baby steps. Again I urge you not to be alarmed. Rosemary, my researcher, says that you may not have told your family about my existence, that this communication may cause you to be upset. Please believe me when I say I am not a threat to you. We can take this as slowly as you like, and you may trust me absolutely to keep our confidences. If there comes a day when we can be a part of each other's lives, however tiny, then it will all have been worth it.

With warmth, your daughter, Lucilla

Then suddenly I am gasping for air, the stabbing in my chest feeling less like a penknife and more like a carving knife. My left arm is tingling and I feel as if someone is strangling me. I rest for a full minute. She has come, after all these years she has come. And in a second I know. I know that I do *not* want her. I do not want her rocking the foundations of my life, breaking the tenuous link I have with my Lowrie. A memory like a sudden drop in temperature freezes out all other thoughts. I am with my mam in the front room of Bedwyr Farm. Lowrie has gone to see the horses with my dad. The words she mouthed that day are carved on my consciousness. 'She must never know. Never!'

All of my adult life I have hankered after the baby I gave to the Pritchards, rejecting the baby that came in her wake. Now I am prepared to do anything, anything, to maintain the brittle bridge that joins me to Lowrie, to the daughter I possess. And so . . . and so for the second time I scheme to give my gift baby away. I write back at midnight. I am becoming a nocturnal creature, one who would be at home with vampires, werewolves and unclean spirits.

The Adoption

Dear Ms Dixon,

I was extremely upset by your correspondence, your enclosure. Honestly I never dreamed the purpose of your writing to me.

Lucilla's letter was a shock. As I suffer from a heart condition it has been quite an ordeal. I am pleased that she has a lovely husband and family. I have a grown-up daughter, Lowrie, and for many reasons our relationship has not been an easy one. She is ignorant of Lucilla's existence, of my past. She would be devastated by such news. I cannot run the risk of her making such a discovery. Unfortunately, however traumatic for Lucilla, I have to factor this in to my decision. It is too late. I wish neither of you to contact me ever again. It is vital that the finality of this is conveyed to your client. As an investigator, I expect that you have a professional code of conduct. I ask that you adhere to it in this volatile situation, and withdraw as I have requested.

Yours sincerely,

Bethan Sterry

I seal it and fumble in the drawer of the dressing table for a stamp. In the early hours, I steal from my bed, shrug on a coat and, while the residents in my road are still sleeping, I walk to the postbox and mail it. The following morning my skin has improved to such an extent you would think I had undergone a miraculous cure overnight.

Chapter 27

Laura, 2000

When the rose gardens at Brightmore Hall are in full bloom, Rosemary Dixon writes to Bethan again. The same reply, only more emphatic, wings back. In the light of it, she announces that she is closing her investigation.

'Why didn't you let Norcap deal with this?' I shrill down the phone. 'You knew how sensitive it was. You should have listened to what I wanted. After all, I'm paying the bloody bill for you to open doors, not slam them in my goddamn face.'

'No need to resort to vulgar language, Lucilla. I have sympathy for you, really I do. But there is no call to take this out on me. I am certainly not being paid enough to swallow abuse.' The angrier Rosemary Dixon becomes the commoner she sounds.

But I am not nearly done. I unleash a condemnatory onslaught, venting my pent-up rage at the injustice of it all. I close with a final surge, using every molecule of my reserve breath.

'For you it's just another job! For me it's my life you've wrecked, you charlatan!' There is a deafening silence at the end of the line into which tears of wretchedness shower from me. 'Do you have the faintest notion of what you've done? Do you? Do you?'

'Contemplating such disruption and . . . and possibly a bitter rejection from her *legitimate* daughter, Lowrie, must be very distressing for an elderly woman in fragile health,' she advises me frostily, having recovered her faux refined intonation. 'She is obviously upset at the prospect of meeting you. I will send all the papers and letters I have back to you. And although, understandably, this is not what you want to hear, Lucilla, you must respect her desire for anonymity and not –'

That is the instant I slam down the telephone. In two bounds, I am on the settee, where Lola gives canine consolation in the form of licks and snuffles. I relay all this to Henry in the evening. He listens, exuding solace from behind a veil of pipe smoke, and inclining his head discerningly. For the passage of an hour, we sit in repose, digesting our supper of lamb chops, arms entwined, my head resting on his chest. I can hear the beat of his heart, hear the reverberations and I imagine it rippling through every cell, every nerve, every fibre, the push of it behind the passage of his blood. I can feel the melancholy in the drag of his heart tonight, because it is my own. Then he clears his throat and says cryptically, '*Dum spiro spero.*'

I break free, wriggle to the edge of the sofa and gaze back at him. 'Translation, if you will?' I ask, suddenly needing very badly to know what it means.

'Cicero,' he growls, keeping me in suspense. 'Roman. Almost as great an orator as I am.'

'Ah! So tell me, Henry, what does the famous orator have to say that may be hawthorn to my bruised heart?'

'While I breathe, I hope,' Henry says.

I inhale a breath as if to test the dictum, and the lift of an involuntary smile tweaks my down-turned mouth.

'Oh Henry!'

Lola gives a gargantuan vocal yawn in appreciation of the gift of philosophy, and sinks back into a deep, deep sleep.

I discuss my next move with my children. Gina, when she, Nathan and our adorable granddaughter come for lunch, is beside herself with anger at the tidings. Lisa complained of an earache when they arrived, causing me to worry that she has inherited my weakness. But Nathan seemed unconcerned, diverting her by taking her for a walk with Lola. This afforded me a chance to exchange confidences privately with Gina while preparing our meal. Having listened carefully she makes her pronouncement. She is all for us springing on a train and beating Bethan's door down. 'She's my grandmother too,' she stakes her claim. 'Lisa's great-grandmother. She can't just ignore us.' Gina is pregnant with her second child, and at the mercy of hormones appears at least as upset as I am. 'She can't pretend we're not real. We'll go together. I know you don't feel you have the courage, but with me at your side you will have.' There is muscle in her tone, but hurt as well. This is not what she has been hoping for either. This is not the history she dreamed of giving her children, that for Bethan Haverd her illegitimate daughter, her granddaughter and her great-granddaughter, all three amount to triple the embarrassment, triple the distaste. I have underestimated the impact of this upon Gina, and now that I fully comprehend how damaging it is for her, I want to protect her. She fixes her attention on the home-made vegetable soup she is stirring on the stove. Her shoulders are raised, tensed. I talk to her back, to her curved spine, knowing these sorrowful tidings have come as a blow her idealistic nature was unprepared for.

'I don't think we'll go, Gina. If she doesn't want to see us it would be futile.' I trace the ridges of her spine over her clingy blue Lycra top, the pressure I exert so light I might as well not be touching her at all. 'Too painful, yes?' She gives the hint of a shrug, and her rigid shoulders gradually relax and drop.

Tim meets me for coffee in Guildford, his mind also elsewhere. He scowls, looking down at his steaming cup. 'I did ask for a cappuccino not an espresso, didn't I?' I open my mouth. 'Oh never mind.' I close it again. 'I had a premonition about this, you know. People can let you down, Mum. It doesn't matter if you've spent a lifetime imagining a reunion between you and your real mother, how wonderful it could be, how healing. Because some people are really fucked up. You've got to let it go.' So intense, raw and honest is the dialogue coming from my son, that I do not remark on the expletive. 'They don't know how to forgive themselves. Do you get it? They run away because the truth is too much for them.' His eyes are cast down, unable to meet mine. He is not comfortable having this conversation with his mother. And yet he forges on, as if he has rehearsed this speech several times. 'All you've done . . . trying to trace her, to put your past together, well . . . it's not wasted. You've faced the truth, Mum, even if she can't. And, as far as I am concerned, that makes you a better person than she'll ever be.' He draws a hand across his mouth, inhales, exhales, chest rising and falling with effort. Then, in one of those surreal role switches that most parents disconcertingly experience, he says, 'And now, Mum, you've got to forgive her, to forgive your mother and get on with your life, our life!' There is a tear in my eye as he finishes. But on a day when rules are broken there is another shock in store for me. 'Mum, I've been meaning to tell you, I'm going to Australia to work for a bit. The contract's for a year but I might stay longer. I'll see.' Tidings that elicit a downpour of maternal tears. Am I about to lose the family I have, as well?

In the ensuing weeks, Henry strides up and down before the fireplace, wearing a groove in the floorboards. Intermittently, he rakes back his hair and shakes his head, while I sit hunched on the settee chewing a thumbnail. 'The blackcurrants have been very disappointing this year,' he informs me dejectedly and repeatedly. 'Don't know what's up with them. Dug in loads of muck and they've had plenty of sunshine. A dud crop, blighted before they matured. I'm going to dig the bushes up and begin over next year. The only way.' He comes across to me and kisses the top of my head.

I obsess for weeks before I pen another letter. It is a begging letter.

I am grovelling in the gutter and acutely aware of it. If I had any pride, I misplaced it decades ago.

Please, please, please, will you just consider writing to me, Bethan? It doesn't have to be often. When the mood takes you. Christmas? Birthdays? If you only scribble down a few thoughts, perhaps relate what it was like, why it had to be, why you gave me to the Pritchards. I don't want to upset you. I don't blame you. I understand that you must have had your reasons, good reasons, for what you did. I appreciate that. The road forked and we separated. You have your own family, as I do now, your daughter, Lowrie. Of course you are concerned at how she . . . she might react if she learned of me. But can't we be pen pals to each other, no more than that? Pen pals who fill up scrapbooks with memories. Do this for me and I promise I won't ask any more of you.

I am lying. I am driven to possess her utterly, as she dispossessed me. A month drags by before her reply is delivered. It is August, unbearably hot and humid. Bethan's answer to my entreaty is as malignant as a curse.

Dear Lucilla,

I am sorry that we have both been inflicted with grievous and, I have to tell you I feel largely unnecessary, torments. You should not have toiled so hard to trace me. And I should have grasped that the past and the present are not to be spliced in two without a little bloodletting. I don't want to see you or to have anything to do with you. I shan't write to you. I shan't send you birthday and Christmas cards. And I won't inscribe stories of yesterday to you. I won't rouse phantoms to enchant you. Leave them be, Lucilla. Don't hold them to account. They were as innocent as you. I am sorry to kill your hope with such a cruel blow, but anything less and you may doubt my sincerity. That you are named my daughter on a birth certificate is meaningless. I am a sick old woman. My heart is too weak for this. I want to end my days in peace. I do not want to remember, I want to forget. I have a daughter and you have a mother. It will benefit neither of us to have another.

My husband, Leslie, has been dead for fourteen years. When he had a stroke, I tended to him. I felt guilty. He deserved more from me. And my daughter also deserved more from her mother. I betrayed them both. The government is marvellous these days. Assistance with all sorts of hardship. My doctor put me on to the carer's allowance. I saved every penny of it. I have my pension and my needs are few. When I last looked, I had savings in the region of nine thousand pounds. I am enclosing a cheque for the said amount made payable to you, Lucilla Ryan. Please cash it, spend it, put it by for your own children, as you will. All I ask is that you receive it in the spirit in which it is given, as full and final payment of my debt to you.

If having read this you begin to despise me, to see what a monster I truly am, I'm glad of it. It will make my resolution to sever any ties between us more bearable for you.

Do not ever contact me again.

Bethan Sterry

I do not make a scene. Nor do I reread the letter. Once is sufficient. I am struck dumb in the heat of the garden. I evade showing the letter to Henry, but I do divulge its general contents. Sharing my devastation, for once the wisdom of Latin proverbs and homilies fail him completely. Transmitted it would seem with spooky telepathy, my very brutal and absolute rebuff is shortly common knowledge in the Ryan ranks. Gina is initially irate, reacting much as she did before. But the scalding temperature of her ire cools overnight, and then freezes into an icy inactive resentment, a mindset that I worry will fester if I do not take some sort of a stand, lead by example. Though the problem is that I do not have the strength. I have been knocked out cold in the last round. Tim becomes a weekend guest, touchingly ringing me daily throughout the week to assess my condition. He advises over and over that I must let it go, let her go, let my mother go. And he implies that I must be thorough, surgically remove her from my mind, my body and my heart. So concerned is he about my despair that he unselfishly suggests cancelling his imminent trip to Australia. But I insist that postponement is not an option, realising in spite of my wretchedness how invaluable the experience will be for him.

It took, we are told in the Bible, six days for God to create the world. Well, it takes me less time than that to descend into lunacy. It is November before I come out of hibernation, emerging on a dripping wet Saturday morning. The beech trees, the sweet chestnuts and the oaks have finally disrobed. They throw up their bare arms and flaunt their gnarled trunks as I go by, like scandalous striptease dancers. The mole traps have been set, making me want to weep. After all, they do not do much damage, the squinting moles. It is all about aesthetics really, wanting perfect lawns, perfect children. I spot a young hedgehog burrowing into a heap of wet leaves. I consider bringing it home, fixing it a saucer of cat food – but on second thoughts we go our separate ways.

Nightfall and the crescent moon is gold, a buttery gold grin, the haze around it a wondrous violet. In the middle of the night, I rise from our bed where Henry is snoring, and slip downstairs. I find the cheque where I left it months ago, in the envelope among the few photographs I have of me as a baby, me as a little girl. I tear it up and rake the ashes in the fireplace over it. I am amused by the whimsy that tomorrow we will have a nine-thousand-pound blaze roaring in our small grate.

The end of my confinement is prompted by the end of Gina's confinement, and the safe delivery of a second bonny granddaughter, Jessica. She has a shock of dark hair, eyes the colour of cornflowers and the cutest button nose. But despite the flurry of activity the baby's arrival necessitates, or possibly because of it, my mind strays to my own absent baby. I miss Tim, my youngest. He started out making musical instruments and has wound up as a nurse in a psychiatric hospital in Sydney. Maybe he wanted to fix people, to fix the tragic inexplicable glitches in their heads, to absolve them of the obsessions that if dwelt on will make them go mad. He flew out in September. It is as I slog about the shops buying Christmas presents desultorily that I decide I want to visit him, to go to Alice Springs and Ayers Rock, to snorkel the Great Barrier Reef. Henry is supportive on my behalf, but adamant he cannot join me. 'Travelling so far you should book a minimum of three weeks. I couldn't take a holiday that length. The gardens would suffer. But you're not to let that deter you,' he says over dinner one evening. 'It's precisely what the doctor would prescribe, change of scenery, injection of culture. Besides, Tim wants you to go. It means a tremendous amount to him.'

I am drifting pleasantly into the realms of sleep when a thought strikes me as a hammer does a gong. 'Henry?'

'Yes?' says my husband drowsily.

'Henry, I haven't got a passport.'

We sit up then as if one spine serves both Mr and Mrs. I switch on my bedside light. It is true. I do not possess a passport. Until this hour, this day, this year, it has not been an issue. I have never ventured abroad. Mainly it is a lack of funds that has kept me from exploring beyond the British coastline. Most of the holidays I went on with my adoptive parents were connected to the temperance movement. In those days, families seldom went abroad. You holidayed in your own country, the seaside being the most popular resort. By the time Henry and I had a family of our own, there was no money to go jetting off to the Mediterranean. But now it suddenly seems imperative that I obtain a passport permitting me to travel anywhere, a passport with my photograph in it, and my name, a document that tells passport control anywhere in the world I choose to visit that I am a British citizen.

'You'll need to apply for one then, quick smart,' Henry says with a yawn.

During my morning walk with Lola, my mind grapples with the scale of my lack of identity, the handicap it is when contemplating distant horizons. It is incredible now I come to think of it, that all these years I have survived without a passport. I sit on the bench that overlooks the green hill – not green today but pearly grey, a carpet of frost under a cloudy canopy. I close my eyes and envision it, me lifting my passport out of my bag and pushing it forwards across a counter. I envision the man in passport control, clean-shaven with quick perceptive eyes, picking it up and thumbing through the pages. I envision him pausing over the photograph and the name, Lucilla Ryan. And then . . . and then I envision him calling a colleague over, asking me to step aside, and me being ushered into a cramped room for questioning. I hear myself saying, 'What exactly seems to be the trouble, officer?' and him replying apologetically that it is my name, that my name doesn't fit. It is borrowed. I am travelling under a false identity. My passport is forged.

And this is how it comes about that at the age of fifty-two, with no previous criminal record, I resolve to enact a murder. Lucilla is stalking me. I keep catching sight of her in shop windows. 'Oh go away,' I tell her, but she will not listen to me. I plan it meticulously. It is pre-meditated, of this there can be no doubt. Murder in the first degree. If caught, I face a life sentence. So the stakes are the highest conceivable. This is survival of the fittest. Her or me? Lucilla has to perish. Lucilla, who as a baby was presented to the Pritchards with as much ceremony as a bag of flour. Lucilla, whose formative years were spent in a house not a home. Lucilla, who was unloved by her adoptive mother, a woman of limited vision, incapable of seeing beyond her German prejudices. Lucilla, whose primary dream of being an artist was stampeded, not long before her secondary dream of becoming a veterinary nurse went the identical way. Lucilla, who was dragged to John Lewis, her nightmare realised when she was assigned to the despised haberdashery department. Lucilla, whose suitor, Henry, was exiled after making her pregnant. Lucilla, whose adoptive father drunkenly groped her. Lucilla, who gave birth to an illegitimate child at nineteen just as her mother had done before her in 1948. Lucilla, whose search for her birth mother ended when she was ruthlessly cast aside for the second and last time by Bethan Sterry. She has not a vestige of her birth family remaining to insure her against identity theft.

This same Lucilla, if I let her live, if I nurture and feed her inadequacies, will destroy me. The only escape is to beat her to it and pull the trigger first. I must unmake her, like the knitted garments Aunt Ethel unpicked, rolling the crenulated wool into balls, casting on and beginning afresh with another pattern. When complete, I often marvelled at how speedily I forgot the previous incarnation. I was blind to the old disguised in the new – all were irreparably transformed, as I will transform, starting with my name. I shall select the name I should have been christened, the name that is as snug as a skullcap. I broach the subject as I fillet fish for our supper, speaking to Henry through the open kitchen doorway that gives on to the lounge.

'Henry?'

'Yes?' says Henry. He is seated in the chair by the crackling fire, cup of coffee on the side table, flipping through a book on Elizabethan knot gardens.

'I'm considering changing my name, changing it legally.'

'Oh yes,' murmurs Henry, still seemingly engrossed.

'To Laura. Laura Ryan. You know I've tried it on, substituted it for some while. Well, I've come to the conclusion that I need to make it permanent, lawful.' The fish scales on the knife blade glint silver as sequins in the lamplight. Head askew, he makes no comment, so that I assume he disapproves. 'It seems sensible to make it official,' I continue. The fire spits. 'You think it's a crazy thing to do at my age?' Lola gives a double sneeze and flicks her feathery tail. 'You prefer Lucilla?'

His considered response is indirect. 'Laura,' he utters the name with respect. 'Laura.' This time there is an unmistakable hint of tenderness in his tone. 'Laura.' I breathe hesitantly and await his pronouncement. '"What's in a name? That which we call a rose by any other name would smell as sweet",' quotes Henry, his timbre quivering with his ardour. 'Should have done it years ago,' he affirms to himself, taking up his pipe.

I need an accomplice in my dastardly crime. Having no previous association with villains, I take pot luck, picking him out of a phone book. Messrs Hawkins and Cowley, solicitors with offices in Epsom. Next day, I dial the number. I am put through to Mr Arnold Hawkins, senior partner. I am seeking an assassin and come straight to the point.

'I want to change my name by deed poll,' I blurt out. 'I want to get rid of Lucilla.'

'Lucilla?' whispers Arnold Hawkins, conspiratorially. Perhaps he thinks the line may be bugged.

I brief him on the mark. 'My first name, the name I was christened. From now on I want to be known as Laura.'

'I see,' cogitates the senior partner of Messrs Hawkins and Cowley. He pontificates with, 'Ho-hum. Well, well. I don't think that will be a problem. So long as it is all done within the letter of the law. Dots and crosses, that's what the court likes.'

A flood of renewed hope has me rising to my toes. I make an appointment two days hence. Having tolerated Lucilla all my life, I am now so eager to do her in that I am prepared to dispatch her with my own bare hands. Mr Arnold Hawkins, senior partner, has a suitably sombre appearance. He is clothed in a dark suit of expensive fabric and cut. He has a low ragged voice emitted without motion of his unsmiling mouth. He is one of those adults impossible to envisage as a child. He is plump, his double chin and the back of his fleshy neck spread over his impeccably starched white collar. Heavy brows preside over sunken eyes. His few black hairs are carefully groomed. I am whisked off to America, a poor Italian woman grovelling before the renowned Mafia godfather to end my affliction and suffering. If anyone can succeed in killing Lucilla and getting away with it, my intuition tells me that Hawkins is the man for the job.

He draws up the deed, as I look on mesmerised, overcome with the solemnity of the proceedings. He does not intrude into my affairs, waving them away with his pudgy pale hand. His client is desirous of a new name. That is all the information he requires, he says. When he has finished tapping away at his computer keys, he prints the document and, handing it to me, invites inspection with a flourish of his stubby fingers.

'Read it through carefully at least a couple of times, Mrs Ryan. And then I'll call in Mrs Billings, my secretary, as a witness and you can sign it.'

I give it my undivided attention. I want no mistakes this time, no accidents of birth. Laura is on purpose, meant. I am naming me for no one but myself.

THIS DEED OF NAME CHANGE is made on the 21st day of December 2000 by me, Lucilla Ryan, of Pear Tree Cottage, Brightmore Hall, Dorking, a married woman and British Citizen under the British Nationality Act 1981, Section 1, WITNESSES AND DECLARES as follows:

1. *Whereas before and after my adoption I was known by the forename, Lucilla.*
2. *I absolutely renounce and abandon the use of the forename, Lucilla, and instead I assume the forename, Laura.*
3. *I declare that I at all times from now on, in all records, deeds and instruments in writing, and in all actions and proceedings, and in all actions and transactions, and on all occasions, will use and sign the name of, Laura, as my forename instead of my former forename of, Lucilla, which is now renounced.*
4. *I authorise and request all persons to designate and address me by such an assumed forename of, Laura, only.*

IN WITNESS whereof I have hereunto set my hand the day and year first above written
    Signed as a deed by the said
    Laura Ryan.
    In the presence of:

I glance up and nod portentously. I am ready. Mrs Billings is summoned. I sign. She signs. Mr Arnold Hawkins, senior partner of Messrs Hawkins and Cowley, solicitors at law, signs. The deed is done. Several photocopies of the document are printed. Mrs Billings withdraws. As my assassin blows smoke from the barrel of his gun, he has these words of sagacity for me: 'You must waste no time in informing the bank, the medical practice where you are registered, your dentist, the tax office, national insurance, not to mention relations and friends.' He presses his hands together as if in supplication. 'You can help the process, Mrs Ryan. Henceforth you are to be addressed as Laura by those you are on first-name terms with. If they fail to comply by using your legal name in addressing you, then you must give no reaction.' He leans close and drops his voice a notch.

'Remember, Lucilla is no more. You cannot talk with the deceased, not in reality.'

I trace my name on the documents, the script that spells out Laura, Laura Ryan. These papers are entrusted with the task of acquainting all and sundry with my new identity. Smiling hugely, I gather up my deeds of name change and hug them to me. Mr Hawkins raises a finger in caution. 'Naturally, you cannot alter the name on your birth certificate or your wedding certificate.'

'But I can on my passport?' I quiz, anxiously. If Lucilla endures there, if I am trapped by her at every border crossing, then all this has been futile.

'Oh most assuredly yes,' vouchsafes Mr Hawkins, getting to his feet. 'I suggest you tackle the passport office without delay.'

My accomplice assists me filling out the forms for such, which I have precipitously collected from the post office in Dorking. He double-checks that all the facts are correct. I write an accompanying letter explaining that I was adopted Lucilla Pritchard, but that I have now changed my name by deed poll. Following post office guidance, I also include copies of all my certificates. The lady at the counter, with the Union Jack transfers on her fingernails, reviews my papers, pencilled eyebrows almost colliding, replying in answer to my query that I should hear in about a week.

The New Year, 2001. Every day I expect to take delivery of a bulky package containing my passport. I have stacks of Australian travel brochures by my bed, and drop off leafing through them at night. I wonder what it will be like boarding an aeroplane, for I have never been airborne – except in my dream, the dream that still comes to me, the dream where I fly off a chalky Empire State Building – Beachy Head. The letter from the passport office and the letter from Tim arrive together. The passport office wishes to see me in person, to examine all my documentation, the originals, and interview me. Tim writes that he is very excited about my forthcoming visit, and that as soon as my dates are confirmed I must tell him so that he can book time off.

My elation at the prospect of such an adventure and a reunion with my son is tempered by irrational misgivings. Born to a Welsh farming girl, reared by the Pritchards, a Welsh man and an English woman, I have only one home. I know no other. For fifty-three years I have resided on this island. I am British, a loyal subject to Her Majesty Queen Elizabeth II. Almost an old age pensioner, I have been summoned to the passport office at in London for interview. Henry maintains this is merely a formality but I am not so sure.

Whatever Henry evinces, the authorities have the clout to say no. *No, Laura Ryan, we are not issuing you with a British passport.* As I near my February appointment, my dread expands until worry beads a mile in length will not mollify me. 'Forsaken by two mothers, now my own country wants to deport me – but to where? Who will take me in? Will I wash up on the streets of Berlin, a pavement chalk artist, scanning faces for my father?'

Henry tunes in placidly to my melodramatic histrionics. 'It'll be a simple process, Laura,' he soothes.

But I spit out this comforter, contemptuous of his faith, waking on the day of my interview nerves jangling. I have had a prolonged ear infection. My right ear is totally deaf, my left whispers sibilantly. There is no discomfort merely an acute sense of isolation, as if my head is boarded up. The weather is filthy, sheeting down with rain, a synonymous climatic backdrop to my emotional desolation. Henry offers for the sixth time to come with me. But I want to go by myself. A bit like dying, I reflect, if that is not endowing the situation with too much pathos. You can't really die with anyone else, can you? So, I reason, that you cannot be reborn with anyone else either. And I know I shall only truly inhabit Laura, when I see her name printed in my passport. So I patch together a faint smile and say, in mimicry of Greta

Garbo, 'I want to be alone.' It doesn't sound anywhere near as sexy, only feeble and bleak. But he nods affably and offers to make the tea.

I expend unusual effort readying myself for the occasion. I wash my hair and, with it turbaned on my head run a scented bath, jasmine essence. I shave my legs and pumice the soles of my feet, pleased that they are still within reach. Getting out, I towel dry, then apply deodorant, body lotion, talc and, finally, perfume, the simple scent of a rose. If the examination is on smell alone, the officer's olfactory receptors will be quivering, and I shall pass with distinction. I dress in a white blouse, a fawn skirt, a navy jacket and suede court shoes. Corporate. Classic. I fuss with my hair attempting to pin it up, but as it keeps sliding free I resort to tying it back in a short ponytail. I put on my oval topaz earrings set in silver, and my locket with a curl of Merlin's hair tucked in it for luck. Even as I go through this ritual I feel absurd, like a bride trying in vain to beautify herself, although she knows she is destined to be jilted at the altar.

I put my life, my letters, my certificates, my few childhood photographs and the one or two I possess of my adoptive parents into a plastic sleeve.

A friend from the estate's gift shop runs me to the station. The weather when I arrive at Victoria can be classed without fear of exaggeration as not just raining cats and dogs, but lions and tigers as well. I trudge along, the envelope tucked under my jacket, my umbrella open, obscuring the dismal drenched streets, my suede shoes sodden and squelching.

We are a brother and sisterhood of sorts, sitting in the waiting room of the London Passport Interview Offices. Our various ancestry is written large over our faces: Indian, Jamaican, African, Chinese, South American, Asian . . . German? From all the corners of the globe we have come, we nomads seeking a land to pitch our tents, to raise our children, a country we can call our own, an identity, a sense of belonging. A squabble of languages buzz in my restricted but still functional good ear; however the cadence, the intonation, the inflexions are all gobbledegook. But fear, insecurity and vulnerability – this tongue is universal. When the bell rings and my number flashes, flesh turns to stone. It takes a supreme effort for me to hoist myself up and out of my chair. With damp, squishing steps, I make my way to the inset compartment where my interrogator awaits. The gentleman sits behind a desk scowling at my paperwork. He looks Indian.

'Mrs Ryan, please take a seat.' I have to concentrate on the process involved in accomplishing this instruction. I am dripping onto the floor, as if gradually melting. Sitting has suddenly become an Olympic sport. I flounder, tip, subside, wibble-wobble into a kind of erect posture. My interviewer introduces himself as Mr Gajarin. 'I'm going to ask you a few questions if you don't mind, Mrs Ryan,' he begins, assessing me shrewdly with darting beady eyes. I half expect him to switch on a lamp and direct the beam straight into my face. And then he is off.

'I beg your pardon?' I say. Then, 'Could you say that again, please?' His voice is soft, his accent treacly. 'Sorry, I didn't catch that?' Still straining my stuffed ears, 'Could you run that by me again?' His eyes pierce me, dark as wet peat. Does he think I am mocking him, feigning deafness deliberately in a wilful attempt at antagonising him? I consider telling him about my ear infections, that I am prone to them, that often when they are healing I am hard of hearing, but that the impairment is only temporary. On second thoughts, he may take this infirmity into consideration. It may cause him to consider whether I will tax the resources of the NHS. I lick parched lips and perform, with an intelligent judder of my chin, a pretence of having heard him. 'What was that? Perhaps you could rephrase that last sentence? A thousand apologies but I was distracted by the bell. If you would only repeat the question more slowly?'

My documents, my certificates and my photographs are strewn all over the desk. Without intending to, I have embarked on my history. I am telling my disjointed story. Granted it is an abridged version, though complete with all the pertinent facts. I gabble frantically, in my excess hoping to include whatever this powerful servant of Her Majesty is listening for, whatever dates may sway him in my petition. Glancing at me now and again, he makes copious notes. When I pause for breath, like a cat that up till now has only been toying with a mouse, he pounces.

'You changed your first name very recently by deed poll from Lucilla to Laura. Why was that?'

I gulp. This man, with his face as closed as a sealed can, has no receptive chink in the set of his features. How can I possibly communicate to him the reason a mature woman in her fifties, married with children of her own, casts off her name of half a century to adopt another. 'I . . . I . . . I . . .' I tail off weakly, eyes curtained.

'You?' prompts Mr Gajarin after a few seconds' hesitation. Mrs Ryan, Mrs Laura Ryan, you?

'I . . . I didn't like it.' And there it is, the card trick extraordinaire, climax of the magician's repertoire, belly-flopping painfully before her one-man audience.

A pause so long it must be reclassified as a silence. 'Ah!' I am unsure how to categorise this exclamation.

I lift my eyes to his and, guessing that he requires more detail, sally on. 'Actually, if you want to know, I've always hated it. My birth mother gave me the name. I was baptised Lucilla before the Pritchards adopted me. I was three and half months old when she handed me over. She didn't really know me at all, what I was like, my personality. I wasn't girly. I was more of a tomboy. Lucilla's a girly name. It didn't feel like me. Besides it sounds like a scream. Then I decided to travel, to visit my son in Australia. For that a passport is a required. I've never been abroad before, so up until now I coped without one. The moment had come to change it, because I couldn't stand to see that name in my passport. It would have been a lie. Because . . . because a passport is going to announce to the world who I really am. And I'm not Lucilla. I never have been. I'm Laura, you see.'

Mr Gajarin has stopped making notes and is looking up, jaw slack, his dark eyes stretched in amazement. Perhaps he has deduced that applicant number sixty-eight is barking mad. But it is of no consequence. I am Laura, legally Laura. Not even the Queen can take that from me. Mr Gajarin flips to a fresh page in his pad. He means business. He flexes the muscles of his down-turned lips. 'What is the date of your mother's birth?' he fires at me, a birth certificate held close to his chest like an answer card in Trivial Pursuit, except that this pursuit is anything but trivial.

Sweat pricks my armpits. My pumping heart seems to rise, blocking my throat. 'Which . . . which one?' I quaver.

Mr Gajarin lifts his impressive eyebrows and brushes a speck of dust from his grey suit. 'Which one?' he queries, alert for my reaction.

'Which . . . which . . . which mother?' I stammer, my film of decorum rupturing in one, two, three tears. Casually, I flick them off my cheek as if they are insects that have randomly alighted there. 'My . . . my real mother? Do you mean her? My birth mother? Bethan Haverd? Well, Bethan Sterry after she married. The one in Wales. Or my adoptive mother? Harriet Pritchard? The one in England.'

His brows relax marginally. 'Bethan Haverd, your Welsh birth mother,' he qualifies after a second's pause.

And suddenly put on the spot, my brain cells are rinsed to a dazzling whiteness, far beyond the realms of biological science. Recalling the names of my children, my husband, let alone my real mother's date of birth, taxes me far beyond my current limited faculties. Distantly, a bell sounds. I spare a charitable thought for the other anxiety-ridden applicants, lives in tow, trouping into the compartments to beg, borrow or steal that most elusive of treasures – a British passport! Now was it the eighth or the ninth? The ninth or the eighth? For the love of God I do not know. I screw up my forehead and slam shut my eyes, prompting my photographic memory. But the certificate that forms there is undeveloped. Mr Gajarin's eyes vacillate from the actual document in his grasp to my anguished face then back again.

'The eighth. No, no, I mean the ninth. No wait a second, it was the eighth. The eighth of August nineteen twenty-seven. Or was it nineteen twenty-eight? No, it was nineteen twenty-seven. Yes that's it. I'm certain of it now.'

The tribulation of the black chair in *Mastermind* does not compare to the agony I am undergoing, toe-curling, thigh-rubbing, buttock-clenching agony.

'The eighth you say?' confirms the crafty Mr Gajarin, eyes locked on mine. I nod desperately. He makes an entry on the pad by his side. 'Do you have a bank account, Mrs Ryan?'

I have to focus. A beat, then, I answer, 'Mmm . . . yes, yes I do. With Barclays.' I give a cardboard smile, a losing smile. 'I've had it for years,' I add, a dash more assertively.

'For years?' Mr Gajarin sits forwards with renewed interest. 'And precisely how many years would that be, Mrs Ryan?' His words ping out, gaining speed, momentum. My tongue is as dry as an airing cupboard. Oh for God's sake, as if it matters. Mr Gajarin's relentless gaze says that it does. How many? How many years have I held the damn thing? I pluck at my watchstrap. Either my wrist has swollen on the instant, or I have fastened it too tightly. 'Mrs Ryan?'

'Twenty-five.' The number bursts from me, as good as any other. 'About . . . well, roughly twenty-five. I can't be quite sure, but it's approximately that. I mean it's an estimate, but probably close. Close enough anyway.' I squirt out a giggle. Mr Gajarin's face says that he is as amused as a gravedigger who has dug himself into a hole he cannot clamber out of.

But he is only teasing me. Now he lets fly his killing thrust. 'Your father, Mrs Ryan, your German father, have you been to see him?'

'No.'

'Never. Not once?'

'No!' I shriek, and then hurriedly collect myself and cough loose my clenched throat. 'Sorry. I'm feeling the strain a bit.' Re-entry at a lower, more sedate pitch. 'I . . . I haven't made any attempt to trace him. None at all.'

The tinned face registers nothing but another entry is made on the pad. 'So you have not communicated at all with your German relations?' says the persistent Mr Gajarin, after a hiatus in which we eye each other like sworn enemies.

'No, no! I didn't see the point. I was going to find my mother initially and then . . .' I sigh as if about expire. 'Well, when that didn't work out, not the way I expected it to, I didn't want to risk it.'

He gives an almost imperceptible nod. 'Thank you, Mrs Ryan. I think we'll leave it there,' he says suddenly, drawing the interview to an abrupt close.

And in trice I am filled with dismay. I have failed, failed the exam. You can see it in his conquering eyes. I have the losing hand. I am not Bethan Haverd's daughter. I am not Thorston Engel's daughter. I am not Harriet and Merfyn Pritchard's daughter. I am not German. And if my own country is disowning me, then who the hell am I? I compress my lips firmly to stop from crying out. Mr Gajarin is rising to his feet, signifying that now the interview really is over and done with. My eyes rove up his smart suit, over his clashing pink and orange tie, and hold his. 'If there is anything else, anything at all you want to know, please ask,' I implore, with impressive vibrato, blinking fast.

'We're finished,' comes Mr Gajarin's clipped tones, as if he is ending a passionate love affair, as if I am a woman irremediably scorned.

'Are you certain?' I ask, fumbling with my certificates, attempting to bundle them together into some kind of order.

Mr Gajarin speaks brusquely. 'If you could leave all these with me, please, Mrs Ryan. We will send them back to you.'

'Oh! But they're the only –'

'Don't worry. We understand that these are the originals. We will look after them, return them to you by registered post,' he informs me, his face impartial.

'Yes, yes. Of course.' I rise in stages, my legs all flesh and no bone. 'Would you like the plastic sleeve?' I offer.

'No, you may take that.' Mr Gajarin is impatient, adjusting his tie and then glancing at his watch. I give a forlorn look at my life scattered over this man's desk, this man who seems impervious to my sorrow. 'You need not concern yourself about your documents, Mrs Ryan. Please. We do this every day. You should hear from us very soon.' He extends a hand to me and I shake it, dazedly. Then it is concluded and I am stumbling out of the passport office into the rain.

Descending to the tube train, I pause to fumble in my handbag for my pocket diary. The previous night I revised like a schoolgirl. I went through all my papers and jotted down the figures I ought to recall if asked. Running a finger down the page, I find my mother, my biological mother, Bethan Haverd's date of birth. It is 9 August 1928. I gave the incorrect date to Mr Gajarin. If it was an exam, and that is what it felt like, I had failed.

I was ill conceived in 1947 in the uneasy quiet of the still primed guns. My father scampered away like a beaten dog. My mother exported me in utero to London to find a couple, any would do, who would import me. The Pritchards had sought a baby the way you might some ambitious plan for improving your home, an extension, or the latest model cooker, fridge or vacuum cleaner. But when the years revealed that I was the wrong specification, their resentments towards me bred like the files of temperance accounts. If they could have exchanged me for a more efficient design, one better adapted for their purposes, say a *Barbara*, they would have. Now, I have been offered to my country. And they too have inspected me and found me wanting. Self-pity threatens to swamp me. I am on verge of going home to broadcast to Henry that Her Majesty's passport officer has seen fit to deny me a British passport. Consequently, I am going to have to throw myself on the mercy of the German government, and how does he like the idea of settling in the Black Forest, when I apply the brakes. I am going to claw back some of this unholy day, I resolve.

Alighting at Covent Garden, I cross Waterloo Bridge and then make my way to the Royal Festival Hall. As I walk along the embankment the rain, which has eased off to a sparkling mizzle, evaporates. The sun, scurrilous wench that she is, immodestly sheds satin grey scarves of cloud. By and by, I come to the London Eye. The clear pods suspended from the circular frame glitter in the burst of afternoon sunshine, like mouth-watering alien fruits, ripe and waiting to be picked. The River Thames is a pewter lizard slithering by. The tang of silt and refuse hits the back of my throat. As it does so the years keel over like skittles.

A girl and her father sit companionably on a bench and peruse river life. She swallows a mouthful of spam sandwich, washing it down with squash brighter than a ripe tangerine. She sniffs sewage, rubbish and oil, all embedded in the muddy sediment of the riverbank. And she reflects, she reflects on Guy, Guy the gorilla at London zoo, who arrived there as a baby in 1947 clutching a tin hot-water bottle, on Guy the adult male who was reputedly said to be so gentle that he caught a fluttering bird in his hand and let it go unharmed.

No longer a little girl, at some invisible stop sign I halt. As I stare up at the wheel it occurs to me that I haven't ridden on it. The showers have dried up. The sky is a glass paperweight. What is the sensation like of standing in the highest pod, at the very tip-top of the great Ferris wheel? North, south, east and west, all of London, the city and the suburbs and the country, must lie at your feet like a map. I crave that altitude for some inexplicable reason. I am officially nobody, an ageing woman without a passport, without an identity. But damn it, I have a right to ride the London Eye, to survey the city I grew up in.

My mind made up, I go and buy a ticket. There is a queue but the minutes seem to glide by. The bubbles are constantly in motion, dipping and rising, but slowly, gracefully, so that I can climb aboard with dignity. Among my fellow passengers are the ubiquitous Japanese tourists, a group all busy clicking their cameras. There is a trio of men in business suits, deep in conference, seemingly oblivious to their surroundings. I guess they have hightailed it out of the London Stock Exchange to clinch a deal in the sky. Two elderly ladies are sharing a bar of chocolate. They munch and look, and look and munch. And there is a mother with her small daughter. They are holding hands, the child and the woman, and pointing in awe.

I am in awe too. I position myself at one of the tapered ends of the pod and drink in the monumental panorama. Distantly, I can make out Leith Hill, the tower, and majestic Windsor Castle. And to the north, Alexandra Palace. Eastwards, I can see all the way to Gravesend. And there is the Greenwich Observatory. I exhale in wonder at the dome of St Paul's, remembering tiptoeing around the Whispering Gallery with my adoptive father, my legs bowing under me, the banging of my heart in my ears. And now I am poised in heaven sailing above that dome. I am high as a bird in free flight. I am flying, not off Beachy Head but over London, the city where I grew up. I think I spot Bowes Park where I lived with Henry and his family and Aunt Ethel. And Primrose Hill. Moving outwards, my eyes sweeping in concentric circles, the tall buildings have thinned to rows of terraced houses. And roaming further there is a patchwork of browns and purples and greens, and the long silver runner of the Thames idling by. The great river with its source in the Cotswolds, meandering through Oxford and Windsor before flowing on to London, and from thence to Dartford, Tilbury and Gravesend, before entering the Thames Estuary, near Southend-on-Sea, coming finally to the North Sea. I look in the direction of Surrey. It strikes me in my pod in heaven what a superfluity of countryside there is. Fields and trees and hedgerows. It is my home, I think. I may not have a passport or a name, but it is where I belong.

Our revolution through 360 degrees of spectacular views ends. I become one of the ant people strolling along the embankment. I ring Henry on my mobile phone.

'How did it go? I was worried,' he says.

'I don't think I got it,' I tell him, resigned.

'Laura, don't be silly. The interview was protocol, that's all. They had to tick a box. It's what they do.'

'But I gave some wrong answers,' I tell him, feeling dejected.

'Wrong answers! Laura, it wasn't a test.'

'It felt like one.'

'There are no wrong answers. Anyway, they saw the paperwork, the proof.'

'Henry, they kept it, all of it. My originals. All I have of my history.'

'That's normal.'

'What happens if they lose them?'

'They won't. They'll send them to you with your passport. Are you coming home, love?' my husband wants to know.

'I'm five minutes from Waterloo. I'll ring you when I'm on the train. And Henry?'

'Yes?'

'I am coming *home*.'

Each day I wait for the post, shuffling through the letters and bills disconsolately to see if there is something from the passport office. A week goes by with no communication, a fortnight. My imagination runs amuck. Henry senses that I do not want to discuss my lack of status. I am a non-entity, a vaporous being, a violin without strings. If it were not for my family, my dog, I would not function at all. I have become an insomniac. The hours after midnight, I occupy sitting in our bedroom by the closed window pulling the mantle of dark about me. I listen to the owls' hoots and the strangled cry of foxes.

Will a letter come couched in official jargon informing me that they have flipped a coin? Heads and I am British, tails and I am German. Perhaps for the remainder of my days I will be batted like a ping-pong ball between Germany and England, as they thrash out which court is mine. Will Henry and the children come to visit me in a refugee camp? And what about my dog, what about Lola? If they see fit to turf me out, maybe the solution will be to sneak back in. An illegal immigrant in my own country? I can harvest fruit, work in restaurant kitchens, pluck chickens, wash cars, sell my body. I strike this last from my list of possibilities. Glancing down at myself in my brushed cotton pyjamas, I decide that at fifty-three there may be no takers. And besides, Henry will not be overly thrilled at the prospect of his wife, illegal immigrant or not, pounding the streets of Soho in her brogues.

Next morning there comes a knock on the door of Pear Tree Cottage. The postman has a bulky envelope for me. Recorded delivery for Laura Ryan. I must sign for it. My signature is an indecipherable scrawl, but he seems content with it. Henry is out assisting a tree surgeon in taking down an ancient oak ridden with honey fungus. It is an hour before I muster the courage to open it, sitting on the settee. When I do, upturning it over the seat, the first thing it disgorges is maroon-coloured, something the size of a compact notebook, something that would fit comfortably into the palm of your hand. As if reading Braille, my quaking fingers tremble over the gold lettering.

EUROPEAN UNION
UNITED KINGDOM OF
GREAT BRITAIN AND NORTHERN IRELAND

Below it is the gold coat of arms, the lion and the unicorn with the crown sandwiched between them. And beneath that: 'PASSPORT'.

I fan the pages daringly, like a gambler shuffling her deck. And now I stop, jam a finger in, open it, my eye caressing the words in italics:

Her Britannic Majesty's
Secretary of State
Requests and requires in the
Name of Her Majesty
all those whom it may concern
to allow the bearer to pass freely
without let or hindrance,
and to afford the bearer
such assistance and protection
as may be necessary.

A hot toddy is spreading through me. Another shuffle and I cut. On this page is an appalling portrait photograph of my face, my thin strawberry-blonde hair, my turquoise eyes. It is, I know, a prerequisite of passports that the photographs of their bearers are uniformly ghastly. I am transfixed by it, as if falling in love with the image at first sight. I dyed my hair to rid it of the encroaching grey, and had it cut shorter for the picture. As if that would improve it! I had two goes as well. Propped on the chair in the tiny curtained booth, I neglected to take off the linen scarf coiled about my neck. In my second sitting, told under no circumstances to smile, my blank expression was inane. There was something of the zombie about the glassy eyes and taut wire mouth. But now as I moon over it, I blink in astonishment, for surely I have more pizzazz than a Bond girl. And adjacent to it the words leap out at me. 'Surname: Ryan. Given names: Laura. Nationality: British Citizen.' I crow with exultation, then rifle in my handbag, grab a pen, bend my head to my passport and sign. I fish out my compact, flip it open and regard my reflection.

Laura Ryan. Laura Ryan. Laura Ryan. That's who I am. I am not the illegitimate daughter of farm girl, Bethan Haverd and prisoner of war, Thorston Engel. I am not the adopted daughter of Harriet and Merfyn Pritchard, crumbling columns of the temperance movement. I am Henry Ryan's wife, mother to our two children, grandmother to our granddaughters. I am an artist and an animal lover. I adore the winter for it is stripped to its honest bones. The city is without inspiration for me. My heart will forever be given to the English countryside. And when I die I want my ashes to fall in a flurry of snow like pale butterflies. I want to be carried off on the snowmelt of spring's nativity. I am Laura Ryan.

I tidy all my certificates into a shoebox and put it away in the small loft space. I keep the photographs of me close by though. Some I put into an album. But the one of me on the furry donkey by the seaside, in my little white dress, my short white socks, my shiny black shoes, holding on to the reins oh so tightly, this one I have enlarged. It's in a frame now on the mantelpiece, a frame Tim carved for me from the wholesome wood he salvaged after a previous storm. When I gaze at it, at the flat grey sea in the background, at the people sunning themselves in deckchairs, what I recall is the plush of those big droopy ears, the mossy plush of them filling my tiny hands, and how good they made me feel, how secure.

Chapter 28

Laura

April and I feel the year rousing itself and stretching. Trees that look bare are cunning. On closer scrutiny they are all busy with buds and sap. The great unstoppable force is on the rise again. It is mid-morning and my cheeks are still wind-kissed from a lovely two-hour walk with Lola. We both have our fresh-air faces on. Coffee is brewing, and the glorious fragrance is filling the cottage. The lounge, all of it, is flooded in an apricot radiance. Through the window I can see the pear trees, and a great spotted woodpecker, a vivid splash of red and black and white, hammering at a tree trunk like a miniature pneumatic drill. A CD is playing baroque music. Henry is at work. Spring is clamouring for his attention. Last year, 2002, I visited Tim in Australia, for three whole weeks in the autumn. It was the most incredible journey. The cities so modern and spread out. And the wildlife everywhere. And the ocean that was the turquoise of my eyes, it really was. But I missed Henry and home, and it was good to get back.

It seems I was not only the one feeling homesick. Tim has arrived back from Australia for good, with a surprise for us. Tonight he is coming to dinner, bringing his new Australian girlfriend for us to meet. I understand that this relationship is serious, so we shall have to be on our best behaviour. I have made chilled salmon, and later this afternoon will prepare a celery and walnut salad, new potatoes with fresh chopped parsley and a lemon meringue pie. But for now I have the promise of a delicious interlude in the day to sort through the family photos.

I am going to make up an album just for our granddaughters, charting their childhoods. I thought I would add my drawings and paintings of them, my home-made cards, as well as theirs, and the stories and poems they write, pressed flowers, scraps that catch their eye in newspapers and magazines. I want it to be something we can sit and look through together as they grow older, as they grow up. I want to be able to talk through the memories of their childhoods, help Lisa and Jessica to cherish them.

I am just settling down with my cup of coffee, Lola at my feet crunching on a doggy biscuit, when there is a knock on the front door. I am a little put out at the prospect of unexpected visitors and a delay, or possibly temporary postponement of my planned project. I set down my cup reluctantly. Lola springs up, tail wagging, ghosting me to the door. Opening it, I see a tall woman in her middle years, her brown hair, greying at the roots, tied back, light make-up, diffident dark-brown eyes. She is smartly dressed in a plum-coloured coat, a scarf knotted stylishly at her neck. She has the appearance of a professional woman, in business selling something perhaps? I have never seen her before in my life.

'Hello,' she says, her voice tentative. She extends a gloved hand. I take it without thinking and then release it. 'Hello,' she says again.

'Hello,' I answer, like for like, peculiarly not feeling suspicious of this stranger. If anything a mild amusement is creeping over me. She looks lost, in need of reassurance. Lola shoulders past my legs and butts her with the dome of her head.

'Oh I'm sorry. Lola! Come back inside at once.' Lola ignores me.

'That's quite all right. I'm used to animals. I grew up on a farm,' the stranger volunteers, petting Lola and even bobbing down to give her a proper greeting. 'Lola is it? Hello, Lola. Aren't you gorgeous?'

I warm to her immediately. Some people have an instant rapport with animals, and for the most part I am inclined to trust our four-legged friends' judgement. Generally, they are very discerning. But my coffee is getting cold and there are photographs to sort through. I clear my throat. 'Can I help you?' I offer, preparing to give directions to some part of the estate, the offices, the shop, the restaurant.

She rises to her feet rapidly, looking distinctly embarrassed now. 'Oh, I'm sorry. I'm a bit nervous. I don't quite know how to –' She breaks off and adjusts the shoulder strap of her bag. Lola stares up at her quizzically. Then, 'Are you . . . are you Lu– Lucilla?' she stumbles, now seeming decidedly anxious.

'Yes, well, yes, I was . . . oh, yes, yes, I am Lucilla,' I tell her all in a rush. And suddenly I have the queerest sensation, as if my life is hurtling backwards, as if the past, my past has come to claim me. I draw in a trembling breath. In a second, my mouth is dry and my heart is beating frantically. 'Is anything wrong? I'm afraid I don't know you. What do you want?' For a long moment, our eyes meet. The pensive look in hers is familiar. I have met it throughout my life – in mirrors. 'Why . . . why do you want me?'

For reply she fumbles in her coat pocket and retrieves two envelopes. She holds them out to me. The handwriting on one of them is Rosemary Dixon's. On the other it is mine. They are the letters I wrote to my mother, to Bethan Sterry. I give a soft implosive gasp and take a step back.

'Please, please don't be upset. It's just that I had to come, that I had to see you. If I wrote, I thought you might not want – My mother . . . our mother has passed away. I was going through her things . . . and . . . and I found –' Again she jars to a halt. She takes a few deep, steadying breaths. We stare at each other. When she next speaks it is slowly, with assurance, and something else, something that makes my heart judder inside me. 'I am Lowrie, Lowrie Sterry. And I think, I think I'm your sister,' she says.